· THE FAERY REHISTORY SERIES ·

# THE ABSINTHE EARL

# THE ABSINTHE EARL

### · THE FAERY REHISTORY SERIES ·

## Sharon Lynn Fisher

**BLACK STONE**

PUBLISHING

Printed in the United States of America

First paperback edition: 2019
ISBN 978-1-9826-8441-9
Fiction / Fantasy / General

1 3 5 7 9 10 8 6 4 2

CIP data for this book is available
from the Library of Congress

Blackstone Publishing
31 Mistletoe Rd.
Ashland, OR 97520

www.BlackstonePublishing.com

*Many times man lives and dies*
*Between his two eternities,*
*That of race and that of soul,*
*And ancient Ireland knew it all.*
*Whether man dies in his bed*
*Or the rifle knocks him dead,*
*A brief parting from those dear*
*Is the worst man has to fear.*
*Though grave-diggers' toil is long,*
*Sharp their spades, their muscle strong,*
*They but thrust their buried men*
*Back in the human mind again.*

**—William Butler Yeats,**
**"Under Ben Bulben"**

# GLOSSARY OF IRISH TERMS AND NAMES

**Angus:** A Tuatha De Danaan king, foster father of Diarmuid, husband to Caer.

**Aughisky:** The Irish water horse, a fairy.

**bean sí (ban-SHE):** Commonly spelled "banshee," a harbinger of death.

**Ben Bulben:** Tabletop mountain in the west of Ireland, near Sligo Bay.

**Brú na Bóinne (BRU nuh BUN-yay):** Ancient fairy mound and ruin on the River Boyne, at Newgrange, near Dublin.

**Caer:** A Tuatha De Danaan immortal, foster mother to Diarmuid, wife of Angus.

**Cliona (KLEE-uh-nuh):** A Tuatha De Danaan immortal, sometimes referred to as queen of banshees (also spelled "Cliodhna").

**Connacht (KAH-nucht):** Region and ancient kingdom in the west of Ireland.

**Dana:** Celtic deity, mother of the Tuatha De Danaan people (also referred to as Ana/Anu/Danu).

**Diarmuid (DEER-muhd):** A legendary warrior of the Tuatha De Danaan.

**Enbarr:** The horse of the Irish sea god, Manannán.

**Knock Ma:** Court and stronghold of Finvara, the fairy king.

**Faery:** In this text, the land where fairies live; also refers to the collective races of fairies.

**Finvara (fin-VAHR-ah):** The fairy king and a Tuatha De Danaan immortal.

**Fomorians (foh-MORE-ee-uhns):** Ancient seafaring foes of the Tuatha De Danaan; often portrayed as a race of monsters; sometimes referred to as the Plague Warriors.

**Grace O'Malley:** Sixteenth-century pirate queen of Connacht.

**Gráinne (GRAW-nyeh):** Legendary lover of Diarmuid, affianced to Diarmuid's chief, Finn mac Cumhaill.

**Kildamhnait Tower:** A former stronghold of Grace O'Malley, on Achill Island.

**Maeve/Medb:** Irish warrior queen from the Ulster cycle of Irish mythology.

**Máine Mór (MAW-nyeh mowr):** An ancient Irish king (fourth century); in this story, the bog king.

**Manannán (MAH-nuh-nawn):** Irish god of the sea; in this story, foster father of Cliona.

**Morrigan, the:** Irish goddess of war, crow shapeshifter; also called "the battle crow."

**pratie:** Irish slang (from Irish Gaelic) for potato.

**púca (PU-kuh):** Fairy shapeshifter usually appearing as part man, part goat.

**Tuatha De Danaan (THOO-a-hay day dahn-uhn), abbrev. Danaan:** Ancient supernatural people of Ireland often associated with fairies; people of the Celtic goddess Dana.

**Note:** Regarding the Tuatha De Danaan, this text conforms to the naming conventions and spellings used by W. B. Yeats.

# PROLOGUE

Fragment of *The Book of Diarmuid*
(author unknown)

*AD 882*

Diarmuid Ua Duibne was the most renowned warrior of the Tuatha De Danaan of Ireland. There lived no fiercer fighter, and his sword, Great Fury, was the terror of his enemies.

His birth date is not known, but his mortal life spanned centuries. While Diarmuid lived for battle, most of his trouble stemmed not from his perilous vocation but from his propensity for falling in love. And, in fact, his decision to run away with the promised wife of his chief, Finn mac Cumhaill, led to his exile from the Danaan and eventually caused his death.

After his death, Diarmuid lived as an immortal in Faery and sometimes even walked the green hills of Ireland, appearing as no more than a shadow except to his own kind and to the fairy seers among the Irish people. During this time, he suffered his most potent love dart, and as a result of that fated event—for reasons known only to him and to the object of his love—he conspired with the last living druid to cast a spell that exiled all the races of Faery from Ireland.

The spell came to be called Diarmuid's Seal.

# FOG AND SPIRITS

**"You must suffer me to go my own dark way."**
**—ROBERT LOUIS STEVENSON,**
*The Strange Case of Dr. Jekyll and Mr. Hyde*

## ADA

*Dublin—1882*

Tendrils of fog, thick and viscous, wended in off the moor on the edge of that midwinter night. I suppose that in Ireland, a moor is more properly a *bog*, but "bog" is a clumsy sort of word, lacking romance.

*It's not a night for romance,* I reminded myself, studying the more uniformly dense mass of fog rising from the River Liffey on my right. I'd never examined the nuances of fog so minutely, but then, I'd never been to Ireland. And in truth, I was stalling—a behavior I had a strict policy against.

"Get on with it, Ada," I murmured, disregarding another of my policies. A young woman traveling alone—and with a head of prematurely silver hair—did not need to give anyone reason to think her queerer than they most certainly already would.

I cast my gaze to the left, lifting my chin to study the sign above the door of Dublin's most popular house of absinthe.

"The green fairy," many call the heady spirit, and this establishment had styled itself after the name. The emblem painted on the sign was a Venusian beauty in a filmy green drapery, a mass of red curls heaped on top of her head. She displayed an ample measure of milky white flesh in the form of softly rounded shoulders and belly and an almost entirely exposed bosom. In her outstretched hand she held a gracefully curving goblet one-quarter filled with bright-green liquid.

*Come hither,* she seemed to say.

And so I must.

I'd been in Dublin four days now, poring over books on Celtic history and mythology at Trinity College by day and visiting houses of absinthe by night. The first three I visited had been cramped little establishments, each containing a half-dozen regulars. Shabby men and women so weighted down by life, or perhaps addiction, that their chins brushed the rims of their glasses as they spoke to me. They took their *alcoholic* spirits as watered down as those residing in their earthly forms, because that was what they could afford.

In the end, their talk wasn't much good to me. They told me what I wanted to hear—stories of recent fairy sightings, either by themselves or by their neighbors—and I offered them a few coins for their trouble.

I had read of a possible connection between absinthe consumption and such sightings, which was what had led to my interviewing them, so you might wonder at my skepticism. It was the feverish desperation in their eyes and the outrageous nature of the stories—as if they were trying to persuade me by showmanship—that caused me to doubt them. Moreover, I was *disposed* to believe them, which is a mental state every researcher should guard against.

In the Green Fairy, I expected to find a more privileged

class of patrons. Not that I believed the wealthy were any less likely to succumb to addiction or low emotional states—in my experience, it was common enough—but the Green Fairy was reputable. A place anyone might stop in for a drop of spirits or a more substantial draught of the dark and frothy national drink. In short, the Fairy's patrons were less likely to want something from me. Less desperation on the part of the patrons also made it less likely I'd need to test my mastery of the ladies' defense techniques that had been part of my physical education requirement at the Lovelace Academy for Promising Young Women. Even so, I kept my umbrella—with its sharply pointed steel tip—close by my side.

Touching the edge of my hood out of habit—it was going nowhere, as I had pinned it to my coiffure—I reached for the brass knob and pulled open the door.

Warm, anise-scented air washed over me, and I stepped inside.

Only a few gazes took note of my entrance, and as I closed the door behind me, shutting out the damp December night, they quickly returned to their glasses and companions. It was a proper Irish pub, with dark wood paneling, leather upholstery, and gas lamps fixed at regular intervals along the walls. The decor, like the sign outside, was a tribute to *la fée verte*. She appeared in all shapes and sizes, from rustic beauties to Morgan le Fay temptresses.

The place was as popular as rumored, though this could be due to the season—Christmas was only six days away. A strange time for vacationing in Ireland, you might observe. "Inhospitable weather" did not do it justice. But I was on break from the Academy and determined to make progress on my thesis, "Anthropologic Explanations for the Exodus of the Daoine Maithe"—the "gentlefolk," as the Irish referred to fairies out of respectful wariness. Besides, even had I not been behind on my studies, I had no family to spend the holidays with.

There didn't appear to be a single empty table, but I balked at the idea of approaching the bar. It wasn't a thing a young miss did—not even an orphan whose parents had left her enough inheritance (*just enough*, mind you) to render her unconcerned about the opinions of others. My courage was failing me when I noticed a small table at the back of the room, at a companionable distance from a blazing turf fire. It appeared to have been recently vacated, as an empty reservoir glass and absinthe spoon rested on the tabletop.

Gathering my skirts and traveling cloak in my hands, I made my way toward it.

It was a cozy corner and a perfect place for observing the room while keeping quiet and anonymous. The only problem was the heat. Perspiration slid between my shoulder blades, and I decided that if I was to avoid a soaking, I must either relocate or remove a layer of clothing.

"For you, miss."

I glanced up as a man placed before me a funnel-shaped glass, the kind preferred for serving absinthe. I locked gazes with the stranger, who wore round, green-tinted spectacles, and it gave me a shock. I don't mean that I was surprised, though in fact I was. I mean that I felt it like a sudden, powerful discharge of static electricity.

My gaze dropped to the glass he'd placed before me. The drizzling-water-over-sugar part of the absinthe ritual had apparently already been conducted, and the glass was nearly full of a clear green liquid.

"Sir," I began, "I haven't ordered—"

"No," he interrupted. "I'll declare myself outright: it's intended as a bribe."

I lifted my eyebrows, though of course he couldn't see this, due to the depth of my hood.

"I do not wish to molest you or suggest anything improper—"

"Disclosures that begin in that way," I interrupted in my turn, "typically prove to be exactly the thing they were advertised not to be." My reply edged on rudeness, but as a young woman traveling without a chaperone, I received my share of unwanted attention. I found it best to quell their enthusiasm right out of the gate. "I had intended to order tea, sir, so please bestow your generosity on someone more receptive."

A chilly reply was usually enough, but the man continued to regard me, amusement now mingling with curiosity.

"I believe you've mistaken my intention, miss. I only wished to beg the favor of claiming your unused chair—if it is indeed unused—so I might rest my feet on the grate." I could not but notice he was a darkly handsome man who spoke a velvety Irish brogue. "I've ridden up from the harbor and I'm soaked through, and there's not an empty seat in the house."

His black hair was tied back from his face, but one stray lock was plastered to his wet cheekbone.

"I'm happy to fetch your tea," he continued.

"No, please." I gestured to the empty chair across from me. "It's not necessary, and I'm too warm as it is. I apologize for my rudeness."

"My thanks to you, Miss …?"

"Miss Quicksilver."

He lifted the chair, angling it toward the fire. "Mr. Donoghue, at your service."

He removed his coat and sank down with a relieved sigh, stretching his boots in front of him. Soon, steam was rising from his garments. His dress marked him as a gentleman—jet overcoat and dove-gray waistcoat cut from fine cloth, and a silver watch fob dangling from his waistcoat pocket. Though, he wore his hair longer than was currently fashionable. It was trimmed to shoulder length and neatly pulled back but for the strands worked loose by the weather. He'd missed his appointment with the razor for perhaps two or three days, and the dark hair softened his strong jawline. His appearance had a blown-in-off-the-bog quality that—studious and unromantic though I was by nature—I found most alluring. I fancied he had a story to tell of himself that would be well worth hearing.

Aware that I was staring—an unsettling habit of mine, I'd been told by schoolmates—I dropped my eyes to the glass before me. So far, I had abstained from partaking of the drink so popular with my research subjects. My work required a clear mind. But it had sometimes occurred to me that by so primly distancing myself from their experience, I might be limiting my effectiveness as a researcher.

Certainly, a taste could do no harm.

Raising the glass to my lips, I just wet my tongue. It had a delicate licorice sweetness that mingled pleasingly with a slight herbal bitterness. I immediately understood its appeal.

"Is it up to par?" asked my new acquaintance. Apparently, he had been studying me as well, though his spectacled eyes were still fixed on the fire.

"I couldn't say," I replied to his profile.

He turned then, arching an eyebrow. Afraid I might have given offense—for I am hopeless at small talk—I explained, "It's the first time I've tried it."

"Ah. And how do you like it?"

"Very well," I replied, pushing the glass a few inches away. I found the drink refreshing, and that was precarious in my current overheated state. Better to remove my traveling cloak and hope that I was tucked too tightly into the corner to attract much notice.

"Are you a wanted woman?" asked Mr. Donoghue, ducking his head to gaze deeper into my hood. The lines of his full lips were firm, but mirth sparkled behind the rounds of green glass. I was suddenly curious to know the color of his eyes. "Or perhaps embarking on an elopement," he continued to speculate, his gaze ranging around the room. "Your bridegroom is late."

"I'm a woman sitting alone in a house of absinthe," I replied. But I unpinned my hood from my hair and unfastened the cloak. Then, holding my breath, I shrugged free of the garment, letting it fall over the back of my chair. "You can understand why I might prefer to avoid drawing the attention of others."

"Certainly, I …" He trailed off as his eyes widened, catching on the silvery locks that had tumbled down around the edges of my face. "I beg your pardon. For a moment, I took you for a dame twice your age."

Had I a shilling for every time I'd heard those words, I could have hired a research assistant to wander the wilds of Ireland in my place. "And have you revised your opinion, sir?"

"Indeed," he said with mock gravity. "I see that you're a youngish lass. One who has perhaps been swallowed up and spat out by a storm off the Atlantic." He was amusing himself at my expense, but I perceived no malice behind it. He continued, "Or was it some shock in early life that wrought this change?"

"While those are imaginative theories, Mr. Donoghue, I—"

"I have it," he said, his gaze brightening. "Miss *Quicksilver*, was it? An inherited trait, then. Your family produces prematurely silver-haired offspring."

"Exactly so," I said, pleased at not having to repeat an explanation I'd given many times. It was my mother, in fact, who had handed down the name Quicksilver, due to a centuries-old legal exception granted to preserve the name. No one in my family seemed to know *why* the exception had been granted, but there were many imaginative theories on that score as well.

"Here you are, Lord Meath."

A young man with a ruddy complexion and stained apron set a glass on the end of the table opposite me.

"My apologies for the delay, sir. We're that busy, what with the holiday bearing down on us."

"Not at all, Michael. Thank you, and happy Christmas."

Michael ducked his head to my companion. "Happy Christmas to you, Your Lordship. And to you, miss."

Michael moved away, and it was my turn to raise an eyebrow. "'Your Lordship,' is it?"

My companion made a disgruntled noise and extended his hands toward the fire. "Please don't start calling me that. My family name is as heavy on the tongue as 'Your Lordship' is on the nerves. You may call me Meath if you like, Miss Quicksilver. Most do."

I understood a thing or two about ponderous names. "As you like, sir. As for myself, 'Miss Q' will do."

He ducked his head and raised his glass. "It's an honor to make the acquaintance of such a unique young lady."

I raised my glass. "And it's an honor to meet …" I tried to think what his title might be, and then recalled that Dublin was in County Meath. "… the *Earl* of Meath—have I got that right?"

He inclined his head slightly. "Since my father died, two years ago."

Our glasses clinked, and I took the tiniest of sips before replacing mine on the table.

"You haven't much of a thirst this evening," he observed.

"I'm not used to it," I explained. "I lead a sober existence. Studious by nature."

He gave me a dubious smile. "Despite all evidence to the contrary."

I reached again for my glass as an occupation for my nervously active fingers but caught myself and folded my hands in my lap. "Things are not always what they seem, sir. I've come to Dublin on a research trip."

"Research! You are full of surprises, Miss Q. May one know what you are researching?"

I straightened in my chair. I mustn't lose this opportunity over a sudden and uncharacteristic case of nerves. "I'm composing my thesis on the disappearance of Ireland's gentlefolk. I hope to find a few souls here who know stories or even have firsthand experience."

Watching him closely to see whether he would scoff at this, I noticed when a shadow passed over his countenance. But he was smiling when he replied, "Well, I daresay you've come to the right place. I'd wager there are many here who have had visions. Of fairies and bogeys, to be sure. Also lions, monkeys, and possibly peacocks."

"My dear sir," I replied, suppressing my own smile, "I believe you are laughing at me."

Then he did laugh. "Forgive me, Miss Q. I've only just left a naval appointment, and I haven't enjoyed the company of a charming young woman in longer than I care to remember. Don't be angry with me for having a bit of fun."

The casual flattery affected me more than it should have. I dropped my gaze to my glass and released the smile I'd been holding back. "No, sir. I'm not so miss-ish as that."

"*That* is a relief." His voice softened slightly as he said this. It was a subtle change, but my heart noticed—and fluttered. "In all seriousness, a house of absinthe seems an unlikely place to conduct research, if I don't offend by saying so."

The earl appeared to have sloughed off the chill. He had angled his chair somewhat away from the fire and folded his sleeves to just above the elbows. He was not quite sitting at my table, but he'd rested his half-consumed drink there.

"I'm sure it seems so," I replied. "Over the past decade, there have been a handful of reports in Paris, London, and Dublin newspapers that suggest a potential connection between consumption of absinthe and the ability to see fairies."

The earl's amused expression had given way to a contemplative one. "You refer to *real* sightings? Not absinthe-induced hallucinations?"

I lifted my hands, turning them out in a gesture of uncertainty. "Who can say? One might argue that they *are* hallucinations, encouraged by the nickname the spirit has earned."

He nodded. "One might."

"Or … one might argue that the nickname was earned as a result of the spirit's effects."

Another nod, slower this time. "But if the sightings are real, would that not mean the fairies have not departed at all?"

I smiled, pleased at his quick intelligence and his interest in the topic. "Precisely. That, or their new country somehow overlaps our own, and absinthe—or perhaps one of its component herbs—creates a sort of gateway between the two."

"Intriguing." He was staring into his glass now, perhaps seeing the spring-colored liquid in a new light. "And you don't wish to test the theory yourself?"

He glanced up at me, and I shook my head. "I'd make a biased subject. I might see only what I wish to see."

"And what is it you would wish to see?"

I frowned, considering. It was an interesting question, and I wasn't sure of the answer. Inspired by his joking manner, I replied, "Anything that might bring me closer to finishing my thesis."

He laughed and drank again from his glass.

"How about you, my lord? Have you ever seen a fairy?"

## EDWARD

I stared at this striking woman, frozen by her question. For all that she was ladylike, mild-mannered, and on all accounts charming, her wit was direct and incisive. Her question was not complicated. It required a simple yes or no, and yet …

Dare I tell her the truth? That at least in my case, absinthe did cause the most troubling hallucinations—though it had never occurred to me that there might be anything real about them—and that only the spectacles kept me from going mad? Yet absinthe was the only thing that staved off the nightwalking, which was far worse. Rising in the morning to find bloodstained bedclothes, my own flesh torn and bruised as if I'd done battle with a host of demons.

Yes, the absinthe was necessary, and the spectacles limited the green apparitions to the edges of my vision. But I could share nothing of this with *her,* however compelling I might find her.

"First of all, Miss Q," I replied, "I've asked you to call me Meath."

She gave an apologetic smile. "I know that you have, but I find myself unequal to addressing a virtual stranger—especially one with a station so much higher than my own—in such a familiar way. Might you be willing to compromise if I promise to avoid 'Your Lordship'?"

It was a very pretty feminine plea, which, of course, I was powerless to refuse. I'd spoken only the truth when I said I'd been too long outside the society of women, and what's more, I couldn't remember the last time I'd found myself so captivated by such society.

"If it will allow us to continue our discourse, then so be it," I replied.

She gave a gracious nod. "Will you then answer my question?"

I eyed her over the rims of my spectacles. The lady's eyes were very close in hue to the undiluted spirit so popular in this establishment: an uncommonly light shade of green. Her lips were dark, nearer plum than pink. She could not be called classically beautiful but had rather an impishness to her features—narrow eyes and arched brows, high and defined cheekbones, and a chin more pointed than round. Not to forget those plaited and piled waves of silver, with loose curls that softened any sharpness in the lines of her face. Together, it created an effect that suggested a way out of the corner she had so innocently backed me into.

"Indeed I have, Miss Q."

In fascination, I watched the flurry of fingers and wrists that produced a notebook and writing implement seemingly out of thin air. "You've seen a fairy?" she replied eagerly.

I nodded. "I believe one sits before me now."

Her gaze took a turn around our fireside nook before returning to my face. She crossed her arms on the table, her pursed lips punctuating the understanding in her expression. I fought a losing battle not to stare at the mouth shaped like a little mauve heart.

"You're laughing at me again, Lord Meath," she said, a hint of vexation in her tone.

"Not at all," I assured her. "I only meant to convey that you yourself are the most otherworldly creature I've met." Strictly speaking, this was true, but I did not much like myself for the flimsy evasion.

She set down her writing implement, the lines of her mouth softening into a self-deprecating smile. "According to my grandmother, an Irish ancestress of ours was kissed by a fairy. All the most interesting family legends have Irish roots, you see."

"Might it not be true?" I couldn't help but ask. "If you accept their existence, why might it be a stretch to believe what your grandmother told you?"

She frowned, and an inch-long wrinkle kissed the spot on her forehead a Hindu would call the third eye. "It's a fair question, Lord Meath. Do *you* accept their existence?"

I shifted slightly in my chair, finally closing the gentlemanly distance I'd preserved between myself and her small table. "I make it a practice never to disbelieve a thing I cannot disprove."

The brightness of her gaze—the almost childlike pleasure in her countenance—caused a swelling in my chest. "Then we have something in common, sir," said she.

I detected motion in my peripheral vision—a swirl of green mist, the hallmark of the otherworldly visitations, which I could never quite ignore. I raised my hand to nudge the spectacles closer to my face and so managed to block my view of the visitor with my hand.

But it did nothing to diminish the shrill cry that pealed like a nightmare across my consciousness. I squeezed my eyes closed. Of all the absinthine visitors, the *bean sí* was the worst. And they often hovered over sailors and ships like great flocks of spectral geese. It had been close to driving me from my commission when Queen Isolde recalled me to attend to affairs of state. But I knew I would return to the Royal Navy when I'd fulfilled my obligation to Her Majesty—I had no desire to remain at my ancestral seat, wasting away my years tormented by mental disease and with an increasing dependence on the infernal remedy. I had to at least remain active, and the sea air soothed my fevered brain.

"Are you well, Lord Meath?"

I opened my eyes to find the lady eyeing me with concern.

"I am, thank you. Just a slight headache."

The banshee had drifted to the other side of my head, her wild rippling tresses and cobweb garments trailing behind. I could not hear the lady's reply over the sudden blast of another shrill death warning.

"One moment," I murmured to my companion, removing my spectacles.

I blinked as my eyes adjusted to the change in light. The barrow woman, having free range of my vision at last, swooped and swirled in the air between us before coiling around the torso of my new acquaintance and whispering into her ear.

"Miss Quicksilver!" I cried in reflexive warning.

The lady suddenly stood and bent toward me with alarm. I felt her cool fingers press the back of my hand. "My lord, what can I do to help you?"

I locked gazes with the wide-eyed hag at her shoulder and, in desperation, gave a nod of acknowledgment. With another shriek, the banshee soared away from my companion and straight through the ceiling over our heads, leaving a trail of green vapor that curled like fog around Miss Q's soft pile of silver hair.

Returning my spectacles to their original position, I looked into the lady's anxious face.

Were I to accept what she had moments ago suggested—that these visions of mine were more than vapors, that they had real substance—I must also accept that I had just been warned of the lady's impending death.

## ADA

Blue. The gentleman's eyes were a light, clear blue. They were striking in contrast to his black hair, which could mean he was at least partly descended from the Spanish sailors shipwrecked near Galway in the time of Queen Elizabeth. The lovely and half-mad Irish queen, Isolde, was said to be descended from those same castaways, and I wondered whether there might be some relation.

Lord Meath replaced the spectacles, and at last he spoke. "Forgive me, Miss Q. I am well now."

I resumed my seat.

"I'm sorry for your headache, sir," I said, and I meant it. He had a kind and gentlemanly manner, and I was little more than a tourist on this island, without family or even friends here to ease my feelings of isolation. He was a handsome, intelligent young nobleman, and I doubt many ladies would fail to appreciate the gift of his time and attention.

He shook his head. "It is nothing. But I must ask you something."

I lifted my eyebrows, uneasy about the sudden somber quality in his tone. "Yes?"

"Have you family in Ireland? Or a friend, perhaps?"

It was as if he'd been listening to my thoughts. The more intimate nature of this question surprised me, and I failed to immediately formulate a reply.

"I don't mean to be impertinent." He touched the base of his glass with the tips of his fingers but didn't drink. He gave a thin smile that constrained whatever true feeling had moved him to ask the question. "I'm only concerned for your welfare, traveling alone and unprotected."

"I appreciate your concern, sir. But I'm afraid—well, I'm an orphan, you see. As such, I'm accustomed to managing my own affairs and am more self-reliant than perhaps I may appear. I assure you, there's no cause for concern on my behalf."

It was perhaps unwise for me to be so honest about my situation. What did I know of him, to be revealing to him just how alone I was in the world? Yet despite my strong suspicion that he was hiding something, my instincts assured me he meant me no harm.

He acknowledged my explanation with a nod. "Do you mean to remain in Ireland over the holidays?"

"I do, sir."

"And then you'll return home?"

"I plan to travel into the countryside after Christmas, until I'm expected back at school. I wish to visit some of the small villages and churchyards. Talk to the people who live there."

His countenance darkened with every word I spoke. "Is there something wrong, Lord Meath? Are you feeling unwell again?"

The corners of his mouth relaxed. "Not at all. But I have a proposition for you."

I stared at him with some surprise. Had I misjudged him after all? "Indeed, sir?"

"Nothing improper, I assure you. Though if you agree, you'll have to trust me as your companion for a few days."

My mouth fell open at this, and I closed it again without replying.

The earl shifted in his chair and again stretched his legs before the fire. I breathed a little easier with his gaze directed away from me, and I studied his profile as he continued. "I was called to shore by Queen Isolde, who, in addition to being my sovereign, is also my cousin."

So he *was* a relation of the queen's, and as an earl, he would by default be a member of parliament. Ireland's government was much the same as Britain's, right down to both countries' independent and strong-minded queens. However, Ireland's monarch had the absolute support of her military and had been known to run roughshod over the Irish parliament. Despite this rather regressive state of affairs, Isolde had raced well ahead of the English queen in advancing reforms aimed at improving the condition of women in the country. For this reason, I had felt easier about embarking on a research trip here than I would have at home.

Even so, I waited with some trepidation to hear the rest of the earl's proposal.

"While I was at sea," he continued, "a ruin of some sort was discovered on my tenant's farm, inside an ancient fairy mound called Brú na Bóinne. The queen believes it is important, and has asked me personally to inspect the site, photograph and secure it, and report back to her."

I don't know what I had thought he'd say, but this was far from anything I might have imagined. Brú na Bóinne, on the River Boyne, not far from Dublin, was a site of great mythological significance. It was associated with two of fairy lore's most beloved figures: the warrior Diarmuid and his foster father, Angus, both members of an ancient fairy race, the Tuatha De Danaan.

"What sort of ruin, sir?" I asked, heart racing at the possibilities this suggested.

"It is believed to be a tomb of great antiquity. Perhaps a place of ritual or worship. Little is yet known. Its construction likely dates back thousands of years, I am told. Due to the nature of your research, I thought it might interest you."

"Indeed!" I could hardly contain myself.

"Let me show you." He reached for his overcoat then and fished inside one of the pockets. He soon produced a box, rectangular in shape, with a drum attachment, and a winding lever on one side. He wound the gears—visible at the back of the device—several turns and then scooted his chair close to mine.

"Are you familiar with stereoscopes?" he asked, and I shook my head.

Raising it to eye level, he asked, "May I?"

I held my breath and nodded.

The box had a goggle-like viewing attachment, which he pressed gently to my face. His fingers tickled the hair at my temples, sending shivers down my neck and across my shoulders.

I heard a loud click and then a series of softer, more rapid ones as a light flickered on inside the box. A succession of photographs began to unwind. The images appeared to have movement and depth, and I gasped at the ingenuity of it. The first series depicted the rolling Irish countryside, and soon a grassy hill slid into view. The next series showed an opening in the side of the hill. The door was framed with stone slabs, its shape very much resembling the dolmen that had been erected in antiquity in County Clare. Beneath the base of the opening was another stone slab, this one carved with spirals. A rocky footpath curved down the hill around the opening and into the photograph's foreground. Beyond the opening, all was in shadow.

"Extraordinary," I said breathlessly. "I wish we could see inside."

"We can." He lowered the stereoscope.

I stared at him, my cheeks warming in response to multiple stimuli. "You are suggesting that I accompany you?"

"I believe your academic background makes you far better suited than I to evaluate its importance."

I pressed my hands into my lap, struggling to rein in my excitement. "I have studied anthropology, history, and folklore," I said. "But I am no archaeologist, Lord Meath."

He waved his hand, dismissing this argument. "Archaeologists are at the site already. But you've interested me with your theories, and I'm eager to hear what you make of it."

I stared at him, shocked out of sensible speech. "I hardly know what to say, sir."

"Why, *yes*, of course," he said with an easy laugh. "But hold—I haven't told you all yet."

I raised my glass, steadying myself with a sip of absinthe while I waited for him to continue.

Removing the spectacles again, he said, "You asked me a question earlier, which I evaded. If you accompany me to Brú na Bóinne, I shall answer it truthfully."


## EDWARD

There's an old Irish tale of a white trout that, when caught, transforms into a beautiful woman. No trout was ever netted so prettily as Miss Quicksilver. Fortunately for her, the fisherman had no intention of devouring her.

"Lord Meath, I ..." Her breath was short, so excited was she at the prospect, and I confess that what had earlier seemed to me a great bother grew more appealing in the light of her enthusiasm. "When do you intend to make the journey?"

"I should have my arrangements made in two days' time. Would that suit you?"

"And how would we …?" Her hands moved restlessly in her lap, and I understood her discomfiture. A battle was being waged within her. It was a highly irregular invitation from a stranger, which she should unequivocally refuse. And yet such a perfect trap for this particular trout. It had the ring of fate, were I a man to believe in such things. But neither did I disbelieve.

Finally, she asked outright, "What would those arrangements be, sir?"

"We shall travel together, but I shall arrange separate rooms, of course."

Her gaze floated around the room in an absent way as she considered. "I would insist on paying my own way."

I shook my head. "As your employer, I would expect to pay your way, and a salary for the work that I've asked you to do."

"I would insist on paying my way," she repeated more firmly. "But I will accept a small fee for the work. I'd rather not, as it is you who would be doing *me* the favor. But for propriety's sake."

"As you like, Miss Quicksilver." I raised my glass and drained the last drops, covering the relief I felt, and rose to my feet. "Now, I've kept you until a late hour, and if you'll forgive me for insisting again, I'll escort you to your lodging. I cannot permit a visitor to our dark, foggy city to walk the streets alone at this time of night."

She glanced around her again, and I saw her start as she discovered we were two of only a handful of patrons remaining in the Green Fairy.

She rose to her feet, and I lifted her cloak from the back of her chair and wrapped it about her shoulders. "I thank you, sir," she said quietly, glancing up at me through eyes that narrowed further as she smiled. "I have enjoyed your company and lost track of the time."

"And I yours," I replied, noting the slight trembling of her frame beneath my hands. Conscious of an adolescent wish that this had somehow to do with my person rather than my proposal, I gestured toward the door, indicating she should precede me.

In the cobbled street outside, she again raised her hood, and we walked in silence until we reached her modest boarding house.

At the door, I said to her, "Shall I call on you tomorrow afternoon and provide you with the details of our journey?"

She eased her hood back far enough to let me see her face. "Thank you, sir. I'm spending the day at Trinity College tomorrow, but I shall make a point of being in by teatime."

"Good night, then, Miss Q."

"Good night, Lord Meath."

I waited until she'd roused her hostess and gone inside before crossing the street to the boarding house opposite and taking a room for this night and the next. I confess I used my station to secure the room of my choosing, and the hostess was surprised when I expressed my wish for one of the small rooms in the front, facing the street.

I'd climbed into bed—without my final nightly dose of *la fée verte,* as I hoped to sleep lightly—before it occurred to me that, while preoccupied with appreciating my own cleverness, I'd managed to lose sight of the fact that the prophesied death of Miss Quicksilver might, in fact, be related to her acquaintance with *me.*

# THE EARL'S SECRET

## EDWARD

I tossed on the narrow sunken mattress, second-guessing my decision to watch over the woman. I was secretive out of necessity. What business did I have engaging a traveling companion? And wasn't it likely *I* who was the dark cloud drifting on her horizon?

Yet I could not bring myself to abandon her. Even if the warning was no more than the product of a diseased brain, she was still a woman traveling alone at a dark time of year. The weather could be more violent than what she was used to in England, and the roads treacherous. I liked her chances better with than without me, even if she was as self-reliant as she professed to be. As for whether I might be a danger to her … so long as I continued my regimen I would sleep soundly. By daylight, I was certainly a gentleman, and she ran less risk in traveling with me than she might with any of my companions of similar age. Not to imply that I was immune to her considerable, if unusual, charms. But my mental affliction had aged me beyond my years, stripping away a young man's frivolity and thoughtlessness.

These deliberations whipped me about like a lifeboat on a stormy sea, and in the end, I took the absinthe. I kept a flask of it on my person always. Without it, I simply could not sleep, for fear of what I would become in my dreams. But the question remained, how was I to watch over her while dosing myself insensible every night?

I would just have to hope that her bed was as safe a place for her as a maiden's bed *should* be, and confine my vigilance to daylight hours.

I dropped off sometime close to dawn, not waking until full daylight, head pounding from the drink. By my watch, I had only a few hours before I intended to call officially on Miss Q. Even less time to catch up with her at the college. Between now and then, I had to settle our travel arrangements and make my preparations for the journey.

It was past noon by the time I arrived at the magnificent old library. I had attended university in England, as my father wished, but I was no stranger to Trinity. Two of my older childhood companions had completed their studies there, and I'd visited them in my rowdier years. I often met them in the library, just before they abandoned their studies to pursue weekend pleasures.

Even if you had no love of books, it was impossible not to appreciate the aesthetics. It was truly a cathedral of learning, with wood-paneled vaulted ceiling, two levels of shelved volumes, and many busts of notable scholars.

But I did not find Miss Q in the Long Room. Tracking her to her actual location, the Reading Room, took considerable time, as I had to proceed with caution. If she caught me following her around like a villain in a gothic novel, I had no doubt our short acquaintance would come to an abrupt end. For she was a sensible young woman.

She was so absorbed in her task of paging through old periodicals, it was not difficult to avoid her notice. I had intended only to mill about the place and keep within shouting distance in case some threat actually did present itself. But I soon found myself unable to quit the room, so absorbed was *I* in watching her at her work. She had referred to herself as studious and dull by nature, or something equally awful, but I think one might more accurately describe her as *determined.* There was nothing dull about her countenance as she read. Or the way her chin lifted, lips slightly parting, when she discovered a passage of particular interest. Or especially the now familiar squinting quality of her easy smile as she handed in one copy of the *Irish Times* to request another. I could have passed the whole afternoon watching her, striking as she was in the plum-colored plaid that accentuated both her womanly figure and her heart-shaped mouth.

But it was not the reason I had come, and neither was it a gentlemanly thing to do. So I left the Reading Room, picking up a discarded copy of the current *Irish Times* on a table outside, and found a comfortable chair to loiter in.

As it turned out, the chair was *too* comfortable, the previous night's rest too brief, and my reading material entirely too dull. I quickly dozed off. Waking suddenly, groggy and disoriented, I checked the time and found that nearly an hour had passed. I returned to the Reading Room, but Miss Quicksilver had already abandoned the desk where I last saw her. Glancing down, I noticed an old edition of the *Irish Times* still open on the desk, and my gaze fell on a photograph of *me.*

The paper contained the obituary of the former Earl of Meath, my father. The photograph of me, as the heir apparent, appeared alongside the announcement. It detailed my personal history: date of birth, education, and naval career, which was predicted to be cut short by my father's sudden passing. But that wasn't all. The article's final sentence mentioned the rumors of mental affliction that regularly circulated about my family, including my high-ranking cousin. Cold crept into my belly, and I turned and left the room.

Of course, she would have heard of it eventually. Even the English referred to my relation as "the mad Irish queen," though they did so with decidedly less affection than did my countrymen. Madness wasn't a trait that much worried a Celt. I couldn't think of a single family that hadn't been touched by it to some degree.

So why did it concern me that she should know?

*Because I damn well don't want her getting cold feet.*

Now that I'd impulsively invited her, I had let myself become attached to the idea and was determined to see it through. I was no longer sure how much it had to do with the banshee and how much it had to do with my own growing fascination with her.

I strode back through the library and passed once more through the Long Room, making sure that she had, in fact, departed for her boarding house, and I noticed a green vapor trail materializing near the entrance. I stopped to fish my spectacles from my pocket. I was usually safe from the visions during daylight hours, but I'd taken my nightly sleeping draught much later than usual. As the vapor took on a more definite feminine shape, I paused in replacing my spectacles. Had the banshee returned?

No. This visitor was younger. A beautiful woman I easily recognized: *my cousin Isolde,* approaching from the other end of the Long Room. She continued striding toward me, though her eyes were on the floor. Her countenance was melancholy, very much in contrast with the brightness of her raiment. Green though she was from head to toe—absinthe-born, like the others—her floral headdress was probably twelve inches high, crammed full of enormous roses and peonies and seeming to defy the physical laws of nature, held aloft as it was by that delicate head perched on a long, graceful neck. Her narrow shoulders did, however, droop, whether from the weight on her head or from that on her mind, it was impossible to say. The long streamers of the bouquet she held in one hand trailed out sadly behind her.

Not many had seen her this way. But we'd played together as children, despite her six years of seniority, and I knew that the melancholy was as much a part of her as the joyful and sometimes wild exuberance she displayed to the rest of the world.

"Isolde," I murmured.

To my astonishment, she glanced up, apparently as surprised as I was. I had only a second to note that her headdress was held together by thorn-bearing vines, and that a drop of blood trickled down one pale cheek, before her forward momentum carried her against—and, in fact, *through*—me. The sweet aroma of anise filled my nostrils, and a chill breeze seemed to blow through the cage of my ribs.

My hand thudded against my chest as if to catch her, and then came a whisper in my ear. *Make haste, cousin.*

## ADA

My trip to the library had been fruitful, but I was relieved not to see the earl immediately on my return. I needed time to compose myself and overcome my feelings of guilt for checking up on his story. It had been the only sensible thing to do—if anything I'd done since meeting him could be classified as sensible.

He was certainly who he claimed to be—if the Green Fairy's bartender hadn't been proof enough, I'd found photographic evidence in the *Irish Times* archive. Furthermore, the Brú na Bóinne ruin did exist and was the subject of a current archaeological study. It was not, however, a new discovery, as he seemed to believe. Two centuries ago, a farmer had set laborers to digging at the earthen mound. After digging far enough to realize they'd struck upon a ruin of some sort—within the confines of a hill that everyone in the county believed to be a fairy mound, and one associated with the Tuatha De Danaan—they dropped their shovels and fled. The farmer, too, had abandoned the project, leaving the grass-covered knoll to his sheep. Fairies were private creatures and had been known to take revenge on mortals who pried into their affairs. Robert Kirk, a Scottish minister and folklorist, was said to have been abducted by fairies in repayment for exposing their secrets in his important book on the subject, *The Secret Commonwealth*. When he died, his body was found on a fairy hill near his home.

But the present-day tenant of Newgrange, thinking to profit either from the structure itself or from whatever it might contain, had excavated further. He found some antique trinkets and sold them for a fraction of their value. When an archaeological hobbyist got hold of a bead necklace and tracked down its origin, the truth had come out and the crown stepped in.

It was a fascinating history, and I'd made careful notes. To say I was eager to visit the site would be an understatement of epic proportion. But truth be told, I'd been equally fascinated by the information I found on the earl and his family. I had to ask myself: was he mad, despite appearances? Might he be dangerous?

More than a figure of dread, he struck me as a man who was suffering. If he would be open with me, as he'd promised to do in exchange for accompanying him to Newgrange, might I be able to help him in some way, if only by listening to his tale and sharing my research with him? I felt that it was too early to dwell on what he might do for *me*, though there was no question my meeting with him in the Green Fairy had been most serendipitous. The impromptu journey would cut short my time in Dublin, but I could always return to the city a day or two early. And it was just possible that last night I had accomplished exactly what I'd set out to in coming here.

But in my enthusiasm, I was running ahead. This afternoon,

we would have a second interview, and I'd have an opportunity to revoke my acceptance of his proposal, should I begin to doubt.

My landlady had tea ready when I arrived, but I retired to my room first to freshen my complexion with cool water and tidy my windblown hair. I studied my face a few moments in the mirror, remembering that he'd called me "otherworldly." Certainly, he had meant no insult, but could it fairly be called a compliment?

*What difference does it make either way?* His opinion regarding my appearance was of no consequence, that was true enough. And yet ... were my brows too thick? Was my nose perhaps too small? Was a smile that tended toward squinting considered a defect? I'd certainly been teased for all this and more—though for none so much as my hair—in my years at that frightful boarding school. It had been some time since I felt a pang over the lost time with my parents, but I felt one now. I turned to make my way downstairs.

I met my landlady on the stairs. Her eyes were wide, and her corseted bosom heaved from having climbed too quickly. "There's a fine gentleman come to see you, miss. Mr. Donoghue, he said his name was, and he's wearing a hat and an odd pair of spectacles. But he's a peer or I'm a Christmas pudding. Go on down with you, and I'll ask Cook for more tea things."

I pressed my fingertips against my chest, where my heart was making clear its feelings on the topic of the earl's visit.

"Thank you, Mrs. Maguire," I replied, wondering whether she detected the hum of excitement under my controlled tone.

She turned, hoisting her skirts as she retreated down the stairs, and I followed.

As we descended I appreciated the good-natured woman more than ever. I'd not been gossiped to or scolded in her house, and even now her interest seemed to run no deeper than making a good impression on the important personage waiting in her sitting room.

Due to the season's limited daylight hours and the gloominess of the weather, the lights were already burning downstairs. As I entered the room, the earl removed his hat. His hair was loose today, but he'd used a little oil—I detected the clean scent of rosemary—to comb it back from his face, and his dark curls gathered behind his ears.

"Miss Quicksilver," said he, smiling warmly. "I'm happy to see you again."

"And I you, Lord Meath," I replied with a curtsy.

"Please, sit down," he urged me, gesturing to the tea table near the sitting room window. A teapot and cup, and a plate bearing a fat slice of cake, were already there waiting for me.

"Will you join me, my lord?" I said. "My landlady is bringing a plate and cup for you." I knew that I should have warned Mrs. Maguire of the earl's visit, but the circumstances were so unusual, I confess I had not been entirely sure he would come, and then what might she have thought of me?

"I thank you," said the earl, taking an armchair opposite me. "It's a bitterly cold day. Please go ahead with your tea, and I shall tell you what arrangements I've made."

Oddly enough after our familiar fireside chat at the Green Fairy, there was now a feeling of awkwardness between us. Perhaps that was only to be expected. The absinthe house was a place for light and easy conversation, while the sitting room during daylight hours was a setting altogether different for a man and woman of recent acquaintance.

Lord Meath removed his spectacles, and as I studied his face in the wan afternoon light, I decided I had mistaken his age. I'd believed him closer to my own age, but now, noting the smile lines at the corners of his eyes, I thought he might be as much as ten years older. Which, admittedly, left him still a young man, as I was only twenty-two.

"Please," he said, reaching for the teapot, "I insist that you not wait."

I watched, bemused, as he filled my cup. I'd never been served tea by a man—at least, not outside a restaurant or café. And I had certainly never been served tea by an earl.

"Blast!" he swore softly, hesitating with the teapot held aloft. "I've left you no room for milk. I shouldn't assume everyone takes tea as I do." He replaced the pot on the table. "Now you'll think I've done it on purpose, to have your cup."

I smiled. "In fact, my lord, you've discovered something else we have in common. You'll have to find other pretense for depriving me."

Lord Meath laughed at this and slid the cup and saucer my direction. "I wouldn't dream of it, Miss Q."

Mrs. Maguire appeared at exactly that moment, bearing a tray with another pot and slice of cake. She gave a woeful groan as she approached. "Begging your pardon, Your—Mr. Donoghue. Let me do that for you."

"Not at all, madam," he replied. "I was only urging your lodger not to let her tea get cold on my account."

Then Mrs. Maguire's gaze did flit to my face. She placed another teacup on the table and filled it for her new guest. "I've brought you a slice of Cook's Christmas cake, sir. I've never tasted better. Can I bring Your Lordsh—you—anything else? Miss Quicksilver takes a light afternoon tea, but perhaps you'd like a bit of cottage pie? Or a drop of sherry to warm your insides?"

"Thank you, no," replied the earl kindly. "Tea is just what I want right now."

Mrs. Maguire nodded. "Then I'll leave you to it, Mr. Donoghue. Ring the bell if you change your mind."

As Mrs. Maguire hurried away with her tray, I said quietly, "I don't think you've fooled her about who you are."

"You may be right about that." Smiling wryly, he lifted his cup and sipped the strong Irish brew.

"You were saying about traveling arrangements, my lord?"

He nodded. "Can you be ready to go tomorrow afternoon?"

My hand slipped on the handle of my cup, and it clinked against the saucer and sloshed tea onto Mrs. Maguire's table.

Lord Meath was quick with the tea towel and wiped up the drops. "Forgive me." He laughed. "Perhaps I seem overeager. It's just that tomorrow is the winter solstice, and as I understand that the day has particular pagan significance, I thought it might be a good day for our visit."

"Yes, of course," I replied, cheeks burning. "How considerate of you."

"Unfortunately, the Drogheda tramway did not have seats available until afternoon," he explained, "so we shall arrive at Newgrange just an hour or so before sunset. But I've taken rooms for us in Drogheda, and we'll be able to return easily to the site the next morning."

I was impressed by his attentiveness to scholarly details. Also, accustomed to relying on myself, I was unused to being so well taken care of. "Thank you, my lord," I said earnestly.

To all appearances, Lord Meath was almost as eager as I was. Frankly, it all seemed too good to be true, and for all my scholarly leanings, I confess to a superstitious vein running through my character.

*It's only sensible to be wary.* It was time to bring the subject around to a topic that would allow me to continue my observation of his character. But how to segue? Subtlety was not my forte.

Lord Meath, as it turned out, was prepared to save me the trouble. "Miss Q," he began, "there is something I'd like to discuss with you before you agree to embark on this journey."

"I have *already* agreed, my lord," I reminded him, feeling uneasy at his altered tone.

"So you have, and true to my word, I'm prepared to reveal to you my secret."

The tension in the air between us had taken on a more somber quality, and to cover my uneasiness, I took a bite of Cook's excellent cake. Unfortunately, I had no appetite, and I chewed and swallowed mechanically.

"You asked me yesterday whether I had ever seen a fairy."

His eyes met mine, and I gave a small nod of encouragement.

"I consider myself a man who looks for a rational explanation of things, and to be very honest, Miss Q, I'm not sure whether I've ever considered a belief in fairies to *be* altogether rational."

"You are far from alone in that sentiment, Lord Meath," I assured him.

"Perhaps so. But I was also honest yesterday when I said I will not disbelieve a thing I cannot disprove. Moreover, I have some personal evidence that your theory is not a frivolous one."

"You have seen *something*," I replied, heart beating faster. But I kept my tone dispassionate.

He nodded. "Until I met you, I considered it no more than hallucination."

The pain it caused him to reveal this was apparent in the downward tilt of his brow line and the furrows above.

"Perhaps you thought you were going mad," I offered in what I hoped was a gentle tone.

The lines of his forehead softened minutely. "Just so."

"And what is it you've seen, sir, if you don't mind my asking?"

He threaded his fingers together, folding his hands on the table before him. His skin had a duskiness to it, and the tracing of hair on his fingers was as black as the curls on his head. "What I'm about to tell you is a thing I've told no one else," he replied.

A warm, fluttering sensation rose in my breast. "I'm honored that you would place your trust in me, sir."

"It may seem odd, considering how little we know each other. But I have good instincts when it comes to people, and they're telling me that you are an honest, good-hearted, and steady young woman."

This was high praise from anyone, but from him … I cleared my throat. "Thank you, Lord Meath. I hope you won't think me obsequious if I say the same of you."

"Certainly not, and I thank you. But I have not been entirely frank with you, and I would like to remedy that now."

I waited for him to continue. He finished his tea, and I reached for the pot and poured him another cup. I believe, had the offer of a glass of sherry been accepted, he would now have drained the glass.

"I take absinthe nightly—less for my own enjoyment of the spirit than for the sleep it affords me. Without it, you see, I suffer from nightwalking."

At first, I didn't understand him. "Do you mean that you walk in your sleep, my lord?"

He nodded, watching the steam rise from his teacup. "The absinthe ensures that I sleep soundly, but it also causes hallucinations. Or what, until yesterday, I had considered to be hallucinations. These visions have a green cast, like the spirit itself, and I've found that I can mask them by wearing green-tinted spectacles, though sometimes they will still appear in my peripheral vision, and I can't always ignore them."

"That's what happened last night, when you took ill."

"It is."

"Do they ever speak to you, my lord?"

"They often try to get my attention in some way, whether through speech or by other means. Other times, they take no notice of me."

"And the one from last night? Did it try to get your attention?"

He met my gaze again, and the intensity of his expression almost frightened me. "The one last night was most provoking."

I felt a prickling sensation at the nape of my neck. "May I know what species of fairy it was?"

"*Bean sí*," he replied. This literally meant "fairy woman," but the banshee was a harbinger of death.

"The keen," I replied. "I've never heard it, but I imagine it to be most distressing. Banshees often attach themselves to noble families. Had you seen one before last night?"

He nodded but offered no further explanation.

"I apologize for my questions, my lord. The topic is of great interest to me, but I do not wish to cause you pain."

"You do not, Miss Q," he replied, earnestness in his dark expression. "On the contrary, you give me some hope that I'm not going mad. I suspect you've heard the rumors about my family."

I dropped my gaze to my cup, my composure shaken by the blunt question. "Yes, my lord. But people love to gossip."

"True enough. But in this case, they may have some cause. Today, I had another vision, Miss Q, and I wonder what you will make of it."

"Please go on, sir," I encouraged him. "You have all my attention."

"You are kind." A grateful smile touched his lips before giving way again to a pensive frown. "In going about my affairs this afternoon, I saw my cousin."

My eyes widened. "Do you mean Queen Isolde?"

"I do."

I pressed my lips together, thinking. "Are you certain it wasn't the queen *herself*? She resides in Dublin, does she not?"

He shook his head. "This time of year, she spends in Connacht— the west of Ireland. The wild and windswept coast suits her mood during these dark, short days. She lodges with our O'Malley cousins, who holiday on Achill Island until the New Year."

I knew of the O'Malleys, a seafaring family of old. In the sixteenth century, Grace O'Malley, a chieftain's daughter, had been both a sea captain and a pirate and was rumored to have been visited by Queen Elizabeth. Historical women of consequence were of particular interest at the Lovelace Academy. In fact, I now recalled a story popular with the Irish: that Elizabeth had fallen in love with an O'Malley on her visit and, months later, returned to bear and abandon an illegitimate daughter. If there was any truth to this tale, Isolde's ancestry was a volatile blend of Spanish sailor, Irish pirate, and English royalty. Did this vision of Lord Meath's mean we must add fairy to the mix?

"Was it like the banshee's visit, Lord Meath? Did she try to get your attention?"

"Not at first. She seemed not to notice me. But I called to her, and then she …" Sighing, he ran a hand through his dark hair. "She walked right through me. And she bade me hurry."

"Hurry? Did you understand this request?"

He frowned. "Not at all. I mean to say, I had a sense that she was referring to my inspection of the ruin. But I could see no sense in that. What urgency could there be? And more to the point, was this *real*, Miss Q, or a hallucination?"

A connection had formed in my mind that I didn't think had yet in his. "I don't wish to alarm you, Lord Meath, but perhaps she was part of the banshee's warning. If this banshee is connected to your family, might the queen be in some danger?"

He studied me a moment, and his expression did not change. But behind his eyes, it seemed to me, he was still contending with strong emotions. Finally, he replied, "That had not occurred to me. It's a keen bit of observation on your part."

"Would it not be best for you to go to her?" I asked, hiding my deep disappointment about the loss of Newgrange. But if he could help his cousin, he must.

He considered this and replied, "It would be two days before I could reach her. The best course would be to send a telegram as soon as I leave you. We'll make our visit to Newgrange on the morrow, and from there I'll continue west."

He'd been studying his tea leaves as he spoke, so he didn't notice the selfish relief that I was unable to conceal.

But now he looked at me. "Perhaps, if you've not tired of me by then, you might consider making the journey with me. If you had to choose the region of Ireland most closely connected with the gentlefolk, the west might very well be it. And in particular, the wilds of the ancient kingdom of Connacht, where legend has it the Tuatha De Danaan first landed on Irish soil." He smiled. "The O'Malley Christmas feast is something to behold."

"You're inviting me to meet the *queen*?" I asked, incredulous.

"Well, I don't imagine you can avoid meeting her if we journey to Achill this time of year. But mostly, I'm taking an interest in your research, and I suspect that you'll get further with your inquiries if you're introduced by a native guide."

This was much to take in. So much that I sank back in my chair and continued to stare at him with my mouth hanging half open, like a child.

"I beg you, don't be scandalized, Miss Q," he said in a softer tone. "Only think about whether it might suit you. And in the meantime, see how you like passing the time with me. Two days hence, you may find you've had quite enough of my company."

I rather doubted it. But even that was no excuse for what I said next. "It sounds quite wonderful, Lord Meath. And an opportunity too auspicious to pass up."

He gave a full and genuine laugh. "I guess it must be true that 'faint heart never won fair maiden.'"

I joined in his laughter but quickly became interested in my Christmas cake to prevent him from noticing my embarrassment at being referred to, even metaphorically, as a fair maiden he had won.

He was lovely, truly. And perhaps a *little* mad. But I'd never felt such excitement in the presence of anyone. He seemed so alive, and it didn't hurt that he had taken such an active interest in my research. If we worked together, mightn't it ease his suffering? I believed that knowledge was power in cases like his. I could imagine nothing worse than believing that your own mind was slipping away from you.

From a practical standpoint, he was correct to suggest the benefit of having a "native guide." While many Dubliners spoke both English and Irish, English would be of limited use in the countryside, and at this point in my career, I was little more than a novice when it came to the Irish language. The Irish had remained wary of the English ever since the failed Norman conquest in the thirteenth century, and I had nothing but friendliness and my nonthreatening appearance to ease my way.

I had expected to pass Christmas in the only boardinghouse in the Wicklow Mountains that was welcoming tourists this time of year, in the village of Glendalough. It was not far from Dublin, and there was a picturesque churchyard and lake. But the prospect of Christmas without friends was something I hadn't allowed myself to dwell on. Now I had been invited to Christmas dinner with the queen of Ireland and her cousin, the Earl of Meath, my new Irish friend. None of my schoolmates would believe it. I could scarcely believe it myself.

Mrs. Maguire chose that moment to bustle in and check on her guests. She entered the room purposefully noisy, so as not to appear to eavesdrop.

"I'll just put a brick of turf on the fire, my lord," said she, apparently having given up pretending not to know who he was. "It's grown dark and drafty."

"Allow me, Mrs. Maguire," he replied, rising from his seat.

A meandering, hand-wringing protest issued from the lips of good Mrs. M, and she stood smiling and blushing like a lass half her age as she watched him build up the fire.

"Will you stay for supper, my lord?" she asked when he'd finished. "We eat simply here, but there will be plenty."

I couldn't help hoping he'd say yes, but he replied, "Thank you, kind madam. I'm sure Miss Quicksilver is by now longing for a respite from my company. And I must away and let her pack her things."

"I do hate to see the child head out into the wilds at this time of year," clucked the good woman. "Perhaps you might persuade her to stay, my lord? At least until Christmas. She hadn't ought to be among strangers."

He would know from this that I had not fully revealed my plans to her, and my face grew warm at being caught in even this small deceit. The fact I had concealed information suggested I thought there was something to be ashamed of in accepting his offer. In truth, I was not sure there wasn't.

But the earl took it in stride.

"I find that independent young ladies like Miss Quicksilver will not be dissuaded from any course they've set their heart on," he replied with a smile that fairly oozed Irish charm. "But I have faith the lady can look after herself."

"Well, I hope you're right, Your Lordship; that I do."

Lord Meath retrieved his hat from a nearby chair. "I'll come round at one o'clock tomorrow to help you with your things. Will that suit, Miss Q?"

"Yes, I thank you, sir," I replied. This drew another quick glance from our hostess.

The earl left us, and I took my leave of Mrs. Maguire to return to my room and begin packing my things. I felt my landlady's eyes on my back as I climbed the stairs, and I sensed she had perhaps begun to have a different sort of concern for me. But if even at this late juncture I decided to revoke my acceptance of Lord Meath's proposal—which I couldn't very fairly do now that he'd shared his secret with me—it wouldn't be due to concern over my reputation. My research had ever meant more to me, though I hadn't exactly been careless before now in my associations with men.

I suspected that in the course of our journey, we'd draw gazes less filled with kindly concern than Mrs. Maguire's, but I was used to strangers' stares.

## EDWARD

I had intended to tell Miss Quicksilver the whole truth about the banshee, but when the moment came, I found myself unequal to the task. I could not bear the thought that she might revoke her acceptance of my offer, deem *me* the danger to her that I very well might be, and send me away. Perhaps she would even leave Ireland, and then I'd never know whether the banshee's prophecy had been fulfilled. I didn't think I could live with that.

So instead, I'd gotten myself in deeper. Thus far, I had at least managed to speak the truth, with only a few details withheld. I *did,* in fact, intend to telegraph my cousin, though only to alert her I was traveling to County Mayo and bringing a guest. But concealment sooner or later will require the service of lies, and I doubted I would avoid it in the end.

Most disturbing was that I didn't feel very much sorry for any of it. I only believed I *should* be. I wanted to keep the young lady close, which was quite against my character. Since I'd grown old enough to care for myself, I'd never tolerated anyone's company for very long. I doubted anyone could have long tolerated *mine.* The nightwalking had started around the time I turned sixteen, and along with it my character had taken a turn toward the morose. A duke's daughter had once sought my affections, and I broke the poor thing's heart. She'd been a lovely English rose, all kindness, sweet blushes, and soft manners. Altogether too delicate a creature to endure a lifetime bound to the mad Earl of Meath. My duty to my father required me someday to produce an heir, but I couldn't even consider such a thing until I could make my bed a safe place for the fairer sex. Perhaps Miss Quicksilver could help me with that. Perhaps that was why I felt so few qualms about endangering her so recklessly.

The proximity of thoughts of my bed to the thoughts of Miss Quicksilver triggered a quake in the clay of my being. Perhaps my determination to keep her close had nothing to do with what was best for her.

*Now we're getting to the heart of it, Meath.*                    •

# INSIDE A FAIRY MOUND

## ADA

Lord Meath was late, and I feared he'd changed his mind. But at a quarter past the hour, he arrived.

"My apologies for the delay," he said to me after Mrs. Maguire let him in. "Fear not, we shall get you to your tram in time."

He had joined in my subterfuge, I assumed, to protect me from the disapproval of my landlady, and I recalled how when we'd first met he'd asked me whether I was embarking on an elopement. That was exactly what this felt like, and the thought evoked an uncharacteristic giddiness in me—unimportant orphan girl that I was, running off to marry a handsome Irish earl.

*But I'm not,* I reminded myself, because I couldn't tolerate such foolishness, not even inside my own head.

His carriage driver came to the door for my luggage, and Mrs. Maguire handed me a parcel neatly wrapped in brown paper. "In case you have trouble finding a meal on the road, love," she explained.

I thanked her and felt a genuine pang on parting with her. I suppose I was always feeling the loss of my mother, but a matron who showed some interest in my welfare did tend to make me feel it more keenly.

I took the parcel and gave the promise she asked for: that if I decided to spend more time in Dublin, I would consider returning to her. "Should you be still in need of lodging," she'd added, with a glance at Lord Meath. A world of meaning passed in that glance. I'm fairly certain it went something like "I wish the two of you well, but should it turn out that you are not the gentleman you appear to be, I'll not keep silent about what I know."

For a moment, it seemed to have rattled him. But he recovered quickly enough, offering his thanks for her hospitality.

A fine carriage was waiting outside, and I guessed that it belonged to the earl's household. When he offered his hand to lift me inside, I felt my first true misgiving. While eating my solitary supper the evening before, I'd overheard Mrs. Maguire talking to Cook, and there were words about young noblemen and their carelessness in their dealings with young women of lower rank. I knew very well that I was *meant* to overhear those words and that her intentions were kind. At the time, I only smiled to myself and went on with my supper.

But planning such a thing and actually going through with it were entirely different matters. I imagined explaining this excursion to my academic advisor, and my cheeks flamed.

The earl noticed my hesitation. "Have you changed your mind, Miss Q?" He stepped closer, and I shivered at the sudden proximity. "Please don't be afraid to tell me if you have," he continued in a lower voice. "Or feel in any way obligated because of the things I've told you."

I took a steadying breath, and I smiled. Reaching for the hand he still held out, I replied, "Not at all, my lord. I only wondered whether I'd left my hairbrush on the dresser upstairs."

Smiling, he squeezed my fingers slightly, causing another shiver. It was a peculiar sensation—warm instead of cold.

"Shall I retrieve it for you?" he asked. I read in his eyes that he hadn't bought this fib, but he would go on the pointless errand to give me time if I wanted it.

I shook my head. "I've remembered. It's in my trunk."

Gripping his hand, I stepped up into the carriage. When I had taken my seat and adjusted my skirts, he followed, sitting opposite me. The driver removed the step and closed the door, and we got under way.

"I've made alterations to our arrangements, which I want to discuss with you," said the earl before awkward silence could descend.

"All right," I replied, trying to keep my tone light.

He reached into his coat pocket and withdrew a folded paper that turned out to be a map. "I've sent a rider ahead to my tenant at Newgrange," he said, "and his family will host you in their home this evening. Their cottage is cozy, but you'll be welcome to all they have. I'll lodge in the camp with the archaeologists and workers."

I frowned, wondering why he would inconvenience himself so. "You've decided against Drogheda?"

He nodded, then bent forward to show me the map. "With these arrangements, we can rise early so you can finish your inspection of the site, and then we'll continue by private coach to Trim. That village boasts an impressive castle ruin, which we can view in the late afternoon. In the morning, we'll take a train to Westport, then on to Newport. From there, we can travel by boat to Kildamhnait Tower." The tip of his finger circled Achill Island. "One of Grace O'Malley's old strongholds."

"And will we find pirates there?" I asked.

He gave a conspiratorial grin. "If we're lucky. With more good luck, and favorable weather, we'll arrive by Christmas Eve." He glanced up at me, eyes alight with boyish enthusiasm. "What do you think? Will it be too much for you?"

I shook my head. "I hardly know what to say, my lord."

"Your honest reaction to all this, please. I don't want to drive you like a sheep."

I smiled, hoping to reassure him. I believed that his case of nerves rivaled even my own. "It's all beyond everything I imagined when I made my plans to come here. You quite overwhelm me with your kindness, sir." The real fondness I was beginning to feel for the earl came through in my tone, and I wondered what he would make of it.

"Well," he replied, refolding the map and tucking it back in his pocket, "it's really you who have been kind to *me*. Agreeing to the trip to Newgrange and not taking fright at my wild schemes." His gaze was downcast, and I knew that my gratitude had made him uncomfortable, but a little smile still quirked his lips. "You're made of sturdier stuff than most young women of my acquaintance. But I suppose that comes of not spending all your time in drawing rooms."

"Don't give me too much credit," I said with a laugh. "Drawing rooms were never offered. Had they been, who knows what sort of woman I'd have turned out to be."

"The sort that would be followed about by every young lord in the county, I'd wager. It appears that may be your fate anyway, despite the lack of drawing rooms."

This was said in such a mirthful tone, there was simply no reason for the coy way I directed my gaze down at my folded hands.

"Forgive me, Miss Q," said the earl quietly. "If my behavior seems overly familiar, I hope you'll set it down to how comfortable I feel in your company. I meant no offense."

"And I took none, my lord," I assured him. "It's only that I'm unused to such compliments. But it does not necessarily follow that I don't enjoy them just as much as your drawing room–variety female."

He laughed heartily at this, dispelling the sudden specter of my landlady and her less-than-subtle warning. Our discourse continued in this lighthearted vein until we reached the Dublin–Drogheda tramway station. I was pleased to find that the melancholy that seemed always to half-possess his mood was not detectable this afternoon.

I had never experienced our next mode of conveyance before that day. The tram had a steam-powered locomotive—very like that of a train, but smaller—that pulled a double-deck passenger car. Lord Meath explained that the trams, not being considered entirely safe, were allowed to operate only in the suburbs of Dublin. Then he hastened to assure me we had nothing to fear. So fascinated was I by the mechanics of the thing, the reassurance was unnecessary. I was eager for my maiden voyage.

The passenger car was clean and simple, and though it was covered, its windows were open to the elements. Having seats on the upper deck, we had some view of the surrounding hills. But the locomotive produced a great lot of noise, steam, and vibration, such that our conversation was scant during the more than two-hour journey.

The driver had been paid to let us off just short of Drogheda, where a small private coach was waiting to take us to Newgrange. As we switched from tram to coach, the clouds suddenly parted, and the sinking sun spilled golden light over the emerald hills and squares of pasture with their low stone walls.

I paused outside the coach, turning my face to catch the sun's warmth. Inwardly, I was warmed by eager anticipation of the journey to come.

## EDWARD

Her hood had slipped back, sunlight transforming her hair into molten silver and raising the natural rosiness in her complexion. I felt a piercing sensation in my chest and knew that I'd taken a fairy dart there.

"How lovely," she murmured.

I cleared my throat to relieve the sudden tightness. "Indeed."

She opened her eyes, and the warmth of the smile she turned on me rivaled the sun.

"Are you warm enough, Miss Q?" I asked. The ground was damp and lent a bite to the air, but she had a good winter cloak with a fur-trimmed hood.

"I am, my lord."

"Shall we enter the coach?"

She allowed me to help her inside, and I offered her the blanket for her lap. She accepted, and I helped spread it over her.

"I fear we're in for a bumpy ride," I warned her. "The weather takes its toll on these country roads, but we should reach our destination in less than an hour."

"I shan't break," she assured me.

She turned her face to the coach window, watching the passing scenery while I gave up my feeble struggle not to watch *her*.

She appeared oblivious to the effect she had on me and on those around her. On the tram, we'd sat together but preserved a polite physical distance that likely made it clear to others we were not man and wife. Before we left the outskirts of Dublin, a wealthy-looking tradesman had boarded our car and stopped before us as if expecting me to make room for him between us. Instead, I had scooted closer to her, leaving room on the other side. I don't believe she even noticed this gentlemanly skirmish. Perhaps she was so used to being stared at for her irregularity, she'd simply learned to ignore it.

She turned from the window then, perhaps feeling *my* eyes on her now, and asked, "Have you heard stories connected with the fairy mound at Brú na Bóinne, my lord?"

Having watched her, entranced, for perhaps a quarter of an hour while pretending to gaze out her window, I struggled to recover my dozing faculties. Finally, I replied, "One of the reasons I thought it might interest you is that over the course of my lifetime, I have heard various reports of fairy activity on and about the mound."

She adjusted her position to give me her full attention. "Much has been said of it in the lore. May I ask what *type* of activity?"

Her scholarly inquiries these past days had started me reflecting on my boyhood and the stories I'd heard from servants on my father's estate, as well as from my grandmother.

"The usual variety," I replied. "Revelries and processions. Sometimes, ghostly figures have been seen atop the mound and walking the surrounding countryside."

"The reports distinguish between fairies and ghosts?"

I was not sure of the answer and said so, but added, "My sense is that in the minds of my countrymen, all inexplicable events are connected to fairies. My grandmother believed—or professed to believe—that those who die of wasting illnesses wake in Faery, their bodies whole again."

Excitement gave her a feverish look. "I have read firsthand accounts of this belief," she said. "They are said to wake in Knock Ma, the palace of the fairy king, Finvara. If I am not mistaken in my geography, we will be traveling quite close to the ruins at Knock Ma, will we not?"

I smiled. How could I help it? It was pleasing to give her such pleasure. "Indeed," I replied. "We shall make a visit there after Christmas, if you like."

"You are too good to me, my lord," she said, laughing.

She then reached into the satchel she always carried and drew out a notebook and pencil. "May I take down notes of our conversation?"

"Of course, Miss Q."

"I cannot express how grateful I am for these personal accounts, Lord Meath. I assure you they will be put to good use."

"To the contrary," I replied, "you have expressed it quite graciously. And I am very happy to be able to help you in return for your agreeing to accompany me on this uncomfortable journey. Now, tell me, Miss Q, what you have learned about Brú na Bóinne."

She took a moment to jot down a few words—an impressive feat given the movement of the carriage over the bumpy road—before replying, "I know mostly what can be found in books, which is why I have made this journey to Ireland. I know that the mound has a strong link to the Tuatha De Danaan. There is said to be an underground kingdom ruled by Angus, who is associated with love and poetry, and his queen, Caer, who could change into a swan. I know that Angus was the foster father of Diarmuid, a legendary Danaan warrior. Diarmuid spent his boyhood at Brú na Bóinne and was eventually buried there."

"I have never understood why Diarmuid is viewed as a romantic figure," I remarked, "having been most famous for stealing the fiancée of his chief and friend, Finn."

She laughed. "The lore has not been kind to his paramour, either. Most stories say that Gráinne enchanted and lured Diarmuid away, and after Finn allowed Diarmuid to be killed by a boar, she went *back* to him."

"We are agreed, then," I replied, laughing with her. "It has more the character of tragedy than of romance."

She sobered a moment, touching her pencil to her chin, and replied, "In scholarly circles, the story is viewed more symbolically, though there is little agreement on what it symbolizes. There is a sort of parallel to the story of Adam and Eve, and it is likely the original story evolved under the influence of the church."

"Ah. Perhaps it was never intended to be a love story."

She smiled. "Perhaps not."

After that, she made a few more notes in her book, and when she lifted her gaze again, she pursued a new line of questioning. "In my studies, there has always been a distinction between the 'big folk' of Faery—such as the Danaan and their enemies, the Fomorians—and the diminutive fairies that Irishmen often refer to as the 'gentlefolk.' Do you find that to be true in your experience, and do you know how to account for it?"

Again I was forced to recall memories from long ago, when my grandmother was still living. I had not thought about her stories for many years, and I confess they turned my thoughts to the cousin I'd grown up with and made me nostalgic for simpler times. I remembered tramping across meadows and tumbling down hills in our searches for gentlefolk and fighting with wooden swords we'd made by taking apart old fences. I always pretended to be one of the ancient heroes—Oíson or even Diarmuid—while she pretended to be the warrior queen Maeve or the Morrigan, the dread goddess of war.

"My grandmother told us stories of both varieties," I replied. "And in them, the gentlefolk were not always small. Here I believe your own learning probably exceeds my own, but I think she viewed the gentlefolk as descendants of the Danaan."

She nodded. "I have read of this belief. Other sources refer to the gentlefolk as faded versions of the ancient heroes."

She grew quiet and focused as she fell again to the task of scribbling. Much as I was tempted to keep her talking—something I sensed would not be difficult, as she was warm to this topic—I left her to her work and fell into nostalgic reverie while watching the scenery pass outside the window.

After much jostling on the muddy road—and a stop to free a mired wheel—we arrived at Newgrange. The sun was setting as we alighted from the coach, so rather than stopping at the farmhouse, we made straight for the ruin.

The workmen's equipment had left muddy ruts in the field, and their tents huddled together on one side of the fairy hill. Miss Q raised the hem of her dress and approached the dark opening in the hillside as calmly as if she were entering a church. There had been some clearing away of turf and stone since the photographs were taken, and the opening was now large enough to walk through. The workmen had also reconstructed the stone frame of the door, supporting it with timbers.

"Come away from there, miss," someone called.

The man strode toward her, and I walked over to intercept him.

"Good day, sir," I said. He turned to look at me. "I'm Edward Donoghue, Earl of Meath. I believe you had word of my coming? This is Miss Quicksilver. We're here by order of the queen to inspect the ruin and the work that's going on here."

I extended my hand, and the man took it. "Honor to meet you, my lord," he replied stiffly. "I'm Tom Deane, the architect in charge."

"Is it unsafe to go inside?" I asked him.

Deane's gaze shifted to the opening in the hillside. "By our accounting, it's stood at least two thousand years. It's not likely to cave in now. The entryway was in a risky state, but we've shored that up." His gaze returned to my companion. "It's safe enough, but I'd prefer nothing was disturbed until the archaeologists finish their work."

"Miss Quicksilver is a specialist in Irish history and mythology,"

I explained. "I've brought her along to help evaluate the cultural significance of the ruin. I assure you, she won't disturb your work."

Deane sized up Miss Q in a way that suggested he was not as susceptible to her considerable charms as I.

"Perhaps you might wait until the morrow, my lord?"

"I'm afraid we have only this evening and the morning until we must continue west to make our report to Queen Isolde. We'd like to perform a brief inspection tonight. Before we do, perhaps your men can share with us any discoveries they've made."

"May I ask if anything was found inside, sir?" asked Miss Q.

Deane shook his head. "Nothing but the bones of small mammals and birds. But we weren't the first inside. Once excavations get under way, I'm sure we'll find more. What was carried away already by the farmer, the archaeologists have classified as 'grave goods.'"

Miss Q looked a little stricken at the word "excavations," but she made no comment. "Meaning items that would have been buried with any human remains interred here?" she asked.

Deane nodded, and I saw a flicker of keener interest in his gaze. "Exactly so," he replied. "We assume ceremonial burials took place here, though we've yet to confirm it."

"I see." She glanced again at the entry. "How large is the ruin, Mr. Deane?"

"The main passage goes back about sixty feet. At the end is a large chamber with three smaller chambers adjoining. We've found large stone slabs throughout, and our geologist says they came from nowhere around here. Which has confounded us a good deal, considering that the people who built this structure must have had only rudimentary tools."

The disapproving Mr. Deane was warming up nicely. It was a special talent of my Miss Q.

"The passage runs straight?" she asked.

"It does, miss."

"Hmm." She continued to study the entryway. "Do you mind if we have a look inside now, before the light's completely gone? I give you my word we'll not disturb anything."

"All right, then," he said, with graciousness, even. "To tell the truth, we were all going for a pint, anyway. Perhaps my lord and yourself would like to join us?"

"We would indeed," I replied, stepping in. "But with our time so short, we'd better go about our business. Don't let us stop you, though, Mr. Deane. Perhaps Miss Q can ask the rest of her questions in the morning?"

Deane nodded. "Certainly, my lord. Take the lamp, and you'll find plenty of candles inside. Without them, you'd not see anything but shadows. And once the daylight is gone, it's black as pitch. Hope you don't frighten easy, miss." Deane smiled at her. "It fairly makes my skin crawl. You're sure you won't reconsider? A pub's a cozier spot to sit out the darkest night of the year."

She returned his smile. "We thank you for the invitation, sir, but you go on. I assure you I'm not easily frightened."

My heart swelled with something like pride. *How ridiculous, Meath,* was my head's answer.

"Good eve, then, miss. Good eve, my lord." He'd removed his hat on our arrival, and he replaced it now. "If you would, put out the lights when you leave."

"Good eve, Mr. Deane," I replied. "You have my word."

Miss Q met my gaze as he left us. "After you, Lord Meath."

"After *you,* Miss Q. I insist."

With a grin of anticipation, she turned and lifted an oil lantern from a hook by the entrance.

We had a bit of a squeeze just inside, where the passage narrowed. As it opened out again and the light from our lantern and others filled the space, I was surprised by how square the passage was. And not earthen at all—stone slabs lined the whole length of it. It was hard to imagine so many of them being transported here by modern man, much less by a primitive people.

"It's close, isn't it?" she said, voice echoing in the chamber. I felt an inexplicable surge of dread and increased my pace to close the distance between us, my head suddenly filling with visions of ancient monsters. But then I realized she was talking about the closeness of the walls. *Steady on, Meath.*

"So it is," I replied.

"It appears not much more than a man-made cave," she observed sedately, but I felt the energy she was suppressing. Was it fear? Excitement? Perhaps both? I confess that to me, it was a large hole in the ground, made interesting by the fair maiden lighting my way. "Whoever ordered the construction left very little evidence for us to follow and understand the why of it," she continued.

"So far as we know now," I replied. "Who knows what they may find when they begin to dig?"

At the end of the passage were the chambers described by Mr. Deane—the one larger chamber and the three smaller adjoining ones.

"I'm wondering whether they *should*," she said, holding up the lantern to examine a spiral design that ran floor to ceiling. It was similar to the one outside, carved on a wall facing the entrance. "Dig, I mean. I'm eager to know more about it, of course. But whoever built it—would they like us digging it up, do you think? Perhaps it's no accident that it has been buried for two thousand years."

I moved closer to take the lantern for her, but instead of continuing her observation of the spiral, she looked up at me. I understood vaguely that she'd asked me a question and seemed to be expecting an answer. For the life of me, I couldn't recall anything she'd just said, not with her attention so fixed upon me.

So I smiled and said, "Perhaps," and hoped for the best.

Seeming to accept this, she set down her satchel. Then she unbuttoned and removed her cloak, for the earth over our heads had apparently insulated the chamber against the cold. I watched her, frozen, as she also removed her jacket. She stood before me in her skirt and a simple white blouse, and I could see the outline of her corset beneath. The blouse sleeves ended just below her elbows, and I found I couldn't tear my gaze away from her exposed forearm and wrist.

"Do you mind if I make a few sketches tonight, my lord? It will look different by daylight, and I'd like to compare."

"By all means, Miss Q."

Smiling, she retrieved a drawing pad and pencil from her satchel. Finding no place else to sit, she sank primly on the edge of a slab that held a large stone basin.

"I hope it's not sacrilege," she murmured.

I sat down a respectable distance away from her and replied, "Now we're both guilty."

But as she scratched away on her pad, I found I could not sit still. I believe I could have watched her for hours without her noticing, so absorbed was she in her work. The small movements of her hands and wrists. The shallow breaths, shortened by excitement, that caused her breasts to rise and fall. The pulse point in her neck that I could just see by the light of the lantern. And that heart-shaped mouth, mauve lips parting as she concentrated ...

Breathing deeply to clear these thoughts, I rose and took a turn about the chamber. Finding a box of matches, I made another circuit and lit fat candles that stood in a series of pie tins. I distracted myself by studying the slabs with their rounded edges, and the spiral carvings that had caught her eye. But none of it was any use. I was fascinated, indeed, but not with these cold stones.

*God help me.*

She had placed herself in my power. Trusted me completely. And I'd believed myself trustworthy. Believed that I could protect her from whatever the banshee had seen. I asked myself for the thousandth time, *What if it is I?* What if *I* was the shadow cast over her short life? The one who would bring her to ruin and destruction?

"Lord Meath?"

I started and turned.

"Are you well?" she asked. "Have you … Have you seen something?"

I forced a smile. "I am well. Perhaps a little fatigued from the journey."

"I'm sorry," she said, rising. "I've been inconsiderate."

"No, please, finish your sketches. I'll move to one of the other chambers so I won't disturb you further."

"It's not necessary, my lord. You aren't disturbing me."

The disturbing, of course, ran the other direction, but I could hardly tell her so. "You are kind to say so. Nonetheless, I'll leave you to it. Please call me if you need anything."

## ADA

As I watched him retire to the adjacent chamber, I knew he was hiding something from me. Perhaps another vision, something worse than before. I noticed he hadn't yet donned the tinted spectacles, so he had no protection from the green visitations.

Selfishly, I had not missed the spectacles. His eyes were bright and alive, something easy to miss when he wore them. He was full of charm and humor, and I couldn't help feeling that the side of him I was seeing now, until the past few moments, was his true self. That the brooding lord was just a projection of his suffering—the nightwalking and the drinking, and the visions that resulted from the cure he took.

*Dear fellow,* I thought. Then I wondered how long I'd been thinking of him thus.

I let my eyes drift from my sketch to find him again in the other room. The furrows had returned to his brow, but even like this he was … I know no better word than "beautiful." It was more than the dark sensuality, the Irish blue eyes, or the sailor's growth about his cheeks and chin. More than the power in his build, hinted at by the fit of his clothing.

*He has a beautiful soul.*

Yet how could I know such a thing, having been acquainted with him for only two days? I was developing a schoolgirl crush.

He ran a hand through his dark curls and removed his coat and jacket, draping them over the chamber's stone slab. Then he rolled up the sleeves of his shirt and bent to light and lift another of the numerous candles. I studied the musculature of his forearms with each small movement, finding it inexplicably compelling. I imagined how his arms might look were his fingers gripping my waist, and the blood rushed to my cheeks.

Pulling my gaze back to my sketch pad, heart racing, I thought back over the day's events. All the little moments that had tugged at something more than my heart. The way he had refrained from pushing me when I experienced that moment of doubt. The man who had tried to take his seat beside me on the tram, and how he'd refused to allow it. The way he rushed to my aid when Mr. Deane came to scold me as if I were a child. The way his gaze had rested on me as the sun slanted across us in the road, and then again inside the coach. Even just a moment ago, as I'd hurriedly made my sketches, hoping to finish before he grew bored.

I closed my eyes and shook my head, collaring these thoughts like disobedient children. Then I continued with my work, shutting out the small sounds the earl made as he moved about the other chamber.

I don't know how much time had passed when I started up from the stone at some new sound. I do know I'd become absorbed again in my work, and it might easily have been an hour or more.

As I glanced about the chamber, the sound came again, and I realized it had come from Lord Meath. He was seated on the stone slab, back resting against the wall. What I'd heard was the heavier breathing that often came with sleep.

The poor man had been so exhausted, he hadn't even needed his sleeping draught.

# SOLSTICE

## ADA

Next, I heard a strange sound like breath blown into the mouth of a bottle—but before I could move about the chamber to investigate, the lamp and candles all went out at once.

It was true that I didn't frighten easily, but it was also true, as Mr. Deane had said, that it was black as pitch inside the fairy mound once the lights were extinguished. I let out a startled cry.

The cry met with silence, and I called into the void, "Lord Meath?"

There came a scraping sound like metal on stone.

"My lord?" I called again, a tremor in my voice now. "Are you there?"

*Don't be a fool.* But I couldn't help it. Certainly, the wind had caused some change in the atmosphere in the chamber and snuffed out the lamps and candles. And Lord Meath had simply fallen into a deep sleep due to mental exhaustion. But the grinding sound … I couldn't account for it. It could hardly be for no reason that the entire Celtic race had a superstitious dread of these fairy mounds. Had I not based my career on such premises?

I circled around the stone basin to the side opposite the direction of the sound. I thought to call out again until I'd woken the earl, but I found myself afraid to give away my location.

The scraping sound came again, and I clamped my jaws closed, breathing shallowly so I'd not make a sound. If it was Lord Meath, he'd speak soon, surely. He would light a match.

*Who else would it* be? I gripped my precious silver propelling pencil, brandishing it like a dagger.

I felt a movement of air in the chamber, and I turned my head to feel it against my cheek, hoping to identify the direction.

The next thing I knew, my pencil-wielding hand had been gripped at the wrist.

"Lord Meath!" I shouted. "I need you!"

Long fingers squeezed, and I reached to pry them loose, but to no avail.

"Please," I squeaked, breathless both from fear and from struggling with my unknown assailant.

At last, my strength gave out and the pencil dropped to the floor.

Strong arms closed around me, and I felt a hand at the base of my spine. My body was tugged forward, and the length of me fell hard against the intruder.

"Let go! Please—Lord Meath!" I called "*Edward,* awaken!"

A growling voice tickled my ear. I could not understand the words. They were certainly not English, nor did I think they were Irish, though I was not fluent enough to be sure.

"I don't understand you," I protested, still fighting him.

He continued speaking, his voice taking on more of a soothing quality now. I interrupted him, demanding, "Who *are* you?"

"*Diarmuid.*"

Now came a word I understood, and I froze from the shock of it. I recalled that according to legend, the warrior's body had been brought to Brú na Bóinne. I recalled the earl's talk of ghosts. But there was nothing incorporeal about this stranger. He must have taken the cessation of my struggling as a sign of resignation—or, at least, recognition—for the next thing he did was coil his arms tighter around me. I felt his hand move into my hair and then gently tug my head back by the bun I'd pinned at the nape of my neck.

I gasped as I felt lips against my throat.

"Stop!" I cried, desperate. "At least let me see who you are!"

He drew back then, and I could hear his labored breathing. I felt its heat on my face. That's when I noticed the familiar smell. *Anise.*

A cold draft raised goose bumps on my flesh, and the candles suddenly flickered to life.

I cried out in shock when I saw it—the face of the man I was beginning to know and yet now could hardly recognize.

"My lord," I croaked.

*Nightwalking,* and absinthe was its cure. Only, he hadn't taken his cure this evening, I was almost certain of it. The anise smell came from his clothing, not his breath. From his skin. From his *being.*

His blue eyes were bright in the shadow, shimmering like moonlit pools. His whole countenance was altered—fierce, and *hungry.* My gaze flickered behind him briefly, where candlelight glinted off metal a few feet away.

*A sword.* I understood the metallic grating sound I'd heard earlier.

"*Moralltach,*" he muttered. When I looked at him, his nod redirected my gaze to the sword. As he repeated the word, its meaning came to me—*Moralltach* was a fabled sword associated with the Danaan heroes Angus and Diarmuid. It was an Irish word that meant "great fury." But where had the weapon come from? Deane's men would never have missed such an important artifact.

The earl's fingers pressed at the base of my neck as he tried to draw me closer.

"Lord Meath," I said in a loud but steady voice, angling my body away from him. "Awake, my lord. You *must*."

He murmured a few more words, his face bending close to mine. My attempts to pull away were foiled decisively by his hand at the base of my neck, and his arm around my waist. His gaze held mine prisoner, and for a moment, I could almost see the earl behind his eyes—gentleness overtaking fierceness. A softness, even, that was almost like reverence.

His expression resembled those in the fantasies my traitorous thoughts had played out in unguarded moments these past two days. So much so that for the space of a heartbeat, I did not fight him, and he pressed his lips to mine.

Suddenly, the howl of an ocean tempest was in my ears. The fury of a fire raging. I heard voices crying out in unison—an opera of violence, blending warlike masculine cries and the keening of a thousand women. A sob rose in my throat as his fierce melody threatened to pull me under.

"My lord!" I protested.

And then he was speaking again. I heard the foreign syllables dropping from his lips, but the sense of it now, somehow, came into my mind. "Your lord," he murmured against my cheek. "And *thee,* my own love, whom I both know and know not."

I shivered. "I am *not,* my lord," I said. "You are not yourself, and this is a thing we both shall regret."

He drew back to look at me then, my face between his hands. "We have been dreaming until now," he told me, his eyes pleading. "We need only awaken."

These puzzling words made me hesitate, and his thumb came to trace my lips. "Let me taste," he said. "Again, and yet for the first time."

*Let me taste.* This was a phrase he had spoken in his first moments in the chamber, though I hadn't then understood. Now that I did, heat rushed to my cheeks.

As he studied me, something caused his grip to loosen. I seized the moment and twisted in his grasp, stumbling away from him. My eye caught the flash of lamplight along the sword blade, and I reached for it, gripping the hilt in both hands.

"God help me," I grunted, but the weapon weighed less than I had imagined, and my physical education at Lovelace had included fencing. I dragged the sword tip along the floor, raising sparks. Then I whirled about, brandishing it between us.

The earl's eyes went wide, and he took a slow step toward me. "My love—"

"I am *not,* sir!" I shouted, pushing the tip of the sword against his chest. "Leave me *alone.*"

"I *know* you," he insisted. "Am known *to* you."

"Of course you know me!" I replied, pleading. "Lord Meath, it is *I.* Miss Quicksilver. Do you not see me?"

He shook his head slowly and backed away. Then he turned and fled the chamber.

I stumbled toward the stone slab and sank down on it, letting the tip of the sword clang against the floor. My heart pounded against my ribs, and my breaths unfurled visibly before me. The chamber had gone cold.

I stared at the entrance to the mound, wondering how far he would wander into this darkest of nights. Wondering when he would return, and whether he would be himself again when he did. I closed my eyes.

*I am out of my depth. I belong in London.*

But that was a decision for the light of day. The hour was late. The workmen had gone, and I dared not venture out in search of Lord Meath's tenant all alone. I let the sword fall to the floor and pressed my fingers to my temples.

"I must wait," I murmured. He had warned me of this, his nightwalking. It had happened before, and he had always returned to himself. I was safer here than I would be wandering the night, especially so near the River Boyne. There were sure to be bogs. I had the sword, should he return to threaten me. And mightn't his tenant or one of the workmen come looking for us?

I lifted the weapon again, resting the blade across my lap, and resigned myself to watching the long night. Hunger gnawed my stomach, its pleas for mercy echoing in the chamber. I studied the runes cut along the edge of the blade—ogham, an ancient Irish alphabet. I wondered again where the earl had discovered it. Tuatha De Danaan heroes had used swords like this one in the lore, but I had always assumed them to be modern embellishments—long blades had come with the Vikings, and the Danaan predated their arrival. I ran my finger over the hilt, which was bound in strips of well-worn leather, while the pommel was overlaid with engraved gold. Not a ceremonial sword, to be sure, but it had belonged to someone important.

*Diarmuid.* Great Fury had been a gift to him from Angus. Diarmuid had been greatly accomplished as a fighter—there were tales of him single-handedly defeating hordes—but as Lord Meath had earlier pointed out, he was best known for his romantic exploits.

What was his connection to Lord Meath? Could the earl be tapping into an unconscious legacy of Celtic memory? And what had I to do with that? *We need only awaken,* he had said. Perhaps, in his delusion, I had seemed to be someone else.

The chill air was biting into me, and I drew my jacket and

coat around my shoulders. Then I closed my eyes, resting against the wall at my back.

The earl's return was likely to be very awkward for us both. Would he remember what had happened? I hoped he would not. And yet, in that case, was I not obligated to tell him? I shuddered at the idea of raising such a topic. I was not overly concerned with the world's idea of propriety, yet I feared how it would alter things between us. I feared his reaction to hearing how I had been … *handled* by his alter ego. He would certainly blame himself, and then where would we be? These thoughts were exhausting, as our journey had been, and it wasn't long before I grew drowsy.

I did not open my eyes until I felt light on my face. The sun was shining directly through the entrance to the mound, on the morning after the longest night of the year. The entrance was so narrow that with the shifting path of the sun, this could very well be the only morning when sunlight could penetrate the central chamber. This was surely significant.

I sat up, bones and muscles protesting the stiffness of my bed. There at the foot of the stone was the earl, fast asleep. Had I dreamt it all? But on the floor beside him lay the sword.

"Lord Meath?" I called softly.

A shadow fell across us, and I glanced at the entrance. Someone was standing inside the opening of the mound.

## EDWARD

The feral cry that woke me—the challenge and threat of it— echoed in the chamber. As I jumped to my feet, my eyes found the long shadow in the passageway, and the backlit figure that cast it. Whatever had come calling was not a man—I could deduce that much from its silhouette.

*Then for the love of God, what* is *it?* Could it be another of the visitations? No, this creature was solid in form.

I glanced about for my traveling companion—whom I'd all but forgotten in the strange sleep fog I was still trying to shake—and a loose stone or anything else I might use to defend us.

"The sword, Lord Meath!" cried Miss Q.

In that same moment, a bright flash caught my eye, and I glimpsed a blade in the swath of sunlight on the chamber floor.

How came *that* here? I wondered. But the beast had started a charge down the passage, and I bent to snatch the weapon up.

While my gentleman's education included various forms of defense, I had never wielded a sword. Yet it felt comfortable in my hands as I raised it. Light washed over the flat of the blade, and suddenly there was a bright blue flash. The beast snorted and froze in its steps.

The sound it made was like nothing I'd ever heard—a goatlike bleating, magnified in chorus as if it had come from a hundred beasts. It had the torso of a large man, though covered in dark fur, and its head was that of a great horned and bearded goat.

"It's a púca," called Miss Q, half in wonder and half in fear. I could hear her moving behind me—the quickness of her breath, and the rustle of her clothing.

The púca was a fairy creature right out of the stories my grandmother told before the feast of All Saints. She had warned us that dark fairies such as redcaps, water horses, and púcas gobbled up children who played too close to waterways or the ruins of old castles that dotted the Irish countryside. As a young man, I had come to view them as tales fabricated by our elders to keep us from danger.

"Stay back, Miss Q," I warned, gripping the sword hilt.

"Take care, my lord!"

The beast watched us with eyes that glowed a luminescent gold,

air moving noisily through its protruding snout. Voicing another
unearthly bleat, it lowered its head to charge. I swung the sword,
but I misjudged the weight of it and my timing was off. The beast's
massive head caught me in the chest and flung me over the stone
slab and into Miss Q. Fortunately, the tips of its horns curved
backward, but still, the blow was enough to knock the wind out of
me. Ignoring the panic of temporarily paralyzed lungs, I untangled
myself from her and scrambled again to my feet.

The púca stamped the floor with one hoof as breath filled my
lungs again.

"Run to the other chamber!" I shouted at Miss Q. "Watch for
a chance to escape!"

She moved to comply, and the beast followed her with its eerie
lifeless gaze. Suspecting that its body would soon do the same, I
raised the sword and, as it darted past me, I lunged and swung.
The blade struck one of the púca's legs, thick as a tree trunk.

It fell with a great bellow of anger, tugging the weapon from
my hand. Before I could retrieve it, the creature lurched again to
its feet and began another charge.

This time, I waited until the last moment and dropped and
rolled aside, leaving it to collide with the stone wall. One of its
horns snapped off a few inches from the tip, and the púca sank to
the ground, stunned.

"Come, Miss Q!" I cried, retrieving the sword.

She obeyed, flying from the other chamber, and together we
fled down the passageway. When we cleared the entry, I shoved
her away from me, into the arms of a very startled Mr. Deane.

"My lord!" he cried in surprise.

Ignoring him, I turned and began kicking at the timbers they
had used to shore up the entrance.

"Stop that, sir!" demanded Mr. Deane, forgetting himself.

"Help me, man!" I ordered.

"Please!" urged Miss Q. "There's something dangerous inside."

Before Deane could argue, the púca made its presence known by yowling another of its eerie and awful challenges. We saw it rise, readying for another charge.

Deane took an ax from a pile of tools near the entrance and began swinging the butt against one of the supports while I continued kicking at another. Miss Q sensibly scrambled a few steps back, and the mouth of the tunnel collapsed with a great groaning of stone on stone, enveloping us in a cloud of dust.

The head of Deane's ax struck the earth as he struggled to catch his breath. "What the devil was that, my lord?" The pitch of his voice was high from the shock.

"Our folklore expert thinks it's a púca," I replied, wiping perspiration from my forehead with the back of my hand.

Deane stared wide-eyed at Miss Q and made the sign of the cross. Then his gaze swung back to me. "And how'd you come by that weapon, sir?"

"I found it inside, Mr. Deane." Before he could protest that this was impossible, I continued, "We need to get to Mullingar with all haste. I want to be on the next train to the west. Is it possible to hire a coach on short notice?"

"Possible," he replied, "but not certain so close to the holiday. I'll look to it, my lord."

"Thank you. We'll wait at the cottage with the family. Will you also set a watch on the ruin and keep everyone away?"

He gave a quick nod. "I will, my lord."

"And it won't do for word to get about, Deane. We don't want to create a panic."

Deane lifted his dark brows. "I heard half a dozen tales at the pub last night that'd make this one seem like child's play. I'd wager the locals are used to such things." He raised a hand to his chest. "Being a Cork man, city born and raised, *I* am not."

"Nor I, sir," I assured him, though perhaps this wasn't entirely true.

"What do you make of it, my lord?"

I shook my head. "I don't know. I want to talk it over with Miss Quicksilver, and I hope we'll make Achill Island by nightfall. There I'll consult with the queen. I'm leaving you in charge here in the meantime. Under no circumstances reopen this passage, Mr. Deane."

"Certainly not, my lord."

"I want you to notify me if there are other strange occurrences. You can direct a telegram to me at Westport. I'll check on our arrival, and when we depart, I'll hire a courier to wait there."

"Very good, Lord Meath."

"Good man."

A chill breeze stirred over my skin, damp with perspiration from the skirmish, and I shivered. I noticed for the first time that not only were my jacket and overcoat missing, but the front of my shirt was ripped open.

The architect removed his overcoat. "Take this, my lord. We've had a frost in the night."

"I thank you, Mr. Deane." I fished in my trousers pocket and handed the man a pound note.

"It's too much, sir," he protested.

"I insist."

As I donned the overcoat, I caught the curious glance Deane cast at Miss Q. My thoughts raced as I tried to recall what had happened before the púca appeared, but I found that I could not. Had we spent the entire night inside the mound? It certainly appeared so. I deemed it best to move along before the man thought to ask the same question.

When I held out my arm to Miss Q, something crossed her countenance as well, but it was more like a shadow. Still, she tucked her hand into the crook of my arm, and we started across the field toward my tenant's cottage.

The fingers on my arm were stiff, and as we progressed through the frosted grass I began to fear that something untoward had happened. Somehow, the whole night had passed without my being conscious of it. Had I drifted off? Panic squeezed my chest as it occurred to me that I might have fallen asleep without my nightly draught. Had I nightwalked? It wasn't unusual for me to return with my clothing damaged or even missing. I could only hope that I had left the tomb and not threatened or molested my traveling companion. I cast a sidelong glance at her profile. Her color was a little high, and those silvery tresses were in disarray, but that was not surprising considering our precipitous departure from the tomb.

"Are you healthy and whole, Miss Q?" I covered her cold fingers with my hand.

# THE FEY EARL

## ADA

Warmth flooded my cheeks. Maintaining my composure required all my concentration. I was relieved that we would not walk in silence, but my thoughts were so disordered, I hardly knew what answer to make.

*Start by answering the question. The rest must wait.*

"I am, my lord," I replied.

"I'm relieved to hear it. You must be hungry. The Doyles will give us breakfast." His tone was solicitous and generous, which was indeed no different from usual. But we were not *as usual,* and I was not sure how to interpret this. I considered whether he would try to insert some distance between us. It was possible he had forgotten the events of the evening before, but he at least must know that we had spent an entire night alone inside the fairy mound.

We walked a while in silence. I had the sense that he waited for me to speak—indeed, the entire business should have had both of us talking—but I was exceedingly uncomfortable and uncertain and could not bring myself to it.

"Miss Q." He stopped in the middle of the muddy track and turned to look at me, features drawn with worry. My heart thumped in anticipation. "I believe that I fell asleep last night and that I walked in my sleep. I have no memory of it, but it's not unusual for me to wake in ... in such a state on those nights when I lose myself. I am alarmed that we seem to have passed the whole night in the fairy mound. And I am racked with fear that I have said or done something to frighten or offend you. If I have, you *must* tell me."

What was I to do now? As his friend, I owed him the truth. But to explain such a thing ... I knew that I could not.

The lie that must be told would far exceed any small deception I had perpetrated thus far in my career. But having determined I was unequal to revealing the truth, I had no other course.

"You did walk in your sleep, sir," I began slowly, "but please rest easy. I was distracted by my work when you emerged from the other chamber. You exited from the mound, and it was dark by then and I dare not follow. I thought it best to await your return rather than walk out into the night unescorted, unsure of my destination. I waited some time, and then I, too, must have fallen asleep."

The release of tension in his body drained some of the charge from the air around us, but I had not yet escaped.

"I want more than anything to believe that was the extent of it," he said, "horrified as I am that you were forced to sleep so uncomfortably. But I sense that you are concealing something, perhaps to protect me. I insist on being held accountable."

"For things that happened involuntarily?" I protested. "Why, sir?"

The expression of dread descended again. "You're a poor liar, Miss Q."

My heart galloped as I rallied my faculties. *Stall.* "I shall take that as a compliment, sir," I replied with a halfhearted smile.

"I meant it as such. But please proceed to the truth."

I felt pinioned by his gaze. Worse than that, something of the look of the Danaan warrior returned to his eyes and brow.

"I have told you nearly all," I continued. There I paused to see whether he would lead me.

"I accosted you in some way."

"You … frightened me with your intensity." As I spoke these honest words, I met his gaze.

He closed his eyes and balled his hands into fists. "And did I harm you?"

Relieved that he had not chosen wording that would require me to lie outright, I replied, "You did not, sir. I am well, as you see."

"Miss Quicksilver," he began, opening his eyes, "I must earnestly beg your pardon. I neglected my sleeping draught last night. I hadn't expected to doze off. I hope you will believe that my actions were outside my control."

"I do, sir. Of course I do."

"Can you forgive me?"

"With all my heart."

"Come," he said, turning again into the path. "We must talk of this further, but first a fire and a hot meal."

He looked more troubled than ever, and I knew that if I wished to maintain our association, I could never tell him the whole truth. Yet how could I, in good conscience, conceal such a thing?

Moreover, was maintaining our association even advisable? Had I not better tell him the truth and flee back to the safety of the Lovelace Academy, where my greatest worries had to do with professors and exams? Never had it entered my thoughts back in London that a research trip could be so fraught with peril. And yet, had I not found exactly what I'd come looking for? More, in fact, than I had dared hope for?

We had almost crossed the field and were now approaching

a modest cottage. Lord Meath led me through a gate, pausing a moment to rest the sword against the low stone fence, and a man came out of the cottage and strode out to meet us.

The earl introduced me to Mr. Doyle and apologized for our tardy arrival. The farmer's confusion upon being told that we'd spent the night in the ruin was plain. Doyle told the earl that he had assumed we were delayed in town or on the road and had not thought to come looking for us. He was launching into a verbose apology, but the earl cut him short, explaining that we were sorely in need of a hot meal, if it was not too much trouble for his wife. Doyle ushered us inside and directly to the kitchen, inviting us to seat ourselves at the end of the table near the fire. He explained what was wanted to his wife, who also welcomed us and expressed concern over our ordeal.

We warmed ourselves by the fire while she busied herself at the stove. No questions were put forward about our night in the ruin, though this was not surprising—a tenant would not think it his place. Mr. Doyle fussed with the turf fire until it was blazing, and then fell into idle chatter about the weather. I assumed that all the awkwardness had to do with our absence the evening before—and perhaps the farmer's speculation about the earl and me—until I recalled that it was Mr. Doyle's sale of beads found inside the ruin that had drawn attention to the place. This could easily have proved a consequential lapse in judgment had the man possessed a less compassionate landlord.

A quarter hour later, a feast was laid before us—steaming bowls of porridge and a pitcher of fresh milk, eggs fried with mushrooms and onions, bread hot from the oven, with a cake of rich yellow butter, and a pot of strong tea. When Mrs. Doyle had poured our tea, she excused herself to check on her children, who were about their morning chores.

My wondering whether the earl would think it advisable to

tell his tenant of the púca came to an end when Lord Meath finally spoke. "Mr. Doyle, I don't wish to alarm you, but I feel that I would be remiss in keeping from you the fact that we encountered a threatening creature inside the ruin."

The farmer turned from the fire, regarding Lord Meath with wide eyes. "Is that so, my lord?"

"It had the appearance of a púca, though I know that must sound very strange."

"A púca!" Doyle regarded him with surprise and what I took for alarm rather than disbelief.

"I know of no better way to describe it," replied the earl, "and I'm at a loss to account for it."

Doyle shook his head. "Sorry I am that ever I poked my nose where I hadn't ought to, my lord."

"I suspect it was less connected with your laborers' foray into the chamber than with the reconstruction of the entrance, but I'm far from an expert in such matters." Lord Meath's gaze came to rest on me.

I swallowed the bite of egg I had just taken. "I would agree with you, my lord. It feels significant that the first rays of dawn traveled down the passage and pierced the central chamber. It's likely the structure was erected for just that purpose. I wonder whether it might even be some kind of gateway." As I warmed to this topic and as the excellent breakfast underwent the chemical transformation necessary to revive my energy, some of the early morning's sense of dread began to dissipate.

I wondered, could this be *the* gateway? If we had left it open, what else might have come through. And was it truly closed?

"Have you noticed anything unusual since the inside of the ruin was first examined, sir?" I asked Mr. Doyle, endeavoring, by my careful wording, to spare him further remorse. "Any sightings that could not be explained without reference to old stories?"

"No, miss," he replied. "But Mrs. Doyle has made me feel how wrong I was to trespass on the gentlefolk, and I'd take it back if I could."

By this answer, I could see that the farmer's main concern was to ease his guilty conscience by confession to his lord—perhaps even to the gentlefolk themselves, who were known to be easily offended—and I did not pursue further questioning. But I confess I was looking forward to the loss of his company so I might discuss the matter more fully with Lord Meath.

"The site is important, Mr. Doyle," replied the earl in a somber tone. "I don't believe you are to blame for the púca's attack, but I'm counting on you to aid the scientists and workmen in keeping the passage sealed until I can return from my consultation with the queen."

"Rely on it, Your Lordship," Mr. Doyle readily assented, clearly relieved for this opportunity to reaffirm his worthiness as a tenant.

"Keep your own family away as well, for their safety."

"I shall, Your Lordship."

"As soon as we reach the train station, I'll telegraph Her Majesty and request a company of soldiers to relieve the excavation crew."

Before Mr. Doyle could reply to this, we heard a sharp rap on the front door of the cottage. The earl walked out with our host to answer it, and they passed Mrs. Doyle as she returned to the kitchen. I overheard enough of the men's conversation to understand that conveyance of some sort had been procured for us, and I was rising to join them when Mrs. Doyle pressed a basket into my hands.

"For your journey," she explained, smiling kindly. She was a young woman still, not yet thirty, and had numerous ginger freckles and a head of curls to match.

"Thank you, Mrs. Doyle. And thank you for the excellent breakfast."

As I took hold of the basket handle, she held fast a moment, pulling me closer.

"He's a handsome lord, miss, but fey," she whispered urgently. "Take warning. I fear you daren't trust him."

Anxiety brought a flash of heat to my chest. Though I knew how right she was, this reminder of my predicament freshened my sense of unease. I was spared the concealment that would have been required for me to reply to this kind warning, by the return of Mr. Doyle, who came to lead me to Lord Meath.

"Thank you for your generosity," I repeated, hoping by my calm reply to ease her distress on my behalf, even if I could not do the same for myself.

She pressed her lips together and made a small curtsy. Then, cutting her gaze at her husband, she seemed to contemplate a moment before adding, "You bear the mark of attention from their kind. You must take especial care." She eyed my silver hair, which I hadn't bothered to conceal under my hood, and curtsied again. "Safe travels, miss."

I thought about my grandmother's story of the fairy kiss as I followed Mr. Doyle out again to the farmyard. I thought again about the earl's words in the ruin: *And thee, my own love, whom I both know and know not.*

Lord Meath waited for us near a small open carriage. "This is all that was available on short notice," the earl explained as I joined him. "Fortunately, the weather is fine for a late-December morning."

This was true enough. The air had a bite, but the sunshine was its balm.

"Will you be comfortable enough?" the earl asked.

"I'm sure that I will, my lord."

I gave him Mrs. Doyle's basket, and he placed it on the seat beside the driver before helping me in and climbing up to join me. We would be rather cozy on this ride, as there was only one passenger seat in the carriage and it was much smaller than the private coach.

"With any luck," he said as we got under way, "we'll make Mullingar in time for the Westport train."

"If we don't?" I asked.

"If we don't, we must stay in Mullingar and resume the following morning."

The open carriage was both a blessing and a curse. With the driver so close, the earl could not resume his questioning about the night we'd passed together. Neither could we continue our discourse on the púca and its significance. Instead, I studied the wintergreen-and-dun countryside, trying not to think about the warmth of his leg pressing against mine.

I found my mind returning to the night before. But now that I was tucked safely into the coach, beside a man I had come to respect and trust, these thoughts raised a warming curiosity. I knew what it felt like to be held in his arms. To be kissed by him. I trembled to think how different an experience it might have been, had he been himself. I wondered whether he could ever feel the same desire for me as the sleepwalker had.

That was no more than mistaken identity, I reminded myself. And as for the earl ... well, he was an *earl,* while I was merely a Miss Q. And I had a decision to make.

## EDWARD

*You frightened me with your intensity.*

It was what I had feared most in persuading her to join me on this journey—that she might come to harm in my care. And the almost certain knowledge that I had acted in an ungentlemanly manner toward her, whether or not it was within my control, sickened me.

Yet she insisted she was well. To all *appearances,* she was well. Her color was still high, but it gave her a healthful glow. She looked even more alive than she had this morning, when she had been flushed with excitement for the journey to come. And she had not fled from me in terror, as I imagine any other woman would have. Not yet, at any rate.

I thought I might be driven the rest of the way mad by not knowing the specifics of what I had said or done. I could not now reopen the topic, not with the driver so near. In truth, I didn't know whether I could *ever* speak of it again. Would not forcing her to speak in more detail constitute a fresh offense? As I eyed her profile, I noticed a purplish mark on her neck—a fresh bruise. Had I caused *that?* Certainly, she would have fled by now had I laid hands on her. Perhaps she had been bruised sleeping on the stone.

*Dear God.* I closed my eyes and gritted my teeth, tormented by my lack of information.

Feeling a gentle weight on my shoulder, I opened my eyes. Despite the rough road and the uncomfortable carriage, the poor woman had fallen asleep, and her cheek now rested against me. I scarcely dared breathe for fear of disturbing her. If she woke, she would certainly move away.

I leaned toward her, lowering my shoulder so she might rest at a more comfortable angle. I resisted the urge to take hold of the hand that lay, palm up and fingers slightly curving, in her lap.

"Rest, my clever and kind Miss Q," I murmured, "and know that I will do whatever is required to protect you—even from myself."

# FLIGHT OF FANCY

## EDWARD

She slept for the duration of the journey. We did, in fact, make it to Mullingar in time to catch the train, though I had only a few minutes in the telegraph office, and I feared that my cousin would find my note incomprehensible. I'd been forced to compose it in French to avoid alarming the telegraph agent, and to call my French "passable" would be generous.

Before we left the office, Miss Q asked the agent to post a letter for her. She told me that it was a note to her mentor at the academy, informing him of her change in itinerary. I felt a pang that she had no parent or other family member looking out for her welfare, and I again vowed to myself that I would take better care of her.

We had some trouble with the station agent over the sword I was carrying, as it was too long to fit in my travel bag. After assurances that the weapon was a family heirloom, a promise to stow it above with our bags for the duration of the journey, and a few shillings for the agent's inconvenience, we were finally allowed to board and take our seats.

Our journey would take several hours, and I had retrieved my absinthe supply from my bag, thinking I was likely to sleep on the train and unwilling to risk another nightwalking episode, though it was yet early in the day.

Miss Q had been paging through her notebook while I settled our baggage, but she glanced up as I sipped from the flask. She offered me a smile that I hadn't seen on her before—shy, even self-conscious—and returned her attention to her book.

"Are you troubled by my drinking, Miss Q?"

"No, sir," she replied earnestly. "I am only sorry for the condition that necessitates it."

"That is kind of you." I sipped again before closing the flask and slipping it into a pocket of Mr. Deane's overcoat. "I must be on my guard to avoid repeating the offense of last evening."

Color rose to her cheeks, and she replied, "What do you make of that creature that attacked us, my lord?" In her change of subject, I had my answer whether it was better to drop all inquiry into the specifics of my behavior.

"I would like to hear your thoughts on the subject," I replied.

She laid her notebook aside. "I think that Brú na Bóinne may be a portal to wherever the fairies reside. Reconstruction of the portal, or perhaps activity in the chamber, may have opened it. I have read accounts of such doorways in County Sligo as well."

I nodded. "My family sometimes traveled on holiday to Sligo Bay. Locals say there is a fairy door in the face of Ben Bulben, the tabletop mountain where the warrior Diarmuid is said to have been killed by a wild boar."

The lady's eyebrows lifted slightly, and her gaze fell to her folded hands as she considered this information.

Her theory was reasonable, and a natural one considering her course of study. Yet I resisted this explanation with its potential threat. "It is also possible that the creature was roaming the countryside and just happened upon the ruin."

"Yes," she agreed, looking up. "It's possible. But according to the tales I've studied, púcas tend to be tied to a place. Lonely, deserted places such as castle ruins and old mills. And its appearance on the night of the solstice could not but be significant. Even had it traveled from elsewhere in the country, we'd be left with the question of its origin."

All this was as soundly logical as I'd come to expect from Miss Q. "And what do you make of the sword?"

Her lips parted, but she hesitated.

"Tell me, please," I urged.

"You named that sword, in Irish, when you were ... sleepwalking."

I stared at her. "I *what?*"

"You gave it the name of Diarmuid's sword, Great Fury. You have no memory how you came by it?"

I shook my head, stunned. "None whatever. What does it mean?"

She pursed her lips together, and I followed the delicate motion of her throat as she swallowed. "I don't know, Lord Meath. But ..." Again she hesitated.

"Please, go on."

"It seems clear that we're witnessing some bleeding through between worlds. And I think it may somehow be connected to your nightwalking and to the visions you see when you drink absinthe."

I let go of some of my resistance to the idea that we had naively opened a fairy door—releasing heaven knows what in the process—in light of this theory that suggested a possible explanation for the madness that plagued me.

"Connected how?" I asked her.

Perhaps hearing the desperation in my voice, she eyed me

with sympathy. "That remains a mystery, my lord. I hope we shall unlock it."

"But you do have a theory?"

She frowned. "Any conclusion I draw now would be nothing more than conjecture."

"I am no less eager to hear it."

## ADA

I knew that he sought relief, and I could not refuse him—even though I must tread carefully to avoid being drawn into further discussion of events the night before.

"Very well," I began. "I think that in your nightwalking, you may be seeking something." *Thee, my own love.* "Something you've lost. The absinthe stops your wandering in *our* world, but only because it opens a gate allowing the other world to reach *you*. The sword, for example, came from the other world, which explains why the workers didn't find it."

His eyes were bright under tensely knitted brows. "But why am I afflicted thus? What have I to do with this other world?"

"I don't know, my lord," I replied quietly. "But I think you may be more than you seem."

His gaze shifted to the window, and his fingers slipped into his pocket. He brought out the flask but only held it in his hand as he watched the evergreen pastureland and whitewashed cottages slide across his view. Finally, he turned from the window and drank deeply.

His distress wrung my heart, just as it had that day in Mrs. Maguire's sitting room.

Replacing the flask, he removed his spectacles. His gaze fixed on me, and I caught a glimpse of the nightwalking earl behind his eyes. No more than a shadow, but I began to fidget under the intensity of his stare. I steadied myself with a reminder that he was taking his cure and I was therefore safe. If I was to remain in his company, both he and I must be more vigilant about his doses.

He dropped his gaze after a moment and reached into the watch pocket of his trousers. But he froze in the act of drawing the watch out, producing instead what appeared to be a folded scrap of old tea-stained paper. Or *parchment*.

"What is that, my lord?" I asked, unable to restrain my curiosity.

He blinked at it and shook his head. "I haven't any idea."

Yes, parchment. I watched him unfold it, and his eyes began to move over it as though he was reading. With no small measure of anticipation, I waited for him to complete his inspection.

Finally, he handed it to me, and my hands trembled as I rubbed my fingertips over the material that was so much softer and suppler than paper. I studied the stark lines of the letters on the page but could read none of it.

"This is Old Irish," I said, breathless from the realization. "A week ago, I would not have been able to tell you that, but I viewed a page from the *Book of Armagh* while visiting the Trinity College Library." The ancient text was highly prized, as it contained information about the life of St. Patrick, as well as rare samples of written Old Irish, the language that preceded Irish Gaelic.

"Old Irish?" he said with surprise. "Are you certain?"

"Fairly," I replied. "I studied the document quite closely, and I have a good memory. I wish we could read it."

"I can."

Now *I* glanced up with surprise. "You can read Old Irish, my lord?"

He frowned. "It would seem so."

I could see that this troubled him, and indeed, I had no way of accounting for it myself. Perhaps I *was* mistaken and it was only written in Gaelic.

"What does it say, sir?" I asked, sliding to the edge of my seat.

"It is a story—or, perhaps more accurately, a history. Shall I read it to you?"

"Yes, please!"

The earl took the parchment from my hand, cleared his throat, and translated for me.

## The Story of Cliona's Wave

The maiden Cliona was the only child of a blacksmith and a fairy seer, born near the prosperous trading village of Cork. Like her mother, the child was marked by Faery, and came to be renowned throughout the country for her beauty. One day, the great chieftain Eochaid asked her father to craft a sword, but in truth he had come for a glimpse of the fair Cliona. When the blacksmith and Eochaid had reached an agreement on price, Cliona happened to enter the smithy, carrying supper to her father. From the moment Eochaid's eyes fell on her, he was in a fever to possess her.

Eochaid bargained with her father, who was ambitious and gave her hand against her will. Tearfully the maiden left her family and joined the household of the chieftain. Her new husband was a Christian and a proud man. He forbade Cliona from worshiping—or even speaking of—the old gods, fearing anything that might diminish his position in the country. He discouraged her whimsy, and she was no longer permitted to wander hill and vale, visiting known fairy haunts. Beyond the early months of her marriage, she was no longer permitted to receive her mother at the hall.

The austerity of Cliona's life became intolerable to her, and after the birth of her first child, she fled her husband's hall with the help of a loyal servant. On a frosty but clear winter morning, Cliona and her infant daughter set out in calm waters for Bere Island, where there was a temple devoted to the goddess Dana, mother of the Tuatha De Danaan. The existence of this holy place had been kept a close secret, and the young mother intended to seek sanctuary there. But not long after casting off from a secluded bay—though there was not a cloud in the heavens—the sea began to roil. Cliona had kept close to the shore for safety, and yet a great wave rolled in, violently rocking the coracle and casting the young mother into the frigid water. Her infant lay bundled warmly in the bottom of the coracle and thus was saved.

Eochaid, warned of his wife's flight by a stable hand, set out in pursuit. He found the coracle washed up on the strand with only his wailing daughter inside. As for Cliona, her lifeless body was discovered under the waves by Manannán, the god of the sea. Grieved by her wasted youth and beauty, Manannán carried her to the Danaan at Brú na Bóinne.

I stared expectantly at the earl, waiting for him to continue. But he shook his head.

"Thus it ends," he said. "What do you make of it?"

I took a deep breath and settled back against the seat while the train rocked gently along the track. The story of "Cliona's Wave" was familiar to me, though I had never read a version like this one. In the others, she had been an immortal, sometimes associated with healing, sometimes with banshees. She had been drowned by a great wave while waiting in a boat for a mortal lover. This was a common paradox among mythological tales—immortals who could be killed and yet remain immortal.

I reached again for the parchment. He handed it to me, and I inspected it more closely. Along the left side, the sheet was uneven, as if it had been removed from a book.

"I would bet that this came from the same place the sword did," I said.

"A sensible conclusion," the earl replied.

"As for its significance, obviously, it relates to Brú na Bóinne, but how it might connect with the events there, and what it might tell us …" I slowly shook my head. "I cannot say, my lord."

I tried to recall whether anything I'd read of Diarmuid connected him with Cliona, other than their both being of the Tuatha De Danaan. Diarmuid had been romantically linked with several women, most notably Gráinne, the high king's daughter who was engaged to Finn but ran off with Diarmuid. That relationship eventually led to the end of his mortal life, and though in some accounts he became an oracle to the Danaan, no further stories had been recorded of him.

While pondering this, I noticed that the earl's gaze had shifted beyond me, and his wary expression caused me to turn and look over my shoulder. I saw nothing but other passengers, reading or dozing, rocked in their seats by the gentle motion of the train.

"Isolde," murmured my companion, and I turned again to study him.

He rose from his seat, eyes still fixed on the same spot.

"You see the *queen?*" I whispered, remembering his story about the vision in Dublin.

Nodding, he reached into the overhead compartment and took down his sword.

"Lord Meath!" I whispered urgently.

"She beckons," he replied.

I rose to my feet, standing between him and his visitor. "My lord, we don't know with certainty that this apparition has any connection to her."

"And thus, I take a precaution." He raised the sword, eliciting small sounds of alarm from the other passengers. "Remain here," he said.

But as he moved to leave the car, I followed. His threatening appearance was sure to cause a disturbance. His vision had carried him beyond reason, which meant I would have to speak for him—though heaven knew what I would say.

I followed him through to another passenger car, but I dared not call after him for fear of causing an even greater disruption. Instead, I hurried to keep up. We passed through three more cars, leaving startled passengers in our wake, before reaching the final car. He stepped out onto the small balcony at the end, and I joined him just as he was stepping onto a ladder mounted outside the car.

"Lord Meath!" I cried as he scaled the ladder.

When he reached the top, he froze. "Miss Q!"

"I'm here, my lord. Can I call the conductor to assist you?"

"I would like for you to come up and tell me whether you see what I see."

*Come up?* The train rumbled along. My heart pounded as I watched the track flying away beneath us. I stared up at the earl, who was looking at the sky.

Gripping the ladder's rail, I took a deep breath and followed him up.

My stomach dropped as the earl crawled on top of the car and out of sight. Placing one careful, deliberate step after the other, I climbed. At the top, the wind tugged at my hair and clothing.

He crouched on top of the car, very near the edge, his eyes still fastened on a point above us. I saw nothing but blue sky broken by wisps of cloud.

"Do you see it?" he asked, looking at me as if his life depended on my answer.

"I see *nothing*, Lord Meath," I cried, greatly alarmed. There was madness in both his look and his tone. "Will you not come down?"

He turned again to study the empty air. "How am I to know that you are who you appear to be?" he demanded.

I pondered this in confusion before realizing that he was no longer speaking to me.

"Here, now, miss!" Glancing down, I saw that the conductor had followed us outside and was now preparing to climb up onto the car. "Come down from there at once!" he barked.

"Stay, sir!" I cried, afraid that he would only make the situation worse. "Please! I'm worried for my friend, who has climbed on top of the train."

He repeated his demand that I come down. I glanced again to the earl's perch near the edge of the car and heard him say, "I could not possibly—"

But I did not find out what he could not possibly do, because at that moment, I heard a shrill cry beside my ear that so startled me, I let go of the ladder.

"Miss Q!" the earl shouted in alarm as I lost my balance.

But before I could fall either to the deck or to the track below, something I could not see grasped me by the waist and lifted me off my feet.

"My lord!"

"Release her at once!" cried the earl. "Cousin! Call off that beast!"

*Beast?* I looked up, but still I saw nothing. I could feel the disturbance of the air, as if a large bird were beating its wings just above me. I reached down to my waist and ran my hands over the mechanism that held me, recoiling in horror at the feel of tough, wrinkled skin and a smooth, hooked claw.

Below my skirts, which the wind had billowed like a purple balloon, the locomotive surged along like a great mechanical snake, a line of smoke and vapor curling backward from its engine. The earl receded in the distance—my invisible captor was not keeping pace with the train. And then the distance played a trick on my eyes, for I thought I saw the earl climbing the air itself, as if it were a ladder. Sunlight glinted off the blade of Great Fury as he ascended.

I glanced at the ground below and felt a swell of nausea, and a burning behind my ears.

"Please!" I cried. "Please, let me go!" I squirmed in the creature's grasp but then came to my senses. A fall from this height would certainly be fatal.

Closing my eyes, I tried to collect my wits. Struggling was foolish. I would simply have to wait until whatever held me chose to land. But what, in the meantime, would happen to the earl? He was obviously seeing many things that I could not, but I now had clear and alarming firsthand evidence that these were no fanciful visions—unless I had contracted madness by association.

I opened my eyes again, determined to make a rational assessment of our situation, only to discover the earl now stood a short distance away, perched on nothing, defying the law of gravity. He stood upright, but with his feet planted in empty air, as the train sped into the distance far below us. Had he, too, been taken by a creature like the one that held me?

He followed my approach, his eyes vivid with anger and alarm. Relief surged in my breast as we drew yet closer to him. Then the claws at my waist opened.

For a moment, I felt an inexplicable weightlessness—inexplicable because I knew that my weight was carrying me toward the ground. My scream stopped half out of my throat, cut short by a sudden impact with something solid.

Pain speared through my knees and the heels of my hands.

"Miss Q!" cried the earl, kneeling beside me.

My breath came in gasps as I stared between my hands at the ground far below. "I fear that I'm going mad, my lord!" I said in a voice cracking from the strain.

He knelt beside me, supporting me so I could rise. "If you are, then you have me for company on your journey. Can you still see nothing, dear lady?"

"Nothing but that which I cannot believe." I looked into his face and saw such a look of pity that I knew I must be a sight to behold. The wind had pulled my hair loose, and it cascaded over my shoulders in a silvery tempest. The waist of my gown had been rent to my very flesh in places. I covered these with my hands.

Lord Meath drew the flask from his coat pocket and held it out to me.

I began to shake my head, then stopped suddenly and took it from him, tilting it to my lips. The spirits inside burned their way into my chest with a licorice brightness. I swallowed three times before I began to cough, and he took the flask from my hand.

I remained doubled over, tears squeezing from under my eyelids, as the fire in my throat moved to my belly and then finally subsided. Lord Meath's hand came to my back, warm and steadying.

"What is the meaning of this, Isolde?" he demanded. "You could have killed her!"

A loud feminine laugh pierced the air, and I jerked up straight. My mouth fell open. At last, I could see. A green woman stood before us. She wore the high, proud hat of an Irish naval officer—embellished with a fanciful brocade—and a man's breeches and boots. The rest of her uniform—a jacket and corset worked in the same brocade—was far from regimental.

"I can't say I've ever been mistaken for a queen, Your Lordship. Though some do call me the Sea Queen of Connacht, and I've styled my ship the same."

She was a filmy apparition, as was the vessel that, I now saw, surrounded us. We were standing on the deck of a ship, an enormous griffin's head at its prow. Sails were hoisted and filled, and glancing over the railing, I saw flat-paddled oars extending from holes in the hull and digging powerfully at the sky. Flying alongside the ship were a dozen ravens more than twice the size of a man. As I examined their huge talons, my fingers stroked the widest of the rents at my waist. On their backs, the birds carried what I at first took for children but, on closer inspection, found to be little people with sparrowlike faces.

"Into the Gap, Captain O'Malley?" inquired a crackling voice from the prow. A creature was seated there astride the griffin's head. He was portly and had literally the face of a toad.

"Into the Gap!" replied the woman, punching at the air with her fist.

"Huzzah!" cried a chorus of crewmen's voices.

"O'Malley?" repeated Lord Meath. I wondered whether he had thought, as I had, of the most famous of his O'Malley relations: the pirate queen. But she was long dead.

She gave a mock curtsy, replying, "Grace O'Malley, my lord."

How was this possible?

She turned now toward the bow of the ship.

"She could be Isolde's twin," murmured Lord Meath.

I now noticed a young man standing beside her. Compared to the rest of this fantastical troupe, he had quite a mundane appearance. Like the earl, he had a pair of tinted spectacles, though they rested very near the end of his nose. He eyed me over them. As our eyes met, he smiled and nodded. "Will Yeats, official scribe. How do you do, Miss …?"

Despite my anxiety and confusion, I managed a civil reply. "Ada Quicksilver. And Lord Edward, Earl of Meath."

"Here we go, Mr. Yeats!" called the captain.

The young man nodded placidly and grabbed the end of a line that had been swinging from the rigging. As he wound it around his arm, he said, "Mind the Gap, Miss Quicksilver."

I glanced at the earl. He raised his eyebrows, indicating that our confusion was mutual. Then he grabbed another line, and without preamble, he pulled me into his chest and began wrapping the rope about our waists. The solid warmth of his body was a comfort, propriety be damned.

As he tied off the line, we heard a loud creaking noise, as though the boards of the ship were warping beneath our feet. The bow began to rise, and I lost my balance. Our feet slipped from the deck, and we swung outward, dangling at the end of the line. As the rope stretched, my body slid down against his, and with a cry of alarm, I flung my arms around his ribs while his legs wrapped around my upper body. I glanced down and saw that the pitch of the ship had opened a clear path for us to plummet all the way to the ground should the rope fail.

The mad creatures that made up the ship's crew were cackling like fiends and swinging from other lines.

The ship was changing, her vaporous green outline solidifying and assuming a more natural hue. This change began at the bow and slowly crept back amidships. As it progressed, the sky around the transformed section of the ship shifted from cloudless blue to thick, swirling fog. But the fog wasn't uniform, and in places I caught glimpses of starry blackness.

Suddenly, the ship pitched forward, swinging us the opposite direction and bringing bow and stern level once again. As the arc of our swing shortened, the deck began to tremble violently, as if it would break apart. I felt the strain of the earl's muscles as he fought to keep us from banging against solid objects fixed to the deck.

At last, everything went still. Oil lamps flared to life along the ship's rail, and we cruised peacefully, enveloped in the strange, foggy sea. The air was warm and wet, as if we'd left the Irish winter for the tropics. The crewmen pelted down from the rigging, hitting the deck like hailstones.

The earl and I lay twisted together like a pile of rope, and I could feel the flat of his abdomen warm against my breasts. As we worked to decouple our limbs, the incidental press of our bodies—and the warmth of his breath against my ear one moment, my throat the next—caused my own breath to shorten and my heart to race.

I breathed deeply, collecting myself as the earl picked apart the knot that bound us, and finally helped me to my feet. I saw that the sword had become entangled in a wad of netting a few yards away.

"My lord," I said quietly, nodding. He followed my gaze and strode over and retrieved it.

"I don't trust this fog, Captain," called the toad man.

"Nor I, Coker," replied O'Malley. No longer viewing her through a veil of absinthe, I saw she had a ruddy complexion and flaming-red curls.

"What is the meaning of all this?" the earl demanded, raising the tip of his sword. "Why have you abducted us, and where are we going?"

The captain cocked an eyebrow. "You don't want to threaten me, young sir, relation or no. Your dun-haired cousin wants that sword, and she said naught about bringing your *person*. I don't care if you *are* descended from the Dan—"

Mr. Yeats cleared his throat delicately. "Captain, that's not exactly what Queen Isolde—"

"Hush, now, lad," barked the captain. She rolled her eyes, and they came to rest on me. "Promised to write a ballad about me if I brought him along, that one did. Stays on me like a mother hen."

"You were sent by the queen?" I asked, astonished.

She eyed me up and down. "I was, as I told your thick-pated

companion. But he chose not to believe me." Her gaze dropped to the torn fabric of my gown and she added, "My apologies for the damage, but I was obliged to resort to more forceful measures."

"But *why* were you sent for us?"

She blinked at me, considering my question. Or perhaps considering whether she would answer. Then she glanced at the earl. "Right. I was to say to ye this: 'The queen has desperate need of the sword and desires the counsel of the Earl of Meath.' She was not prepared to wait for Your Lordship until the morrow."

"You're taking us to her?" I asked. "To Kildamhnait Tower?"

"That I am." She gave a brisk nod. "And I'll get you there a mite faster than that great smoking iron serpent would have done. Until then, by way of apology for your gown, I'd be pleased to offer you—"

"How is it you still live?" Lord Meath interrupted. "You must be three hundred years old."

Captain O'Malley stared, wide-eyed. "Who taught the whelp manners, I wonder?"

"I'm sure he means no insult," I said, casting the earl a warning glance. "He's had quite a shock, meeting his ancestor under such circumstances. How *is* it you still live?"

The captain folded her arms over her chest, and her gaze slid away from us, seemingly to examine the ship's rigging. "As it happens, I'm a bit stuck in between, for murdering and the like. The Land of Promise awaits me once I've paid for my misdeeds. But the *Queen* here is the best and fastest of the Gap galleons, and 'tisn't such a bad life—is it, boys?"

"Huzzah!" shouted the crew. I flinched as a hedgehog-like creature scurried up a line dangling beside me.

"The Land of Promise" referred to a paradisiacal Celtic afterworld. That much, at least, I understood. "What do you mean 'stuck in between,' Captain O'Malley?"

"The Gap is 'in between,' Miss Quicksilver," inserted Mr. Yeats. "The nowhere between worlds. It must be crossed to reach Faery from Ireland, and vice versa. These are, of course, only dimensional distinctions, as these countries occupy the same space."

I stared at him. If I had correctly interpreted his explanation, it sounded very much like confirmation of my theory about overlapping worlds. "How is it the captain is stuck?" I asked. "We boarded her ship from a train crossing the Irish countryside."

Yeats nodded. "And I boarded from the summit of Ben Bulben. But the *Queen* was not physically in either location. We boarded only her shadow."

"And how is *that* possible, sir?"

He offered another of his placid smiles. "We are all *touched,* Miss Quicksilver. Did you not know it?"

The meaning of this declaration was unclear—he might very well have been saying we were all mad. But before I could question him further, the captain said, "This life is no hardship if you've a taste for adventure, lass." She winked at me. "Now, if you'll join me in my cabin, I'll stand you a drink to bolster your strength."

O'Malley held out her arm, indicating I should precede her.

"No, Ada."

It was only the earl's voice—speaking my Christian name for the first time—that called my attention to the fact that I'd moved to follow her. I glanced at him, and he shook his head. "We'll neither drink nor eat while on board."

Indeed, what had come over me? Had I really been about to take the fatal step of a novice? According to lore, accepting an offer of food or drink while among fairies would exile me from the living world. I felt a tickle against my cheeks, like a cobweb, and swiped at them with the back of my hand. It seemed that a translucent veil had fallen over my eyes, blurring the edges of the earl's figure. I swiped again.

"Fairy glamour," he said, reaching out his hand. "Stand close to me."

"My lord …" I grasped his fingers and moved beside him. The veil dropped. "I'm sorry, I should know better."

He squeezed my hand but did not release it. "Learning from books is not the same as being lectured by your grandmother since before you could walk."

"Surely you'll not be so rude as to refuse to take refreshment with me," the captain protested. "Not when I've saved you a long, uncomfortable journey."

"I don't imagine you will shorten your sojourn in purgatory by luring unsuspecting Christians," replied Lord Meath. "Do as the queen has bidden you. We shall wait here on deck."

"The devil take ye," snapped the captain. "Hard to find good help in the Gap. A pretty little maid she'd make too. It's only a matter of time, Lord High and Mighty." Her gaze moved over my disarranged silver locks. "She's been claimed by the gentlefolk, and they'll have her in the end, mark my words."

I took hold of a lock of my hair. Was this what Mr. Yeats had meant by "touched"? Marked by Faery? I recalled the earl's remark about my ancestress and the fairy kiss.

"Captain O'Malley!" shouted the toad man suddenly. "Fomorian galleon to starboard!"

No sooner had he uttered the words than a stone ball the size of a beer barrel smashed a hole in the deck directly behind the captain. I fell backward against the earl, and throwing an arm about me, he staggered back further.

"Ah, *Queenie!*" the captain cried in shocked anguish. "Ye'll pay for that, devils!"

The stone ball was tethered by a chain, and figures began scurrying down the length of it toward us. They were jaundiced-looking creatures, shaped like men but moving on all fours.

They had heads of wiry gray hair, and the pointy tips of their ears rose several inches before curling toward the back of their heads. They did not appear to be armed, except for their fangs and claws. Fomorians were described in the literature as a race of monsters—ancient sea raiders and enemies of the Tuatha De Danaan. They were connected with plague, blight, and drought. With darkness and death. Their king was a demon named Balor, whose gaze could level an army.

The crew, armed with swords, swarmed over the invaders, and the captain shouted, "Prepare the catapult!"

I turned to look in the direction of her shout, and indeed, a catapult was mounted on the afterdeck.

"Don't ask about it, miss," Mr. Yeats cautioned. "The captain considers it uncivilized. But powder is tricky among fairies."

I supposed this was meant as an explanation of the catapult in place of cannon—that fairies somehow rendered the firing mechanism unreliable.

Crewmen began shouting, and I glanced up to see a dark prow cut through the fog off the *Queen*'s starboard bow. On the hull, the name was inscribed in black, slashing letters.

"*Death Rattler*," the earl translated.

The ship's figurehead was a creature of nightmares: demon-like, with fire glowing in its gaping eye and mouth openings. The chain extended from the figurehead's mouth to the *Queen*, and more of the creatures were moving along its length.

"Release!" cried the captain, and the catapult hurled a volley of cannonballs at the ghastly boarding party, knocking half a dozen of them off the chain and into the void.

"Reload!"

"Captain," called Mr. Yeats in a cool but cautionary tone, "remember our cargo. Remember what Her Majesty said: 'for Ireland!'"

Captain O'Malley swore and muttered, "Uppity, ungracious child." I took this to be directed at Mr. Yeats, but then I recalled that Grace O'Malley was the queen's ancestress.

"All hands, prepare for the jump!" ordered the captain. "Set the navigator for Achill."

The toad man, still resting astride the *Queen*'s figurehead, held up a smoke-filled glass globe mounted in a metal casing. "Setting course," he cried. He turned a crank on the side of the casing, and a small ship mounted on a hoop inside the globe shifted position. The color of the smoke changed from gray to red.

"Flee the Gap!" shouted the captain.

The earl fumbled for the line he had anchored us with before, and I went into his arms without waiting to be invited. As he worked to coil the line around us, the ship nosed out of the strange fog, and the solid edges of the bow softened to wispy outlines.

But before the ship had passed out of the Gap completely, another stone projectile struck, this time stripping away the mainsail.

The deck went out from under our feet, and the next thing I knew, we were falling away from the ship. The line halted our descent for only a moment before it snapped. Shouting, we made a panicked grab for each other but failed to catch hold in time.

The setting sun had washed the face of the sea, many terrifying feet below us, in brilliant orange light. We seemed to plunge toward the mouth of a volcano.

We broke through the surface of the water, and the cold forced the breath from my lungs, stopping my scream.

# INTO THE DRINK

## EDWARD

The breaking waves meant we were close to shore, but I could not feel the bottom.

*Don't panic, Meath.*

The first thing was to rid myself of the overcoat that threatened to drag me under the waves. I ripped it open and released it into the surf, shouting, "*Ada!*"

I heard a woman's cry and swam toward it, ducking under a wave as it curled over me. I had always accepted that I might die at sea, but not this way.

"Ada!" I shouted again when I surfaced. This time I was rewarded with a mouthful of seawater, which I had to swallow to avoid choking. Striking out with my hands, I caught hold of something—the line that had bound us together, which was still loosely wrapped about my waist.

Kicking to keep my head above the waves, I towed in the line, fist over fist. I found Ada at last, clinging to the other end. I caught her under the arms, but we both began to sink. Giving in to the drag, I worked blindly to release the buttons of her jacket, finally ripping it open and tugging it over her shoulders. Her skirt, too, I shucked off her. Freed at last from the heavy yards of fabric, she began to kick upward, and I followed.

Our heads broke the surface and we gasped for air.

"Swim!" I shouted, guiding her in the direction the waves were rolling. "Hard as you can!"

Her eyes were wide, teeth chattering, her cheeks washed in pink from the reflected sunset. "Go!" I cried, and finally she began to swim.

I kept pace beside her, glancing back every few moments to watch for cresting waves. There was no sign of the *Queen of Connacht*. Had she gone back through the Gap? Or perhaps into the sea? The Fomorians were age-old enemies of the Tuatha De Danaan; that much I knew, and little else. Miss Quicksilver would likely be able to tell me more if we ever found ourselves on land again. I could see the dark outline of the craggy shore ahead of us now, close enough for hope. If we were where I thought we were, there was a very real danger of being flung against the rocks at the foot of the highest cliffs in Ireland. But just east of those cliffs, I knew there was a softer landing spot, and though I could not see it, I guided us that direction.

On instinct, I glanced over my shoulder—and saw a wall of dark water framed by bloodred sky. It heaved toward us, the crest already forming.

"Hold your breath!" I cried, towing her with me and ducking under the curl of white water. I wrapped my body around hers as the water surged, dragging us like fish on a line. The violence of the wave spun our bodies, making it difficult to ascertain which direction was up. The rushing water roared in my ears, and for a moment I believed that this was the shape of my death.

Then one of my boots struck sand. I helped the lady to her

feet and half-dragged her toward shore, banging toes and shins on sharp rocks and mussel shells. The wave that had swept us so violently to safety now made its return, tugging at our ankles, sucking away the sand that supported our footsteps. I curled my fingers around her waist, holding fast, and when the strength of the undertow ebbed, we hurried the rest of the way to the small strand, where we fell to our knees.

She was still struggling to recover, heaving and coughing, ripping at the buttons at her throat. I bent over her, tugged up the tail of her blouse, and worked loose her corset laces. She sank onto the sand, lungs finally taking in their full measure of cold sea air, and I scanned the landscape before us. Dark peaks bookended the strand, which glowed golden in the light of the rising moon.

*Keem Strand.* And indeed, just over the ridge to our left rose the highest cliffs in Ireland. It was a near miss. I'd had other near misses in this spot. As a boy, I had played with Isolde near the drop-off—a place we were strictly forbidden to go. It was a thing I'd learned from my cousin—that we are most alive when death is near. As an adult, I came to realize that in death's company was where my cousin found her existence most tolerable. It was a wonder we both had survived.

My companion's breathing finally quieted, and I knelt beside her. "There's a cottage at the back of the strand. Can you walk there?"

"Yes, of course," she replied, bracing herself against the arm I offered as she rose to her feet.

She was shivering violently. I whispered a prayer as we crossed to the cottage and opened the door.

The inside was nearly as bleak as the exterior, furnished with only a bench and a pair of hard chairs. But my prayer had been answered—a stack of turf bricks stood by the hearth. Fishermen used the cottage as a warming hut on wet winter evenings, and they had left a striker, a basket of straw, and another of driftwood. Everything was wonderfully dry, and soon we were warming ourselves before the flames.

Only when golden firelight was dancing over wet, chilled skin did I let myself look at her. Her state of undress came as a shock—I had done it out of necessity and forgotten. Her wet blouse, which clung to her slender form, had been ripped open to the top of her corset. Her hair hung in heavy curls that released sparkling rivulets over her flesh. The swell of her breasts above the loosened corset was a thing I could not allow myself to contemplate, lest I lose myself in their soft beauty. I raised my eyes and found hers resting on my chest. My borrowed coat gone and my shirt in tatters, I was as good as half naked.

When our gazes met, she looked away quickly.

"I apologize for this awkward state of affairs, Miss Quicksilver," I said. "Rest assured that I know where we are. We have overshot our destination only slightly, and in the morning we'll find someone to take us to the queen."

She made a valiant effort at smiling. "That is a relief, my lord."

"Have you any injury?"

She shook her head. "Only bruised and chilled. And you?"

"I am whole." I glanced at the fire. "There's enough turf to last the night. We'll be safe here."

"Do you think it was all a dream, my lord?"

My eyes moved again to her face, but she was staring into the fire. Though I suspected her question was rhetorical, I tried to answer her anyway. "As you know, I struggle to distinguish dream from reality. Had we not shared the experience, I would assume that my hallucinations were increasing in severity."

Her eyes were oddly bright in the firelight. "Do you recall what Captain O'Malley said when she was vexed with you?"

I shook my head. "I'm afraid I don't."

"Before Mr. Yeats interrupted her, she'd begun to say she didn't care whether you were a descendant of the *Danaan*."

Laughing quietly, I replied, "She did not strike me as an especially trustworthy person. I wouldn't put stock in anything she said."

Miss Q frowned. "Lord Meath, I'm sure I needn't remind you that the most famous of the Danaan warriors was Diarmuid."

I studied her a long moment. "You believe this is important because of the sword?"

"I believe this is important because inside the fairy mound, you told me you *were* Diarmuid. You spoke to me in a language I never learned—Old Irish, I now believe—and yet I understood you. And then you fought the púca with Diarmuid's sword. I know that you want the world to take no notice of the fact you're an earl, so I can only imagine how you might feel about a connection to the Danaan. But, my lord, I fear we no longer have the time for … for gentlemanly humility."

All this came out in a rush, her chest rising and falling rapidly in her excitement. For an outburst of this kind to issue from such a patient and sensible lady, I knew she must be trying to draw my attention to something she believed vitally important.

And yet I could not see beyond the inconsistency in her story.

"I said that *I* am Diarmuid?"

Her lips parted, and she hesitated. "You did, sir."

"What else did I say to you, Ada? What else did I say *in Old Irish?*"

I watched her throat work as she swallowed. "You said very little, my lord."

I rose from my chair and stood with my back to the fire, facing her. Trying to intimidate her, I confess. "Anything I said could be important, could it not? Please tell me again what happened last night. No omissions this time."

## ADA

He stood nearly in silhouette, and yet his eyes flashed fire. Like the Gap galleon that had brought us here, he seemed to drift between Irish naval officer and earl, native of wind and wave, and restless ghost of all of Ireland's wasted, lonely places. Places once sacred to Faery and blighted by their exodus.

A vision came to me then. I know of nothing else to call it.

*The earl's visage faded, and I saw a woman lying in a field of flowers. The skirts of her gown billowed around her middle— she was heavy with child. Her glistening hair fanned out over the moss that her head rested on. She was sleeping peacefully, one hand on her belly. A cloud passed in front of the sun, shading her form, and I noticed she was ringed by perhaps a dozen twiglike yet animate figures. They danced around her, their laughter like autumn leaves stirred by the wind.*

*"Be gone," a voice commanded, and a man stepped into the clearing.*

*Now came a sound like flames licking dry wood. The twig dancers' movements became jerkier and more insistent.*

*"Fate has woven together the threads of our being,"continued the speaker, still half veiled in shadow. "You shall not take her."*

*The twig circle tightened around her, their crackling protests intensifying.*

*"The child of the child of her child, and still many generations hence," he continued, stepping closer and speaking as though to disobedient children. His countenance was very like the earl's but with a strange light behind his features. He was ageless and heartbreakingly beautiful. "I have foreseen that I shall know her."*

*The twig dancers paused now, waiting and watching, and I could see they each wore a thimble-size red cap. In a single motion, each removed its cap and tossed it onto the resting lady.*

*The man bent low over her. With his head near her belly, he drew a sword, and my heart stopped. But he laid the sword beside the maid, and the twig dancers scattered with shrill cries of alarm. The man bent still lower, pressing a kiss onto her belly, then lifting her hand and placing the palm over his kiss.*

*"But, for now, we all go," he whispered against her hand, "taking with us the Plague Warriors so that you may live."*

"Ada?"

I blinked once and then again. What was it I had seen? And what did it signify? The words he had spoken—*I have foreseen that I shall know her*—reminded me of the strange things the earl had said at Brú na Bóinne the evening before.

"*Answer* me, Ada," the earl insisted, drawing closer.

Something reached out of him then. Something I couldn't see and yet could *feel* deep in my throat. Words spilled like marbles from my lips: "Thee, my own love, whom I both know and know not."

I clamped my hand over my mouth, astonished. I had not meant to speak, but had been unable to stop it. Somehow the earl had compelled me.

"What else was said?" he persisted, brow darkening.

I covered my left hand with my right, but unseen fingers prized apart my grip and I answered, again without meaning to, "*Let me taste.*"

"And then what?" His voice was taut with anger.

My fingers touched my lower lip of their own accord, and I gasped. He stared at me, eyes widening, as my fingertips continued moving independently of my will, tracing the outline of my mouth. I remembered the press of his lips in the chamber at Brú na Bóinne—how both the kiss and my reaction had confused me—and I closed my eyes.

"Stop, my lord!" I protested. "You are wrong to do this."

"I ...?" He took a step back from me, horrified, realizing what he had done. "God help me," he choked out. He shook his head and sank down on the bench, gazing into the fire and repeating softly, "God help me."

He reached for his flask, forgetting that his coat was lost to the sea. He dropped his head into his hands.

Dismayed and confused, I watched firelight play over his gleaming skin and dark curls. He appeared to be in the throes of a transformation. A kind of fairy enchantment, perhaps. Or was there a true connection between him and the Danaan? Even to Diarmuid himself?

"I don't know what's happening to me," he murmured. "I was wrong to lure you as I have. I've risked your life, and I—I've taken terrible liberties. It's driving me mad that I cannot remember what I've done, yet I have no right to force your disclosure. How is it possible that I can force you to anything?"

He looked up then, meeting my gaze. "Please believe that to my knowledge, I have never before done such a thing. I was not conscious of ... of the trespass, until you demanded that I stop."

His eyes had lost their fierceness. Now I saw only pain. The firelight danced along his cheekbones and jawline, and he very much resembled the man from my vision, with his ageless masculine beauty. I recalled that the mythical Diarmuid had been marked with a "love spot," and any woman who saw him fell in love with him. Yet he himself had once fallen victim to a love spell that eventually destroyed him. Irish folktales were riddled with such contradictions.

"I do believe you, my lord," I said quietly. "And I am sorry for your pain."

He grimaced. "Do not apologize to me, madam. I have kept something from you that I should not have. I could not bring myself to tell you before—I believed that it might frighten you away from me. You *should* have been frightened away from me."

I stepped closer to him and the fire and sat down on the bench, leaving a forearm's distance between us. "What is it?" I asked in a clear and firm voice, bracing myself for what was to come.

"Do you recall that the night we met, I saw a banshee?"

"I do, yes."

"Though I professed not to understand it, it was clear to me the banshee's keen was for *you*. And though I'd only just met you, I could not bear the thought that harm might come to you. I feared that you would meet with some accident on the road, or worse. So I proposed that you accompany me to Brú na Bóinne."

I sat a moment absorbing this confession, turning over the various ways in which it was troubling. "You did not intend to consult with me about the ruin."

"Certainly, I did," he countered. "Discovering you in the Green Faery was nothing short of serendipity. I mean to say it is not the *only* reason I made the offer. I had the idea that if I kept you close, I could protect you. But I was a fool."

My overtaxed mind grappled feebly with this new information. Unless I misunderstood, he was telling me that a banshee had predicted my death. Not only that, he was confessing a protective impulse I could not understand in view of our brief acquaintance.

"How were you a fool, my lord?" I asked.

"Because surely I'm the reason your life is in danger. How many times have you almost died in my company?"

He had a point, and yet … "We cannot know that. We cannot even be sure that your interpretation of the warning is accurate."

"But I should have told you," he insisted. "It should have figured in your decision."

"Yes, you should have," I replied.

"I don't know whether you can forgive me. I do know that if anything should happen to you, I—"

I held up my hand, and he fell silent. "You should have told me," I continued, "but I doubt that it would have dissuaded me. I would have reasoned, as you did, that the danger lay in continuing on my intended course. And there was no way to be sure on which path danger lurked, except by setting out on one of them. Furthermore, the alternative you offered was very appealing. In short, my lord, I very much doubt that a more complete disclosure would have changed anything."

Gratitude shone in the cool deep blue of his eyes. My words had had the intended effect of soothing his troubled mind. "As for our present perils," I continued, "you have been as much at risk as I. And I have not died, sir. In fact, it is your quick thinking and action that have prevented my death up to now. I consider myself safer in your company than out of it."

He gave me a pained smile. "It is kind of you to say so, and yet difficult for me to believe, considering my behavior in the past quarter hour." He dropped his gaze, studying his hands now. "And also my reprehensible behavior at Brú na Bóinne."

"I do not believe you are to blame for that," I said. "Something unusual is happening to you, Lord Meath. Something transformational, perhaps. We have not yet understood it, but I believe that it has to do with Diarmuid and the Danaan, and that it is the reason your cousin is so anxious to speak to you. I fervently hope she will have some of the answers we seek. Until then, I hope you will cease to shoulder the burden for your … uncharacteristic behavior."

He angled his body away from the fire to face me fully. The

golden light washing over his practically bare torso loosened something in my belly. I half expected him to take me in his arms, and I confess I more-than-half wanted him to. Instead, he said, "I can cease to blame myself only if you will reassure me that I did not force myself on you, as I forced you to answer my questions just now."

I broke eye contact, my heart racing. I could not truthfully reassure him on this point, and with him watching me so closely, I was unequal to lying to him. Not knowing what answer to give, I said nothing.

"Ah," he said bleakly.

For a time, only our breathing and the crackle of burning turf were audible, but at last he said, "And may I know how much I have to answer for? May I assume that I stopped short of ... of compromising you? And that if I had not, you would have called me out when I was myself again? Or at least fled me when you had the chance in Mullingar?"

"Yes, my lord, you were stopped short." I realized too late that my overly precise wording was sure to raise even more questions.

"*Were* stopped ... by you, Miss Q?"

I nodded. "Using Diarmuid's sword."

He made a choked sound, and I looked at him and decided that it was the result of unhappy laughter. The color had drained from his face. "Well, I am grateful for your self-sufficiency. Can you now explain to me why you did *not* quit me at Mullingar, as you certainly should have?"

In his shocked expression, I read all his thoughts. He was considering the fact that he had taken me into his protection and then subjected me to insult. He was a gentleman, after all, and I knew I would not easily talk him out of his self-recrimination. So, I didn't choose the easy path.

"I will tell you why, my lord."

He pressed his lips together and waited while I stoked my courage.

"First, because I know that you were not in your right mind, and second, because of the distress that you now feel upon hearing of it." I dropped my gaze. "You are a gentleman, sir—in truth, one of the best I have known. Your pain and confusion trouble me, and I agreed to travel with you partly in the hope … in the hope I might find some way of easing your suffering. I have no wish to abandon you to your fate, whatever that may be."

As I said these words, I knew that I'd made my decision. For better or worse, I would not flee back to London. Not yet, anyway.

My fingers had knotted themselves together in my lap, and a bead of perspiration collected above my lip. The earl's hand moved toward my fingers, covering them and gently squeezing.

"And so we each have acted precipitously in the hope of helping the other," he said. "I think that cannot be such a bad basis for a friendship."

I raised my eyes to his face, hopeful. "I quite agree."

A smile touched his lips. "And now, though we both have confessed that we'd rather not part, I fear that we must."

I have no doubt that a stricken look crossed my face as I repeated, "We must?"

"You should rest. I, on the other hand, must not sleep without fortification against nightwalking."

"You must be exhausted," I argued, but of course, he was right.

"You have recently demonstrated your ability to look after yourself," he replied, "yet I am unwilling to take the risk. And our sword, I fear, is lost. I insist that you try to sleep."

One glance about the cottage was enough to convince me that my prospects for sleeping were grim. The chairs were of bare wood, and the bench was too narrow to lie on. The floor was earthen and no doubt damp and cold.

"Perhaps you might think of me as your brother for the night."
My eyes darted back to his face. "My lord?"

"In that way, perhaps you won't find it awkward or distasteful to rest against me and find both warmth and some measure of comfort."

My heart throbbed, warm and eager, as he scooted to the end of the bench, resting his back against the wall. Shifting one leg to the other side, he made space for me.

My breath caught in my throat, and I began to tremble. There was simply no way I could think of this man as my *brother*. But neither could I find voice to reject his offer.

I moved closer, sinking down beside him on the bench. I hesitated, unable to meet his gaze, and he held open his arms. I wanted nothing so much as to feel whether the flesh of his chest was as warm as it looked.

"You may trust me, Miss Q," he said softly. "I will watch over you. I will not sleep."

Scooting closer, I tucked myself into him. One of his hands came to rest on the back of my head while the other fell at his side. I longed to feel his arms around me, but I also appreciated this demonstration of his pure intention.

Breathing deeply, I inhaled his salty warmth, still mingling with licorice sweetness despite the recent wash. I knew that I would never feel safer.

But in this quiet moment, I considered a thought that had been looming since his confession: Mightn't the banshee's keening mean that my death was imminent *whatever* path I set upon?

# THE MAD QUEEN

## EDWARD

I had much to think on: my companion's theories and her disclosures, and the fresh evidence of her regard for my welfare. But I could not turn my mind to any of it at present. Her womanly softness—the light sweetness of her scent, her weight on my chest—had subdued every faculty. It took all my strength of will not to fold my arms around her.

Even when my mind could approach the topic of the night before, the images that bloomed before me cast my composure to the winds. What, exactly, had been my trespasses, that she had been compelled to raise a sword against me? How frightened she must have been! And I had thought it was the *not* knowing that would drive me mad.

My actions weighed far more heavily than the lady on my chest. Whatever demon might have possessed me, it was my own body that committed the offense, and I therefore bore the responsibility, never mind the excuses she was kind enough to make for me.

*Let me taste.* I shivered at the thought that I had spoken these words to her—and it wasn't solely shame I felt. Just now I had spoken the words "friend" and "brother" to reassure her that she was safe in my care, but there was nothing brotherly about the fire coursing through my veins in response to the soft, sweet curves of her body pressing into mine.

She murmured in her sleep, stirring against my chest. I lowered my hand lightly to her back, not wanting to take liberties after the intimacies I had forced on her in my altered state. The light touch was enough to quiet her.

*You are a gentleman, sir. In truth, one of the best I have known.* I marveled that she had spoken these words. The women of my acquaintance—especially those Irish and English beauties introduced to me as potential Lady Meaths—were skilled at the sort of teasing compliments whose purpose was to keep a man guessing. I was touched by her openness and honesty, by her warm regard.

But it had come time to ask myself—what, exactly, was I about? What did I intend by keeping her with me and by naming myself her protector? By cultivating an intimacy with her, be it circumstantial or otherwise?

I no longer had mother or father to disapprove of me or remind me of my duty as a peer of the kingdom of Ireland. While she might not have the bloodline, she had all that I considered more important: sense, wit, a kind heart, and an open and curious mind. I had met no other woman with whom I could imagine sharing my ancestral seat.

But in offering her myself, *what* would I be offering her, really? Something was happening to me that neither of us understood. I was determined to overcome it, but what if I could not?

I passed a dreadful night, owing in part to these swirling thoughts but also, I think, to addiction to my elixir. Even had I wanted to sleep, the tremors would have kept me from it. I had waking dreams as well—not the absinthe visions, but lucid nightmares of battle. I saw roiling hoards, fields soaked in blood, and skies teeming with battleships and airborne monsters. The battle crow—the Morrigan—circled above it all, and her ragged cry seemed to mock the tortured souls below.

By dawn, I was feverish and exhausted and had begun to drop off to sleep despite my resolve, when there came a sharp rapping on the cottage door.

The party outside did not wait for an answer but pushed open the door and stepped inside. "This time, cousin, I've come to fetch you myself."

## ADA

I was woken by the sound of a banging door. Lord Meath sat up suddenly, arms clutching around me. But I pushed myself free of the protective embrace so I could see what was happening.

Backlit by the sunshine streaming through the open doorway, a figure moved into the room. I jumped up, blinking at the brightness.

The earl rose more slowly beside me. "It appears that you've not lost your love for dramatic entrances, Your Majesty," he said, bowing low despite his disapproving tone.

I stared wide-eyed and then dropped into a drunkard's curtsy, blushing like a lovesick maiden. "Your Majesty," I murmured. I closed my eyes, pressing my lips together, feeling the mortification wash over me. I'd just been discovered by the queen of Ireland, half-dressed, with torn undergarments and in the arms of a bare-chested earl who just happened to be her cousin.

"How delicious!" cried the queen, clapping her hands together. "Please tell me I've interrupted something clandestine and wicked, Edward."

She angled my direction, and the light fell across her features. Despite my chagrin, her beauty quite literally stole my breath. She was statuesque, with ivory skin and luxuriant dark hair. Her dress was crimson brocade, her jacket trimmed with white fox fur. Her lady's top hat, also crimson, was decorated with coral-pink Christmas stars—poinsettias from the Americas. For all these elegant accoutrements, in her face was the mirth of a child.

"You have not," replied the earl in a sober tone. "We've been shipwrecked by your agent, who claimed to be our ancestress and nearly killed us no fewer than three times. In fact, I believe it was four, Miss Q, was it not? I had not included the raven. So what you have interrupted, Your Majesty, is us taking shelter from the night to which your transportation arrangements abandoned us."

"Well, happy Christmas to you, too, cousin," grumbled the queen. "I had thought you might thank me for abbreviating your journey. Was it not considerate of me?"

The earl's eyes widened, and he offered a satirical smile. "And yet here we are at the same time we would have been had we stuck to the train—by the grace of God alone, I'm certain. Except that now we are cold and hungry, and I have a pounding headache." At the end of this minor rant, the earl bowed and added, "Your Majesty."

The queen rolled her eyes. "Well, I can help with the latter, at any rate." She snapped her fingers, and a servant appeared in the doorway. "Earl Edward has need of my tonic, Gordon."

The man bowed and crossed to the earl, offering him an emerald-studded flask. Lord Meath hesitated a moment, frowning, before he took the flask, sniffed it, and drank. The scent of anise rose bright and sweet against the brittle sea air. Was the queen subject to nightwalking as well?

"This is astonishing rudeness, Edward, but I'll put it down to your current ill health and prickly temper. When do you plan to introduce me to your companion? 'Miss Q,' was it?"

The queen stepped closer, and I curtsied again, heart drumming frantically.

"Your Majesty," replied the earl, "this is Miss Ada Quicksilver, an Englishwoman and student of the Lovelace Academy for Promising Young Women."

"Lovelace, indeed!" she cried. "How charming. I'm quite jealous."

"You know of the academy, Your Majesty?" I asked in surprise.

"I do, in fact. Founded by naughty Lord Byron's daughter, was it not?"

I raised my eyebrows, flushing again.

She laughed. "Forgive me, my dear. I mean the daughter of naughty Lord Byron, Countess Ada Lovelace, of course. And are you perhaps named in her honor?"

"Yes, Your Majesty. My parents admired her."

"Quite a clever woman. Did not neglect her maths. I adore clever women. Are you one as well?"

"I …" I knew very well that I was, though I would not presume to compare my intellect to that of my namesake. Yet to assert such a thing to a queen while I stood in rags before her—it was quite beyond me.

"Miss Q is very clever, I assure you," replied the earl. "She is a student of our folktales and mythology. I offered to help her in her research, but she has gotten rather more than she bargained for."

This last statement was no doubt intended innocently enough, but judging by the queen's amused expression, she had taken the less respectable—but no less accurate—interpretation. "Well, it would seem to agree with her. She is the very picture of youth and healthfulness, though I don't know quite what to make of that hair."

"I daresay we've all at least one hereditary trait that we're prone to be judged by."

The queen's countenance sobered to match the earl's tone. "Too true, cousin Edward. It suits her, at any rate." She returned her gaze to the earl, and her smile reappeared. "Come, it's Christmas Eve. Let us return to Kildamhnait and continue this business in comfort and the company of friends."

"Hold, Isolde," said the earl, "did you say Christmas Eve?"

I glanced at him. Lord Meath was right. We had set out for Newgrange on the day of the winter solstice, two days ago now. "December twenty-third, is it not?" I asked.

"Yes, well," replied the queen, "Auntie said the miscalculation by her navigator was due to the need for … expediency. Count yourselves lucky I found you at all. Now, where is that sword, Edward?" She scanned the interior of the cottage.

He lifted an eyebrow. "Lost, to the waves, I presume."

The queen's eyes went wide. "You jest."

"I do not. Even if I had managed to hold on to it in our fall from the ship, it would surely have been lost in our consequent scramble for dry land."

The queen squeezed her eyes closed, hissing, "Blast. We *need* that sword, Edward."

He frowned at her. "Had you been as frank with me as you apparently were with our pirate ancestress, I might have taken better care. And not to belabor the point, but if you hadn't put us into her hands in the first place—"

A shout from outside interrupted the earl's tirade. The queen turned and hurried out of the cottage. Lord Meath and I followed.

The morning was clear and bright, but I gasped at the shock of cold air against my bare flesh.

The queen joined her servant and a richly dressed gentleman, both bent over something on the strand. As I drew closer, I saw that it was the sword, half buried in the sand, waves pulling at its graven gold hilt.

"Great Fury," whispered the queen.

The gentleman reached for the hilt, but touching it, he recoiled with an oath.

"As I suspected," said the queen. "Edward?"

The earl bent and lifted the sword. The weapon was apparently particular about who handled it. Why had it permitted me?

The earl turned the blade in his hands, and the gentleman gave a low whistle. "She's a beauty." His gaze moved beyond the earl when he noticed me standing behind him. His eyes went wide as they moved over my form, and I hugged my chest. The frigid air made my cheeks feel all the hotter.

Removing his coat, the gentleman stepped closer. "If you'll permit me, Miss …?"

"Miss Quicksilver," I said, voice trembling from the cold. "I thank you, sir."

"Duncan O'Malley," he replied in a heavy Irish brogue, helping me into the coat. He shot a disapproving glance at the earl. "What transpired here, Edward?"

Isolde gave an unqueenly snort. "You may call out cousin Edward at a later time," she said. "I've not had my breakfast. Edward, bring the sword. Duncan, bring Miss Quicksilver."

Lord Meath's countenance was grim, but when O'Malley held out his arm to me, the earl nodded, and I took it.

O'Malley's heavy wool coat had a wide offset collar and reached all the way to my ankles. I felt like a child in it but was grateful for its warmth.

He was a handsome and rather dashing fellow. His coarse dark hair formed tight ringlets that were lit with burnished gold. Like Edward, he wore it pulled back from his face, and also like Edward, he had clear blue eyes—all the more striking against the warm brown of his skin.

We followed the queen and her servant to the small dock,

where a vessel awaited—a snug copper tugboat, gleaming in the morning sun. "*Medb*" had been painted on her hull—Old Irish for the mythic warrior queen Maeve—and she flew the Irish flag, a green banner emblazoned with a golden harp.

We boarded the tugboat and settled ourselves in the wheelhouse, where we could both enjoy the view and warm ourselves by the stove. O'Malley took the wheel, and we soon pulled away from the dock. The servant placed a kettle on the stove, and a breakfast tray on the small table before us—brown bread, butter, and bright-orange smoked salmon.

"Please accept my apology for endangering your lives," said the queen, a sudden earnestness overtaking her.

Smiling, she lifted a slice of thickly buttered bread from the table, turned, and exited from the wheelhouse. We could see her make her way to the bow, where she removed her hat along with her hairpins, inviting the wintery air to whip through her long dark hair.

Shivering, I murmured, "How cold she must be."

"You needn't worry about Izzy," replied Duncan over his shoulder. "If anyone was ever kin to the four winds, it is she."

*Izzy?* "You are cousin to the queen?" I asked.

"Aye," he replied, glancing back. "And to His Lordship as well."

"Isolde and I used to travel from Dublin with our families for the holidays," the earl explained.

"And my brothers and I used to try to drown the wee jackeens in the sea," said O'Malley with a bark of laughter.

Grinning, the earl replied, "They thought to scare us, but Izzy never met man, woman, nor beast she was frightened of."

"She'd pick herself up laughing as if it was all a great joke," said O'Malley. "Unsatisfying, it was."

The servant placed cups before us and filled them with tea. I wrapped my hands around my cup, savoring its warmth.

O'Malley spoke gravely to the earl then, but he did so in Irish and with an accent so different from my language professor's that I caught only a word or two.

I glanced at Lord Meath, who eyed me a moment before replying. And just as on the night in the fairy mound, I heard *him* speak a phrase and understood it clearly.

"*I haven't harmed her, Duncan, nor have I any intention to.*"

My cheeks warmed, and I knew I should warn him that I was listening—yet I did not.

O'Malley then asked a question I did partly understand, and the earl replied:

"*From London. It's a long story, but we've come to consult with the queen on some strange business.*"

Earl Edward, countenance darkening, listened to a second question from his relative before offering an emphatic, "*She is not, but I consider her to be under my protection nonetheless.*"

O'Malley laughed softly and muttered a few conciliatory-sounding words in reply—roughly, "no offense intended"—and I felt a deep blush spread over my face and chest.

Unlike Isolde, O'Malley seemed to be struggling to overlook the impropriety of the situation, which again reminded me of my vulnerable position. Had O'Malley and the queen assumed that I was the earl's mistress? Wasn't it likely the others we met on the island would draw the same conclusion? I'd never embarked on such a venture before and had therefore never been exposed to this sort of scrutiny. It somewhat dampened my enthusiasm for the idea of spending the holiday with Lord Meath's relations.

The servant began dishing out breakfast, and the conversation dropped. We had not eaten since the luncheon of cold sausage and bread from the basket provided by Mrs. Doyle. The moment a plate was set before me, I realized I was ravenous, and temporarily put O'Malley's probing questions out of mind.

While we ate, the tugboat chugged southeast along the ragged coastline, which was broken once by a long, golden strip of sand that the earl called Keel Strand. There was very little activity along the shore, but then, it was Christmas Eve morning.

"I understand you're here on official business, Miss Quicksilver," said O'Malley as he navigated around the southern tip of the island and into Achill Sound, "but I hope you'll partake of the festivities this evening."

I glanced at the earl. "There will be a banquet and a ball," he explained. "I had meant for us to attend, and certainly the queen will expect me to, but no offense will be taken if you'd prefer to rest and recover."

I studied him a moment, trying to ascertain his preference. I had no desire to intrude on his family gathering, and I worried about what would be whispered about the two of us. But neither did I care for the idea of spending the evening apart from him, especially in a strange place.

"I'm afraid I have nothing suitable to wear, my lord," I replied, avoiding a direct answer. It was no more than the truth—my trunk was likely resting unclaimed alongside his inside Westport station. "Nothing *at all* to wear, in fact."

O'Malley laughed heartily. "That's an easy thing to manage."

I glanced again at Lord Meath, still uncertain. "Duncan's right," he agreed. "The queen will have brought her seamstress. If that is your only objection, I hope you'll agree to accompany me."

My hand fluttered to the front of O'Malley's coat, and I squeezed the overlapping edge of wool. "All right, my lord," I replied.

"Since Edward has got the jump on me in asking," O'Malley said, glancing over his shoulder, "I must settle for the first waltz. If you'll have me, Miss Quicksilver."

Having spent nearly all my adult life in the company of other women, I was unsure what to make of the young nobleman's eager attention. "If you like," I replied with a note of uncertainty.

"And since my cousin appears determined to set himself up as a rival for your attention," said the earl, smiling, "I had better claim the second."

I confess I'd begun to bask in the glow of this gentlemanly sparring when the queen reentered the wheelhouse. "And I the third," she announced.

## EDWARD

Poor Miss Q was unused to my cousin's eccentricities. I could not even assure her the queen was speaking in jest, because she might very well be in earnest. But Isolde was flighty, and likely as not, by the time of the ball she would forget she'd proposed such a ridiculous thing.

"Oh, don't look at me that way, Edward," the queen complained. "I'll not eat your Christmas sweetmeat."

Which was little comfort since, after making similar declarations many times as a child, she had proceeded to do precisely that.

Miss Q could only stare at Isolde as she plunked down on the bench beside me, grinning in a self-satisfied way, like a child with a secret. She lifted a cup of tea to her lips, humming a somber Irish Christmas carol with a jaunty rhythm that made it sound more like a jig. I turned to Miss Q to offer her what I hoped was a reassuring smile, and she did her best to return it despite the crease that had formed across her forehead.

The medieval tower now in sight, the tugboat glided toward the dock. Servants were busy about the grounds of both the tower and the far more inviting manor house, which the family had erected only twenty-five years ago. The tower itself was not large enough or comfortable enough for the modern O'Malleys to lodge in—and certainly not for their royal relative. Nor was such a fortress necessary in the modern age. The only O'Malleys who spent any time in the dilapidated structure were the children, just as Izzy and I had once done, ignoring our parents' warnings that the tower, with its many missing blocks, was unsafe.

We disembarked and followed Isolde to the house, and she immediately placed Miss Q in a servant's care. Orders were given for a bath, followed by a visit from the seamstress, and then she led me up to her suite of rooms, which were in the modern structure's tower, overlooking the sound. I was grateful that my companion's comfort had not been neglected, yet I also recognized this as polite maneuvering by Isolde, who intended to claim my full attention for this first interview.

The queen ordered a fresh pot of tea and directed me to a sofa near the windows. I laid the sword on the gleaming floor planks—all the tables in the vicinity appearing too dainty to support the ancient weapon—and took my seat. Isolde began to pace before me.

"I'll order a scabbard and belt made for that," she said suddenly. "I expect you to carry it at all times."

I intended for her to answer many questions in this meeting, but this was as good a start as any. "What is it you want with me and that damned sword?" I demanded. "None of your riddles now, cousin. You've involved Miss Quicksilver and me in something quite dangerous."

The queen froze, turning her head to pierce me with her gaze. "I sent you to Brú na Bóinne to fetch Diarmuid's sword. We need our fiercest Danaan warrior now." She shook her head. "How was I to know you'd have a maiden in tow? It's so unlike you, Edward."

"Isolde," I said gravely, "I don't think you realize how nonsensical all this sounds."

"Indeed?" she demanded, raising a hand to one hip, and an eyebrow high on her forehead. "Did you not fetch Great Fury from inside the fairy mound? Did you not *wield* it, defeating the púca?"

I eyed her warily. "Do you imply that I am somehow connected with Diarmuid?"

She laughed. "Do you maintain you are not—all evidence to the contrary? And in the same breath that you dare call *me* nonsensical!"

Miss Q's words rang in my ears: *I fear we no longer have the time for gentlemanly humility.* The idea of a link with Diarmuid seemed to me something only the most arrogant or deluded of Irishmen would embrace, but my reasons for resisting it were more complicated—foremost among them being the implication that I might not be in control of my own destiny. But of the two women insisting I consider the possibility, Miss Q, at least, I trusted not to be carried off by flights of fancy. I took a deep breath and strove to moderate my tone.

"Cousin, for pity's sake," I pleaded, "speak plainly. As usual, you are running out a mile ahead of me. What is all this about?"

Blowing out a great agitated sigh, she sank down beside me. She removed her hat and set it on the table, stroking the leaf of a pink Christmas star with one fingertip. Her dark hair hung in heavy waves about her shoulders.

"People say they are poisonous," she murmured.

I assumed that this observation was related to the flower and, possibly, in some oblique way, to our debate—or just as easily *not*. Before I could inquire there was a knock at her door, and a servant entered with a tea tray. He placed it on the table before us, and the queen waved him away. She lifted the pot and filled both our cups, dosing her own heavily with milk and sugar. Then she angled her body so she could tuck her legs beneath her and leaned against me. We had been this familiar as children, but not since she was crowned, and I remained a stiff support for her loosening form. The heavily sweet scent of lilacs rose from her hair.

"You've no idea how difficult it is, Edward," she said. "To rule, I mean. I know we'd have made a violent couple, but there are times I regret opposing my parents' wishes about the marriage. If only I had someone to talk to. Someone to discuss things with. It's such a burden—you've no idea."

"Well, I'm here now," I reminded her gently, hoping to preserve this more somber quality of thought. "Tell me."

She sat up and raised her cup to her lips, draining the contents before placing it back on the table. "We, and all of Faery, are about to be at war."

"War?" I frowned. "What do you mean?"

"Just what I said, cousin."

*Patience,* I reminded myself. It was Isolde's way. It would come out by degrees, *if* I could contain my frustration.

"Are the fairies not gone?" I asked.

"Yes," she replied, "they left centuries ago. But they haven't gone far, and I know absinthe allows you to see through the veil over their world—just as I do."

I had begun to suspect we had this in common, even before the events of the past twenty-four hours. "I take absinthe to stave off nightwalking," I clarified. "The things I see are side effects. I always believed them to be hallucinations."

The queen fixed her gaze on me. "You no longer believe this?"

"Miss Quicksilver told me she thought they might not be."

"Ah, so she *is* clever," observed the queen. "We—you and I—see them because we are *of* them. And your nightwalking is related ... Your restless ancestor has been borrowing your unconscious form."

I stared at her. "Diarmuid."

"Diarmuid."

"What makes you think he's my ancestor? He's just a story, is he not?"

"Wasn't *that* just a story?" She touched the hilt of Great Fury with the toe of her boot. "Did you know, cousin," she said, "that adjacent to the library at Trinity College is a library of Faery?"

"Adjacent? Where?"

"Dimensionally adjacent."

I recalled something Miss Q had said in our first meeting: *their new country somehow overlaps our own.*

"It's wondrous, Edward," the queen continued, pouring herself another cup of tea. "Winding staircases made from carved whalebone. Bookshelves supported by living trees. Vining roses and honeysuckle creeping over everything. I've spent hours and hours there. They have *such* books. Recipes for *flowers,* Edward. Recipes for *kisses.* Songbooks filled with ballads that weave dreams and spin nightmares. There's a tune for calling a ray of sunshine on a cloudy day. For mending a sparrow's wing. Even for saving a cake that has failed to rise. And there are endless volumes of history and genealogy. Complete forests of family trees. More *begats* than the Bible. And in one of those books, I traced the roots and branches from the Tuatha De Danaan and the houses of Ulster right down to you and me."

"I saw you there," I realized suddenly. "At the Trinity Library. Just a few days ago." I raised a hand to my chest. "You walked right through me."

She smiled, lightly touching the back of my hand. "*Now* you see."

"Indeed, I do not. What is this about a war?"

"Do you know why the fairies vanished?"

I shook my head. "I only recall our grandmother telling us that long ago, the Danaan yielded Ireland to the Celts. In fact, I was helping Miss Quicksilver investigate that very question—where they'd gone, and why. It's her course of study at the academy."

Isolde laughed softly, and I knew her well enough to guess the reason: She was thinking about how close to her answers Miss Q had been when conducting her research at Trinity. How close and yet how far.

"In the Faery library," she said, "I found books of history that never happened."

I shook my head at the puzzle. "What do you mean?"

"Histories alternate to our own. Things that *might* have happened, and perhaps did in some version of reality unknown to us. Each of these alternate histories described a great famine in Ireland that began in 1845. The causes of this famine varied among these histories, but in every case, it was responsible for the death of at least a million Irish, Edward. And a million more fled the country because of it."

I drained the tepid contents of my teacup, waiting for her to explain the significance of a history that never happened.

"There is a history in the library that matches our own in every respect—up until 1845. In this history, the Fomorians—the ancient enemies of the Danaan—were responsible for releasing a blight that caused a famine in that year." She studied me. "You remember Grandmama's stories about the Fomorians?"

I nodded, but I did not need to refer to my grandmother's stories, as I had very recently experienced them firsthand on the *Queen of Connacht.*

"Also in this history," Isolde continued, "once the famine had done its work, the Fomorians flooded back into Ireland, slaughtering those that remained and claiming our island for themselves."

"Cousin," I began, masking my impatience, "forgive me, but I cannot understand how this pertains to your summoning me here."

"*Listen,* Edward. This history that was meant for us—it was prevented only by the departure of all the fairies. Diarmuid worked a powerful spell that carried Faery, along with its foes, out of our world. The Fomorians were forced to return to the watery country of their origin." She paused, sitting up and refolding her hands in her lap. "Diarmuid's seal between Ireland and Faery was made strong by ancient magic, but the spell is now a thousand years old and has begun to fray."

For a few moments, I could do nothing but stare at her. If not for my own strange experiences, I would have believed her to have, at last, gone well and truly mad. But still, how could she know all this? Isolde loved drama and adventure, as I knew from our childhood. Mightn't she be exaggerating the threat?

"You believe the Fomorians are coming back to carry out their interrupted plan to conquer Ireland."

"I do."

"And you read all this in books in this library?"

"Much of it can be found there, and I have read it, but that's not how I came to know. I learned of it from Diarmuid himself."

She was coming around now to what she expected from me. I could feel it in the way she watched me—like a cat watching a mouse. "How is that possible?" I asked.

"Your Danaan ancestor has a gateway from his world to ours."

I stared, waiting for her to continue, but then it dawned on me.

"You mean *me.*"

# THREE WALTZES

## ADA

After a gloriously hot bath, I was measured and made to try on half a dozen gowns while the queen's dressmaker and hairdresser and their various assistants looked on. They discussed my features—which to emphasize and which to downplay—what colors would best suit, and so on. At Lovelace, I shared sleeping quarters with two other women. Also, the house mother had a habit of entering without knocking, so I lacked the modesty that would likely make this uncomfortable for another woman who had not been raised in society.

When the women at last left me with a promise to return an hour before the ball—by which time the queen would be dressed and ready—tea was brought in. I nibbled cream cheese sandwiches and slices of cold roast beef while making a closer examination of my room—modern and comfortable, though furnished with pristinely preserved antiques. Above the fireplace was a painting of the very strand and cottage where the earl and I had passed the night. I studied it while I finished my meal, reflecting, in the sober light of day, on the fact that I'd spent the night in the arms of a man.

And *such* a man—a peer of the kingdom of Ireland, with a strange connection to one of the country's beloved folk figures. A man both compassionate and capable, with warm, gentle hands and a penetrating gaze.

As I replayed the evening's events and conversation, heat bloomed in my cheeks and spread out over my chest. My breaths shortened, and I chided myself for this schoolgirl giddiness.

Turning from the painting, I looked for another place to sit and drink my tea. The canopied bed was so richly adorned, I was afraid to disturb it. Instead, I chose a fainting couch by the large picture window, which offered a view of the surrounding countryside.

Though I had never in my life fainted, I was sleep deprived and physically exhausted. I meant only to rest until the maid returned for the tray, when I would ask for fresh writing materials. I had mourned the loss of my notebook, though happily, it had not contained the entirety of my research. There were several more notebooks in my trunk, which the earl had assured me he would have sent from Westport station. I wondered then for the first time what became of the poor man who had tried to recall us to safety on the train. How had he made sense of what he had seen? *We* had hardly begun to make sense of it.

I wondered whether Lord Meath would be given an audience with the queen, and whether she would be able to shed more light on recent events. She ought at least to be able to explain what she wanted with the earl and his sword.

I did not make it any further in my musings before waking to a brisk knock at the door. When I opened my eyes, the white light of the full moon was streaming through the window.

"Come in," I called in a creaky voice, disoriented from the long nap.

Stiffness had set in, and I rose slowly from the couch as the half-dozen women who had attended me earlier streamed in, chattering and making disapproving noises over the darkness of the room and the lateness of the hour. In moments, all the lamps had been lit and blocks of turf set ablaze on the hearth. Warm firelight took the place of cool moonlight.

One of the attendants gave me a glass of orange water, which I drained gratefully, and I was made to undress and stand at the foot of the bed. The ladies helped me into layers of undergarments before slipping a beautiful gown of silver brocade over my head and shoulders. The gown had a corset that fitted over rather than under the bodice, and small emerald-green leaves laced through its silver-on-silver floral pattern.

When the ladies had finished hoisting, hooking, and tying, the seamstress, Mrs. Colby, moved behind me to fasten and arrange an emerald necklace. "A loan from Her Majesty," she murmured.

I touched my fingertips to the large, glittering pendant, which was accented with diamonds and hung from strands of small pearls. I was grateful for the queen's ordering of these preparations, without which I could not have attended the ball, even though I did not quite understand her reason for doing so.

My costume complete, I was directed to the stool before the vanity, where Mrs. Lamotte, the hairdresser, took over. Most of my silver tresses were perfumed, plaited, and wound atop my head, with a handful of heavy curls left to fall freely at the back. The attendants worked emerald- and pearl-tipped hairpins into the coiled plaits.

Then the two ladies took my hands and raised me, leading me before the full-length mirror beside the armoire.

I drew in a quick breath, which was quite a feat considering the tightness of my corset. I had never worn such a gown, and I had certainly never worn such a valuable piece of jewelry. The color selected by Mrs. Colby boldly emphasized my most singular feature, and the necklace drew attention to the color of my eyes. Growing up, I had discovered that for some, my appearance held an exotic interest, while others judged it as downright odd. The earl had not been the first to compare me to an otherworldly creature—in my experience, such comparisons had not always been complimentary. But what I saw before me now was a beautiful woman. I had never been bold enough to wear silver or even light shades of gray, but I saw now that this had been a mistake—that the deep jewel tones I'd always favored, while flattering, had been my way of drawing attention away from my silver tresses.

Mrs. Colby was eyeing me expectantly, so I closed my dropped jaw and smiled. "It's beautiful," I said. "Thank you."

Mrs. Lamotte chuckled. "Colby can make even the dullest diamond sparkle, but in your case, my child, very little embellishment was required."

I warmed under this praise and, to my chagrin, even felt my throat tightening. Curtsying to hide my emotion, I thanked them both again. The two women then fell to congratulating each other, and just as I was wondering whether I'd be given a moment to compose myself in private, there came another knock at the door.

Mrs. Lamotte hurried to open it, and Lord Meath stepped into the room.

Due to the distraction his own transformation provided, there was no awkwardness in his openmouthed stare when his gaze fell on me. Seeing him clean and polished, I was freshly reminded how generous a measure of masculine beauty this man possessed, and I took a moment to appreciate that fact. He was an earl and always dressed smartly, so his transformation was perhaps not as dramatic as mine. But his dark curls were freshly washed and combed back from his face, and he wore a suit of dark wool with a silver waistcoat. He'd lost his spectacles, so there was no longer any barrier between those intensely probing eyes and me. And there was another difference. Great Fury, now sheathed, hung at his side.

"Miss Quicksilver," he said at last, "I think you must already know how lovely you look, but let me congratulate you, ladies"—this he directed at Mrs. Colby and Mrs. Lamotte—"on a job well done. I would not have thought you could make her any more beautiful."

A light titter of laughter rose behind me, and the two ladies thanked the earl. Such praise might be common in society, but it was far outside my experience, and my cheeks felt scorched—less from the compliment itself than from the warming sensation I felt low in my belly as he spoke it. This heat spread across my chest, and I was reminded that between the corset and the gown's plunging neckline, I was much more exposed than I was accustomed to being.

"My lord," I said with a curtsy and a racing heart.

He held out his arm. "Shall we go? The ball will be in full swing by now, but we should arrive in time for you to take some refreshment before every O'Malley in the house asks you to dance."

He was all smiles and impeccable behavior, but his eyes had betrayed some fresh trouble on his mind. "Are you well, my lord?" I asked, taking his arm.

"Indeed, I am," he replied, covering my hand with his and guiding me out of the room. He led me down the corridor toward sounds of merriment issuing from deeper in the large house. "I have much to discuss with you, but the queen will not stand for us to miss the ball."

"Have you learned something about the sword?" I asked, unable to mask my eagerness.

He smiled, but it was a different sort of smile than the ones he'd bestowed on the ladies in my chamber. He was not happy. "I have," he said, "and I promise to share it with you before the night is over."

We descended the stairs and made our way through a maze of corridors. As we rounded the last corner, servants opened a set of doors for us. Laughter and music burst from the hall out into the corridor, and the earl gave my hand a supportive squeeze as he led me inside.

"Heavens!" I couldn't help uttering. "Are these *all* O'Malleys?" The hall contained easily a hundred people.

"There are also minor dignitaries and nobility from the nearby counties—Sligo and Galway as well as Mayo. But the rest are O'Malleys, and families of those who have married O'Malleys." The earl stopped suddenly and turned to face me, the shadow that had overtaken his features a jarring contrast to the gaiety surrounding us.

"What *is* it, my lord?"

"I'd hoped to wait to tell you this, but the one time I held something back from you, I regretted it."

My heart gave a sickening lurch. "Then tell me."

"I'm sending you away, Miss Q. Back to London. After what I've learned from the queen, I can no longer in good conscience continue exposing you to such risks. It's much graver than either of us imagined."

The room seemed to spin, and the floor to tilt. It was much like the sensations I'd felt aboard the *Queen of Connacht,* and I slid one foot away from the other to steady myself. Many words waited on the tip of my tongue, and I was surprised by the ones my lips finally spoke.

"I won't go."

"Ah, Miss Quicksilver! There you are."

Glancing up, I saw Duncan O'Malley approaching. *Not now,* I muttered inwardly. But the gentleman either missed or chose not to notice the hail of bullets the earl's eyes were firing at him.

"I believe you are promised to me for the first dance." Smiling broadly, he held out his hand as the first strains of the waltz filled the hall.

I glanced at the earl, who was grimmer than ever. Then, seeing no escape, I reached out and took O'Malley's hand.

*I'm not going anywhere,* I told myself by way of bolstering my strength for the performance to come. *The earl will have to accept that.* And somehow the encouragement, though self-delivered, did seem to have the desired effect. For after all, the earl had no power to force me.

I joined my hand with O'Malley's, and his other hand came to the small of my back. He, too, was smartly dressed, though his jacket was longer and his waistcoat was a lively red that matched the Christmas stars in the banquet tables' centerpieces.

"Cousin Edward looks like a thundercloud," he observed, beaming at me. "Do you suppose he's jealous?"

"I'm sure I don't know what you mean, Mr. O'Malley," I replied. But his mood was festive and the teasing good-natured, and I found it difficult to suppress a smile.

He gave a bark of laughter. "I'm sure that you *do.* But it's good for him to be a little jealous."

While I suspected that the earl's grim countenance had more to do with my defiant reply to his pronouncement, I could feel his gaze following us as we glided across the dance floor.

O'Malley's arm drew me a little closer, so our bodies brushed with each turn. "You're a beautiful woman, and if I thought you didn't want him, I'd run off with you myself, and Edward be damned. But I'm fair certain there's been something compromising between you, and I believe it only wants a nudge to make the man do the right thing." He shook his head. "My cousin's spent far too much time among the English, no offense to present company. His blood runs a little cold."

I laughed, though I couldn't avoid a mental rejoinder that

the earl was anything but cold. "What makes you think I want to marry Lord Meath, if that is, in fact, what you're suggesting?"

O'Malley shrugged. "I've a good ear for the things folk say to each other without speaking. It's one reason Her Majesty keeps me close—Izzy is shrewd but doesn't read faces well. That's not to say I've never been wrong." I had directed my gaze over his shoulder, where I caught a glimpse of the earl, watching us with arms folded across his chest. "Thundercloud" was an apt description. O'Malley shifted his head to force our eyes to meet again. "I'd be happy to find I was wrong in this case."

I sighed, sobering as my thoughts returned to the reality of the situation. I did not feel at liberty to discuss my present troubles with the earl's cousin, but I might take another tack to stem his enthusiasm for matchmaking.

"Mr. O'Malley," I said, "your cousin is an earl. I am a scholar of modest means. He is not at liberty to make such a choice."

O'Malley snorted. "His parents are dead. The title is his. Unless he's a fool, he'll do as he pleases."

His boisterous manner was compelling, and I couldn't help laughing. But I countered, "You yourself are likely to marry a titled young lady, are you not? Will your family not expect you to?"

He shook his head. "I'm a fourth brother and a bastard, though my parents eventually married, and my mother was Jamaican—born a slave, later a pirate. I'll never be Lord Mayo, thank the Maker. I could marry a selkie and I doubt my father would notice."

There was no bitterness as he said this, and in fact his mood appeared completely unaffected. "You have quite an interesting history, Mr. O'Malley," I observed. "Moreover, you're a charming and handsome fellow. There will be no need for you to marry a selkie—unless, of course, you fall in love with one."

He gave me a conspiratorial smile. "I stand out from the

crowd in a room like this, that's certain. And I like a girl who does the same." The waltz was drawing to a close, and he halted our progress across the floor. Kissing the back of my hand, he bowed and then continued, "Makes her easy to find when a fellow wants to dance with her."

He passed my hand to Edward, who had come upon us without my noticing. "You don't look fit company for such a beauty, cousin," O'Malley said. Then to me, he added, "If you get tired of scowls, come and find me."

He winked and then was off, just as the musicians finished tuning and began the next waltz.

The earl's hand was hot in the small of my back, and his mood was prickly and dark. We danced a while in pained silence, and I waited for him to open the inevitable argument.

Instead, he said, "Duncan is gay, is he not?"

I smiled. "Indeed he is. I believe he fancies himself something of a rogue, but he's actually quite charming."

"Many women find rogues to be so. Quite unaccountably, to my thinking. But Duncan is, in fact, a pirate, and pirates have their charm, or so I'm told."

"A pirate! Truly?"

The earl nodded. "Truly."

"How fascinating. Clearly, it runs in the blood."

Lord Meath gave a dry laugh. "Clearly."

"Mr. O'Malley thought that you might be angry with him," I probed carefully. "He said you looked like a thundercloud."

"That sounds like Duncan," replied the earl. "And perhaps I was, in a way. You and I had not finished our conversation, and he could see that well enough."

"Well, I *had* promised him the dance." My gaze fluttered down to the top button of his shirt. *Courage, Ada.* "But you and I know that it was me you were angry with."

The earl gave a weary sigh, and I glanced up. "I'm not angry with you, but you must go. This adventure of ours has become quite dangerous."

"Are not all adventures, by definition?"

He frowned. "Perhaps. But as much as I've enjoyed your company, as much as I have benefited from your … your insights and quick intelligence—and, moreover, your compassion and warmheartedness—I am unwilling to expose you to further risk. I care about your *life*, Ada. Do you not see? It's selfish of me to keep you here."

He had again used my Christian name, and I was trembling. But I pressed on. "It is good, in that case, *Edward,* that you have no authority over me. I will remain because I am unwilling to leave you to your fate, whatever that might be. Because I *know* that something dangerous is happening, and I believe you need my help. And you may stop feeling selfish about it, because, in fact, you have no say in the matter."

He might have looked less affronted had I slapped him, and I was sorry for that. But he was a naval officer and an earl and, therefore, unused to being opposed. It would require all my strength of purpose to hold my ground.

"You are refusing to conform to my wishes in this matter?"

"I am," I said, softening my tone. "And I hope you will not be angry with me for long, because that will pain me."

The waltz had ended, and he released me. We remained facing each other but not touching, drawing curious gazes.

"You will not so easily defy Queen Isolde." He sounded defeated rather than angry now, pressed to measures he'd rather not take. How was I to stand against the queen?

"There will be no need for that." The queen had joined us on the dance floor. "I'm of no mind to force a clever young woman to do anything other than what she chooses." Isolde smiled at me and held out her hand. "Are you ready, Miss Quicksilver?"

My eyebrows lifted, and I glanced at the earl. I had assumed the queen to be jesting when she claimed a dance with me.

"Cousin," he pleaded softly, "can't you see you're frightening her? Leave off with this nonsense."

I *was* feeling something rather close to alarm, but it was time to disabuse him of this persistent notion that I needed protecting. And unless I was mistaken, the queen had just stated her intention to let me stay, and I was grateful.

"I'm not frightened," I assured them both. I took a step toward the queen. "Merely surprised." I placed my hand in hers. "Who shall lead, Your Majesty?"

She laughed and swept me onto the dance floor. "I shall, of course!"

The queen was an excellent dancer, and she was resplendent in deep emerald green. Her hair towered impressively on her head—dark coiling plaits embellished with large white roses and deep-pink peonies.

"I misjudged you, my dear," she said.

"Did you, Your Majesty?" A tremor sneaked into my voice.

"Twice now. You are not a plaything, and you are not meek."

I acknowledged this with a bow of my head. "I hope not, Your Majesty."

"What remains to be seen is, are you brave?"

"I believe I am."

"Mmm, well, you shall need to be. Do you know that Lord Edward is sometimes overtaken by Diarmuid, his ancestor?"

So it was true. "I suspected that to be the case."

We spun to the edge of the dance floor, and I caught Duncan O'Malley's eye. He nodded at me and continued conversing with … thin air. But I had no time to make sense of what I'd seen.

"Ah, but do you know why?"

"No, Your Majesty," I admitted. "Both Lord Meath and I had hoped you might be able to help us answer that question."

The queen proceeded to relate a story that was by turns illuminating, fascinating, and frightening. Isolde's mother had been an Ulsterwoman who descended from the warrior queen Maeve, just as Edward descended from Diarmuid through his father. In researching her family tree, the queen had also learned that the Fomorians were coming to carry out an ancient plan of conquest—setting a curse on the people of Ireland, with the expectation of claiming the island for themselves.

"A million lives," I replied when she had finished. "That is quite a burden for Lord Meath to carry." I began to understand why he had tried to dismiss me.

"So it is. But it would seem to be his fate. And he will not fight alone."

"Certainly not," I agreed. "But do you think it must come to that? Fighting, I mean."

"The Fomorians are coming, there's no doubt about that. And my soldiers must fight alongside all of Faery if we are indeed to prevent this tragedy."

"And Diarmuid will lead them?" I asked.

The waltz was slowing, and the queen halted abruptly but did not release me. "Diarmuid will lead his warriors; I shall lead mine. What remains to be seen is what part *you* shall play, Miss Quicksilver."

I swallowed and forced myself not to break away from the intensity of her gaze. "I do not know, Your Majesty. I am not an important person like you and your cousin. But I do have knowledge that may be helpful. And I do ... I do care about him. Childish as that may sound to you. I'll not abandon him. I'll not abandon either of you."

The queen smiled at me then, less like a queen than like a

sister or friend. Then she leaned forward, and before I understood her intention, she had touched her lips to mine. The kiss was brief but soft and full-lipped, and it so startled me that I stepped back, warmth flooding my cheeks. Before I had regained my composure, she walked away.

"You looked as though you could use this." Duncan O'Malley reappeared, pressing a champagne glass into my hand.

I raised the glass and swallowed a mouthful—and discovered that it was not champagne, but a potent punch containing champagne and absinthe, cut slightly with fruit juice. Allowing myself one more sip for courage, I then placed the half-emptied glass on the tray of a passing servant.

"Has Edward been a gentleman this evening?" asked O'Malley.

"Lord Meath is never other than a gentleman," I assured him, though in my experience that was not entirely true. "In fact—"

I failed to complete my sentence, because I suddenly noticed a vaporous apparition next to Duncan O'Malley—none other than his pirate ancestress.

"Captain O'Malley," I said in greeting, recalling Duncan's conversation with what had appeared to be thin air. The absinthe-induced second sight appeared also to run in the blood—both his and mine. "I'm relieved to see you survived your ordeal. I take it the Fomorians have been subdued?"

"Aye, for now," she replied, but she was moving away from us, toward a knot of revelers that had formed around the queen. "I need a word with the high-and-mighty miss."

She moved briskly, and I gasped as it appeared she would collide with Lord Meath, who was striding our direction. Then I watched him pass directly through her without even seeming to notice.

"May I help you to a plate, Miss Quicksilver?" he asked, joining us. He fixed a warning glare on O'Malley. "There is more I would say to you."

"If you wish," I managed to reply calmly despite the worried movement of my heart.

"If you'll excuse us, Duncan," he said to O'Malley, who raised his glass with a grin.

"Go to it, cousin."

O'Malley might be as good a judge of people as he claimed, but he was quite mistaken in this case. I could not speak to any jealousy on the part of Lord Meath, but he was certainly *not* about to ask me to marry him.

He led me to the banquet tables, handed me a plate, and offered to serve me from each dish. There was roasted meat of every variety, salmon and shellfish, potatoes and apples cooked a dozen ways, a dizzying selection of cheeses, and an entire table loaded with pies, cakes, and puddings.

I was feeling a little queasy in anticipation of our next interview, but to mask my unease, I accepted portions of fish and vegetables. Then I followed him to the end of a table, where it looked as if we might enjoy some modicum of privacy—as much as we were likely to get in a room full of a hundred revelers. We were the object of many curious gazes, but Edward's dark looks were more effective in frightening off his other relatives than they had been with Duncan. Clearly, Duncan felt that his cousin took himself too seriously, but I doubted he was fully aware of the burdens the earl was carrying.

As soon as we were seated, the earl said, "I've begun badly, Miss Quicksilver—Ada—and I hope you will forgive me and allow me to begin again."

I frowned, wary, but replied, "All right, my lord."

"What I had wanted to address first with you is our position with regard to one another."

Confusion supplanted wariness. "What position is that, my lord?"

The earl appeared nervous and would not meet my gaze for long. But he continued. "This spirit with whom I'm involuntarily communing has caused me to take liberties."

"Yes, but we've—"

He raised his eyes to my face. "Please hear me out, Ada."

I nodded and waited for him to continue.

"Furthermore, we spent an evening alone together—in a way that must have appeared quite compromising. It will not be long before that fact is common knowledge, if it isn't already."

I wondered whether he meant that the queen or O'Malley would speak of it to others. I believed this unlikely, but servants had been on the strand that morning. I had overheard something on the boat that led me to believe Duncan O'Malley had speculated I was Lord Meath's mistress. If *he* thought so, as the queen initially had, would not the servants draw the same conclusion? I did not like to think of the whole O'Malley party whispering about us.

"I know that you do not wish to return to London," continued Lord Meath. "But I wonder whether my concerns and my wishes might carry more weight with you were we … were we man and wife." The fork that I had raised when he began speaking now clattered noisily onto my plate. But he forged on. "I know that I would rest easier knowing that you had not been tainted by your association with me. I would also rest easier knowing I had a claim to come to you should I survive the ordeal that's threatening my country. And *should* something happen to me, you would be left a widow with means to do whatever you like with the rest of your life."

The booming laugh of Duncan O'Malley rang out from a distant corner of the room. Most likely unconnected to my conversation with the earl, yet highly coincidental. Lord Meath had carried a glass of punch for me, and I took it now and drank half. I drew a deep breath, let it out, and fixed my gaze on him.

"You wish to marry me to save us both embarrassment," I said. "You also wish to marry me so that I will be obliged to obey your commands."

The earl's mouth opened, but I held up my hand. "And the queen, of course, would be unlikely to intervene in an argument between us once we are man and wife. I can think of no more promising setup for marital disaster, my lord."

I rose from the table, shaking. So many emotions warred within me, I hardly knew which to voice. My heart had involuntarily swelled at his proposal—had warmed like a lovesick fool at the thought he might have fallen in love with me. Then my mind reeled from the cold realization that he had proposed to me so he could feel justified in giving me orders. Did he expect that a scholar of modest means would be so enchanted by a proposal of marriage from an earl that she would readily assent? The fact that he was so obviously concerned for my safety only added a twist of sweet to the bitter.

Knowing I was very close to tears, I fled, unwilling to give the O'Malleys further cause for gossip. Lord Meath called after me once, and I could hear the pain and frustration in his voice, but I could not stop. I crossed the hall to the double entrance doors, which now stood open to circulate the air. Passing through them, I believed I was safe, but as I paused there catching my breath, another voice called my name.

Madly, I scrambled away, scheming to dash for my chamber and escape the much taller and certainly much swifter Duncan O'Malley. But moments later, I was hopelessly lost in the labyrinth of corridors, and I halted with a groan of frustration.

O'Malley joined me silently, reaching for my hand and tucking it into the crook of his arm.

"I'll see you there safely," he said with a gentle smile.

Tears of hurt and anger stung my eyes, and I let loose a

strangled sob. To his credit, O'Malley kept his gaze straight ahead, and soon we'd found my chamber door.

"I see that he's mangled it worse than I feared," he said.

"I am well, Mr. O'Malley," I choked out. "Thank you for your assistance." I wanted nothing more than to escape to my chamber and close the door between myself and the whole O'Malley clan.

"I'll leave you to your rest," said O'Malley. "But first, I promised to deliver a message."

I hesitated with my hand on the doorknob, and he held out a slip of paper. I took it from him and opened my door. Once it was closed, my back pressed against the other side, I opened the note. The lamps were too low to make out the hastily scrawled writing, so I carried the note closer to one of them. Turning it up, I read:

*Please understand, I've been ordered by the queen to give up absinthe. I can no longer answer for your safety. —M*

# A QUIET AND UNIMPORTANT ENGLISHWOMAN

## ADA

I sat up for some time, gazing over the moonlit countryside, not bothering to take off my ball gown. I wasn't even sure I could do so by myself. When a maid came to tend to the fire and turn down the bed, I could have asked for her help, but I needed to be alone so I could think.

The earl had not intended to wound me; I had accepted that. He simply hadn't known what else to do. He felt unable to continue being responsible for me—he had the weight of a million Irish men and women on his shoulders, after all. I believed that he asked me to marry him out of pity, in a way. To protect my reputation, but also to lessen the sting of his dismissing me after a measure of intimacy had been forced on us.

I began to think that perhaps I *should* go home. The coming battle was not mine. These were not my people.

"I would only be in the way," I murmured.

In any case, I would not be accepting his unusual offer of marriage. I could not agree to marry someone who didn't love me, not even an earl. Furthermore, I had such an independent nature, I might not be suitable for marriage *at all.*

As for my own feelings, I could not defy him and remain by his side simply because I fancied myself falling in love.

But what if he needed me? The thought resurfaced persistently. What if I *could* help in some way? If I truly cared for him, did it not mean that I must try?

These questions had no ready answers. I was tired, and somewhat muddled from the strong drink. At any rate, I could not leave on Christmas Eve. Nor even on Christmas, probably. Which meant I had some time to think.

Even a resolution to do nothing was still a resolution, if only a temporary one, and it gave me some peace.

I had just resolved to ring for the maid to help me undress when I heard loud voices in the corridor. Arguing voices—masculine ones that I recognized. Suddenly, there was a heavy thud against my door, shaking it on its hinges, followed by sounds of a struggle.

"So help me, Edward," shouted Duncan O'Malley, "if Izzy hadn't ordered me not to kill you, I'd have done it already!"

The reply came in Irish: "*This is not a fight you want to start, bog crawler.*" Lord Meath. Or, more likely, his Danaan ancestor. "*Out of my way.*"

"She did not, on the other hand, place any prohibition on shooting you in the leg."

I sprang to my feet, running to the door and yanking it open.

"Stay inside, Miss Q!" barked O'Malley, who stood in front of the door, with his back to me.

Opposite O'Malley, I could see the earl, eyes glittering, watching me like a cat. I shivered to see the stranger staring at me out of his eyes.

"Diarmuid?" I said, just to be sure.

O'Malley's head jerked in my direction, and the earl, possessed by his ancestor, nodded. "*You remember.*"

"Duncan," I said, stepping closer and gripping his arm. "Give the pistol to me."

O'Malley shook his head. "Let me handle this. I don't trust his look. Something's wrong with him."

"I know," I replied. "I've seen it before. I'll be fine." Or I wouldn't. But I wasn't going to stand there and let him shoot Lord Meath, which he would certainly have to do before long if I didn't intervene. "I need to speak to him in private, Duncan."

Blowing out a sigh of disapproval, O'Malley backed toward the door, and I made room for him to pass. Once he was behind me, his arm still extended into the corridor and pointing the pistol at the earl, he took hold of my right hand with his free hand and raised it to the weapon.

"It's ready to fire. Just pull the trigger."

I gripped it in my palm.

"You'll shout if you need me, agreed?"

"Agreed."

"And if he doesn't behave like a gentleman, you'll shoot him?"

"I will."

He stepped around me again and moved away from the door.

"Come inside," I said to the Danaan warrior as I backed away from the door. "Slowly."

Duncan and I watched as Lord Meath strode toward me. He was half dressed, wearing only trousers and boots, and a loose nightshirt that left most of his chest bare. In the lamplight, I noticed a number of pale-pink scars marking his flesh. He clutched the hilt of Great Fury in both hands, and just as in the fairy mound, the flash of light along the blade made it seem a living thing in his hands.

I continued backing into the room until my legs brushed

the edge of the fainting couch. The earl entered my chamber and closed the door behind him. With one hand, he picked up a chair beside the door and propped it under the knob before starting toward me again.

"Stop," I warned. "Leave your sword by the door."

He complied with the second request but then took another slow step toward me.

"I don't know if you understand," I said, "but this weapon can kill you. Actually, it can kill your descendant, Edward Donoghue, Earl of Meath, whose body you are inhabiting. If he dies, you have no gateway to our world."

I did not know whether this was true, but I had to find a way to reason with him, for Edward's sake. And it seemed to work, for he did at last stop.

"He and I are not separate," said Diarmuid.

"What does that mean?"

"Immortals and mortals," he replied. "Our life cycles are different. Through my children, I have passed down to him."

I frowned. "You mean that you're ... *part* of Edward? Tangled up with him somehow?" Poor Lord Meath. No wonder he thought he was going mad!

He nodded. "So if you love him, you also love *me.*"

My mouth went dry, and I tried to swallow. "I am not sure I believe that. Neither have I said that I love him."

His gaze ranged around the room, settling finally on the bed. "And yet I know it." Again he looked at me, eyes rising to the top of my head. "You are the very image of *her.* And the first to bear the mark."

Mrs. Doyle's voice echoed: *You bear the mark of attention from their kind.* Captain O'Malley, too, had spoken of it: *She's been claimed by the gentlefolk, and they'll have her in the end.* I recalled the absinthe vision of the woman sleeping in the meadow.

"What is it you want?" I asked. "I know that Queen Isolde has agreed to fight with you. She's persuaded Edward as well. Why have you come to *me*? I'm an *Englishwoman*, and a quiet and unimportant one, at that."

"I have waited centuries for you," he said, taking another step. "I have dreamed of you, the mortal woman who stands with the Danaan, and I wrought ancient blood magic to be here with you."

I shivered. Blood magic was sometimes associated with druids, though it did not necessarily require a death.

"My people have watched you watching them," he continued, his intensity softening. "Fey runs in families, and it was your blood that led you here. Your blood that led you to him." He glanced at himself in the mirror above the dressing table. "To *me*."

I closed my eyes. More riddles. I jumped only a little when his hands enfolded mine and then took the pistol from me. I wasn't going to shoot Edward; he knew that very well. He laid the weapon aside on a table.

He stepped close to me, and his voice was a low rumble near my ear as he said, "He keeps his distance, does he not?" His fingers grazed my jaw, and I sucked a breath through my parted lips. I was unprepared for this gentleness—his behavior was much more Edward-like now than it had been in the fairy mound. Since that night, I had longed to feel Edward this close. His heat and proximity, the brightness of passion in his eyes.

"I do not understand this age of manners," Diarmuid said, his breath a caress. "This age of politeness and unspoken passion. There is no shame in passion. Yet he would send you away rather than acknowledge it."

He drew back to meet my gaze, and I was again confronted with his otherworldly beauty. His face was inches from mine.

"Women were warriors in your time, I know," I said, a tremor in my voice. "We've done away with all that now. He would send me away to *protect* me."

"From me, yes. But you refused to go. Why?"

My body was responding to his proximity and his gentle touch in ways that confused and frightened me. I could not organize my thoughts well enough to answer him. Why, indeed?

Then I felt a strangling sensation in my throat and realized that it was happening again. Words were being dragged out of me even as my body fought to hold on to them. Fey though I might be, I was no match for an immortal.

"Because I love him," I choked out. A tear trickled down my cheek, and I glowered at him. "If you want this discussion to continue, you won't do that again."

"All I want is for you to remember what you know. So many years I have waited to be with you here. *Please,* Cliona."

Cliona! I stared at him and shook my head slowly. "Is *that* who you think I am? You are mistaken, my lord, I assure you!" I stepped away from him and turned. "What, may I ask, is your connection to her?"

His brow furrowed. "My connection to her is *everything.* I breathed immortality into her. I cast all Faery out of Ireland for the love of her."

*Immortality.* I recalled that Cliona had been brought, lifeless, to Brú na Bóinne. Had Edward's parchment been only the beginning of her story? Before I could further question him, he closed his eyes, then stumbled and fell.

"My lord!" I cried, moving quickly to kneel at his side.

He panted from some unseen strain, and his hand pressed mine to his forearm.

I bent and studied his face. "Lord Meath?"

He righted himself and lifted me to my feet. "Are you well?" he asked.

"Yes, my lord, perfectly. But are *you*?"

He nodded. "But I grow weary of these transgressions."

"How is it that you have returned?" I asked.

"I did not like the way he was ... thinking of you," he replied, eyeing me darkly. "He believes you *belong* to him."

I swallowed thickly.

"*Why*, Ada? Why did you allow him into your chamber? Why did you let him put his hands on you?"

I turned from him, uncomfortable under the intensity of his gaze. "I allowed him in for your sake, my lord. I wanted to try to understand him."

Had he heard the words the Danaan warrior forced from my lips? If he had, it did not appear to have softened him toward me.

"And why did you not use the weapon at your disposal, as you did the last time, to require him to keep his distance?"

I flushed, hot with shame. Confused and dismayed, I blurted the truth: "It was too difficult, my lord. He was so like *you* that I—"

I broke off, shaking my head, my throat tightening from conflicting emotions—tenderness, frustration, fear ... *longing*.

I felt him moving behind me.

"Shh," he whispered. His hands came to my shoulders, and he gently turned me. "Ada, look at me."

Trembling, I raised my eyes to his face.

"I had no right to ask you such a question." He raised his hand to cradle my cheek. "Can you forgive me?"

I could not trust my voice, so I nodded.

"He tried to shut me out, to draw a curtain between us." Edward moved closer, and the noise of my heart threatened to interfere with my hearing. "I couldn't stand that he might steal something I myself had worked so hard to resist stealing."

My breath caught in my throat, and his gaze descended to my

parted lips. I felt his other hand, warm against my waist, and then his chest pressing against mine.

I lifted my lips, unable to hold back any longer.

He bent his head, and his mouth brushed softly against mine—once, then twice. I had initiated the kiss, but the earl took possession of it, silken lips moving, exploring this new territory. I felt a shudder go through him.

His mouth grew firm, insistent, as it covered mine, though his lips were full and soft. I raised my hand, slipping my fingers into the hair at the back of his neck, and his tongue pushed gently between my lips, deepening the kiss.

His arms came around me, and the heat in the full press of our bodies shortened my breath. As the flames licked between us, he broke from the kiss, lips trailing down my chin to my throat. His hand glided up my corset, coming to rest beside my breast.

Then he froze. "You *must* agree to marry me, Ada," he said breathlessly, raising his head to meet my gaze. "Else I must go before this … progresses."

*Here* was the passion I had found wanting in his proposal. His fingers pressed against my ribs as he drew me against him. I could hear the blood pulsing in my head. It made me dizzy and hot, and I was grateful for the support of his arms.

"I shan't, my lord," I said firmly. "Not now. If we survive what is to come, perhaps there will be a time for that."

He closed his eyes, nodding, and I felt his grip loosen. "Then I must go."

"You must *not*," I said. "We have not seen the last of Diarmuid. You *know* we have not. For reasons I still don't fully understand, he considers me to be his. *You* are the reason he muddies my thinking and weakens my resolve. Will you not fortify me against his coming?"

He stared at me and muttered, "God help me." His lips

crashed against mine like waves on the rocks of Keem Strand. He tasted me again, deeper and deeper, until I felt myself prostrate on the sand, opening to the saltwater caress that worked rhythmically against my body.

He broke free, slipping behind me without ever completely letting me go. He swept my hair over my shoulder, and his lips came to the back of my neck. My limbs loosened again at the rush of warm sensation, and I sagged against him. Then I felt his fingers moving along my spine—he was unhooking my corset.

His hands slipped inside the back of my dress, peeling it away from me until it dropped and hung loose at my waist. He unfastened the stiff petticoat with its complicated bustle and pushed my skirts past my hips until they fell and pooled at my feet. I stood close against him in nothing but lace drawers and stockings and a silk shirt that scooped low over my breasts.

My body ached deliciously. My breasts felt swollen, and the cleft between my legs had begun to throb.

His lips brushed the back of my ear, and his hands came to my shoulders, sliding down my arms. As his fingertips grazed the bare skin above my nipples, my heart pounded and I could feel my own hot breath.

Suddenly, he lifted me in his arms. He carried me to the bed, laying me across the parted white sheets before covering my body with his. I felt the press of his stiff wool trousers between my legs, and I felt him trembling.

Hunger darkened his countenance, and he moved closer, curls falling softly around his face. He lowered his mouth to mine, hard and hot, lips parting instantly. His tongue pushed into my mouth, sliding against mine, and he groaned. I arched, pressing my body against his.

Dipping his head, he used his teeth to pull back the neck of my shirt, baring one breast. Groaning, he took the nipple in his mouth. With the hot, moist pressure of his tongue, I felt a deepening ache, like the shore longing for the tide's return.

"I don't know that we will be able to stop this," he warned. "You were so beautiful tonight, Ada. You shattered me."

His words so inflamed and engulfed me that I was almost senseless with desire, but I whispered urgently, "I don't wish to stop, my lord."

He took my mouth again, showing me his hunger. His legs pressed against mine, spreading them farther apart.

Rising to his knees, he pulled his shirt over his head and tossed it to the floor. I lifted the hem of my own shirt, and he helped me to remove and discard it. Then he bent to grasp the last layer of modesty between us, tugging the soft fabric down past my hips and over my thighs, his gaze lingering on the part of me that, in this moment, felt most alive.

As his eyes moved slowly over me, mine feasted on his flesh. On the strength of him, taut muscles that formed graceful flowing lines. His body wove a powerful spell.

He reached down, touching gently between my legs, and I gave out a tremulous little moan.

My flesh was wet and slick, and his fingers tickled between the folds. The aching of the cleft just beyond suddenly became more than I could bear. When his fingers finally ventured within, my back arched, raising my hips toward his hand.

Unfastening his trousers with one hand, he moved closer, and I had only a moment to assess that part of him that sought, above all else, to lose itself in another. I held my breath as he pushed slowly inside me, then let it out with a moan. I could recall no sensation like this—no sensation that at once satisfied and stoked a desperate need.

"Edward," I breathed, the muscles inside me clenching over him, my body welcoming that hot, hungry tide.

Raising himself on his arms, he began a rhythmic thrusting. I followed the sinuous motion of his body and then wrapped my legs around his waist to keep him from driving me into the headboard. I dug my heels into his back, seating him deeper, and worked my hips against him, rolling with his rhythm, reveling in this new sense of fullness. Little cries escaped my throat as beads of perspiration dripped from him and trickled down my breasts.

One of his hands slid across me, rolling my breasts. He bent, hungrily tasting my mouth and driving his tongue between my lips. Both our bodies went rigid.

Our sharp cries broke the tension. My release was a burning star that burst from me, throwing light over the walls of the darkened room. Again I heard the voices I'd heard inside the fairy mound when Diarmuid stole his first kiss—the war cries and wails, now mingled with the cries of souls lost to ecstasy. I knew that Edward's ancestor was with us, and I deemed it a small price to pay for feeling the earl's body against mine at last.

# EDWARD

*You are the reason he muddies my thinking and weakens my resolve.*

With these words, she had undone every gentlemanly impulse. She had encouraged every wrongheaded, proprietary feeling. She wanted me. She cared nothing for my title or for any honor conferred by my proposal. She wanted *me.*

But as the embers of passion cooled, uncertainty returned.

Feeling the rise and fall of her chest beneath me, I came to myself and lifted my weight off her. "Forgive me. I'm suffocating you."

The room had gone chill, and I drew the counterpane over her before fastening my trousers and pulling on my nightshirt. Then I went to the fireplace and added turf to the fire. I felt her eyes on my back and knew that I should not have left her so quickly.

Should not have moved away from the bed without so much as a glance at her face. The atmosphere of the room felt thin, as if the act we shared had sucked away all the air.

Had we married before this act, I would have known how to be with her now. It would have been proper to kiss and caress and perhaps even indulge my appetite for her again.

The thought of it set my blood afire. But I did not know how to manage a woman who had rejected me almost in the same breath that she had asked me to make love to her.

Before I had marshaled the courage to face her, three knocks sounded on the chamber door. Turning, I saw her take a dressing gown from the chest at the foot of the bed. After covering herself, she rose and went to the door, removing a chair that someone had propped there, before opening it a few inches.

"How do you fare, Miss Quicksilver?" *Duncan.* Had he been outside in the corridor all along? I squeezed my eyes closed. In asking him to protect her from me, I had put her squarely in this awkward position. There was nothing I could do to help without exposing her further.

"I'm well, Duncan, thank you," she said in a low, earnest tone. "And safe."

Her use of his Christian name caused a pang. I thought of all that had passed between us before she used *mine.*

"You're certain?" he asked.

Ada repositioned her body, and by this I knew that Duncan had tried to see beyond the door.

"I'm certain."

A pause. "Then I'll leave you to your rest."

"Please wait a moment."

Closing the door, she crossed the room and retrieved the pistol from a table by the window. She went back to the door and held out the pistol to Duncan. I was astonished by her composure.

"Hadn't you better keep that?" Duncan asked.

"There's no need," she replied, reaching for his hand and closing it over the weapon.

There was a long pause, and I felt certain he had held on to her hand, for she did not withdraw. Finally, he asked, "Has he agreed to do right by you, then?"

"I assure you, Duncan, Lord Meath is in no way blameworthy."

"And what of ... what of the *other*?" asked Duncan.

"Even he," she assured him.

She was always far kinder to me than I could be to myself. Far kinder than I deserved. I knew that I had injured her with my bungling proposal. In believing I was doing the honorable thing, it had not occurred to me that she might like to be wooed. Was she not a pragmatic young woman? But more than this, I feared that in some dark corner of my mind lurked the notion that a woman of her status was unlikely to refuse such an elevating offer. Whatever my reasoning might have been, I had certainly taken her acceptance for granted. And in doing so, I might very well have lost her, all evidence of the past half hour to the contrary.

"Good night to you, Duncan," she said. "Again, I thank you."

"You are quite welcome, Miss Quicksilver. Send a servant if you need me."

She closed the door, hesitating with one hand on the knob and one pressing against the panel. Then, finally, she turned and met my gaze.

"When I received your note," she began, "I understood why you had pressed me to leave you. Forgive me if I was ungracious in refusing you."

I shook my head. "It is I who must beg forgiveness. You were right to call my offer cold. It was not due to lack of warm feeling, I assure you."

She blushed prettily at this, which charmed me. "So you have demonstrated," she said. I took a step toward her. She had donned her dressing gown hastily, and the neckline dipped low, exposing the upper curve of her breasts. Had my lips touched her there not a quarter of an hour ago? It seemed impossible now, yet I had the memory of it, and I burned afresh with desire.

Her sudden frown stamped her forehead with worry lines. "Edward, I don't know how to—"

Closing the distance between us, I folded my arms around her. "Neither do I," I murmured into her hair. "I am grateful beyond expression for the gift you have given me, but I confess that I am ill at ease with these circumstances. You must understand, I was raised a gentleman, and it goes against all that I was taught concerning the proper way to treat a woman."

"I do understand. Certainly, I do, and I … I admire you for it."

She raised her head from my chest, and I took her face in my hands. "And you won't reconsider? Even if I vow never to command you?" Was I equal to such a promise? I wasn't sure.

Her hands came to my forearms, and I pressed my forehead against hers.

"Ask me again, Edward," she whispered. "If you like, ask me again when we are more sure of each other."

Her words settled like a lead weight in my chest. Was she unsure of me, or did she believe I was unsure of her? With a protest on the tip of my tongue, I pressed my lips together. She was right, of course. Did she love me? Did I love her? Was it possible for either of us to know after so little time? I had never expected I would marry solely for love, but she might never have imagined marrying for any other reason. She had an independent nature and did not require support. And though she had told me her mother's family possessed an old name, she had no ancestral seat that required an heir. In short, she did not need me.

*She fires your blood. So long as she wants you, what does the rest of it matter?*

The thought was intrusive, and I couldn't help wondering to what degree my mind was under my own control. Yet, instinctively I knew that if I dwelt on that question, I might very well go mad. Only yesterday, I had compelled her to speak without my even being aware of it. And I felt the presence of this "other" in the same way one sometimes feels another's eyes on his back.

"We should speak of Diarmuid," she said, perhaps giving up on waiting for my reply.

"If you wish," I agreed. Though it was certainly the last thing I wanted to be doing. I resented the being that kept co-opting my body to make advances on the woman I had tried so hard to protect.

I led her to one of the chairs before the now blazing fire and sat beside her. "You wouldn't prefer to wait until the morning? You must be tired."

"I'm not sure that we can afford the delay," she replied.

"All right. Tell me what he said to you."

She hesitated, gazing into the fire as she collected her thoughts. Her head still wore the crown of bejeweled plaits, waves of silver cascading below. Her profile was regal and radiant, and she was completely unaware of it.

"Diarmuid seems to believe ..." she began. "He seems to believe that he and I have been lovers. That he has been with me in his own time, somehow. Or perhaps that we have been lovers in the future—though I realize that must sound nonsensical. The woman we read about—Cliona—she is tied up in it too. He once called me by her name. But I can't make sense of that, either."

Resentment took a step toward jealousy, and the wrongheaded proprietary feelings rallied.

"He speaks in riddles," she continued, meeting my gaze. "I

don't think he means to. It's as if his heart is too full to speak plainly."

"What else did he say?" I asked quietly, hiding my uneasiness from her.

"He called me 'the mortal woman who stands with the Danaan.' He also said that 'fey' runs in families and that it was my blood that brought me here."

I nodded, but I broke away from her gaze. I did not want to share her with this cause any more than I wanted to share her with my ancestor. I wanted to send her away somewhere safe. But there was an answer to this riddle that she was not seeing, perhaps because she was so close to it, and it would draw her in even deeper than she had yet imagined. I was not ready to admit it to her, not even to myself.

"How well I know it," I said.

"Know what, my lord?"

I looked at her. "That *fey* runs in families. But I'm not sure that I agree with this assessment of your character. You are one of the most sensible people I know."

She smiled, taking my honesty for a compliment. "I pride myself on good sense, I admit. But I have what some might consider an unhealthy fascination with a race of beings that many believe are no more than children's stories. He seemed to be suggesting there is a reason for that."

"Did he not offer any more specific explanation?" I asked carefully.

She shook her head and dropped her gaze to her folded hands. "As I said, he speaks in riddles. And he is always very ... distracted."

"Yes, by more interesting topics." My words carried a bite, and she shot me a troubled glance. I covered my ill humor with a smile. She in no way deserved my ire.

"He did say that I had been marked." Her fingers played absently with a lock of her hair. "If you'll recall, Captain O'Malley—"

She suddenly looked up, her gaze focusing beyond me. I turned to look at the door.

"Do you see them?" she breathed, her tone anxious.

I continued to scan the space where her gaze had settled. "I see nothing."

"What do they want?" she cried, and I turned to find she had clapped her hands over her ears.

*The absinthe.* She had drunk it. I had not. "Ada," I said, reaching out to take her hand, "tell me what you—"

The words froze on my tongue as her body rose from the chair without any movement of her limbs, as if gravity had released her. And then I did see "them": banshees, a dozen or more of them. They were not formed of green mist, like the other times I'd seen them. Though still ghostlike in form, their features were ashen and they wore gowns of black or gray. They clearly had more substance, as they managed to support Ada with their arms and backs, lifting her into the air.

I jumped to my feet, reaching for her with both hands, but she was torn from my grasp.

"Edward!" Her eyes were wide with fear.

I stumbled across the room after her as she shrieked. The window shattered, and they bore her out into the night.

# OUT OF SHADOWS

## EDWARD

Her white dressing gown fluttered and flapped in the breeze, reflecting moonlight and rendering her a luminous spirit.

"Ada!" I cried, cursing my compliance with the queen's abstinence order. But for that, I might better have anticipated what was happening to her.

I moved quickly, yanking my boots on and fastening the sword belt. Then I returned to the window, eyeing the distance to the ground. I could still see her pale form aloft over the winter-dormant fields, but she was moving away, and I couldn't afford to lose sight of her.

*Neither can you afford to break your neck.* The intrusive voice had returned.

"Blast!" I shouted. "If you want to help me, then *help* me. Come out of the shadows!"

Wind gusted through the broken window, and I took a step back. The room filled with chill sea air, as if the house had taken a great breath. The wind carried on its back a shrill, inhuman cry.

On the ground floor, there was a disturbance—excited and fearful voices drifting up the staircase. A loud crash sounded; then came a series of heavy footfalls accompanied by shouts, as if a family of giants were running up the stairs.

The door burst open and crashed to the floor, rent from its hinges. I shouted and raised the sword. Over the toppled door thundered a living nightmare—a great black horse, trailing rivulets and seaweed across the floor. Breath puffed from the beast's nostrils, loud as wind from a bellows. She pawed the floor with a barnacled hoof and tossed her dark head, that same eerie cry issuing from her jaws.

*Aughisky.*

I tightened my grip on Great Fury. As a child, I had feared the Irish water horse, said to be a fierce and dangerous fairy. And like the púca at Brú na Bóinne, this was no absinthe-induced vision. Water pooled at her feet, the smell of low tide filling my nostrils. Her eyes glowed orange, bright as the coals of our fire.

*What are you waiting for?* demanded the voice in my head.

"You've sent for this beast?" I said, for I did not find it easy to converse without actual speech. "She'll carry me to my death." I was perhaps not as versed in fairy lore as Miss Q, but every Irishman knew better than to mount a water horse.

*If you want to catch a troop of banshees, you need Aughisky.*

I recalled the warning in the pub the night I first met her, and panic urged me to action.

I took a few steps toward the water horse, and she continued to toss her head and paw at the floor, gouging the wood. Her steaming breath had created its own weather in the chamber, so that there was more mist inside than out. She was clearly agitated—whether over the summons itself or from some sense of urgency, I did not know.

She stood tall as a draft horse, my head reaching only a little higher than her shoulder. I hesitated in supernatural dread despite my frantic worry over Ada's fate. Finally, I dragged the tea table to the beast's side and stepped up on it, steeling myself as I buried one hand in the dark mass of sodden, slimy mane. I heaved myself onto her back and had barely found my seat when she bolted. I flung my arms around the thick neck, powdery with salt deposits and sand, just as she vaulted through what remained of the window panes.

"Edward!" I heard the queen shout from the chamber. Then, "Diarmuid!"

Glass fragments rained down, clinging to Aughisky's forelock and mane, catching the moonlight like diamonds as we arced toward the ground. The landing should have buckled her legs, and nearly did break my neck, but she hit the ground at a run and was soon thundering inland across the field behind the manor house.

Aughisky rocketed across the uneven landscape, clearing stone walls and streams without any break in stride. I clung to the long tendrils of mane as best I could—they seemed to be coated in "starshine," as Highlanders referred to washed-up jellyfish because the glistening blobs were once believed to be the remnants of falling stars.

Beyond the fields lay miles of peat bog, which under normal circumstances would be suicide to try to cross on horseback. As I had no idea of our intended destination and no control over the creature's movement, I could only hold fast and hope for the best.

As we galloped over the island's interior, the frigid air bit into my flesh, and pools of acidic bog water reflected the glittering stars. Soon, hulking masses of moonlight-limned cloud began to push like great ships across the sky. Mist rose from the vast, empty landscape, and I could no longer see anything below my waist. Aughisky skimmed across the treacherous ground, light-footed as a palfrey.

Our path began to rise beneath us, and by this I knew we were leaving the blanket bog behind. The swirling mist cleared as we approached a lake, oddly situated on a bluff overlooking the sea and surrounded on three sides by oak trees and flaming beacons. The lake had a distinctive shape, like a lumpy crescent, and I recognized it as a place I had visited as a child. Yet the oak trees should not have been there. Nor should Ada Quicksilver.

But there I found her on the north side, between lough and sea, surrounded by perhaps two dozen keening women, half of them clad in gray and half in black.

Aughisky slowed to a silent walk, and the group did not seem to notice our approach. But suddenly, the beast reared, neighing loudly against the night, and the women turned. I slipped from the jelly-slick back and struck the ground with force.

Half the women—those in black—opened their mouths, and their desolate cries filled the air. I covered my ears and squeezed my eyes shut, gritting my teeth against the sound. Inside their cries were the retreat calls of defeated armies. Weeping mothers whose sons had been lost at sea. Howls of the plague-cursed and starving. My heart swelled with sorrow, and tears seeped from beneath my eyelids.

"Enough!" cried Ada, and I could not understand how I had heard her over their unearthly wailing.

The keeners, too, had heard her, and they obeyed.

The air rang in the sudden silence as I rose to my feet.

"Edward!" called Ada, stepping forward, though a narrow body of water lay between us. "Are you all right?"

Before I could answer, the other half of the gathering began to keen. But this chorus of cries was entirely different. Their sorrow was just as pronounced, but they struck a high, clear note. It carried a call to hope that was as painful in its solemn beauty as the other had been in its desolation. Again I felt raw in the throat.

"Enough," repeated Ada, but in a gentle tone this time, and the voices fell silent.

The tightness in my chest eased. The woman who stood before me shone with beauty and strength. The gems in her hair and at her throat caught the starlight and danced. In her countenance, I caught only a trace of the uncertainty that I would expect my Miss Q to be feeling right now—that I myself felt at seeing her among those supernatural beings. My heart swelled again, but this time it was the swelling of a heart divided, a swelling of recognition.

*Cliona, my own love, you have awoken.*

## ADA

The beast that Edward had ridden reared again with an equine shriek that tore the night. I flinched at the great horse's proximity to him, but the earl staggered back a few steps, and she recovered her footing without harming him. No sooner had her front hooves struck the earth than she galloped toward the lake, leaped cleanly over it, and plunged down the bluff behind me before charging into the sea.

As I turned back to Edward, a dark shape erupted from the surface of the lake. A crow larger than a man winged its way around the ring of trees several times before landing only a few feet in front of me. The great wings shook, scattering droplets like pearls in the air, and then closed around the bird's body. A moment later, they unfurled to reveal the figure of a woman.

How old she might be, I could not have said. At first, I thought her close to my own age, but as her head turned, I glimpsed the profile of a much older woman. Though her black hair was piled high on her head, thick ropes of it had fallen about her shoulders, hanging nearly to her waist. She was sheathed almost completely in black crepe, with only her chest, shoulders, and neck revealed behind panels of dark lace. Her skin was deathly pale, but a band of black had been painted from one temple to the other, crossing over and around her eyes, causing the whites to glitter like the cold, brittle light of the winter moon.

"Ada, step back!" cried the earl. He had raised Great Fury and stood at the very edge of the water, opposite me.

I did not need encouragement. The woman emanated power, and my instincts told me she was dangerous. But the beings who had brought me here pressed around me in a tight circle—protectively, it seemed, but they inhibited my movement.

"Do you know me, child?" the woman asked. Her voice was disconcertingly uneven, shifting between youthful and clear, and ragged with age. She punctuated the question by knocking her staff against the ground, and I noticed it was not wood, but the chalky leg bone of some large beast. Where it struck, a tendril of white vapor unfurled into the night air, like smoke from a pipe.

My lips parted, but I could only shake my head.

She smiled, blackened lips peeling open to reveal gleaming white teeth. "The Danaan warrior does." Her head craned slowly downward and left as she looked askance at Edward across the narrow reach of water between us.

"You are the Morrigan," said Edward, sword held high.

*The Morrigan.* The battle crow. She was associated with war and death and, more philosophically, with change and rebirth. But there was nothing philosophic about the creature before me. She was a dark and palpable menace.

"The time draws nigh for the seal to be broken," she told Edward. "You must be ready."

"What does that mean?" he demanded, his voice clear and strong. His bright eyes, damp curls, and gleaming chest gave him a savage appearance. The light of the Danaan was not in him, and by this I knew that he was Edward still, but I wondered how long that could last.

"The battle is coming," she replied. "The boundary between our worlds has been weakened, but if you are to meet your ancient enemies on the field, that boundary must be erased. Diarmuid made the seal. Only Diarmuid can unmake it."

"What stake have you in this fight?" asked Edward.

She smiled again and returned her attention to me. Cold seawater seemed to trickle down my spine. "Shall we ask your scholar?"

"Her stake is the fight itself," I replied, a tremor in my voice. "She takes no side."

The Morrigan gave a satisfied nod.

"Hardly an inducement to trust your counsel," observed Edward.

She gave a slow, creaking laugh. "Perhaps not, my boy. Take it as you like. But if you do not wish to leave the fate of your countrymen in the hands of the bloodless race, you'll consider my words."

"Bloodless" was a poet's or bard's word describing fairy creatures, who were considered ephemeral and cool-bodied—without souls, even. Yet folktales bore out that they could be quite hot of temper. To me, "bloodless" had always suggested their immortality.

"Ada Quicksilver is an Englishwoman," Edward replied. "Why are your creatures holding her?"

The Morrigan raised her dark eyebrows and glanced at the keening women. "The banshees are not *my* creatures, though I asked that they lead her to this place, where the boundary is weak, knowing that you would follow."

Edward glowered. "Why not have them bring me instead?"

The Morrigan shifted, resting her weight on her staff and readjusting her wings. "Had you been listening for the voice of your ancestor, you would not need to ask *me*. Your Englishwoman has a drop of Cliona Airgid's blood in her veins.

Once she arrived on these shores, they could not but seek her out." The crow woman gave a chilling smile. "No more than could you, my boy."

I stared at her in shock. She seemed to be saying that what I had taken for Diarmuid's mistake—that I was his long-lost love— was, to some degree, *true*. And the word I had heard as *Airgid* ... In the same way that I had this night begun to understand all the Irish spoken to me, I knew that this word meant *silver*.

This was a puzzle piece that allowed many others to come together—including Edward's banshee vision on the night we first met, for Cliona was also referred to in some texts as queen of banshees.

Yet I could not wrap my mind around such a thing.

I studied the faces of the odd creatures who surrounded me. Some of them still watched me expectantly, while others had settled on stones near the shore, where they seemed to be washing items of clothing—blood-stained garments of the dead, according to legend. Some were aged and some youthful. Their hair and garments were trailing and vaporous, but they did not have the green cast of the absinthe visions, and their voices were substantial enough. Did this mean I was not seeing through the veil to Faery? That they were actually *here*?

I perceived no threat from them and hadn't since I found myself safely on solid ground again. Perhaps it was imagined, or merely a result of my previous studies of the fairy death heralds, but I did feel something like a connection to them. I sensed vulnerability and even empathy, and I felt a protective impulse, as I had toward younger orphaned girls at Lovelace.

And now the question I must face: Was I like Edward? Would I, too, soon find myself in the thrall of a powerful ancestor?

"I know of Cliona and her tragedy," I said to the Morrigan, "but what is her connection to Diarmuid?"

The goddess frowned. "When Cliona drowned, the sea god, Manannán, carried her body to Faery."

"To Brú na Bóinne," I said, remembering the story the earl had read to me. "Where Diarmuid was buried."

"Where he dwelled after the death of his mortal body. The Danaan warrior was so struck by her beauty that he woke her to immortality with a kiss. But she grieved so over the loss of her child—the living daughter whom she could not reclaim, and who was your own ancestress—that she drew all the fairy keening women to her, and thus she came to be called queen of banshees."

"And she and Diarmuid ..." I began uncomfortably. "They became lovers."

"Which is how you were able to use Ada for bait," the earl fumed.

The Morrigan offered a wry smile. "Had you been listening for the voice of your ancestor," she repeated, "there would have been no need."

"Lord Meath is truly descended from Diarmuid?" I asked, preferring to confirm as many facts as possible rather than argue with the goddess of war.

"From Diarmuid's mortal descendants by the lady Gráinne," she said, "before his death."

Legend did say that Gráinne, the fiancée stolen from Diarmuid's chief, had borne Diarmuid sons.

"Diarmuid created a seal to protect Ireland from the Fomorians," said Edward. That much Queen Isolde had told us, but he was clearly struggling, as I was, to understand all this. "The seal is now failing, and you brought us here because you want me—or Diarmuid—to break it and go to war with the Fomorians."

"The battle will come," she replied. "If you are first to take the field, you have a chance."

"What will happen when the seal is broken?" he asked.

The Morrigan frowned. "That which was divided will be joined. Those once separated will find themselves reunited."

The glower returned. "*That* is not an answer."

"Watch for your moment, Danaan warrior. Watch, and prepare." The goddess's wings unfurled, and she rose from the ground. She swooped once around the perimeter of the lake, the wind of her great wings extinguishing the beacons—and with them the great oaks themselves—before cawing loudly into the night and diving again beneath the gleaming surface.

# "I SHALL WALK"

## ADA

Great clouds scudded across the sky, reducing visibility of our surroundings now that the beacons had gone out. Even the light emanating from the fairy creatures surrounding me had faded nearly to shadow.

"Edward?" I called out.

"I'm here," he assured me. "Stay where you are, and I'll come to you."

Peering into the gloom, I assessed the distance around the small lake. "How?"

"I shall walk."

Oddly, a bubble of laughter rose in my throat and escaped before I could stop it.

The rustling sounds accompanying the earl's movements quieted. "Ada?" he called, his voice wary.

"Forgive me," I replied, mirth lifting the ends of my words. "I just ..." *I'm hysterical,* I thought. No, I didn't believe in hysteria. "Diarmuid, the Morrigan, Cliona, the water horse, and the banshees … Such powerful patrons, and here we are fumbling about in the dark like …"

"Like mortals," he said, still making his way to me. There was grounding in his words. "We *are* mortals, Ada."

"Do you really believe that? That we are now as we were before? For myself …" I hesitated, for my voice had thickened with an emotion opposite from the one I'd felt only a moment ago. I cleared my throat. "For myself, I am no longer sure what to believe."

A frigid wind gusted off the sea, and I shivered, crossing my arms over my chest.

"There's a path down to the strand," said Edward, coming around the horn of the crescent-shaped body of water. "We'll go and collect driftwood. There's also an old stone hut nearby. We'll build a fire to keep us warm until dawn, then discuss what to do."

The calm and cool in his tones quieted my anxiety, as did the warmth of his hands on my arms when he finally reached me. He was an anchor for my unmoored state.

"What shall we do for light?" I asked.

He pulled my hand through the crook of his arm and led the way. "I'm a sailor," he said softly. "I see well enough in the dark."

The path down to the strand was rocky and rough. Edward had his boots, but I wore only thin slippers that were never meant to be used out of doors. My ankles were bruised and scraped by the time we reached the strand, but the light color of the sand made it easier to see there. When we each had collected an armload of wood, he guided me to the beehive-shaped stone hut. I could see the indistinct outlines of the banshees gathering around the ancient dwelling. They did not approach or attempt any interaction but rather appeared content to serve as otherworldly escorts.

The hut was not currently occupied but had recently been in use—probably by hunters or fishermen, Edward said—and had straw mats on the floor to prevent the chill rising from the ground. He managed to start a fire using stones and beach grass, and the structure was snug enough to keep out most of the wind.

After we warmed our hands before the flames for a few moments, he asked, "Are you feeling better?"

I nodded. "Please forgive me for … for my lapse."

He laughed at this, and I glanced up. "You needn't apologize for being human," he said. "I was beginning to think nothing could shake you."

I gave a self-conscious smile. "I assure you, that was a mistaken impression, my lord. I merely have a gift for maintaining a stoic appearance."

This, too, made him laugh, and the sound of it warmed my heart. "My dear Miss Quicksilver, 'stoic' is the very last word I would use to describe you."

At the end of this observation, his tone took on a fond— no, *intimate*—quality, and I shivered. Mistaking this as a sign of chill—though a chill I did feel—he said, "I know it is cold. We shan't stay here long. When the light returns, we will more easily find someone to help us. And I wish to hear your thoughts on our next course of action."

I stared at the opening to the dwelling, and lest I forget all that had happened in the past hours, a banshee passed before it, her figure ghostly in the gathering light of dawn.

"If we believe all that we've been told," I said, meeting his gaze, "I think we must try to understand more about the events that are unfolding."

He nodded. "I agree, though I confess myself at a loss how that is to be accomplished. The obvious course would be to consult further with my cousin, yet …"

"You don't entirely trust her."

Another small nod. "I believe she wants what is best for

Ireland, but in my long relationship with her, I have not always approved of her methods."

"The queen mentioned her connection to a powerful ancestor—Maeve, the warrior queen. If Isolde gained access to Faery through this ancient bloodline, we should be able to do the same."

"Through our own connections to ancient bloodlines."

"Yes."

He studied me in the firelight. "Shall we speak of that? Of Cliona, I mean?"

Sighing, I shook my head. "I hardly know what to make of it."

"It does not surprise me, Ada," the earl replied. "I know little of the Danaan woman, but I do know that had my grandmother lived to know you, she would have pronounced you fey after your first introduction."

I gave an incredulous laugh. "There was never anyone so ordinary as I, I assure you."

"You *say* that," he countered. "You with your crown of silver locks, your possession of an ancient name, your choice of Irish mythology as a course of study, and not least, your family mythology of congress with fairies."

My lips parted, and I studied him as I thought on all he'd said. "Well, when you put it like that ..."

We both burst out laughing, and it shattered the tension and uneasiness that had pressed in close around us in the darkness before dawn.

"What we have now learned of Cliona," I said, sobering, "is not a story I am familiar with. There are echoes of old tales in the story of her husband and her death beneath the waves, but I've read nothing of the part Diarmuid played. My knowledge of the Danaan warrior's exploits ends with his death, and his burial at Brú na Bóinne."

I studied the flames of our fire, turning it all over in my mind.

"Yet I have always imagined the mythologies to be incomplete—mere fragments of the originals. And they are also inconsistent among the various sources. If we add the fairies' exile as orchestrated by Diarmuid, and the possibility of unfulfilled timelines, as discovered by your cousin … well, it is all unsettling, to say the least. It means that with all my years of study, I may actually know very little."

"What are we to do about that?"

I met his gaze. "Update our knowledge, I think. I should like to return to Brú na Bóinne, but not the one at Newgrange. There is another Brú na Bóinne, perhaps below or somehow beyond our world. The sword must have come from there, because the archaeologists would not have missed it in the tomb. Perhaps the scrap of parchment you found, as well. I'm willing to bet that the ruin is another place where the boundary is weak, which would also explain the púca. After that, I should like to visit the Faery library."

Edward gave a nod of commitment. "You shall set our course. But what of the seal between Faery and Ireland?"

The seal remained vexingly mysterious. "From what little the Morrigan told us, you will not have to seek out the seal, but it will somehow seek *you* out. I hope that we will be more knowledgeable by the time that happens."

"Agreed." He tossed the last bundle of sticks onto our fire.

Rubbing my hands over my arms and shoulders to warm them, I said, "Of course, we shall be able to accomplish none of these things unless we can discover how to cross into Faery."

## EDWARD

*Don't be such a coward.* This time, the critical voice in my head was all my own. My ancestor had, for the time being, receded.

"Come, Ada," I said, reaching for her. "I have little to contribute to our current strategy, but I can at least keep you warm."

She moved tentatively closer, and I wrapped my arms around her. The combination of her scent and her warm, soft skin managed to be both soothing and arousing.

"There were two times this evening when I thought I had lost you," I murmured.

She did not reply but stirred against me as if she would move closer, were it possible. My heart swelled with a pure and mounting joy that I recognized from experience. A sign I was doing something I was meant to do—I had often felt it at the prow of a ship in fair weather. The blood moved through me with vigor and purpose.

*Thee, my own love.*

With the echo of my ancestor's words, the music of my heart faded until I could hear it no longer. I didn't want to be used this way. I didn't want to wonder whether the feelings inside me were truly my own. The lady stiffened almost imperceptibly, and I knew that I was communicating these conflicted emotions.

"How shall we cross into Faery?" I asked quietly, reaching for the peace I'd felt only moments ago.

As she replied, I felt the vibrations of her words in my chest. "The Morrigan said *this* is a place where the boundary is weak. She crossed between worlds, as did the water horse, and the púca at Brú na Bóinne. We know that Isolde has done so as well. And Captain O'Malley—she used the Gap to cross the Irish countryside in little more than a blink. Because of our connection to our ancestors, we, too, may have such means of travel at our disposal."

I nodded, warming her back with my hand. "But how?" Indeed, *how* was I to properly consider her characteristically logical hypothesis, with the fullness of her breasts pressing against me? With the memory of her body before my mind's eye, and the taste of her still on my tongue?

She straightened and looked at me, eyes lit with determination. "I think we must make a trial of it, my lord."

She got up and ducked out of the hut, and my body protested the sudden loss of her. Chiding myself for this boyish lack of focus, I kicked apart the burning sticks of our fire and followed.

Outside, the risen sun had all but erased the nebulous forms of the keening women. But I could make out their dim outlines as we walked back to the lakeshore. They arranged themselves along the water's edge, and Ada waded in, sucking in a sharp breath.

"What are you doing?" I asked her.

"I think I must go in," she replied, watching the mist rise from the lake's dark surface. "Like the Morrigan."

"Like the Morrigan," I repeated, uneasy. "How will you do that?" She looked at me. "I shall walk."

## ADA

The water was shockingly cold, and sharp stones jabbed the bottoms of my feet through the thin slippers. I took one slow step after another until the water lapped at my knees, and my body quaked from the chill. The death messengers still watched from shore but offered no suggestion. If my hunch was wrong, they would soon have a job to do—I could not long survive this cold.

"Ada," cautioned the earl, "remember that we are trapped here for the time being. If you soak your clothing, I don't know how I shall warm you."

His thoughts were obviously running in a similar vein, and perhaps I *was* being foolish. The cold was now all I could think of, and I could no longer understand why I had thought this a good idea. I had made up my mind to return to shore when I felt the water rush around my legs, tugging at my ankles and knees. The earl shouted a warning.

I could see my feet resting against the bottom of the lake—but the lake itself was somehow melting away from me. My eyes followed the rushing motion of the water, watching it rise like a wave on the opposite shore. The water collected there, its surface diagonal, much like water in a glass that has been tilted. The movement of water revealed the mucky lake bottom, and a few yards in front of me, I noticed a round opening.

"What is that?" Edward gasped, joining me.

"I don't know." Heart pounding, I took a couple of steps toward the opening and noticed rocky stairs leading down.

Edward shouted an oath, and I looked up. The high end of the diagonal of water was slowly curling, as a wave does just before it crashes to shore. And then that curl was racing downhill toward us, building power and speed. The banshees began to wail.

"This way!" I cried, running for the stairway.

I hesitated a split second at the mouth of the opening, confused by a stairway that plunged into the ground yet also, somehow, up into the sky. The stairs did for a fact lead downward, but below I saw only star-flecked blackness.

As I hit the first stair, my wet slipper slid, and I skidded down several more, landing painfully on my backside.

"Edward!" I shouted, glancing back. He dived into the opening and rolled down half a dozen stairs, thudding to a stop just below me. I screamed as the water roared over our heads—but by some miracle, not a rivulet, not even a trickle, penetrated the opening, as if a pane of glass separated us from the lake.

"Cliona's Wave," I said breathlessly, heart pounding against my ribs as I watched the violent waters swirling above us. It was the title of every version of Cliona's story I had read, and it referred to the wave that had taken her life. But in the Morrigan's version, Cliona had died only to reawaken in another world, much as we just had.

Rubbing my bruised back, I turned to look down the stairs. I hadn't imagined it—what seemed to await us at the bottom of the rocky tunnel was a field of stars.

"The Gap," said Edward.

"Of course!" I replied.

I glanced again at the opening, wondering about the banshees, who seemed not to have followed us. "Shall we descend?" I asked.

"It appears to be our only option," replied Edward. "Give me your hand."

We made our way carefully down the stairs. The stones were sharp in some places and slick in others, and we had only the filtered, watery sunlight streaming through from the other side of the lake. It's how I imagined it would feel to stand at the bottom of a well, or perhaps in the cave of a *merrow,* the Irish mermaid. But it was not cold here, and that was a vast improvement.

In fact, the air was warm and humid, as it had been when Captain O'Malley's ship passed into the Gap. Ferns the color of absinthe, and an odd kind of moss grew in clefts in the rock walls. The moss was phosphorescent and velvety to the touch. It left a glowing gold residue on my fingers, reminding me of the time, as a child, I had accidentally mashed a firefly between my fingers.

I gasped on discovering that the stairway ended abruptly not more than a dozen steps below. There was no landing, and nowhere for us to go but into the open star field. What would happen if we fell? Would we plunge as from a cliff? I gripped Edward's hand.

We lingered there, wordlessly assessing our severely limited options. Edward had just turned to say something when we heard voices. A vessel of some kind was moving into view below us, at the foot of the stairs. Edward flattened himself against the rough wall of the stairway, and I did the same. His hand closed over the hilt of Great Fury.

The voices rising from the vessel—a tugboat like the queen's, but whose hull was pitted and thickly crusted with verdigris— were gravelly and growling. Their speech was at first unintelligible to me, but after a few moments I began to understand them. They were arguing, it seemed, about which of them would carry an item of value that had been entrusted to them.

Catching my eye, the earl held a finger to his lips.

We watched as a ladder rose from the deck of the tugboat to rest against the bottommost stair. Two men with rust-red caps mounted and began to ascend. They were wiry, armored fellows, their knotty hands the color of an apple cut open and left out to brown. The leader's head tipped back as he glanced up, and I held my breath as he surveyed the tunnel, the bluish whites of his bulging eyes glowing brightly. We held our breath, pressing ourselves even flatter against the wall, and the men continued to climb.

No sooner had they clambered onto the stairs than the earl stepped out of the shadows, raising Great Fury.

"Who are you?" he demanded in a voice that echoed loudly in the tunnel.

The foremost of the men gave a piglike squeal and raised a spear in threat. His wide, bloodshot eyes sparked with malice. His lower jaw protruded beyond the upper, and two long canines spiked upward, giving him a fierce appearance. He wore a rough and filthy tunic, leather armor, and heavy boots. His exposed forearms and calves were all sinew and ropy muscle.

The heavily browed eyes narrowed. "'Tis thou, is it?" he snarled.

The second man also brandished a spear, and he let slip to the stairs a large burlap sack lumpy with unknown contents. The sack thudded against the stones and then began a slow, awkward roll that carried it past the last step and back down to the deck of the tugboat.

"You know me?" Edward asked, sword still raised.

"Aye, I know *thee*," replied the man, spitting onto the stair. "'Twas thou that laid us under this bondage. All for foolish woman's sentiment." The creature narrowed his eyes. "But I see that Diarmuid has forgotten old Billy Redcap, King Under the Millstone."

I felt a slight drift of air against my face. It carried a sharp metallic odor that soured my stomach. Redcaps were a type of fairy with a dark and vicious reputation. Their caps were said to be kept red by frequent dyeing with human blood.

"What was that you were carrying?" I called, drawing the fairy's attention to me. His gaze sharpened, and I shivered.

"The banshee woman herself," he said with malicious interest. "And well met too. Roup here was not relishin' the swim."

"Answer the question, Billy Millstone," the earl snapped.

The redcap's lips peeled back in a gruesome grin. "Gifts from Lord Balor to the Celts, m'lord. Best for thee to step aside."

*Balor*, the legendary king of the Fomorians. And by "Celts" the redcap could very well mean the Irish people.

"Don't let them through," I cautioned the earl.

"You'll not pass, redcap," said Edward.

The man was perhaps two-thirds the earl's height but sturdy as a farmer's cart. The redcap's bulk did not prevent him from swinging his spear with a quickness that caught Edward off guard. He stumbled backward, and had he not tripped on the stairs, the swing would have caught him in the ribs.

Both redcaps surged forward, and the earl and I retreated. Edward regained his footing and raised his sword in time to parry another thrust of the spear. I expected the wooden weapon to snap in two, but it held fast.

Before the combatants could attack again, I felt a sensation I could only describe as a humming in the blood. The keen of the banshees also rang in my ears, and I recognized it as a warning. Glancing over the earl's shoulder, I saw that the second redcap,

Roup, had flung his spear at me. I should not have been able to watch the progress of the pointed tip, but the spear progressed slowly, as it might in a dream. In the heartbeat before it reached me, I leaned out of its path and plucked it from the air.

I stared at it, astonished.

*Weapon of thorn and iron. It will serve you well.*

Before I had a chance to wonder about the power that had allowed me to do this, or the source of this whispering in my mind, I heard the earl shout.

The combatants tumbled, colliding with Roup, who was knocked backward down the stairs.

"Edward!" I cried, watching helplessly as redcaps and man rolled and dropped from the bottom stair, landing in a tangled heap on the deck of the tugboat below.

Gripping the spear in one hand, I turned and stepped onto the ladder. It wobbled under my weight, but I steeled my grip and my resolve and started down while, on the deck below, the fight resumed.

"Now, thou Danaan poxbottle," snarled the redcap king, "Billy will end thine heirless descendant and bid thee farewell for good."

Stepping down onto the deck, I saw that Roup's arms were clenched viselike around the earl's torso, and Billy had aimed his spear at Edward's chest. Diarmuid's blade lay on the deck a few feet away. As the weapon appeared to be selective about who handled it, I assumed there was no danger of its being used against us.

Raising the spear, I charged forward.

"M'lord, the lady!" Roup shouted.

The warning came too late. I swung the spear with all my might, and it cracked hard against the leather jerkin, causing Billy to stumble. The iron tip sizzled against the leather, leaving a brand.

*When traveling on a moonless night, remember, iron is a fairy's blight.*

I couldn't recall where I'd read or heard the old rhyme, but some folklorists did cite iron as a protection against fairies. Since I was wielding the redcap's own weapon, the threat appeared to lie in direct contact with the metal.

Edward, still in Roup's grasp, thrust outward with his legs, kicking the off-kilter Billy. As the redcap fell, I jabbed at him with the spear, catching him in the shoulder, below the protection of his jerkin. The skin sizzled and Billy squealed in pain.

Edward's lunge toppled his captor, and Edward scrambled for Great Fury. Roup made a desperate grab for the earl's legs, but it wasn't enough to stop Edward from grasping and swinging the sword. Roup's ill-timed lunge was halted by his head's sudden parting from his shoulders. So powerful was Edward's strike, both head and helmet flew over the tugboat's rail. The earl thrust a foot against the redcap's chest and sent his body after.

Such violence was alien and shocking to me, yet I was surprised by the small volume of blood—as well as by its color. Thin, silvery trails dribbled down the rail, glowing in the low light. The head and body of Roup did not plummet as they should have according to the law of gravity, but drifted away from us in a ghastly, dreamlike fashion, trailing mercurial beads of fairy blood. I glanced at my feet, planted solidly on the tugboat deck, and wondered. I took a step back from the rail.

The word *aether* came to mind—a so-called fifth element that appeared in some ancient alchemical texts. Modern physicists also used this word when referring to a theoretical substance that formed a medium for the travel of light through space.

The grunts and curses behind me drew my attention, and I saw that Edward had immobilized Billy with the tip of Great Fury. Each time the panting redcap squirmed, the sword's tip touched his armor and sent up a curl of smoke.

"Don't kill him, Edward," I urged.

"Billy and I are merely coming to an understanding, are we not?" growled the earl, raising the point to Billy's face.

The redcap's eyes went wide, and spittle dripped from his thin lips.

I scanned the deck until my eye fell on the burlap sack, a few feet away. It had partially spilled its contents. I walked over to examine two brown lumps, which I took to be stones.

"What is this, Master Redcap?" I asked, poking at one lump with the tip of the spear. The object was easily pierced—not a stone after all.

I glanced back at Billy, but he only stared balefully.

"You said 'a gift for the Celts,' did you not?" I recalled. "What sort of gift?"

"Do as thou wilt to oul Billy," he whined. "Lord Balor will deal out worse for betrayal."

"Get up," Edward snarled, kicking him.

Billy obeyed, making disgruntled noises in his throat, and the earl's sword followed his movements closely.

They walked over and joined me, and Edward toed one of the lumps. "Potatoes," he said, grunting in surprise. "Rotten, by the look of them."

I frowned at Billy. "Why are you carrying rotten potatoes?"

The redcap kept his stony silence.

"Answer the lady," Edward said, again pressing the point of the sword into the redcap's armor.

Billy faltered back at the hiss of singed leather, and Edward thrust the sword in his face.

"*Answer* the lady," repeated the earl, "or I shall send your head after your fellow's!"

Billy cried out, cringing in terror. He raised his arms in front of his face and made a sound very like a sob. "Sure, 'tis praties for the journey, is all," he wailed, sounding even less convinced by this answer than I was. "Or did ye think oul Billy had no need to eat?"

"It's no use," I said, sighing. "He's more afraid of 'Lord Balor' than he is of us."

Edward, still training his sword on Billy, glanced at me. "You believe this is important?"

"I think it might be."

As he considered this, something about the change in his countenance made me uneasy.

He turned his attention to Billy again, and my heart quaked at the power in his voice when he said, "What does the King Under the Millstone want with a sack of rotten potatoes?"

The redcap's bulging eyes stuck out even farther, and he reached a hand to his throat, clamping shut his menacing jaw. He made a choking noise and clapped his left hand over his right.

I recognized his distress; Diarmuid was compelling him.

"The black rot," he answered in a high and grating voice, panting from the effort of holding back further disclosure.

Apparently, my suspicions were well founded. "Queen Isolde told of blight and famine visited by the Fomorians," I said. "'Balor' is the name of a Fomorian king, is it not?"

"It is," said the earl. Though from the light in his face and the deeper timbre of his voice, I knew I was speaking to Diarmuid. "Balor is an age-old foe of the Danaan. A horrible brute with a deadly gaze. I have met him in battle before."

Holding his gaze, I said, "I am willing to bet these are for spreading disease, my lord." As I watched him, the familiar intensity burned down, marking the earl's return. His brow furrowed.

"Many people in the Irish countryside eat little other than potatoes," said Edward, studying the prostrate redcap. "They are easily grown here and require no processing, and they don't fetch the high prices of exported grain that are so appealing to landlords."

"Why here on Achill, I wonder?" I replied. "Would it not be to greater effect on the Irish mainland?"

The earl considered. "The boundary of Diarmuid's Seal is weak here," he recalled. "Perhaps it is the only place they can pass through."

I stared at him with a creeping sense of unease. "But this is not the *only* place the boundary is weak."

Low laughter, bitter as dark ale, bubbled up from Billy Millstone. "The hour is late," he cackled. "Ye'll not stop it now. Neither of ye, nor the warrior queen herself."

"We must find the other locations where the seal has been weakened," I said to Edward, ignoring the redcap's taunts. "The queen is looking to the battle to come, but the Fomorians—are they not masters of plague and blight? Is it likely this threat is limited to potatoes?"

The earl eyed me darkly, shaking his head.

"*This* is the first threat to be faced," I continued. "If we can stop it, perhaps we might prevent the battle."

"Or at least even the odds."

"Not to mention all the lives that may be lost if we don't try."

Edward frowned. "But how?"

I swallowed, reluctant to say what I knew he would not want to hear. "We need Diarmuid."

# "THE STORY OF US"

## ADA

The dread in his expression pained me. He glanced at the redcap. "I don't think I will be able to compel him further. He is in mortal terror of Balor, and more than that, I sense a ..." He drifted off, considering a moment before going on. "Something like a blood oath. If I try to break it, I may kill him."

As if to reinforce these words, Billy Millstone's eyes went wide, and the already protruding jaw jutted further. I felt encouraged that the earl seemed to be in some manner communicating with his ancestor without ceding control to him.

No sooner had this idea crossed my thoughts, however, than I watched the rekindling of that otherworldly brightness in his eyes. Turning suddenly, he surged forward with the sword, making Billy stumble backward onto the deck. He planted a boot on the redcap's chest and thrust the tip at his throat. Billy gave an ear-rending squeal.

"So be it," were the potent words of Diarmuid. "It would be no more than he deserves."

"My lord," I called, drawing his attention. I would never grow accustomed to his intensity. The more time I spent in his presence, the more my body answered with a welcoming heat—a simmering anticipation that caught fire in my belly. Was I Miss Quicksilver falling for the Earl of Meath, or Cliona responding to the presence of her lover?

I stepped toward him. "Can you tell me the other places where the boundary is weak?"

He did not bother to mask a feverish longing as he studied me. "Almost from the beginning, the seal was threadbare in sacred places, and Faery peoples have sometimes found their way back to Ireland. In some of these places, the Morrigan's alchemists constructed Gap gates to make it even easier to pass between worlds."

Fairy lore contained descriptions of such places, usually referred to as "fairy doors." They tended to be located in ruins like those at Newgrange, in enchanted lakes, or in notable landscape features like Ben Bulben, the tabletop mountain recently mentioned by both the earl and Captain O'Malley's scribe, Mr. Yeats.

"You're saying the Gap gates were created *intentionally*, inside fairy doors, to make it easier to circumvent the seal?" The Morrigan's role in all this was complicated indeed.

Diarmuid frowned. "They were."

"Do *you* use them to travel to Ireland?"

"Immortals inhabiting living descendants require neither fairy doors nor Gap gates."

*Edward* was his fairy door, and I was Cliona's. "You mean we might have traveled to Faery without passing through a Gap gate?"

He nodded. "But not to pass from Achill Island to Brú na Bóinne," he admitted. "We may pass easily between worlds, but only the navigator devices can fold the distance between locations within those worlds. Without one, we must employ more traditional means for cross-country travel."

"Ah. Captain O'Malley uses such a device."

"And Billy Millstone." Diarmuid shot a disdainful glance at the prostrate redcap. "But if you're thinking to catch up with the other servants of Balor, we shall be too late."

My heart sank. "We know now what they plot. Is that not an advantage? What is your counsel?"

"My counsel is as it has ever been: prepare to fight."

Of course. He was a warrior. "But what of those who will die in the famine, my lord? Farmers and their children. Their aged ones. They will be most affected."

Diarmuid lowered his sword but kept his heel planted on the chest of his foe. With some impatience in his tone, he replied, "They shall be avenged."

"If it could be prevented, you would do nothing?"

His eyes glittered. "You must know, there is only one mortal I care for. It was for her—for the child that she pined for, and for her descendants—that I worked the magic to exile my own people. I will fight for her. You are of her line, and I will fight for *you*. All else is distraction."

*I cast all Faery out of Ireland for the love of her,* he had told me at Kildamhnait. At the time, it had seemed yet another riddle, but I had learned much since then.

Now I understood that his creation of the seal had not been out of regard for the people of Ireland, or over hatred of his old enemies, the Fomorians. This rendered his motives, at least to some degree, disconnected from our own, which meant that we could not entirely trust him.

I took a step toward him, holding his gaze though I trembled. "You need the earl. Without him, you can never reach *her*. Without *me,* you can never reach her. And the earl and I are for Ireland."

He cocked a dark brow, eyes lit with fierce amusement. "You would threaten a warrior of the Danaan?"

I willed myself not to flinch. "If I must."

He dropped the sword, and it clattered to the deck. I gave a startled cry as he grabbed for me, pulling me against him and locking me in his arms. His lips came down on mine.

My body erupted in fire.

*The fire of making. It consumes us. Yet for us, it burns without issue. We forge nothing but passion between us. But across the centuries we have found each other, my love. And our mortal bodies can do things our immortal ones could never dream of...*

## EDWARD

*Then let us burn.*

Four passions raged in two bodies, and I feared it would tear us to pieces. Yet I knew it would be the most exquisite pain I had ever known.

*No.*

With a growl of desperation, I gripped her shoulders to pry us apart. What I had intended to be gentle separation resulted in more of a shove, and she stumbled. Cursing my clumsy control of my own body, I reached out to steady her, but my attention was diverted by Billy's lunge toward his fallen spear. Recalling the preternatural strength with which he wielded that weapon, I snatched Great Fury from the deck and struck him across the back with the flat of the blade. With the redcap once again immobilized, I looked at her.

"Forgive me," I panted, hoping it would suffice for both the ardor and the violence.

She shook her head, dismissing the apology as she struggled to recover her own breath. "What now?"

I studied the cringing Billy Millstone, considering. Each of my ancestor's visits left behind a kind of memory residue. I knew things about his life that I hadn't before, though the picture was far from complete.

"Brú na Bóinne," I replied. "I trust your instinct that there are answers there. I believe we may even be able to consult my foster father—Diarmuid's foster father—Angus."

She stared at me, and I knew she was curious about the merging of my ancestor's and my intellects, yet also wary of it.

"Perhaps we shall not find this Faery version of Brú na Bóinne deserted, like the ruin we visited at Newgrange," she said.

"It is by no means deserted." I thought for a moment about how to explain something that I barely understood myself. "Ireland is the domain of mortals, but Faery is inhabited by what is left of the Danaan, and the gentlefolk—the fairies. In Faery, Brú na Bóinne is the domain of Angus and Caer."

Ada's expression was composed, but very keen and active. "You've learned much from your ancestor. This will help us."

"Perhaps so," I replied. "I hope that is true."

"Do you know how to reach Faery?"

I frowned, reluctant to answer this, of all questions. But I needed her counsel. "If I give myself over to Diarmuid completely—and you to Cliona—we shall be boundaryless. In fact, Diarmuid has been able to use my slumbering form to cross between Faery and Ireland already."

"Your nightwalking."

I nodded. "Understand, Ada, my ancestor wants this surrender more than *anything*."

She considered, and I waited, counting heartbeats, as if she held my fate in her hands. And indeed, she did—the fate of us both. I strongly suspected that if we relinquished control of our physical forms, we might not ever recover it. There would be rich rewards for such a choice—I could feel the promise of those rewards every time Diarmuid's gaze branded her—but it might be the last choice we would freely make.

"No," she replied, and I let out my breath. "Their motives for wanting this may well be very different from our own. We have a navigator who can take us there."

Following the turn of her gaze to the redcap, I saw his eyes move between us as if we were two wolves fighting over a lamb.

Grateful for her steadiness of mind, and even more for her vote in favor of our autonomy, I ordered, "Take us to Brú na Bóinne, little man."

"Wait, Edward," said Ada. She used the ill-fated Roup's spear to push the diseased tubers back into the sack, as if afraid even to touch them. Then she moved behind Billy, pointing the iron spike at the back of his knobby neck. Glancing up, she nodded at me.

I lowered my sword and bent to lift the moldy sack. Then I heaved it over the rail. Like Roup, it floated rather than plummeting, and we watched it sail away from us into the void.

With these small but formidable weapons disposed of, we marched Billy into the wheelhouse. Inside, we found one of the fog-filled globes that the ship's navigator on the *Queen of Connacht* had used. What appeared to be a tin cutout of the tugboat floated in the mists of the Gap.

Billy moved to the globe and began operating the gears with his long, knobby fingers.

"We want to go to Faery," said Ada. "To Brú na Bóinne, the domain of Angus. Is that clear?"

"*Ach*, aye," replied the redcap in a voice thick with sarcasm. I whacked the back of his head with Great Fury. He flinched and yelped, grizzled hairs smoking, but continued with his manipulation of the device.

Once the navigation had been set, the helm began to spin

seemingly of its own accord, and the tugboat drew away from the tunnel.

I didn't like trusting this rough fellow who had applied himself so enthusiastically to murdering us—along with the whole population of Ireland, albeit less directly. But our choices were dismally limited. He, at least, could be controlled by fear, and for the moment, he appeared to fear Diarmuid more than he feared his master.

I eyed our surroundings by the light of the wheelhouse's greasy lanterns, imagining what Captain O'Malley might have to say about the state of this vessel. As an officer of the Irish navy, it fairly made my skin crawl. Bones of birds and other small animals littered the deck and had accumulated in piles in dark corners. Empty ale and wine jugs lined the walls, a few of them tipped over and rolling gently back and forth with the motion of the tug. Gazing out the wheelhouse window, I discovered that what I had taken to be a battered and frayed standard was actually a portion of blackened human skeleton that had been hung from the flagpole. The bones rattled gently together with the movement of the tug.

The engine room resided in an open well behind the wheelhouse. Rather than the rattle of steam pistons, there was a grimy gearworks that produced rhythmic mechanical clicks. The decks and hull were in a sorry state of repair, verdigris-coated and containing gaping holes that would sink a seagoing vessel. For all that I could understand by studying its workings, the operation of the tugboat might as well have been magical in nature.

I glanced at Ada, wondering what her inquisitive mind made of all this, and found her watching me.

"What is on your mind, my love?" I hadn't meant the presumptuous endearment to pass from my thoughts to my lips—I had slipped into a habit of shielding her from the Danaan warrior's ardor, but sometimes I was not quick enough. This time, it had rolled so naturally off my tongue, I realized that marking any kind of solid boundary between Diarmuid's and my intellects would become more and more challenging.

*It is the boundary you so unnaturally draw between yourself and the lady which is doomed to fail* was the helpful suggestion of my ancestor, who would have my body for his own if he could.

She broke from my gaze and appeared to study our captain's back. "I was thinking of what you said. You implied a risk of losing ourselves. Do you believe that might happen?"

Frowning, I replied, "If we give in to their wishes, I think it very well might. But what is your opinion?"

"I think you have grounds for that fear," she agreed. "They are clearly devoted to each other, holding on to their bond for centuries. And we know they are powerful."

"I cannot help wondering whether they are why *we* found each other," I said, unsure that I really wanted to know.

"It would be hard to dispute that we have been touched by fate," she admitted.

My thoughts had run in a similar vein even from the earliest moments of our acquaintance. "And what of our own will?" Her eyes returned to me, and I continued, "Our own choices, I mean. Do they exist anymore?"

She smiled. "For now."

She was right. She had encountered no difficulty in rejecting my request to bind us under the law. Yet I was uneasy. "I worry about the price we will pay for their aid."

## ADA

The earl spoke of a *personal* price, I knew.

"As do I," I admitted, "and yet I am grateful for their aid. Perhaps we should feel encouraged by Queen Isolde, who seems to have embraced her otherworldly connections and yet remains her own sovereign."

Edward frowned. "An advantage, perhaps, of being half mad. What worries me most ..." He drifted off, leaving me hanging on a partially voiced sentiment that my instincts told me was important.

"Tell me," I said.

His eyes met mine. "I had begun to know you. You had begun to know me. I fear now that we will be consumed by their passion. And, Ada, don't mistake me—I *yearn* for that. Its siren song is almost irresistible." His gaze took in all of me, and under the sudden heat of his regard, my thoughts drifted back to our night together. "But if that happens," the earl continued, "will we lose the opportunity to write the story of *us,* whatever that may be? Will we not be a mere footnote to their epic?"

I was astonished by his eloquence. Misgivings very like these had been taking shape in my own mind, but I would have failed utterly to voice them. And I could not overlook the tender sentiment underlying his words. *The story of us.*

Longing to feel his arms around me, I said, "These are questions we share, and I fear it will be some time before we know the answers. For now, I think all we can do is allow ourselves to be led by our better natures and hope that fate will be kind to us."

Edward smiled, replying softly, "Hear, hear."

# HOUSE OF IMMORTALS

## ADA

The tugboat had just nosed into a bank of warm fog when the stillness was suddenly broken by cracking noises along the deck, as if the little vessel were under strain.

"What's happening?" the earl demanded of Billy Millstone.

The redcap grumbled in annoyance as he fiddled with the navigation device. The fog inside the globe shifted from gray to green. "We're nigh on the River Boyne, or is that not what ye were after?"

The tugboat drew up beneath another stairway inside a tunnel. Glancing to the top of the hewn stone steps, I saw the same watery sunlight filtering down. It might be the same gate, for all I could tell.

"Can you not take us there more directly?" I asked, recalling that our brief journey on the *Queen of Connacht* had not involved Gap gates. "We recently traveled by Gap galleon without any need for climbing or descending wet staircases."

Billy gave a frustrated squawk. "And did the madwoman carry ye to Faery?"

By "madwoman," I assumed he was referring to Captain O'Malley. "No, only cross-country."

"*Well*, then," he replied, raising his eyebrows and shaking his head in impatience. "Ye can get out here or not. It's all the same to Billy."

I glanced at the earl, who nodded.

"What are we to do we do with *him*?" I asked.

Edward let out a sigh. "I suppose he'd better come with us. We don't want him carrying his story to his master."

"*Damn* thee for a—"

"Desist, redcap," Edward hissed, raising the tip of Great Fury, "if you want to keep your head."

He sent Billy up the ladder first, and I followed. The wretched, foul-smelling creature kept up a steady stream of muttered recriminations, which Edward and I ignored.

I had kept Roup's spear, feeling more secure with some method of defending myself—especially as I now believed that it had been Cliona's voice that recommended it to me. I was intensely curious about my ancestress, and more trusting of her counsel than the earl was of his ancestor's. Perhaps because she herself had been mortal once. She also had yet to overpower my intellect—as Diarmuid certainly had done many times with Edward—and for that I was grateful.

*What has happened to the banshees?* I inquired experimentally, keeping an eye on Billy Millstone as he stepped from the top rung of the ladder onto the first stair. Edward's boots continued tapping against the rungs below me.

I had not dared hope for a reply, but it came as a whisper in my mind: *They are spectral and easily pass between worlds.* There was a sense of effort behind the words, as if it had cost the speaker something to make them heard. *They will find you again in their own time.*

I understood her to mean that like Diarmuid and Cliona, the banshees did not require Gap gates in order to move between worlds.

As I joined Billy at the top of the stairs, I saw the calculation in his eyes—on this uneven footing, a sudden charge would easily have overpowered me, even with the spear in my hands. But Edward and Great Fury were only a few steps behind, and I could see the redcap soon abandon his scheming.

I stared into the liquid sky. As the water drifted overhead, Edward and even Billy watched me with expectation. Tentatively I reached up, dipping a finger into the current. Cold water pulled gently at my skin, and I slowly submerged my whole hand. Beside me, Edward held his breath.

The river's flow ebbed and stilled to become like the waters of a lake. Then, with the roar of a breaking wave, the water parted and peeled back from the opening. Ignoring the twist of panic in my stomach, I hurried up the last few stairs and stepped onto a riverbed slimy with drooping water weeds. As I glanced back to make sure the others were following, my instincts screamed at me to escape, and I shook, thinking of the potential energy curling directly over my head.

We hurried across rocks and mud and the occasional flopping trout, to the bank. I lost first one, then both slippers. Not knowing how long it would be before the river returned to its course, I didn't pause to retrieve them. They were ruined in any case and did very little to protect my feet from the hazards of the riverbed.

We climbed onto the grassy bank, and I watched with wide eyes as the parted waves rolled and crashed into one another. Witnessing this explosive event from aboveground was even more shocking. I thought about Cliona and how terrifying it must have been— snatched from the coracle and carried to her death by the violence of the ocean, all the while worrying over the fate of her child.

Suddenly, a sense of the horror of that moment washed over me, and I stumbled to my knees with a fearful cry.

*The water was icy, the shadows deepening as she sank. Willfulness is a sin. The weight of her garments carried her beyond hope, and she had never learned to swim.* God punishes the selfish. *But the child was innocent! Where was she? Washed overboard like her mother? Drifting alone out to sea?* Manannán save her!

"Ada!"

Edward knelt beside me, alarmed.

"I am well," I assured him, yet I struggled to catch my breath, and tears stung my cheeks. The sadness was heavy, like the young mother's soaked gown. The soul-rending shame was unbearable, and I choked back a sob.

"Ada, what is happening?" demanded the earl.

Gripping his hand for support, I rose slowly to my feet. "I am well," I repeated, my voice stronger this time. "A difficult memory, that is all."

*More curse than blessing, though Manannán meant it as a gift.* My ancestress's voice was soft and mournful in my ear. I understood that she was referring to this power of parting the waters. Every time she used it—every time *I* used it—she was reminded.

"*Your* memory?" the earl asked. "Or Cliona's?"

I squeezed his hand. "Her death."

I eyed Billy Millstone, who stood behind Edward, half turned away from us and as wretched as ever. I wished him far away. This grief was too raw, too private, to share with an enemy.

"It is fading," I assured Edward. "Let us go."

The waters of the Boyne had returned to their normal peaceful course, and Edward and I turned to take stock of our new surroundings. His hand pressed the small of my back, and the warmth and concern in that gesture seeped into me, dulling the edges of a now shared sorrow.

Directly behind us, a manor house on a hill dominated the landscape. Most artists' renderings of fairy palaces depicted them as light and airy confections. But this was a blocky medieval structure, with heavy wooden beams, and plaster that had aged to a buttery yellow. Stables and other outbuildings surrounded the dwelling, but beyond the grounds in every direction stretched acres of dense oak forest. I saw no sign of a stone structure like the ruin at Newgrange, but then, there would be no need for a tomb in the land of immortals.

The forest and the manor house were not the only ways that this Faery version of Brú na Bóinne departed from the modern-day site. Something about the very atmosphere was different here. There was a golden glow, a saturation of color ... I could only liken it to the quality of light on an autumn afternoon when warm sunshine has gently dried an early rain. Everything my eyes fell on had that richness imparted by slanting afternoon sunlight, and yet the light here was directionless. In the sky, which was a beautiful duck-egg bluish green, I saw no sun. The air was clean and crisp, neither warm nor cool. The gentlest of breezes caressed my cheek, carrying the scent of wild rose and rich, dark earth. Even a hint of the sea.

"What shall we find inside, do you think?" I asked the earl.

He shook his head. "I hardly know what to expect. But Diarmuid considers this his home, and its inhabitants his family."

The earl directed Billy to precede us as we walked toward the manor. The redcap looked by turns angry and frightened, and as we walked, he carried on a muttered conversation with himself.

When we were within a few yards of one of the outbuildings, several figures strode out to meet us. As they drew closer, the redcap began to snivel and growl.

"Wispy sylvans," he spat. "Bloodless sprites."

"Hail, Diarmuid," called a lofty, slender woman whose medieval dress of sage and gold included an armored bodice. "And Cliona," she continued, dipping her head respectfully.

"The master and mistress are within," said one of her companions. "They have been expecting you."

The other two of the welcoming party were male. All were tall and regal. The complexion of their angled faces was dark and flawless, their hair straight and raven black, and the pointed tips of their ears protruded between gleaming locks. Their dark irises blended with their pupils, lending their gazes an unsettling bottomless quality.

"You speak of Angus and Caer?" asked Edward. "They knew we were coming?"

She studied him a moment before replying, "They knew that you would seek them. And they are aware of your mortal … encumbrances."

The earl frowned, and he opened his mouth to reply. I diverted him as politely as I could. "May we know who you are?" I asked them.

The woman offered a chill but, I believed, genuine smile. "I am Ash. We are the people of the forest, and we serve the king and queen at Brú na Bóinne, who protect it."

"Woodland fairies," grumbled Billy.

"Your companion must remain without," said one of the men, flaring his nostrils. "He exudes an unwholesome odor."

I glanced at Billy, who glared malice from under his frowsy eyebrows. "I fear that he will flee if we don't keep him close," I replied.

"He will not escape us, lady," replied Ash. "If you wish, you may claim him when you depart." Though her smile remained fixed, her expression made it clear she did not know why we would choose to do such a thing.

I bowed my head. "We thank you."

Billy began to protest, but the woman gestured sharply with her spear, and he stalked off in the direction she indicated, the others following in his wake. I began almost to pity him. Billy had been sent to harm the Irish and would happily have killed Edward and me. But was he not bound by a blood oath? He had also, wittingly or not, been the source of very useful information.

The Tuatha de Danaan were no true friends of the Irish people—at least, according to lore—and I knew I must remember that. They had, in fact, been foes once and seemed to be bound together now only because their bloodlines had at some point become intermingled. *And* because the Danaan's most accomplished and revered warrior had fallen in love with an Irishwoman and made her one of them.

"Are you ready?" the earl asked.

I nodded. "I wish I did not look like …" I broke off, glancing down in dismay at my stained dressing gown and muddied bare feet. I was not sure *what* I looked like, but it was neither genteel nor dignified.

The earl laughed. "You are beautiful as always, while *I* am a half-naked savage. But they must take us as we are."

My eyes fluttered down to his chest, which was mostly revealed by the deep V of his nightshirt. Dark hair traced the curve of his breast and the sheer wall of his stomach. I knew that it was silky to the touch and that the flesh beneath it was warm.

I felt the heat of his gaze on my face, and he reached for my hand. I gasped quietly as he drew me forward, splaying my fingers across his chest. I shivered as he leaned over me, dipping his head. I lifted my chin, and his lips brushed mine. Another small, helpless sound escaped my throat, and the pressure of his lips increased while the distance between our bodies closed. I felt the taut muscles of his torso against my breasts as his arm hooked around my waist, pulling me close.

His lips trailed across my cheek, and I whispered, "Edward."

"Yes," he softly confirmed.

He released me then but took my hand and led me to the manor's entrance as my heart slowly returned to its normal rhythm.

An impish face wrought from metal had been fixed to the great oak door. It held a knocker in its mouth, and Edward lifted and let it fall. A moment later, a tall, lithe woman opened the door. Her hair was white and glossy like cream and hung in a sheet to her waist. Her complexion was so fair that I could see a tracery of silver veins beneath her skin. I had assumed her to be corporeal like Billy and the woodland fairies—until she shifted slightly in the doorway and I noticed that I could see through her to the corridor beyond.

I felt another throb of sorrow that I knew was not my own, and along with it came a new and startling understanding.

*Ours was a winter love that never enjoyed its springtime.*

In the time of Diarmuid and Cliona's love, they had never possessed mortal bodies. They had craved *carnal* passion but never experienced it. What they shared had been more like a blending of spiritual energy, or a mingling of souls. Suddenly, I understood the desperate quality of their desire. What torture it must be, finding themselves once again in physical bodies yet unable to reach for each other without our acquiescence.

"Welcome to you both." The woman's kind voice roused me from these thoughts. She smiled, gray eyes brightening, and opened the door wider, inviting us inside. "We are well known to each other," she said, her voice light and pure as a songbird's. "But perhaps you do not recognize me?" She studied Edward's face.

"You are Caer, my foster mother," he said in a gentle tone, returning her smile.

Caer was Danaan royalty—Angus's shape-shifting queen.

The lady bowed her head. "So I am. It pleases me that you remember. Come inside. Your chamber stands in readiness. You and your lady may refresh yourselves if you like."

"We are grateful," replied Edward.

"Your foster father and I and the others will await you in the hall."

Fostering was a common practice in the time of the Tuatha De Danaan and, indeed, in ancient Ireland in general. Rival kings or chieftains would send their sons to be reared by each other as a gesture of their intention to keep peace between them, much as a daughter might be given in marriage to a rival. The only story told in the lore about Diarmuid's true father was an account of how he had inadvertently played a part in Diarmuid's death. But the love between Diarmuid and his foster father, Angus, was well established.

Caer stepped back and gestured to a passage that led left from the entryway, and we stepped inside.

"Thank you, lady," I said, wondering what she had meant by "the others."

"Of course, child." As she turned from us, I noted that the skirt of her gown was constructed of long white feathers, their tips whispering around her ankles as she walked. According to legend, the wife of Angus could take the form of a swan.

The house of Angus and Caer was immaculate. Our movement along the passage disturbed neither dust mote nor cobweb. Light spilled into the dwelling through the large windows of the open chambers we passed, burnishing the honey-colored beams of floor and ceiling. The rich tapestries that covered the plaster walls depicted scenes from Tuatha De Danaan legends. I studied them as we walked, stopping suddenly as my gaze fell on an image of a woman and child in a coracle. An enormous wave curved menacingly over the small figures, causing a stir of panic in my belly. The wind whipped the woman's silvery hair back from her face. I touched the face of the bundled infant in her arms—if I believed all I had been told this day, the babe was my ancestress.

*By the grace of Manannán,* whispered Cliona, and I could feel the warmth of her gratitude.

*Where is he now?* I wondered. Like the battle crow, Manannán was an ancient and powerful Celtic deity. Were we destined to cross paths with him too?

*Manannán no longer leaves his own kingdom,* was the mournful reply, and by this I knew she meant the sea.

Edward had walked on, gazing into each doorway as he passed. But he stopped now, saying, "here."

I followed him into a high-ceilinged chamber with a heavy oak bed, a desk and chair, a sitting area, and two large cases filled with books. An impressive collection of weapons covered one wall, among them a single empty mounting bracket. There were more tapestries, three depicting battles and one of a man and a woman in a state of partial undress, locked in an embrace at the center of a woodland scene. The man had a head of dark curls, and the woman had flowing red hair. I did not know who she was—the legendary Diarmuid had taken various lovers—but I wondered whether she might be Gráinne, his most famous conquest.

*And the mother of his children,* I was reminded. Which made her an ancestress of Edward. The flicker of longing I felt reminded me of Cliona's reference to "the fire of making," and a passion that burned "without issue." Her lack of a physical body had also prevented her from bearing Diarmuid a child.

At the opposite end of the chamber, I saw a gleaming copper tub resting on the floor near a dormant fireplace. Steam rose from its surface. Beside it stretched an enormous wolf-skin rug. The windows had been thrown open, allowing in the fresh, naturally perfumed air.

Edward came to stand beside me, and I asked, "Do you find yourself at home here?"

# EDWARD

Dirt smudged her cheek, and much of her hair had pulled loose from its pins. She had retied the belt of the dressing gown multiple times, but it stubbornly gaped to reveal the curves of her breasts, and the lovely hollow in between.

"I do," I replied. "And I don't."

She nodded, and her gaze returned to the tub.

"Please," I said, "I insist that you have the first bath."

Turning from her, I drew Great Fury from its sheath and placed it in the empty bracket. I had intended to give her what privacy I could, for I would not leave her alone in this strange place, however comfortable my ancestor might feel here. But I found myself turning in time to see the soiled dressing gown slip from her shoulders. I held my breath as she bent to grasp the edge of the tub and then stepped over the side.

Her figure had been worthy of worship *before* she was a fairy queen. She gave a guileless sigh of pleasure at the water's embrace, and I felt a surge of raw lust, like nothing I'd experienced even in my hot-blooded youth.

*I am heartily ashamed to claim kinship with you,* said the impatient voice in my head. I turned from the bathing beauty, blocking my ancestor's fevered gaze as I focused on the implements of battle mounted on the adjacent wall. *Why do you hesitate, fool?*

"Because I am a gentleman," I grumbled in reply, "and I respect the lady. Two things you cannot understand."

"Edward?" the lady in question called out. "Is anything wrong?"

"Not at all," I replied as steadily as I could. "I am wondering whether you ought to have a proper weapon." I touched the hilt of a slender sword with a blade crafted of white metal, and its history came into my mind. Diarmuid had won it in a fight with the champion of a clan of invading *huldre*—elves from Scandinavia. "This is a shieldmaiden's sword, light and strong. Though I imagine you have never wielded such a weapon."

"Only once," came the faint reply.

In response, my mind produced an image of her standing before me, threatening me with the very sword I had taken from the ruin. Her eyes were wide, her brow furrowed in dismay.

"In fending off the brute," I said quietly.

There was no immediate reply, and from the sounds of displaced water, I knew that she had risen.

"No doubt he could have taken it from me had he truly wished," she said at last.

I had to acknowledge the truth of that. Raising my hand, I ran my thumb across the edge of the blade.

"Have a care, my lord," she said. "Ancient swords of power are often said to possess uncommon and dangerous qualities."

I dropped my hand and turned. She stood on the rug, wrapped in a bath sheet.

"Right you are," I replied, hardly aware of what I was saying as I noted the way the thin white cloth clung to her wet figure.

"Please," she said, indicating the tub. "The water is still warm, though not nearly so clear as it was before, I'm afraid."

I stepped forward as she had bidden, and our shoulders brushed lightly as she moved away. The contact robbed me of breath.

"With your permission," she began, "I shall see if your ancestor possessed any clothing that might be made to serve a lady."

"Of course. Consider anything of mine, or his, to be at your disposal."

When she turned to pursue her search, I shucked off my trousers and sank into the tub, occupying myself with the business of washing.

A few minutes later, she said, "It appears that Diarmuid shared this chamber with one of his ladies." Glancing up, I found her kneeling beside a trunk. She produced a green gown and laid it across the foot of the bed. How she maintained her characteristic poise and calm under such circumstances was beyond me.

She stroked the silver needlework embellishing the gown's bodice. I was no expert in ladies' fashion, but it was obvious even to me that the gown had been crafted for another age. Both skirt and sleeves were voluminous and trailing.

With her back to me, she let drop the bath sheet, and my breath stopped. Her silver waves swung free, the thick, damp ends coming to rest just above her hips. My eyes traced the softly flowing lines of her body, and my mouth watered.

She lifted the gown above her head and let it fall over her, pushing her arms through the sleeves. Turning her head, she glanced over her shoulder. The laces hung loosely at the open back of the gown.

"I fear I shall never manage this on my own, my lord."

I swallowed, then dunked myself once more under the water. Stepping out of the tub, I dried quickly and then wrapped the bath sheet about my waist. Water sluiced down my back and chest as I crossed the room.

After glancing again toward the out-of-reach laces, she raised her eyes to mine. Her lips curved in a small self-conscious smile, and my heart stumbled.

As I took hold of the lace ends, my fingers trembled. I could just see the top of the outward curve of flesh below the small of her back, and try as I might, I could not will my fingers to tighten the laces that would restrict my view.

"I …" Clearing my throat and clenching my jaw, I did finally tug the gown closed.

She had lifted her damp hair away from her back, and I found myself staring at the well between her shoulder blades. This sweet indentation of flesh drew me closer, against any possibility of resistance, and soon I had pressed my lips to the spot. I closed my eyes as the ocean roared in my ears.

Releasing the lace ends, I slipped my hands into the back of her dress. I worked the laces loose again by sliding my fingers down and around her waist. Drawing her backward, I tucked her rounded backside against me, and she gave a little gasp of surprise.

Her head came back to press my shoulder, and I breathed hot, dark lust into her pale and delicate ear.

My ancestor had gone silent, but I felt his presence. He had goaded me mercilessly, but now that he was so close to fulfilling his ancient desire, I knew that he feared to break the spell.

But there was no need for words. He was ravenous, and his feverish hunger had robbed me of gentler passions and even gentlemanly consideration. I'd made a pact with the lady to keep my distance, and now I had wantonly broken it.

"Tell me to stop," I murmured, either daring or begging her (even I wasn't sure which) to do something that I could not.

"I am unequal to it," she breathed, leaning into my chest.

I gave a half-choked laugh. "May God have mercy on us."

"For good or ill, my love, I fear we have traveled beyond God's mercy."

I froze at these words that seemed to spring from the voice but not the mind of Ada Quicksilver.

Freeing my hands from her dress, I took hold of her shoulders and turned her. "Ada?"

She pressed the front of her gown to her chest. Her eyes were wide and bright. "That was not I," she said.

I took her hand and pressed it between mine. "I understand," I assured her. She was not as accustomed to these invasions as I was. "Do you know what she means by it?"

She stared at me bleakly. "A long desolation has stretched between them," she said, and I could hear that desolation in her voice, as though it had traveled across a windswept English moor. "They have lived here together for centuries, but having lost their mortal forms, they have been unable to experience more earthly, blooded passions. This is why they reach for each other through *us*."

To hear her talk so openly of "earthly passions" was enough to stir my blood again, but I was determined to be master of these impulses. "And why does she say they have traveled beyond God's mercy?" I asked.

She frowned. "I'm not sure. But I think because they are immortal and drifting." Her gaze, too, had taken on a drifting quality as she spoke, and it troubled me. She stared beyond me as if she was seeing something that I could not. I worried about her communing more closely with her ancestress.

"They are two of only a few Danaan with surviving descendants," she continued. "Cliona clings to her humanity still, and to her bond with the daughter she lost." I noted the flash of some new understanding in her eyes, and her focus returned to my face. "Diarmuid exiled his people not just out of love for her, but also to assuage his guilty conscience. His decision to gift her with immortality separated her forever from her daughter."

So relieved was I over the return of my Miss Q—and so struck by the passionate concern in her expression—I gathered her in my arms. I wanted her so desperately, I felt it would be the death of me. I wanted to climb beneath the furs and coverlets heaped on my ancestor's bed, make love to her, and sleep an age in her arms, the rest of the world be damned.

I had no way of knowing whether this was my desire or his.

If anything, her disclosures had reaffirmed my instinct to preserve some boundary between us—between our ancestors—for as long as I possibly could.

"Let us join the others," I murmured, "and we will see what aid they may offer."

# OF TWO MINDS

## ADA

The earl donned a simple dark tunic and breeches and then watched, barely suppressing a smile, as I tried to subdue my hair. In the end, I settled for a loose plait coiled at the base of my neck.

"I suppose it will do," I murmured.

"You are beautiful," said he, "and endlessly fascinating. Had I such a remarkable feature, I would leave it wild for the world to admire."

I laughed. "Had you been 'admired' by the world so often as I, you might hesitate in such a course. But you are kind, my lord." I continued to use his title out of habit and also, perhaps, due to uncertainty about the nature of our relationship. But even to my own ears, the words sounded like a caress, kissed with tenderness.

Smiling at last, the earl replied, "Shall we go?"

In truth, I was loath to leave this sanctuary. The path ahead was unknown, and I longed with all my body and being for the intimacy we had aborted. "I suppose we'd better," I replied.

"I believe we will be safe in this place," he said. "But let us keep close to each other."

We made our way back down the passage and along the route Caer had followed when she left us. We soon found ourselves in a central chamber with a large banquet table. Four people were seated at the table, but what first caught my attention was the tapestry that ran the length of the wall opposite the table. It depicted two figures in a close embrace in some woodland bower, which reminded me of the tapestry in Diarmuid's chamber. I found I could not shift my gaze from the lovers—and soon discovered that the couple bore a striking resemblance to the earl and me.

Heat crept from my cheeks down my throat and across my chest.

"If it isn't the Bog King of Connacht," said the earl suddenly, and I felt him stiffen. "What is *your* business here?"

My gaze fell from the tapestry and alighted on a familiar face—and an angry one.

"Duncan!" I cried, stepping forward. He had stood up, his brow so dark I anticipated a rumble of thunder. And indeed, there was lightning in his look—his eyes were bright and strange, reminding me of Diarmuid.

"Finvara, please sit," the lady of the house urged.

She seemed to be speaking to Duncan, and I glanced between them, confused. According to lore, Finvara was king of the fairies, and he resided in the west of Ireland. In the stories about him, the fairies went to war with the ancient Irish, lost the war, and then were said to be exiled to an underground world that was probably Faery.

But what had he to do with Duncan? And what was it that had set Edward off?

Turning to question him, I could see by the light in his eyes that Diarmuid was ascendant.

*An ancient rivalry,* whispered my ancestress.

Could it be that Duncan, like Edward and me, was a descendant of Faery? I glanced at him again, this time noting that beside him sat the resplendent queen of two worlds, Isolde, looking bored and annoyed.

"Must we?" she muttered.

"We must," replied Duncan, "if he will begin by insulting me."

"Please," said Caer, glancing at the earl and me. "Won't you join us?"

As we moved to take the seats she indicated, I discovered that my eye had greatly deceived me about the tapestry. The scene depicted a sword fight between two men. How could I have been so mistaken about its subject?

Then I realized that the tapestry's combatants were the very men now bristling at each other across the banquet table.

"Welcome, friends and allies." This greeting came from the man who occupied the raised seat at the head of the table, and it had a dampening effect on the ireful looks passing between Edward and Duncan.

The man's countenance was kindly. His dark hair was streaked with white, and he wore a circlet of some plain, lusterless metal. But a large moonstone was set in the center of the band at his forehead. His eyes, like the stone, were a nearly white shade of gray. Caer sat at the place beside him, and I realized that this must be Angus, Diarmuid's foster father and the Danaan chieftain at Brú na Bóinne.

Caer poured an amber liquid from a pitcher into two goblets and handed them to us. The vessel felt strangely light, and the metal caused a slight tingling in my fingertips. I placed it on the table before me.

"Thank you, my lord," said Edward, sounding himself again. "And my lady."

Glancing at Isolde, he continued, "I must confess that I am both confused and surprised to find us all gathered here."

"We have assembled to discuss our plan for battle," said the queen, frowning at him. "Had you done as I asked, you'd know that. But the important thing is, you're here. I thought you'd gone mad entirely, jumping out the window like that."

"I'm not sure that I haven't," replied the earl. "But we're here, primarily, because we've caught a creature who's sworn fealty to the Fomorian king, and he has told us of a plot to spoil Ireland's potato crop. We foiled his attempt, but he has indicated there are others in progress—perhaps directed at other crops—and that they are too far along to be stopped. I assume this to be the blight you spoke of at Kildamhnait."

"Potatoes?" asked Duncan—or Finvara—sounding dubious.

"We caught him carrying a sack of diseased potatoes through a Gap gate," I explained. "We inspected and disposed of them ourselves. If other servants of Balor crossed successfully into Ireland, many people could starve."

"Many Irishmen *will* die," agreed Finvara. "'Tis but a foregone conclusion now. We are here to talk of the battle to come."

"It could be that something may yet be done," I countered, holding his gaze. If Duncan was also Finvara, our situation had been greatly complicated. The Finvara I knew from the lore certainly had no love for the Irish, despite his fabled penchant for mortal women. Was it possible to appeal to his Irish counterpart?

"Think of your family, Duncan," I pleaded. "Your brothers and their families. Perhaps they would survive, but what of your father's tenants?"

Finvara stared at me as he considered, and I prayed that my words might wake his descendant. But after a moment, he shook his head. "These ideas—they are cut from the same cloth as those that brought about our exile. I, for one, have had enough of it.

For you, lady, I will fight for Ireland, but it is not my business to save her people."

I detected only traces of Edward's charming and high-spirited cousin in the countenance of the man sitting opposite me. It appeared that when it came to their descendants, the male immortals among us were more interested in conquest than in alliance. I could only hope that in time, Duncan and Finvara, like Edward and Diarmuid, might at least agree to an uneasy truce.

"Isn't it possible we might find a way to stop the Fomorians without the need for war?" the earl asked reasonably. "If they are somehow foiled in their attempt to reduce our numbers beforehand, mightn't they think twice?"

Finvara's fist came down suddenly on the table, making the goblets jump. "*You* are the reason for *all* of this. If no one else here will say it, I will. And I'm not interested in your proposals!"

The bench we were seated on quaked as Edward lunged across the table, knotting his fist in Finvara's shirt. "Blasted bog-crawler!" he growled, and Finvara took a swing at him, just grazing his chin.

"SIT. DOWN." Angus's deep voice rumbled through the hall. "Both of you."

The combatants gave each other a shove and stumbled back from the table, seething.

I stared at them, baffled. *This enmity is about the exile?*

*And a woman who made her choice,* came the answer.

Somehow, I knew which woman, and I had a suspicion about the choice. More complications.

"Sit," repeated Angus, and the men obeyed. "These decisions belong to the four of you," he continued. "For Caer and me, the time has passed." He glanced at his wife, and the look she gave him was loving and contented, yet tinged with melancholy. When Angus returned his gaze to the rest of us, he added, "But I would encourage you not to waste time playing out old dramas."

"What is 'old' to timeless beings?" growled Finvara. "We are as we ever were."

"Upon that, we can agree," the earl muttered.

"In some ways, immortality is a curse," Caer agreed. "Without birth or death, there can be no true change."

"Our hall is host to beings of two minds," Angus continued. "The Irishmen among you will, of course, desire to preserve their race. You of Faery will not abide a Fomorian takeover of Ireland. Some motives are more complicated." He looked from Edward to Duncan. "If you cannot strive together, none will get what he wants. You will squabble and fight and accomplish nothing. It is as simple as that."

He eyed each of his guests in turn, allowing his words to work on them. A faint smirk curled Queen Isolde's lips, and her gaze rested briefly on me. Her disdain for our masculine companions was apparent, and I could at least empathize with her impatience at their behavior.

"As for this business of potatoes," Angus continued, "the men and women trapped under the bogs of this country fall under your banner, King Finvara, do they not?"

Finvara gave a short nod. "They do."

Edward—or, more likely, Diarmuid—gave a snort of quiet laughter, and I kicked him hard under the table.

"If the ground has indeed been poisoned, might not their aid be enlisted?" asked our host.

Finvara, after considering for a moment, gave another nod. "It's possible. They have communed with the earth for centuries and are sensitive to disturbances." He lifted his goblet and drained it. I thought I caught a softening in his expression, and he sank deeper into his seat before continuing, "Through the ages, many instruments of murder have been cast into the bog, only to be found the next morning lying on bare patches of ground in plain sight."

I understood now what Angus and Finvara were referring to: bog bodies. Several had been discovered by farmers cutting peat, or turf, the fuel used in Irish hearth fires. The bog waters were acidic and prevented the natural process of decay. In essence, the bodies were mummified. But what these two men seemed to be suggesting was that they were not entirely *dead.*

"You know how to find these bog men, my lord?" I asked Finvara.

His blue eyes, bright with the light of immortality, fixed on me. "Aye, lady. But it is you yourself who should speak to them, so they understand what they must look for. I will serve as your escort."

The earl stiffened beside me, and I, too, understood this trick—or perhaps it was Cliona who understood. At its heart, it was a bid for the lady's companionship and attention. But it was also a compromise—or perhaps, in a less charitable light, a kind of bribe. He would help us, but he expected something in return.

My companionship was an easy price. My ancestress and I had a stake in this game, and both she and Finvara had a connection with the dead. And while a request from the king might carry force, it would certainly lack the passion of my own.

Movement behind him caught my eye, and I stared at the tapestry as the lines of the figures in the scene softened and disappeared, some colors fading while others intensified. New lines were drawn as the tapestry reorganized itself, and the scene now depicted Finvara and me, galloping on a great white horse across a wasted landscape. Did it foretell the future, or merely reflect the topic of conversation at the table?

My eyes returned to the king. "Yes," I replied. "Of course I will accompany you."

"*No.*" It was Diarmuid's voice that now echoed in the hall.

I turned to meet his fiery gaze. "My lord," I insisted, "I must. Do you not see?"

I pleaded silently with him, and at length he turned to glower across the table at the king. "Then I will go too."

"You will *not*," interjected Queen Isolde, stern and incredulous. "You have warriors to command, as do I. We have strategy to plan. Have you even *called* your fighters? Broken the seal?"

"You do not command me," growled the Danaan warrior.

"But I do command the body you inhabit, and he shall *not* defy me in this."

Before Diarmuid could retort, Caer interjected, "Queen Maeve is right, my son. Even as we speak, the minutes slip away from us. We must begin this battle on our own terms and not wait for our enemies to attack. You are two of Faery's most renowned generals. You must set the course for battle and entrust these other concerns to your allies."

"Let us waste no time," Finvara agreed. The light of triumph was barely, halfheartedly concealed behind Duncan's clear eyes. "I must rouse my own court to readiness as well."

"The Danaan can expect the aid of the fairies?" said Angus.

"I can speak for most," replied Finvara. "But some will have allied themselves with Balor. The Sluagh most certainly will stand no friend to us."

The Sluagh was said to be a host of the restless dead. And there were other fairies more associated with evil doings than with good—redcaps like Billy, for example, and the púca. Aughisky, the water horse, had a dark reputation, though she appeared to answer to Diarmuid.

"Sounds like a failure of leadership to me," Diarmuid observed dryly, and I held my breath.

"The fairies are fickle," replied Caer before Finvara could respond to the taunt, "and their alliances ephemeral. King Finvara is to be commended for keeping what peace he could."

Finvara nodded in acknowledgment of the praise. "We shall

first return to Ireland and speak with Máine Mór, the bog man. Dana knows I would be pleased to live out the rest of eternity without traveling again under the flag of that O'Malley woman, but if we don't, we'll lose time in the journey to Connacht."

"I may be able to help with that," I said. "Unless the others have need of him, we can take Billy Millstone. If there is a Gap gate near our destination, he can guide us there."

"Billy?" said Finvara, frowning. "What's he got to do with this?"

I explained that Billy was the redcap we had intercepted at the Gap gate.

"The old wretch," growled the king. "Aye, there is a Gap gate at Knock Ma. The bog man resides an easy distance from there."

I knew of Knock Ma, or at least the Ireland version of it. There were important ruins there, said by folklorist William Wilde to be associated with the first major Tuatha De Danaan battle. More to the point, the stronghold of King Finvara was said to have been at Knock Ma.

"Gather your things, my lady," said Finvara, rising. "Warm clothing, a weapon if you have one."

"Hold a moment," said Angus, his gaze on me. "What of the banshees, lady? Will they take a side in this conflict?"

The Danaan chieftain, fair minded and wise though he obviously was, presented an intimidating personage, and I hesitated in giving an answer I knew to be insufficient. But before I could inform him of my uncertainty on this point, I received guidance from my ancestress.

*The banshees will follow their queen.* I repeated this answer to Angus, sounding much more convinced of it than I felt.

Angus nodded, satisfied, and before rising from the table, I glanced from the corner of my eye at the still-smoldering immortal on my right, willing him to keep his peace.

I made a small curtsy to Angus and Caer. "If you'll excuse me, my lord and lady."

"Travel safely," said Caer kindly.

"Finvara will take care of you," her husband added.

I moved slowly away, more than half expecting one of Diarmuid's eruptions in my wake.

In truth, I could sympathize with his unhappiness at this turn of events. Leaving Edward at this time was the last thing I would have chosen, but it seemed our stars had other ideas.

On my return to Diarmuid's chamber, I made another search through drawers and chests until I'd found suitable items for the journey—a fur-lined cloak, a pair of sturdy boots, a less ostentatious gown that had chain mail sewn into the sleeves, and a leather bodice that might deflect a blade.

I was struggling with the laces of the emerald gown when suddenly the door slammed shut behind me.

I spun around. "Edward!" I cried in surprise.

He crossed the room like a rainsquall, halting a few feet before me. "Promise me you will return when this business is completed. Do *not* follow Finvara back to his court."

"What is it that frightens you, Diarmuid?" I demanded, unable to keep a note of scorn from my voice.

"It is *I,* Ada. Edward. And I don't want you following him back to Knock Ma, because he's a woman-stealer."

"*Diarmuid* has told you this?" I demanded. I knew, of course, of Finvara's reputation—the story most frequently told of him had to do with kidnapping the most beautiful woman in Ireland from the home of her betrothed. But it was a *severe* case of pot and kettle, and I resented the earl's sudden bluster. Which may explain why I tried to rouse him further by asking, "Are you sure this isn't about Duncan O'Malley?"

The earl's eyes widened and his nostrils flared. He stepped

closer, until the toes of our shoes almost touched. "At this point," he replied, "there is no difference."

I gave up wrestling the fastenings of my gown and drew myself up to my full height, little good that it did when he had a half-foot advantage. "Do you fear that he will hold me against my will, my lord, or is it *I* whom you do not trust?"

His hands gripped my arms. "Why do you test me?" he demanded, and I wondered at this change in him. But I could not expect him to share his mind with the Danaan warrior and not be affected.

"Why do *you* not answer the question?" I replied with no quaver in my voice. "Do you not trust me?"

"We have no *arrangement*, Ada," he said, as if this explained everything. "You are not my wife, or even my mistress."

"I am glad that you have remembered it."

The argument was pointless, but my blood was rising, and not only in anger. A kind of energy swelled between us, like a gas lamp flaring to life.

"There was a time before all this when you were less indifferent to me," he said, bending over me so I was forced to tip my head back.

He was baiting me. We were baiting each other. Which of us would first feel the hook?

"You once asked me to fortify you against the charms of another," he continued, his thumbs hotly rubbing the insides of my arms.

The loosened gown had slipped down my shoulders, revealing the visible quaking of my chest. I followed his eye there. My heart was near frantic with desire, and a tremor entered my voice as I replied, "And were you satisfied with the result, my lord?"

He made a dark rumbling sound in his throat. "Indeed, I was."

I swallowed past the thick, hot pressure in my throat. "Then why not test its efficacy again?"

His hand came to the side of my neck, tilting my jaw, and he covered my mouth with his. Heat, hunger, even anger—I took all of it into myself through his lips and tongue. With his free hand, he yanked loose the laces of my gown and pulled down the bodice.

## EDWARD

Bending to her chest, I dipped my head and closed my mouth over one breast. Opening my lips wide, I took as much of the sweet, supple flesh into my mouth as I could. The hard, dark pebble I woke with a thrust of my tongue—the breath hissed between her teeth and she slackened in my arms.

I *was* mad. Mad with lust, mad with fear, mad with the impotence of a lover overruled by cooler heads.

Curling my hands under her buttocks, I lifted her, tucking her legs around my waist, resting her full weight atop my throbbing cock. I took three steps, luxuriating in the pressure and slow friction, before tossing her onto the bed.

Her arms and legs splayed as she fell, and before she could recover a more dignified position, I grabbed the hem of her gown and shoved it above her waist.

I watched her face as I reached down to loosen my breeches, and instead of offering protests or scooting away from me, she issued a challenge with her eyes and slid her legs farther apart. Taking her thighs in my hands, I dragged her toward the edge of the bed and fell on top of her. Reaching between her legs, I parted her silken flesh with one finger, uttering a groan as it slid inside her. I could lose myself in that warmth and wetness and never miss the light of day.

I added a second finger, and she made a sound halfway between cry and plea. The muscles of her sex closed over me.

I teased her only a moment more before pulling my hand free.

Then I sank my cock into her until my abdomen was pressed up against her mound.

Taking hold of my shoulders, she wriggled until I understood that she wanted me on the bed. When we had managed this reversal, she sat up, straddling me, the green gown pooling about her waist. Thus mounted, she seemed to hesitate, as if unsure what came next. I took hold of her hips, grinding her sex down hard against me. Her head tipped back, and a long feminine moan worked its slow, delicious way out of her.

Hands bracing against my chest, she began to rock under her own steam, the center of her pleasure grinding against me, trailing moisture across my flesh. Her swollen breasts rolled with the violence of her movement, and my hands were now free to knead them, drawing from her a piercing cry, and a stronger spasm of contracting muscles.

I was not equal to this sensual attack. I could not continue to man the battlements. Gripping her hips again, I held her in place and thrust as hard as I could—*one, two, three, four, five*— deepening my seat with every motion, voicing a shuddering moan with my release. Her body went rigid, the muscles between her legs wringing pleasure from me, and she gave a final cry of surrender before collapsing, breathless, onto my chest.

My sense of relief at her weight resting on me, and the physical contentment of sated desire, held at bay my sense of alarm at her determination to leave me—to flee from my protection into danger, and in the care of a rival. This was a moment I would wish to hold on to forever.

On this subject, my ancestor and I were in accord. He did not trust the king, and I did not trust my cousin. Duncan would never harm her, I knew, but he had made it quite clear that should the lady feel mishandled by me, he would know how to treat her better. These possessive impulses were alien to me, and I was not proud of them.

For now, I must content myself with this victory of the flesh. She had met and matched my desire, and we had not been overcome by powerful ancestors. Diarmuid had kept to the shadows, and I believed I understood why. Only in feeling unthreatened by his presence could I give in to the demands of my body, which had only grown more insistent since the lady first gave herself to me. And if he could not be with Cliona, Ada was the next best thing. I should have been sickened by such a thought. And I might later be. But while she was here, nothing could disturb the warm contentment flowing through me.

*You understand nothing,* came his voice in my mind. *For me, she is Cliona. And I was not about to send her away without a reminder of what burns between us.*

So my ancestor's motive had been the same as my own. Did Cliona love Finvara, I wondered? Had the choice been real, or merely a case of unrequited affection?

*Only the lady knows,* came the answer. I did not find it reassuring, though I did consider it a point in his favor that he had not compelled the information from her, sorely as he must have been tempted.

*Had I, I would have lost her forever.*

Closing my eyes, I stole a few more moments of uncomplicated enjoyment of my mortal lover's scent, her soft skin, and her sweet sighs of contentment.

"The king waits for me," she murmured.

I coiled my arms more tightly around her. "He'll wait a moment more."

"I would not choose to …" She trailed off, and I stroked her back, encouraging her to continue. Her body rose under my hand as she breathed deeply and said, "I would not choose to part from you just now."

My heart sang with relief. "Ah, love," I replied, kissing the top of her head, "nor would I. You needn't go, you know. He can most certainly manage the errand on his own."

"I think you know that's not why I agreed to go."

I sighed, feeling heavy and resigned. "You agreed because you thought he wouldn't go otherwise."

She gave no reply, but none was necessary.

"I don't trust him, Ada," I said. "Nor does Diarmuid."

"I'm not sure that I do, either. But somewhere within him resides Duncan, and I trust *him*."

I laughed dryly. "Duncan, I assure you, is a thorough rogue *and* an opportunist. But he would protect you, of that we already have evidence."

"I shall try to call him back to us," she replied. "I think that eventually he will find his strength, as you have."

"Ada," I said, and she raised her head to look at me. Mesmerized by her clear green eyes, I brushed a lock of silver away from her face. "I hope you can forgive my brutish behavior. I hope you understand that I am not entirely myself."

"I do, my lord."

When first we met, this courtesy title had made me feel all too keenly the distance between our stations. But for me, it had now taken on sensual connotations, and hearing it from her lips never failed to warm my blood.

"I hope you also understand how ..." My courage failed me on the word "dear," and I finished with "... how important you are to me."

She parted her lips to reply, but I continued. "I do not ask for assurances or declarations. I merely wanted you to know it before you go. My most fervent desire is that you return safely ... whether or not you return to *me*."

She raised her eyebrows, and she touched her thumb to my

lower lip. "Return to you I shall," she said softly. "As expeditiously as possible."

Another warm current of relief coursed through me, and I took her hand, kissing the palm. "Then let us reunite you with your gown and send you on your way so that you may return all the sooner."

*And before the Danaan warrior finds the strength to brutishly revoke my acceptance of this distasteful arrangement.*

# THE BOG KING

## ADA

I fought a choking tightness in my throat as Edward snugged the leather corset against my spine, his warm breath tickling the hair at the nape of my neck. As the time for leaving approached, I began to second-guess my decision. I had ever felt safe in the earl's company, but this fairy king and even his descendant were relatively unknown.

More to the point, however, was the strong attachment I had formed to Edward.

"I shall be the worse for the loss of your counsel," he said.

I turned and took his hands in mine. "Trust yourself, my lord. Your heart and your intentions are ever in the right place, whether you realize it or not."

He smiled and pulled me into his arms. "If you believe in me, I must surely believe in myself. For you are the cleverest person I know."

I laughed. "We must believe in each other."

"I believe in *you* unquestionably. Only promise me that should you find yourself in need, you will get word to me somehow."

I nodded against his chest, and he held me tighter.

"And trust that if an undue length of time should pass, I will come for you. Never feel that you are abandoned."

He released me then and retrieved Roup's spear from its resting place against the weapon wall. "You're certain you'd prefer this to the shieldmaiden's sword?"

I reached for the spear. "I am. I wouldn't know how to manage such a powerful weapon."

"Dare I hope you've had some instruction in self-defense?"

"Certainly," I replied, laughing again. "Lovelace heartily embraces the idea of physical education for young women. I'd not call myself formidable, and never in my wildest imaginings did I suspect that these skills might one day be put to use, but I am not entirely a novice."

There came a knock on the chamber door. "My lady," called Duncan's voice from the other side, "I've come to collect you if you're ready."

The earl muttered an oath, and I reached up and touched my fingers to his lips. *I love you*, I thought but did not speak, for I could not be sure whose thought it was.

Then I bent and collected my cloak and crossed to the door.

"Dana guard and keep the jewel of my heart," he said as I opened the door. Diarmuid, I assumed, for this poetry was not like the earl. As my eyes fell on the king, the Danaan warrior added, "And the battle crow take Finvara should the slightest harm come to you."

"Only Diarmuid would send off his beloved with a curse," muttered the king. "Come, my lady."

I glanced once more at Edward, and he watched, grim-faced, as we departed.

We left the manor house and liberated Billy Millstone from his guardians. He appeared not to have suffered in their care. And in fact, when he took note of my new companion—whose sword was drawn as a precaution—I would bet my small fortune that he would have returned to the woodland fairies rather than proceed with us.

"So you've cast off the old oath and taken a new," King Finvara accused.

The redcap screwed up his courage and glowered defiantly. "Billy sees that the lady and he have it in common."

Finvara raised the sword to knock the redcap a blow with the pommel, but I stayed his arm. "Let it pass, my lord."

He lowered the sword but growled, "How soon you forget the kindness you've been shown by your king and by your Danaan ancestors."

"Is it not the fault of *they* that we are exiled from the sun?" demanded Billy. "From the moon and stars? Is Billy to be blamed for castin' his lot with those as would return them to us?"

Glancing up at the sky, I noticed that the light had not changed at all during the hours we spent inside the house of Angus. Was Faery cursed, then, to exist as no more than a shadow of the living, breathing world?

"Has Faery not always been like this?" I asked. "Was it caused by the exile?"

Finvara looked surprised by the question. I suppose he assumed that as Cliona, I would know.

"Faery is as it ever was," the king replied. "But the fairies are more tied to Ireland and the Irish than to the Danaan, so exile has been hardest for them."

"Are fairies not *descended* from the Danaan?"

"Aye, but their ties to their forefathers severed when the immortals departed for Faery. They are soulless creatures, drawn to the light and dark in men. Without it, they have no compass." He looked pointedly at Billy. "Their loyalty is transient. They don't always make choices that align with their interests."

The redcap's lip curled, and he spat on the ground.

"Billy here would poison the Irish to suit the Fomorians," the king continued, "never thinking how he shall exist or occupy his time in a world without men."

"S'pose that's nobody's business but Billy's," grumbled the redcap, but I could see a glint of uncertainty in his bulging eyes.

I began to see what a heavy price *all* the races of Faery had paid for Diarmuid's actions. As we continued to the river, I found some sympathy in my heart for Billy Millstone.

The little copper-hulled tug carried us to the Gap gate at Knock Ma, and we emerged inside a mossy cave concealed behind a waterfall. I used Cliona's gift to stop the waters, but we could have managed it without supernatural aid—though we would certainly have been soaked to the skin. I asked Billy whether all the Gap gates were concealed by water. He was inclined to be rude, but one threatening glance from Finvara was enough to loosen his tongue.

The Gap gates were not so much concealed by water as *enabled* by it, he told me. Water was sacred to the druids—conjurers of "old magic"—and it was also important in alchemy. Billy had a meandering turn of mind, but I believed I understood him to say that Diarmuid's seal—or "Diarmuid's curse," as he called it—was old magic that covered Ireland like a blanket, its stitches straining in sacred places like this, where the boundaries preferred to remain fluid. And alchemy, as Diarmuid had already told us, had been used to establish the Gap gates. When I asked him how those who could not part the waters accessed the gates that were submerged, he simply replied, "By swallowin' a great deal of water." Thus it became clear to me why Ireland was not already overrun. And gave me hope that the servants of Balor were not yet so far ahead of us as Diarmuid believed.

"This gate is relatively easy to pass through," I said to Finvara. "Perhaps we should set a guard."

The king nodded. "I will give the order, my lady. Bear with me a few moments while I return to my fortress at Knock Ma." He turned to Billy. "It's time you returned home, redcap."

Billy backed away with a startled yelp, but Finvara collared him, and the two of them disappeared, leaving naught but faint green outlines of their forms hanging in the air. I stood alone in the gloaming, watching the vapor dissipate. If I correctly understood Edward, had he and I allowed ourselves to be overtaken by our ancestors, as Duncan appeared to have been, we, too, could flit between Faery and Ireland.

I wondered now about my ancestress, who had been quiet since I left the house of Angus and Caer. Before I could seek her with my thoughts, the king reappeared.

"Come, my lady," he said, offering his arm. "The stones are slippery."

"What will happen to Billy?" I asked.

"My servants will watch over him until I decide what's to be done with him."

"I can't think why I should," I said, "but I find myself with a desire to urge mercy, my lord."

Finvara smiled and folded his hand over mine. "Because you have a kind heart, my lady. And for your sake, he shall be spared."

"Thank you. I hope that we won't regret it."

We climbed a stone stairway, its edges worn and smoothed by time, and emerged from the grotto into an ancient forest. Naked oak branches traced stark lines against the winter-gray sky, but emerald moss covered the stones and tree detritus that littered the forest floor. Dry leaves crunched under our feet, and the air was biting and damp. I pulled the fur-lined cloak closer about my shoulders.

"There are but few remains of Knock Ma in Ireland," said

Finvara, indicating the circular ruin of a building. "But this one will serve as shelter for the night. You're certain you wouldn't prefer a warm, dry bed? My court would be pleased to welcome you."

I would have *infinitely* preferred a warm, dry bed, but the earl had warned me away from the court of the fairy king.

"I'm sure I will be comfortable here, my lord," I replied.

The light was failing, and I suddenly felt weighted down by fatigue. It occurred to me that I'd not had a full night's rest since my last evening under Mrs. Maguire's roof. And even *that* night's rest—which now seemed a lifetime ago—had been disturbed by excitement and trepidation about the next morning's journey.

"What day is this?" I asked, considering the timelessness of the place we had left. I also recalled that we had *lost* time in the voyage aboard the *Queen of Connacht*.

"The evening after the ball at Kildamhnait," said Finvara as he moved about the ruin, gathering wood. He glanced up at me and smiled, reminding me of Duncan. "Happy Christmas."

I stared at him. I had forgotten entirely. "Happy Christmas," I replied, and the words stirred a longing for things currently out of reach: hot meals, warm firesides, mulled wine … loved ones. In recent years, I had spent my holidays in London with other orphaned young women, but the academy was festive and even homey at this time of year. My academic advisor was something of an orphan himself, his aged mother still living in Ireland, and he always invited us to his "garret," as he called it, for Christmas tea. His garret was, in fact, a high-ceilinged attic chamber in the history building, with windows overlooking the little wilderness of a park across the lane. He possessed shelves full of wondrous old books, and on most winter days, a cheerful fire blazed on his hearth, with reading chairs cozying round. I couldn't help thinking how astonished he would be at my current situation. I wondered whether I would ever have the chance to tell him about it.

But my current pang, I must confess, had more to do with the earl and the Christmas I had expected we'd spend together among his relations.

I moved to join Finvara in gathering wood. Everything was so damp, I had my doubts it would burn, but I tossed what I could find onto the pile he was accumulating inside the ruin.

The fact that the fairy king recalled it was Christmas suggested a closer communication with Duncan than was apparent, as I assumed that Finvara himself was not a Christian.

"Do you remember leaving Kildamhnait, my lord?" I asked him by way of opening the topic of his descendant.

"Aye," he replied.

"You left after we did? Diarmuid and I?"

"Aye. The queen was anxious to recover the Danaan warrior. And I—"

He broke off suddenly, and I stood and studied him in the dim light. "Yes?"

He met my gaze, his expression uneasy.

"Are you well, my lord?"

He frowned. "Miss Quicksilver?"

I stepped closer. "Duncan?"

His gaze dropped, and he shook his head. "Duncan O'Malley is my descendant."

"Yes," I said, hiding my disappointment.

He began arranging the wood for our fire.

"I'm curious, my lord, why you chose Duncan. He has three older brothers, and a father who is an earl. Are they not all your descendants?"

"There is less choice in it than might appear. He is the most like me, and therefore, we are more connected." He glanced up, adding, "And it was he who led me to *you*, my lady."

*Oh, dear.*

"My acquaintance with Duncan has been brief," I said carefully, "but I do esteem him. He has been very kind to me."

His eyebrows rose. "Because he has been captivated by you." I was grateful when he returned his attention to his fire preparations, but then he added, "A predicament I can appreciate."

As I considered how best to respond to this declaration, the king flicked open his hand, and a white flame sprouted from his palm. He held his hand over the woodpile, and the flame slid down onto the wood.

"How extraordinary!" I breathed.

"Conjuring a fairy light is the easiest thing in the world," he replied. "But without fuel, it provides no warmth."

The small flame licked at the wood and grew larger. Once the fire was blazing, the king opened his traveling bag, and out of it came a Christmas feast. Or so it seemed to me at least, as I had not eaten since the night before. There were apples and cheese, spiced and candied nuts, sturdy brown bread with butter, scones, and even a bottle of brandy.

"How did you come by all this?" I asked, laughing.

"The queen insisted we pack provisions before traveling to Brú na Bóinne," he said. "We were unsure how far our journey would carry us. Inconveniently, these earthen forms require sustenance."

My stomach chose that moment to rumble, and the king laughed and arranged the food on a cloth on the ground. "Please, my lady," he urged, pouring brandy into two metal cups. "This will warm you."

"Are there no meals in Faery, then?" I asked, taking a cup and a slice of bread.

He gulped his brandy. "Oh, there are. Like nothing you've ever seen. But citizens of Faery don't require them with the regularity of mortals. In Faery, we feast when it suits us. Some feasts last for six days and nights at a stretch, breaking only for the holy day, when even the fairies generally rest. But Faery fare will not sustain a mortal for long."

Before I could inquire further, I heard light echoing laughter, like children playing in the distance. Rising, I moved quickly to the wall of the ruin and peered through a wide chink between the stones. Above the rim of the grotto from which we had climbed, golden lights floated like fireflies toward the sky. Then a troop of creatures, their exotic little faces lit strangely from within, swarmed over the edge and scrambled across the ground.

"My lord!" I called softly.

I felt him move close behind me to peer out through the crack between the stones. "They're celebrating Christmas and know not that their king has spied them crossing out of Faery."

Apparently, construction of the Gap gate had not disturbed the original fairy door.

"Shall we keep our peace and see what they will do?" he asked.

I nodded, and together we watched. They were the merriest band of creatures I'd ever seen. Forming a ring around the structure where we were sheltering, they flew, tumbled, and skipped in a circle, playing instruments and singing a most discordant but jolly tune. Their dress ranged from cloaks of muted forest hues to brilliantly dyed coats and gowns, and most of their small bodies had insect wings. In skin tone, they were as varied as eggshells: some pale, some tan, some brown, and a few verging on green or blue.

"How extraordinary," I found myself repeating.

"Indeed," murmured the king, and his low voice started a tickle in my ear. I realized now that I could feel his breath on the back of my neck.

Clearing my throat, I said, "I am surprised to find they celebrate Christmas."

He laughed quietly, and again I could feel it on my skin. "They will celebrate any occasion, including funerals—you can see their influence in the Irish wake. But fairies love Christmas primarily because Irishmen do."

A clearer understanding of the bond he'd spoken of between the Irish and the gentlefolk began to dawn on me.

Then, as suddenly as they had appeared, the fairies gathered in a knot and swept right over the rim of the grotto with small cries of alarm.

"Have we frightened them?" I asked.

"No," replied the king. "Something is coming."

From farther down the hillside, I could just see a group of figures moving toward us, and my heart skipped. The waning moon peeked through the clouds, throwing a pale light over them.

"Keening women," said the king.

And so again they had found me. I watched them moving up the hill. As with mortal women, their legs propelled them forward, yet it seemed to me their bare feet did not touch the ground. When they reached the ruin, they settled on the stones outside and appeared content to remain there. There were twice as many of them as before.

"What is it they wait for?" I wondered aloud.

"Your command, lady," murmured Finvara.

I gave a bleak laugh. "I know not what to ask of them."

The king hesitated, as if considering, and then said, "That may change." I heard him moving away. "Let us finish our meal and take our rest," he urged. "We'll travel to the village of Gallagh at first light, and there we'll find the bog man Máine Mór."

"How long is the journey?"

"About ten miles. We'll need a carriage, or at least a horse."

I remembered the white horse I had seen in the tapestry at Brú na Bóinne.

*Enbarr,* whispered Cliona, startling me.

"Enbarr?" I repeated. The name was familiar, but I could not recall its significance.

Finvara, assuming I had been speaking to him, replied, "An excellent idea, my lady. She'll make the journey faster than any fairy steed."

*The horse of my foster father, Manannán. He lends her to no one, but he will to me.*

*But how?* I wondered.

I was carried then toward the doorway of the ruin—I say "carried" because my movements were not directed by my own will. It was strange and disorienting to feel my limbs move under someone else's command. As a very young woman, while riding on a crowded horse tram in London, I had discovered I possessed an irrational fear of restricted movement—the panic I had experienced that day was similar to what I felt now, and I found I was holding my breath.

*Forgive me,* whispered my ancestress. *I can help you if I may speak to them.*

*Yes,* I agreed, letting my breath out slowly as I willed my limbs to soften.

I had lost sense of language since Cliona revealed herself. At times, I was aware that those around me were speaking one of the forms of Irish, but I understood them, and they seemed to understand me. As I stepped outside the doorway, I spoke Irish to one of the banshees, a young woman dressed in gray.

"Good woman, find a sea bird to carry a message to Manannán. I have need of the white mare."

The banshee bowed her head and vanished into the shadows.

I returned to the fire, and the king and I finished our meal and cleared away the remains. I confess that by now my eyes were closing of their own accord, and it did not go unnoticed.

"Rest now, lady," murmured the king.

Rolling his traveling cloak into a pillow, he offered it to me, and I was too exhausted to protest. It smelled of fir, heather, and a spice I could not place, as had the coat Duncan loaned me on Keem Strand. After that, I noticed nothing more.

I slept a black sleep. No dreams, no restlessness, no starting at sounds in the night. I woke at the first gray light to the timid song of the winter thrushes in the lacework of branches overhead.

Finvara stooped over the fire, stirring the coals to life. He bade me good morning, and we breakfasted on what remained of last night's supper. After, I made my way down to the waterfall to wash my hands and face and drink the cool, sweet water. When I returned to the ruin, I found Finvara outside, speaking in a gentle voice to a great horse. Her coat was creamy white flecked with caramel, like sea foam, and her mane hung long and straight like a woman's hair.

Low though the tones of Finvara's voice were, the magnificent mare was not having it. She tossed her head and danced away, and I feared that she would bolt. I daresay the banshee women were not helping matters, though they kept to their posts around the ruin, only eyeing the creature curiously.

"Enbarr," I called, holding out my hand. She glanced up, and the whites of her eyes receded as her gaze went soft and liquid. She lowered her head and approached me, nickering.

I touched her velvet muzzle and felt her warm breath on my fingers. "If we hoped not to attract notice," I said softly, "I fear it was in vain."

"Not to worry," replied the king. "A little fairy glamour will render her less …"

"Dazzling?"

He nodded. "Mortals are easily deceived."

He approached Enbarr again, and this time she allowed him to lay a hand on her creamy shoulder. He spoke a few more soft words, and her sea-foam coat grayed before our eyes.

"She will appear smaller, too, to those standing at a distance," he continued. "Shall we go, my lady?"

We gathered our belongings and stood on a block of stone from the ruin to mount up. Finvara settled behind me, reaching his arms around me so he could grip Enbarr's mane—a position I found both unwelcome and unavoidable.

Before our departure, I again addressed my banshee companions, requesting that they await our return to Knock Ma rather than follow. The king said he expected our errand to require no more than a couple of hours.

The ten-mile journey passed as little more than a blur. Enbarr galloped nearly the entire distance, slowing only for other riders or carts on the road. I caught glimpses of landscape—an occasional ruined medieval tower or picturesque bridge—and we arrived in the village of Gallagh in not much more than a quarter hour.

The bog man, Finvara explained, had been unearthed earlier in this century by a laborer cutting turf—and had been immediately (and superstitiously) reburied, with a gravestone added by way of apology for disturbing his sleep. The landowner, a member of the Gallagher clan, avoided the area entirely for fear of rousing or angering the spirits of his ancestors, so we had the patch of bog—blocked from view of the manor house by a small rise—to ourselves.

Navigating a bog was perilous, as the human eye could not distinguish solid ground from soft, and many unlucky travelers had been lost without a trace, some of them led intentionally astray by the "fool's fire," or will-o'-the-wisp. We had set out in daylight hours, but visibility had decreased over the journey's course, cloud cover thickening until finally the sun was but a dim beacon hanging low in the southern sky. Still, Enbarr found no difficulty picking a path across this treacherous ground.

We soon found the bog man's resting place, marked by a relatively modern Celtic cross now half submerged.

"He'd not thank them for that," said Finvara, gesturing at the cross. "This man has been in the ground for many hundreds of years and knows nothing of priests or prayer books."

"What else do you know about him, my lord?" I asked, my heart thumping from a creeping sense of dread. I was grateful for the king's companionship—I could not imagine attempting this alone.

"He is an ancient king of Connacht," replied Finvara. "A chieftain sacrificed to the gods, in the hope of ending a plague."

"Heavens," I breathed. "And yet he somehow lives still?"

"He is not alive," replied the king, "but neither is he dead."

I studied the coarse, low plants that covered the grave. "How are we to speak to him?"

"Máine Mór," called Finvara, his tone deepening. "Show yourself."

The bog scrub in front of the stone cross began to tremble and shift and finally to *rise* as a hillock pushed up beneath it. The plants tumbled aside, and tea-colored water sluiced down the sides of the newly formed hillock.

I saw then that the "hillock" was not earthen or even peat, but rather a human figure, wrinkled and brown as last year's apples, its leathery hide burnished to gleaming by the bog water. This was the figure of a man, emaciated to little more than skin over bone. Surely a human form in such a state could no longer contain any spark of life.

Finvara and I remained astride Enbarr, but I bent toward the rising figure. I felt the king's arm tighten about my waist.

The skull jerked suddenly toward me, eyelids peeling back to reveal glassy black slits. I gasped, and Enbarr reared and shrieked.

"Easy!" Finvara shouted at the mare, gripping fistfuls of mane. But I was seated sidesaddle and slipped from his embrace, splashing into the icy water of the bog.

# DIARMUID'S TRUTH

## EDWARD

"How good of you to join us."

The queen was in high dudgeon; that much was apparent in her pursed lips and red cheeks. Ignoring her, I returned to my place at the table. The blasted tapestry made clear the reason for the delay in my return. I wondered whether it mirrored my thoughts, or had our frenzied lovemaking been a topic of general speculation?

*If it wasn't before, it is now,* I realized with a simmering anger.

With Ada gone off with Duncan, I was in no mood to be chastised, and I carefully avoided meeting Isolde's gaze.

"Have they gone?" asked Caer.

I nodded, lifting my untouched goblet to my lips. "They have," I replied, not bothering to mask my foul mood.

*You were a fool to let her go.*

I drained my goblet and replaced it rather noisily on the table. The mead was strangely airy—more scent than taste—but it warmed my chest nonetheless.

"You were wise to let her go," said Caer, and I glanced up. "You need Finvara's aid, and he was not inclined to join your cause."

"He's only agreed now in hopes of somehow holding on to her," I countered.

"It was a price that had to be paid," Isolde replied.

I glowered at her.

"Finvara has long loved Cliona," said Caer.

I shifted my glare to Diarmuid's foster mother. Was this meant to comfort me? "Finvara has loved *many*."

Isolde snorted at this, and I knew that the hypocrisy was not lost on her. I resented my ancestor's reputation and the fact I was now being conflated with him.

"I don't say this to anger you, my son," replied Caer. "But he feels, somewhat justly, that we all have been led a merry chase."

"By you and your—" Isolde began.

"My lady," Caer interrupted, not unkindly and yet not gently, "*peace*." Isolde returned to sullen silence.

Turning to me again, Caer continued, "Edward, Earl of Meath, I cannot know what knowledge Diarmuid has shared with you and what he has kept to himself. But there are certain things that you—and he, whether he likes it or not—must understand."

I drew in a long breath, relieved to be granted even this temporary and hypothetical separation from the Danaan warrior. The warmth of the mead had spread out from my chest to my belly and even into my limbs, and I let my folded arms come to rest on the table.

"Please, lady," I urged in a more reasonable tone. "I shall be most grateful."

With a bow of her head, she continued. "The exile resulting from Diarmuid's seal has not so much affected the Danaan. Our kind were in decline already, many of us with no surviving mortal descendants, and many of us content to leave Ireland to the Irish. Even those Danaan warriors who had survived the many battles had mostly faded to Faery by the time of the seal. But it has been hardest on the fairies."

"How so?" I asked.

"They do not thrive under exile, let us say. They blame you—they blame *us*—for their plight."

"The exile freshened an old resentment," said Angus. "The fairies have ever felt that we viewed them as our inferiors."

"For good reason," said Caer. "They are descended from the Danaan—and, in some cases, Fomorians—who were abandoned in Ireland when the immortals began to withdraw. We have ever regarded them as lesser beings. And yet, with a few exceptions ..." Her gaze moved between Isolde and me. "... they are almost all that remain of us. Finvara, though Danaan himself, has become like a father to the fairies. He believes that Diarmuid has stirred up this ancient conflict with the Fomorians because he wishes to return to the glory days of the Danaan."

My lips parted as I stared at Diarmuid's foster mother and worked at the puzzle she was trying to unlock for me. "Is this true?"

The question was meant for my ancestor, but Caer replied, "That, Diarmuid alone can answer. And only *Finvara* can say whether he, too, might wish for the same. But one thing we can be sure he does *not* wish for."

I held my breath, waiting for her to continue.

"He does not wish for the earthly union of Diarmuid and Cliona."

"Has that not already happened, lady?" My face grew hot, and I added, "Have Diarmuid and Cliona not returned to Ireland already, in the forms of Ada Quicksilver and me?"

Caer nodded. "And Finvara has agreed to join us because

he believes he has a chance to interfere with their union. It is necessary to the success of your cause that he believe he may be able to do so. Your lady glimpsed some part of this, Lord Meath, and so she agreed when you could not."

I felt all my own wrath and Diarmuid's roiling within me, despite the soothing effects of the mead. "Then I *have* been a fool!"

"You have done what was needful," she asserted.

"Seeing how you and your obsession with this woman have played games with all our fates," retorted Isolde, "it was the very least you could do."

I squeezed my eyes shut, cursing my ancestor for this ghastly mess. He had raised the woman from death, never considering whether she would have consented. He had agreed to help preserve the descendants of her mortal daughter, not out of love but out of guilt for stealing her mortality. Now, not liking the fate to which he had consigned them both, he had seized this opportunity— not to save Ireland, but in hopes of returning to his old life.

*Why does she love you?* I wondered.

*Only Dana knows,* came the answer. *But everything I've done, I've done for her.*

"For *yourself*!" I countered, not realizing I'd spoken the words aloud until I felt a cool hand covering mine.

"Recall, my good Irishman," said Caer, gently squeezing my hand, "that many of your countrymen were saved by Diarmuid's actions, whatever might have been his motive. If you're to make that count for something, you have no choice but to join this fight."

I wasn't sure how long I'd been sitting there, silently observed by the others, when I finally glanced up at the tapestry and saw a scene of battle. Four armies, three smaller and one seemingly innumerable, met on a field. At their heads were Diarmuid, Maeve, Finvara, and a large one-eyed figure out of nightmares—

Balor Evil Eye. A whitish film covered the eye, and it came to me that when the film lifted away, destruction would rain down on all he beheld. I had at first overlooked a smaller group in a corner of the tapestry nearest the Fomorians—Cliona and her banshees. These luminous beings seemed imprisoned in this tableau of violence.

Studying the tapestry, I could feel Diarmuid's eagerness for battle. As a lieutenant aboard the flagship of the Irish Royal Navy, I had seen battle, though only with Spanish pirates. The outcome of the fight now impending was by no means certain. I was no coward, but I knew I could never keep Ada clear of it, not without locking her away. Her ancestress was, of course, immortal, but if there was truth in these stories that Ada had made her life's work (and little doubt remained that there was), "immortal" did not equate to "cannot be killed."

*This is why you must enable me to protect her.*

I frowned and set a guard on my thoughts. I was in no mood to negotiate with the Danaan warrior. And there was a thought that had not *quite* crossed my mind … I pushed it away and returned my attention to the others.

"It seems there is no avoiding it," I said at last. "From what the Morrigan has told me, the battle will come, with or without my joining it. And if Isolde's forces are to join it, it must take place on the fields of Ireland."

The queen released an audible breath, and her posture eased. "Agreed. For that, the exile must be lifted." She fixed her gaze on me. "The seal must be broken."

Nodding, I glanced again at the battle scene on the tapestry. "What is the status of our armies?"

"As you have heard, Finvara has committed his forces," said Caer. "As has Cliona."

"As we speak, my army is crossing to the west by train," said

Isolde. "My navy is taking up a position in Sligo Bay." She leaned forward, resting the palm of her hand on the table. "Let the battle commence on the plain below Ben Bulben."

I noticed movement behind her and glanced at the tapestry. The scene now depicted was that of my death—of Diarmuid's death—gored by a wild boar while hunting with his old chieftain and former enemy, Finn, whose bride-to-be he had once stolen.

"Ben Bulben was the site of your betrayal and death, I know," the queen continued. "But there is a fairy door there, and that hill has ever been part of the country of Finvara and his subjects. The Fomorian raiders will certainly approach from the Atlantic. It makes sense."

*Let it be the place of my rebirth,* came the voice of my ancestor.

"Very well," I agreed, as I had no practical argument against it. Moreover, symbolic significance could be a deciding factor, as even an amateur historian knew. "What can we say of numbers? Ours? Theirs?"

"We made calculations while awaiting your return," said the queen, limiting her disapproving expression to a slight frown. "We expect our combined numbers to be as many as fourteen thousand, though I must reserve at least a thousand to guard the other known Gap gates, lest they sneak up from behind."

"Will that be sufficient, I wonder?"

"The other gates are less accessible. But Captain O'Malley and the others under her command will watch them from inside the Gap. As for the Danaan, we have no way of knowing how many will answer the call."

"They will answer," I said, feeling the conviction of my ancestor in this statement, though still with no idea how I was to summon them. "What of the Fomorians?"

Isolde shook her head, sighing, and Caer replied, "We have no way of knowing that, either. Many thousands, certainly."

"Have you considered approaching Queen Victoria?" I asked. "I daresay she'd not favor a takeover of her nearest neighbor by outside forces."

Isolde shook her head briskly. "This is our battle. If we invite them here, we shall never be rid of them."

There was foolish national pride in this assertion, yet I wholeheartedly agreed. Also, we could ill afford to waste precious time persuading the English queen to believe a story we ourselves could scarcely believe, even with new evidence arising hourly. The two queens were strong-minded, their relationship tenuous and mistrustful at the best of times.

"Irishmen for Ireland, then," I said.

Isolde raised an eyebrow. "And Irish*women.*"

I glanced over her shoulder at the tapestry, which bore a solitary image: a woman gazing out the window of a high tower. I scrubbed my face with my hand and reached for the pitcher of mead.

# A CAPTIVE AUDIENCE

## ADA

The bog water was frigid, but this I hardly noticed, because mere inches from my face was the hide-covered skull of the bog man. There was no focus to his pupilless eye, and yet there was no question he was looking at *me*. His head was strangely oblong, as if it had been pressed inward at both ears by heavy weights.

My lips parted, breath clouding as I involuntarily made a soft stammering sound.

Finvara's boots plunged into the water beside me, and Enbarr neighed and bolted. The king knelt, his arm at my back. "Are you injured, lady?"

*"Does it suit thee, fair lady—the bitter cold of my watery hall?"*

The bog creature was *speaking* to me, though the mouth opening, with its thin dark lips, hardly moved. His speech was halting and ragged.

"Let me help you," urged Finvara, trying to raise me.

"He is speaking," I hissed, resisting. Though heaven knew,

my preference would have been to return to the relative safety of Enbarr's back and ride away from here.

Finvara stopped pulling at me but did not let go. I watched the shrunken features for other signs of life and found one I had not been looking for: a shiny beetle crawled out of the bog man's ear, across his cheek, into his mouth and back out, before disappearing on the far side of his head. My body shook with revulsion.

"I see that it does not," continued the bog man, making a rasping sound that I strongly suspected was laughter. "If not for my hospitality and comely visage, why is it thou hast roused me?"

"By order of King Finvara," I replied, a tremor in my voice. "For the sake of the people of Ireland."

The bog man's head shifted as he turned his eyes to the belly of dark cloud overhead, and I breathed easier. He made a sound like drawing breath, accompanied by a rattling in his chest. "Why is Máine Mór to be moved by the cares of a people so distant?"

*Why, indeed?* I thought about what Finvara had told me. "Did you not make the ultimate sacrifice for the hope of ending plague? To save your people?"

"Mmm. To appease the gods. To save my own sons."

"Your sacrifice was not in vain," observed Finvara. "Your sons and their sons ruled Connacht for centuries. The mighty O'Malleys trace their roots to the warrior women of your line."

I looked at Finvara. *This* man was also Duncan's ancestor? I recalled Diarmuid's "bog crawler" taunts.

"Who can say what purpose it served?" replied the bog man. "But it gave them hope, and sometimes hope is all that is required."

"For the cause of which I speak, we will need more than hope," I said. "Your descendants face a plague to end all plagues. A famine, in fact, that will end the lives of more Irishmen than any battle in ancient or modern times. If you cannot aid them, I fear that no one can."

The skull rolled slowly as he again turned his gaze upon me. "What is it thou thinkest I may do for thee? Raise a blade? Lead an army?"

I glanced at Finvara, who nodded encouragement. So I told the ancient king my tale of blighted potatoes, and my suspicions about the broad scope of the plot.

When I finished, he remained silent for so long that I wondered whether he was still with us.

Finally his jaw opened slightly and he said, "So many generations under the earth, and still the Fomorians threaten. The Plague Warriors, we called them in my time. Fortunate we were that they hated the Danaan more than they hated us. Yet it was they who poisoned our villages."

"Can you help us, sir?" I asked quietly.

Again came the rasping laugh, and he replied, "His Lordship of the Bog will serve thee if he can, fair lady. If there is a thing I do know, 'tis dark earth, sour bog water, and the ways of the mud creepers. Passionless are they, and a thing that has been touched by ill intent is a thing that does not escape the notice of a bog crawler."

"Do you think there are others who may help us?" I asked.

"Aye, could be. I will do what I can to enlist them." His attention shifted to Finvara. "You say there is to be a battle?"

The king nodded. "Almost certainly."

The bog man made a sound very like a sigh. "Would that I could join it."

I reached toward his arm but froze before making contact with the withered flesh. "You will, sir, in your own way," I said. "I earnestly thank you."

He seemed to study me a moment and then said, "I could not guess how many years since I felt the touch of another."

I shivered, and my stomach twisted. But it was not a moment

for squeamishness. Bending over him, heart racing—fighting reflexive revulsion—I pressed my lips against the damp, rough hide that stretched over his skull. Though my very flesh crept at the idea of it, the reality was not unpleasant. No smell of decay reached my nostrils, and mercifully, no insect crept forth.

When I sat up, the bog man said faintly. "Thank you, lady."

And before I could reply, his body began to sink back into the bog.

"*Máine Mór,*" I whispered, recalling the name Finvara had used for him.

Finvara rose, helping me to my feet, and I watched the water wash over the ancient king's remains. My hand trembled on the fairy king's arm, and as the frantic beating of my heart subsided, I realized I was desperately cold.

"Call Enbarr, lady," said Finvara. "Let us return to Knock Ma so we may wash and change clothes before we catch our death."

As Enbarr bore us back across country, Finvara's warmth against my back helped counter the frigid blast caused by the mare's breakneck speed.

When we reached the glade at Knock Ma, a bright, glinting winter sun had broken through the clouds, and mist rose as it burned off the morning dew.

"Perhaps we should ask her to carry us to Brú na Bóinne," I said as Finvara slid down from Enbarr's back.

"Indeed," he said, but he reached up to help me dismount. "But let us travel warm and dry, and meanwhile, I may show you my home. I also have business to discuss with my people before our return."

Something about his words ignited a warning flare in my chest, but before I could voice my concern, I found myself slipping into the king's waiting arms. He lowered me gently to the earth, and a ray of misty sunlight fell across his face. His eyes were the clearest blue I had ever seen, or so it seemed to me now. I felt his arms encircle my waist.

*Have a care, daughter,* came the voice of my ancestress, from seemingly far away.

I imagined then that I heard the keening of the banshees. I say "imagined" because this, too, seemed to come from far away and, a moment later, was gone.

A moment after that, so were we.

The ground dropped from under me, and the heavens above me spun. When the dizziness abated, I found that we did indeed stand on solid ground, before a proper fortress. All hard lines and dark stone, it was a stark departure from the comfortable hall at Brú na Bóinne, though the surrounding woodland was just as picturesque. The oak trees crowded in closer here—right up to the fortress walls, which, I was certain, broke a basic rule of defensibility.

*Nothing sneaks past us, lady.*

The sound was like a thousand whispers, and I spun about, heart jumping. I had the sudden and sinking sense I was not supposed to be here.

"Duncan?" I called.

"I'm here," he said, suddenly beside me. He took my hand.

At his touch, I felt a rush of warmth, like sinking into warm bathwater. Something tickled my cheeks, and I wiped a hand over my face. I forgot what had disturbed me only moments ago.

"Is it you, Duncan?" I asked.

He smiled. "Trust me, lady. I won't let anything happen to you."

He led me toward a gated bridge that spanned the castle moat, which was filled with still black water, its surface like a mirror. We passed through the gate, and I noticed a disturbance of the water's surface, as if something large moved beneath.

I gasped, and he said, "Pike."

The tip of a fin rose and cut a wavy line through the water. "They must be enormous!" I exclaimed.

"Indeed," he replied. "Some larger than a man."

I shuddered and moved farther from the bridge's railing.

"We will wash ourselves here and then return to Brú na Bóinne and the others?" I inquired, as I was finding it difficult to recall conversation from even a moment ago. I brushed again at the hair or spider thread that tickled my face.

Before he could answer, I heard the peeping call of a kestrel and glanced up. The speckled hawklike bird spiraled down slowly toward us, and Finvara held out his arm. After a graceful landing, the creature tipped back her head, and I saw that her beak held a small folded paper. Once my companion had taken it, she lifted off again. He opened the note and, after a quick perusal, refolded it and tucked it into his pocket.

"Let us go in," he said.

"What was in the note?" I asked.

"Nothing important," he replied with a shake of his head. "My greatest concern at present is getting you dry."

His tone was light and easy, but as I studied his profile, I got the sense this might not be genuine. Moreover, I could not be sure whether I was speaking to Finvara or Duncan, and the strange tickling sensation on my cheek distracted me unrelentingly, making me forget the things I wanted to ask him.

The only course of thought I seemed able to follow had to do with his person. I could admire the smoothness of his chestnut skin. Study the fine, light freckles across the backs of his hands. Trace the full lines of his lips and compare the color of his eyes to the sea. All these thoughts I could follow without difficulty, and after a while I grew fatigued and let my questions fade into the background.

Stately woodland fairies, like the ones at Brú na Bóinne, guarded the inner gate. They stood silent, their spears crossed before the entrance. They uncrossed them as we approached, allowing us to pass.

Stark though the fortress appeared outside, within were luxuries and comforts similar to those that adorned the house of Angus and Caer. As we walked around the perimeter of a great hall, creatures like the ones we'd caught in their Christmas revels flitted like mice around columns, tables, and chairs, their bright laughter echoing through the hall.

It all had the quality of a dream, and I began to feel heavy and slow. I was grateful when at last we reached a chamber door, which the king opened, ushering me inside. He spoke to someone in the corridor for a moment before joining me.

"Rest, lady," he said. "A bath will be drawn, and fresh clothes brought. After that, refreshment, and we will talk of what comes next."

"My lord, I fear that ..."

I broke off, unsure what I had been about to say. He waited, but finally I shook my head, feeling that the effort of recalling it was too great.

"You are tired," he said, brushing my cheek with the tips of his fingers. "And cold, I fear. Not for long."

He bent then and touched his lips to mine. I felt a pulling inside me, as though I needed to get away, yet his mouth was soft and warm, and he smelled of heather, with just a hint of the spice of evergreens. His hand came to the small of my back, and the scant space between us closed. His body, too, was warm, but with edges firm and strong, reminding me of ...

He drew back and I closed my eyes, drawing a long, shuddering breath. I felt his hands on me as he eased me back onto the bed.

I sank onto the crimson coverlet, and he moved away, leaving the chamber and closing the door behind him.

I woke with a start, clear-eyed, and sat straight up. My breath came fast, almost in panic, and I struggled to remember where I was.

I found myself on a great, soft bed. Flames crackled in the chamber's fireplace. Glancing down, I found that I was dressed in a gown of medieval design: dusty plum, with embroidered flourishes at the neck, above the elbows, and along the edges of the draping sleeves.

Recalling now where I was, I wondered who had dressed me—as well as who had *bathed* me.

As I rose from the bed, I caught my reflection in a glass. The gown's fabric was soft and supple and thin, revealing the lines of my body in a way that brought warmth to my cheeks. My hair had been washed and becomingly arranged.

Behind me in the glass, I noticed a table next to an armchair, and on it rested a goblet and a plate of small cakes. I also saw a slip of paper, and I went immediately and picked it up.

*Keep up your strength, my dear Miss Q. —Duncan*

The note did much to relieve my anxiety. Finvara had been kind, and true to his word, but there was something about this place …

Suddenly, I remembered. I was not supposed to come here!

*Do not follow Finvara back to his court,* the earl had said in a fit of jealousy.

I had made up my mind to follow his advice despite his ungentlemanly behavior, and yet here I was.

I picked up the goblet and one of the cakes and crossed to the window to look out. We must have climbed many steps to arrive here, as my chamber appeared to be situated in the top of a tower. Oddly, I remembered none of it, only that a great fatigue had come over me the moment we crossed the castle threshold.

Nibbling at the cake, which tasted of honey and cream, I stared out over the tops of the trees and thought that I could make out the frosted-white ridges of ocean waves in the distance. The window was barred but in no way covered to keep out the elements. The outdoor air was still and comfortable, with neither breeze nor bite.

I sipped the mead and remembered something that made me choke. Had I not *kissed* Duncan? Or Finvara?

Closing my eyes, I shook my head. I had dreamt it, surely. And yet even *this* thought made me uneasy.

*Glamour.* The voice of my ancestress reached me as if she approached from a distance.

I recalled the tickling feeling on my cheeks that had so annoyed me. And I recalled that I had felt it once before—aboard the *Queen of Connacht.*

*Mortals are easily deceived,* Finvara had said when he spoke of disguising Enbarr. And mortal I was. How could I have been such a fool?

I plunked the goblet down on the windowsill and went to the door, just as Finvara opened it from the other side.

"My lady, I am pleased to see that you are—"

"Let me pass," I demanded. "I'm going back to Brú na Bóinne."

I pushed past him as he replied, "I fear that won't be possible."

Ignoring him, I stepped across the threshold—and found myself suddenly alone and unmoored. Floating in a field of black perforated by thousands of pinpricks of light, hard and clear as diamonds. I spun about, digging my arms into the emptiness, like a swimmer, and panicked upon discovering no way back to where I'd been.

I cried out, or thought I did, but no sound escape my lips.

*We are trapped in the Gap.*

I listened to the sound of my own breathing, quick and

shallow. *Trapped?* I demanded. *How can that be?* My thoughts churned furiously, and I remembered something important. *Can you not free us? Can we not pass between worlds?*

*No longer,* came the reply.

Suddenly, a hand gripped my arm, and I stumbled into a firelit chamber—I had returned to the room in the tower, and Finvara stood eyeing me gravely.

"That is dangerous, my lady," he said. "Please do not attempt it again."

"I want to leave here, my lord," I insisted.

He frowned. "As I said, that's impossible now."

"How so?" I demanded.

*An enchantment was cast on your breakfast,* Cliona informed me mournfully. *Your mortal body is trapped here, and I along with you.*

"Blast!" I cried, realizing the truth of it. I spun away from my captor, squeezing my hands into fists as I stared into the fire. I had walked right into a well-known fairy trap *for the second time.*

"Diarmuid will kill you for this," I said, my voice rising in anger. "You must know that. He will be overjoyed that you have given him an excuse."

In the silence that followed, I could not hear him breathing, or any other sound but the crackling of the fire. At length, he replied. "I have his word that he will not."

I turned on my heel, glaring at him. "What are you talking about?"

His arms were folded, one elbow resting in the opposite hand, one thumb and forefinger rubbing the tip of his sand-colored beard. His eyes were round, his expression clear, as he studied me. Even now I felt the pull of his beauty, worldly and preternatural at once. I fought this physical and untrustworthy response, clinging desperately to my anger.

"Well?" I demanded.

"Do you wish to see the note he has written?" he asked in velvet tones.

"Note!"

He reached into his pocket, and he handed me a bit of folded paper. *The kestrel.* My fingers trembled as I opened it.

*I think—at least, I hope—that there is one thing on which we can agree: she does not belong in battle. Her ancestress may be powerful, but her mortal form is fragile. Nothing in her experience could have prepared her for the danger and horror of war. Confine her somewhere safe, somewhere comfortable, and I will not seek vengeance when I come for her. If you need further reason to acquiesce to this request, consider the possibility that after my role in this is revealed, she may never wish to see me again.*

*—Meath*

I turned and flung the note into the fire. A sob welled up in my throat and came forth more like a gasp.

*Damn him, he is right!* I thought. *I shan't.* Hot tears ran down my cheeks.

*This is not Diarmuid's doing,* said Cliona.

"How well I know it!" I said aloud. "He wouldn't dare. Only Edward is capable of this. And *you.*"

I rounded on the king. "*You,*" I repeated. "I care not what agreement you've made with him. I demand that you release me."

Slowly, the fairy king shook his head. "For once, I agree with him. I would not for all the world see you bloodied and broken. You will be safe here."

"And what of your *word*? You promised to help them."

"And so I shall. I will be rejoining them as soon as my preparations are complete."

I stared at him, incredulous. "You're leaving me here *alone?*"

"Not alone. My servants will attend to your every need," he repeated. "Food, drink, entertainment—you have only to ask."

"A curse on both of you!" I cried, shaking with anger. "Get out!"

"Lady," he pleaded quietly, "let us not part in this way."

"Let us not part *at all,*" I tried once more. "Take me with you and I will forgive you wholeheartedly for your part in this."

I thought for a moment that I had shaken his resolve, but if so it was fleeting. I could see the effort it cost him to turn from me, but turn he did, and left me alone, closing the door behind him.

I picked up the delicate table beside the armchair and hurled it at the wall. It exploded satisfyingly against the stone, the pieces clattering to the floor.

*Never feel that you are abandoned.* The earl's parting words echoed painfully in my mind. I sank to the floor, covering my face with my hands.

# ONE GOOD DEED

## ADA

Finvara did not come again. My only visitors were servants who brought my meals. When they entered the chamber, I could see guards outside my door, and it seemed an unnecessary precaution. Did the king fear that Edward might change his mind? *Might he?* No, I realized, it was Diarmuid he feared. My only hope for escape lay in a circumstance I had dreaded up to now: that the earl might be overcome by his ancestor.

*The king cannot keep you in Faery indefinitely,* Cliona said. *Else you would waste away.*

Which meant that eventually I'd have a chance. But would it come before the battle?

As I paced between window and chamber door—the activity that occupied most of my time now—I could not help wondering about what had transpired between Cliona and Finvara in the past. He clearly believed he had a claim to her. Had he reason for that? Cliona had implied she'd chosen between them. I thought about how I'd watched him, admiring his comeliness, and how I'd permitted him to kiss me. Had it *all* been glamour?

*I have long known Finvara,* Cliona replied to my train of thought. *Longer even than I've known Diarmuid.*

I halted in my pacing. "Have you?"

*He visited me in my childhood and even into my maidenhood. Like my mother, I could always see the gentlefolk.*

"You were a fairy seer." Cliona had, of course, been born before Diarmuid's seal exiled the fairies. But fairy folk had a reputation for shying away from mortals.

*He proposed to carry me off, many times. And I had been tempted, handsome and honey-tongued as he was. But my mother had warned me against him, and I would not go. When I married, my husband put a stop to my wandering, and I thought I would never see King Finvara again. But he sent a servant from his own house, and it was she who arranged for the coracle, and the horse that carried me away from my husband's hall.*

"The king helped you escape your husband!"

*He did, though it did not end in the way I expected. It is often the case when one accepts gifts or favors from fairies.*

"He caused your death?" I said, aghast.

*Not in the way that you mean. There are forces more powerful than Finvara. It is myself I blame. I have ever been fond of the fairy king.*

This information shined a very bright light on the hostility between the two men at Brú na Bóinne. "But you *chose* Diarmuid."

*I chose Diarmuid, yes. I should be by his side now, and he would wish me to be so. He will come for us.*

I had no doubt about that. But how *long* would we be confined here? If I had to stay in this tower, waiting and wondering, my very sanity would be in peril.

"There must be a way," I muttered.

With some difficulty, I unlaced and cast aside the plum gown and again donned the armored dress, which Finvara's servants had cleaned and returned to my chamber.

"The banshees!" I suddenly recalled, rushing to the window. "Mightn't we call them?"

*I called them when first Finvara began weaving his spell. And they did try to warn you, but it was already too late. The fairy king's enchantments are old magic—very powerful. Neither I nor the banshees can counter them.*

Sighing, I moved to the bed and sank down. I tried to recall everything I'd read about charms against fairies, and fairy enchantments. But in all the stories and accounts, I'd never read of anyone returning from Faery without being either released by the fairies or aided by someone on the outside. Abduction enchantments *were* strong, especially when sealed by food or drink.

There were a few things I might try—turning my clothes inside out, making the sign of the cross—but I could not know whether these charms had worked without again trying to escape, which was obviously risky. I had my doubts Finvara's spell would be so easily defeated.

Again I paced, staring first into the fire and then out at the forest, exhausting myself by fretting. I had been at this some time when I heard a noise near the door. I turned, expecting a servant, only to find Billy Millstone standing in my chamber.

"How do you come to be here?" I demanded, taking a step backward. I glanced around the chamber for my spear, though I'd already made a thorough search for it earlier.

"Shush, lady," he hissed. "Billy's after helpin' thee."

I frowned, momentarily hung up by his odd dialect. "Helping *me*?"

"*Ach*, aye," he said, gesturing. "Make haste now."

I stared at him, wary. "Why would you help me?"

The redcap grumbled with impatience. "'Twas thanks to *thee* that oul Billy was spared."

"Spared from what?"

"'I'd flay thee alive, Billy,' says the king, 'if not for the lady askin' me to show mercy. Count yerself lucky.' And so I do, lady. And grateful too."

My gaze flitted from him to the door. How had he bypassed the guards?

"How are we to get out?" I asked, afraid to hope.

"Sure it's the same way thou camest *in*!" he replied, as though I'd asked something foolish.

"But the enchantment …"

*The enchantment has opened a door to the Gap,* explained Cliona. *Billy has used it to come to you, and he can use it to get you out.*

*Mightn't this be a trap?* I wondered.

She was silent a moment. *The alternative is to remain here.*

"Are we after waitin' here to be caught?" demanded the redcap. "I'm coming!"

He turned for the door before I reached him, and as he stepped toward it, I took hold of his jerkin. I braced myself for the spinning sensation, and it came. But a moment later I stood on the deck of his tugboat.

"Heavens!" I cried in surprise and relief. I stared at Billy in wonder. "I am in your debt, sir."

He muttered something unintelligible and made for the wheelhouse. I followed.

"How did you know I was Finvara's prisoner?" I asked. "How did you manage to get free of your captors?" Billy took hold of the navigator, and I said, "Where are we going?"

He made an exasperated noise and whined, "Just be still a moment, lady, or Billy will get addled."

I stood fidgeting, waiting for him to finish. *Dare I trust him?*

*Have we a choice?*

We had, and we'd made it—whether for good or ill would soon enough be revealed.

"Where are we going, Billy?" I repeated when he'd concluded his fiddling with the device.

"The Faery library," he replied. "There is somethin' thou wilt wish to see, havin' to do with Diarmuid's curse." He stuck out his chin and continued staring out the wheelhouse window.

I frowned. "Can you not simply tell me?"

The redcap turned then and met my gaze. "Billy swore an oath, as the Danaan warrior told thee. Some things he mayn't say. Not without invitin' a fate worse than death."

Billy shuddered, and he continued staring at me strangely. I got the sense he wished me to understand something he had left unsaid. Could it be that he truly wished to help me but was prevented from doing so directly by his blood oath to Balor? Could it be that some book in the library would explain how Diarmuid's seal was to be broken? I didn't like the delay in joining the others, but this detour could prove valuable. When I left Edward at Brú na Bóinne, he had not yet come to understand how or when he was to break the seal.

"All right, Billy," I said. "Let us go there."

Billy returned to his navigation, and I said, "What of my other questions, Billy? How did you know I needed rescuing?"

"Billy knew he'd lock thee away," he replied. "It's in the king's nature. As for how Billy got free—they've almost all of 'em left the castle. Pocketed Billy in the dungeon, did they—leavin' in such a rush as not to be mindful a redcap can pick a lock like no other folk. And the wee rat-faces they left to mind Billy?" He sniffed in the air, flicking his thumb and finger as if at an insect. "*Meh!*"

"Well, again I thank you," I said. His story held enough water to let me breathe easier for now. It was true I had asked the king to show mercy. And heaven knew I was happy to be out of that tower.

I left Billy to his navigation, but after a moment, he said, "Why, lady?"

"Why *what*, Billy?"

"Why ask the king to show oul Billy mercy? After them praties, an' all?"

I frowned, considering. It was a question I'd asked myself without receiving a satisfactory answer.

"I'm not sure," I admitted. "I suppose it seemed to me you had your own troubles that caused you to make the decision you did, and not all of them were of your own making. The same may be said of us all."

"*Hmph*," he grunted, scratching the rough stubble on his chin.

Both Billy and I fell to musing. I wondered why the library, but perhaps it was an obvious choice. Isolde had found information there about her family tree and the alternate histories. And I had planned to visit there myself before agreeing to go with Finvara to Gallagh.

*I have seen it,* offered Cliona.

*Have you?* I prompted. When first I learned of my connection to the Danaan woman, I had striven, I realized now, to preserve some distance between us out of fear of what was happening to the earl. Either she had respected this or she, too, had preferred to preserve a separation. But as our peril increased, I knew that I would need her—I certainly could not expect to survive the battle without her aid—and I began to feel it was important to understand her better.

*My husband was a hard man,* said she, and I could feel the mournful flavor of her words. *My mother had taught me to read some Latin, and I wanted to continue my studies, as well as to read the books and documents my husband possessed. Especially during the time of my confinement with our daughter. But I was not permitted. He was God-fearing, and he believed that his neighbors would think me a witch. When I came to Brú na Bóinne, Diarmuid continued my education, and he introduced me to the library so I could read the history of my new people. It was there I found the histories of Ireland and learned that my child's children could be lost.*

Since the night I danced with Queen Isolde, one thing that had puzzled me was the idea of the Danaan warrior poring over history books. It hardly seemed in his nature. Now I understood.

*So you went to Diarmuid with this information,* I said.

*I cried over my daughter. I railed at him for making it impossible for us to be joined again in death. I told him the least he could do was save my mortal descendants. He had perhaps been selfish in some ways, but had I not also been, in trying to take my child from her father? Diarmuid deserved better from me. But he did what I asked, and it affected us all. It is no great wonder Billy hates us.*

It was impossible not to be moved by this tale of woe. *I cannot fault you,* I told her, *and you should not fault yourself, for trying to make a better life for your child, or for your grief over your permanent separation from her. I am deeply sorry. I believe I can imagine what that might be like.*

Heaven knew I thought about my own mother every day.

*Someday, you will have your own child to worry over, Dana willing,* she said. *But I have been blessed to find you, and there are others—distant relations you know naught of. I have Diarmuid to thank for this.*

*Why the connection between us, lady?* I couldn't help but ask. The answer Finvara had given to this question had been illuminating. *Why not an Irishwoman?*

*You are in part an Irishwoman, and you are the only one who bears my family legacy, the mark of Faery.*

*I suppose that we also have scholarship in common.*

We had something else in common, but I could not quite bring myself to question her on that point. I had to believe that some choices had been entirely my own.

I glanced up at the helm then, wondering how long it would take us to reach the Faery library, which I understood to be superimposed, dimensionally speaking, on the library at Trinity College.

I noticed we were approaching a larger ship—a Gap galleon. I thought at first it was the *Queen of Connacht,* but then I glimpsed the baleful eyes of its figurehead.

"Billy!" I cried, starting to my feet. "That's a Fomorian ship!"

"*Ach,* aye," he muttered grimly.

# THE FAIRY GATE

## EDWARD

I had never seen so many soldiers gathered in one place. Standing with Isolde and Finvara atop a hill beside Drumcliff Castle, near Sligo Bay, we surveyed the queen's army. They were arrayed on the plain between us and the southern slopes of Ben Bulben, green coats vivid against the winter grass. Thousands of bayonets shone sharp and bright as the clear December day. Columns of smoke rose from their breakfast fires. Did they understand what would happen this day? It was a soldier's lot not to question, but I did not envy them the awakening they were about to receive, and I hoped against my suspicions that Isolde had adequately prepared them.

In these quiet moments before the battle, I permitted myself to wonder about Ada. What was she doing at this moment?

*Cursing your name,* was my ancestor's reply. Within the tone of reproach, I detected a note of smugness. Diarmuid, I knew, would never have let her out of his sight. I wasn't sure which of us was the more selfish.

Finvara would not speak of her other than to confirm the

success of their mission to the bog and assure me that she was unharmed. He made it clear that he considered it his business— that he now considered *her* his business. For the time being, I would have to tolerate him.

I knew that my ancestor's thoughts were at least half occupied with the vengeance he would seek against the fairy king despite my promise to exact none.

I had guarded my own thoughts well in this endeavor, and my ancestor had not become aware of my intention until I wrote my brief letter. At that point, I had only to present it to my feathered courier, procured for me in advance by the lady Caer, before any coup over the body we shared could be mounted. "Rage" was too mild a descriptor for Diarmuid's reaction, but by then, even he understood that nothing could be done. This business of war could not be postponed while he was off rescuing his lady. Also, I got the sense he believed he would see Cliona before the battle was decided. I could only hope he was wrong. It would probably mean loss of the aid she had promised—that of the banshees— but it was difficult to imagine that this loss would significantly affect the outcome.

When this was over, I would return to Faery and free her. It might very well be the end of our association. But I would sooner lose her than sacrifice her—along with anyone else who may have become part of this bargain. She and I had never spoken of the more earthly hazards of our coupling, but they had never been far from my mind. I intended to do right by her if she would let me, but if not, I would at least do all I could to prevent her suffering in any way for her decision to give herself to me.

One of Isolde's generals joined us on the hill to discuss battle strategy. I viewed this as premature, as still missing from the scene before us were both the fairies and the Danaan warriors. But as I observed her discourse with her female commanding officer—noting the difference in the queen's demeanor, not only her respectful tone and lack of archness, but the way she leaned in, lightly touching the other woman's arm, and the softness in her gaze—something occurred to me that hadn't before. I realized that I'd been a fool not to see it, and that there had been less whimsy in some of her actions than I had imagined.

"It is time, Edward." The queen addressed me in a tone of command. "If you cannot do it, you must give over to Diarmuid."

"It is time," I repeated faintly, my gaze shifting beyond her to a rock face high on the southwestern end of Ben Bulben. Many compared the mountain to a table, and indeed its treeless summit was nearly flat and crookedly oblong. The north side featured a formidable cliff-like face considered too dangerous to scale. The slopes on this southern side were gentler, yet still stark and imposing.

For some time, I had been studying the bleak slab, and now a square of white limestone directly above the queen's crown of dark plaits caught my eye. *The fairy door.* With this discovery came another realization: *this* was the weakest point of the seal. Once it was broken, through that door would cross fairy, Danaan, and Fomorian alike.

But how was I to break it? How was I even to *reach* it?

A ragged scolding cry tore at the morning, and I glanced skyward. A huge crow circled high overhead, and with each circle it wound closer to us.

*The Morrigan.*

It became clear she would land, and we shifted to make room as her great wings beat wind in our faces. A sinuous movement of her neck brought her black-beaded gaze to bear on me.

A wordless understanding passed between her and my ancestor, and in that moment, I knew what I must do. I moved to her side, and she bent low, inviting me to climb onto her back.

"Edward?" said the queen.

Reaching between neck feathers, I grasped a hard quill at its base and hauled myself up. I checked that the pistol at my side was secure, and then drew Great Fury. Turning to the queen, I said, "Be ready."

The Morrigan lifted from the hilltop. If I'd found travel on the back of the water horse hair-raising, it was nothing to this. Soaring high above the battlefield, I could see across mountain, plain, and bogland to the east, and beyond the white-capped breakers rolling through the bay to the west, where ships of the royal navy approached like great storm clouds.

We climbed high above Ben Bulben, where the atmosphere was cold and thin, and then suddenly we were dropping back toward the earth. Cold air blasted the hair back from my face, and I tightened my grip on the hilt of Great Fury, locking my gaze on the fast-approaching face of the mountain.

*Be ready,* my ancestor admonished as I had admonished the queen.

At the last moment, I raised the sword higher and swung with all my might in a downward arc. There came a blinding flash as the ancient blade clanged against the square of limestone, striking so hard that the weapon vibrated out of my hand and slipped from my fingers. The impact deflected the Morrigan's light avian form, and we tumbled away from the mountain. I gripped a quill in each hand, closing my thighs against feathered sides, and somehow managed to remain astride as she righted herself in midair—just in time for me to watch the prow of a ship materialize directly before us.

"Good God!" I muttered as the vessel pushed through a gaping hole in the side of the mountain, sailing right into the sun-washed Irish morning, dragging a black storm cloud behind her. At once I recognized *Death Rattler*—the Gap galleon crewed by the Fomorians who had attacked the *Queen of Connacht*.

And suddenly, my heart, like the sword, plunged away from me. For on the deck of that ghastly vessel stood Ada Quicksilver. Over her loomed my enemy, Balor Evil Eye, the Fomorian king, commander of the Plague Warriors.

"Close the gate!" bellowed Balor. His voice came at me like howling wind, rolling boulders, and raging rivers. Six-inch talons curled around the slender neck of the woman I loved, and something twisted horribly in my gut. "Close the gate behind us, and we shall negotiate the terms of your surrender."

Closing the gate would prevent both Finvara's subjects and the Danaan from returning to Ireland to aid us; this I understood. And had I any idea how to do it—or any assurance that it would really save her—I would not hesitate.

*It will not, so we must find another way.*

"Fire!" The wind carried the voice of the queen's general from the battlefield below us, followed by the din of perhaps a thousand rifles firing at once. I expected to hear bullets whizzing past my ear. Half expected them to pierce my own hide or the Morrigan's, as we were so close to the target. I shouted for Ada to get down, knowing it was pointless.

But in the aftermath of this violent noise, there was silence, and it appeared to me that neither ship nor captain had been hit.

I reached for my sword before remembering that it was gone, and then drew my pistol.

"Land on the figurehead!" I shouted, and the Morrigan's flight path adjusted accordingly.

The moment she lighted atop the fiery demon, I raised my weapon and fired directly at Balor's white-lidded eye—and heard the click of a misfire. Then the weapon exploded right out of my hands, its barrel striking my right cheekbone painfully before it bounced off the demon's snout and plummeted toward the ground.

Anger boiled inside me—the anger of Diarmuid, who recognized interference from the Morrigan.

*Treacherous hag!*

Thus I was reminded she was not on *our* side, but on the side of the battle itself.

I reached out for Great Fury with my thoughts, and the thrum of blood lust revealed its location on the battlefield below. But I could not leave Ada on *Death Rattler*.

## ADA

"Call the Danaan!" I shouted at the earl, and the viselike grip on my neck closed even tighter, choking off my voice.

Pulling hopelessly at what felt like iron pincers at my throat, I stared in horror at my captor. He was a dark-scaled monster with an oversize block of a head. The fangs of his lower jaw protruded several inches above gray lips, and his bare broad chest was the color of soot but covered with chalky burn marks that looked like Nordic runes. He watched the earl with one catlike eye while the other remained covered with a filmy white lid.

Suddenly, the Fomorian king flung me aside like a child's doll, and I struck the deck with force, not far from the booted feet of my betrayer, Billy Millstone. I watched, horrified, as Balor reached up and, with two talons, plucked at the film over his eye.

"Diarmuid!" I screamed. If the lid was raised, we would not survive. Frantic, I scrambled to my feet so I could see the Morrigan. She and the earl were circling *Death Rattler,* dodging the spears the Fomorian crewmen were now hurling at them. The light of the Danaan shone out brightly from the earl's countenance.

"The foe is upon us!" shouted Diarmuid in a voice that surely carried across the Irish Sea to England. "For the Danaan! *For Ireland!*"

Balor roared balefully, and my hands flew to my ears while

the deck vibrated beneath me. A beam of crimson light streamed from the opening eye, knocking Diarmuid and the battle crow from their orbit.

Crying out in alarm, I scrambled toward the rail, but a thunderous battle cry took my attention. Behind us, the fairy gate still yawned open, a black tunnel in the side of the mountain. Far below us, at ground level, warriors began pouring out of the blackness, roaring like wild beasts and waving swords in the air.

*Now come the Danaan!* cried Cliona in relief, confirming my hopes.

Balor turned his head slowly, but the Danaan, directly beneath us, were out of range of the deadly beam. He stepped forward, tipping his head over the rail, and the red beam swept down and across the battlefield, wreaking a wide swath of destruction right through the queen's army. Gunpowder exploded, horses shrieked, and soldiers screamed as they were hurled into the air. When the beam cut off, the great eyelid closing at last, I saw that the ground had been scarred black in the shape of a lazy S. There were hundreds of broken and bleeding bodies.

At this rate, the Fomorians need never lift a sword.

"Why will their rifles not work properly?" I shouted at Billy, having no one else to ask.

"Simple spells," he muttered, "them that interfere with mechanicals. Especially them that need fire."

*Of course.* I remembered what Finvara had said about the spell for conjuring a fairy light—*the easiest thing in the world.* Rifles used combustion. Fire, water, air, earth—fairy peoples were masters of elemental manipulation.

*Powder is tricky among fairies,* Mr. Yeats had told me.

"This is dire," I moaned, digging my nails into the railing. "They are defenseless."

The crow bearing Diarmuid suddenly appeared again to the ship's port side, and the Danaan warrior held Great Fury high in the air. *Death Rattler* appeared to be creating weather around it, darkening the clear winter sky. Lightning cracked in the clouds, making the ancient blade flash.

"Billy swore a blood oath, lady," said the redcap in a pleading tone. "He could not help himself before, and he cannot help *thee* now."

"What!" I snapped, annoyed at the timing of this useless confession.

But Billy wasn't looking at me. He was staring at his spear, which lay on the ground between us.

Gasping, I grabbed for it, and the wailing of the banshees filled my ears. *The warning keen*—I knew it by now. The moment I snatched up the weapon, Balor's talons closed around my other arm, and time itself seemed to stutter and slow.

Agony seared a path from shoulder to fingertips, and I screamed. Balor had yanked me from the ground by my arm, and something in my shoulder had given way. The pain was nauseating, nearly blinding.

He thrust me up so I dangled between him and Diarmuid, and a cruel laugh bubbled up out of his throat as, with his other hand, he reached to lift the membranous covering from his eye.

I felt faint from the wrenching pain in my shoulder, but my right hand still gripped the spear, and I focused on the feel of this sturdy weapon in my hand.

*Weapon of thorn and iron. It will serve you well.* It wasn't the spear I had lost, but it was the same in every other respect. I squeezed the shaft with my palm and fingers. I raised it, feeling its heft.

As the first beams of red-hot light stabbed outward from beneath the eye's covering, I took aim and thrust the spear with all my strength.

It had only a few feet to travel, and the iron tip cut through the eye like a hot knife through butter. As putrid steam hissed from the wound, time spun free once again, and Balor gave a roar of agony. Silver fluid fountained from beneath the eyelid. The talons at last released me, and I fell again to the ship's deck, tears of relief and pain hot on my cheeks.

The great hand swept out blindly, and I rolled aside. But the knuckles caught Billy, hurling him across the deck to crash against the rail. He crumpled and fell to the boards, and there he remained.

I heard feet pounding the deck beneath me and looked up to find Fomorians swarming over it, forming a protective circle around their king—all but the four who were running toward *me*, fangs bared and gazes rabid.

The next thing I knew, I'd been gripped at the waist, but these hands were warm and familiar. *Friendly.* He lifted me, placing me before him on the back of the crow and reaching his arms around to grip her glossy black neck feathers. I let myself sink against his chest as the pain knifed through me, hot and searing like a blacksmith's forge.

# FOR IRELAND

## ADA

I awoke to the loud blast of a horn and looked around me. I was lying on a hard surface.

"You are safe." The voice was Edward's. He bent over me, intently focused, the black clouds dramatically framing his dark features—and those vivid blue eyes. It stopped my breath.

"Your arm was pulled from its socket," he said. A fresh wave of nausea washed over me, and I closed my eyes. "I believe I have successfully reset the joint. You should feel some relief."

He touched my face, gently pushing back a strand of hair, and I opened my eyes. "I must go," he said, "but may God strike me down should I ever underestimate you again."

He stood then and moved away.

"Edward!" I cried, sitting up.

The sudden movement triggered a dull, hard ache in my shoulder, and I sank back with a groan. But the sharper pain, thank goodness, was gone. I used the uninjured arm to support myself as I rose to my feet and discovered I was alone on what appeared to be the roof of a tower, facing the battlefield and the southern slope of Ben Bulben.

Hugging my injured arm to my chest, I glanced about me and tried to get my bearings. The field below me was a seething mass of bodies. I made out Fomorians, the green-uniformed fighting men and women of Ireland, and many species of fairies. The Danaan were distinguishable by their ancient dress and leather helms and shields—as well as by the wild abandon in their faces—and the Fomorians by their gruesome forms. Many were like the gaunt, fiery-eyed creatures aboard the enemy galleon. But there were also gray demons with wrinkled elephantine flesh that reminded me of gargoyles, fearsome giants with the torsos of men and the heads of boars or wolves, and cloaked spearmen whose faces I could never quite glimpse. There were also beings very like the woodland fairies—larger and with painted faces—who fought viciously against the Irish allies.

The clash of weaponry—spears, swords, bayonets, daggers, axes, and clubs—blended discordantly with shouts of pain, grunts of colliding bodies, and fierce battle cries. Volleys of arrows fell like rain, some thunking against shields, some piercing flesh, others whizzing off crazily, apparently repulsed by spells.

As my mind struggled to order the chaos, something drew my attention skyward. Not birds, but half a dozen huge stones, were soaring in an arc above the battle. Though I was out of range, I ducked instinctively as they slammed down on the east end of the field, ground mostly held by Isolde's men. A loud cheer went up on the opposite end of the field, and I saw *Death Rattler* suspended above the western tip of Ben Bulben, her Fomorian crew swarming over a catapult.

I understood why Edward had wanted to protect me from these horrors, though I could not countenance the choice he had made.

*Where is Diarmuid?* asked my ancestress.

"I don't know," I replied.

The din around me was not as loud as it *should* have been. I did not hear rifle fire, which was troubling. I assumed that these weapons had been defeated entirely. But I also detected no sign of the deadly eye of Balor. Had I killed him? I lifted my gaze again to *Death Rattler* and located the Fomorian king's dark form, standing on the foredeck. He seemed to be directing his army using horn blasts that differed in pitch, tone, and length.

I scanned the battlefield again for Edward, and as my eyes began to make sense of this constantly shifting tapestry, I saw banshees moving through the violence and carnage. They were the only shapes without solid lines and forms. Indeed, sometimes they passed directly through the bodies of the soldiers in their midst. The men, otherwise engaged, seemed to take no notice of this, but it was an eerie sight.

*They can help us!* said Cliona.

The women appeared to be on a course for the castle—seeking me out, as they always did. Yet they did not travel in a group as they had before. Instead, they moved individually and slowly, stopping at times to keen over the fallen. Their keening was diluted by the sounds of battle, but I noticed that whenever they uttered these heartbreaking cries, the warriors in the immediate vicinity—no matter which army—sank to their knees with expressions of despair until the keen had ended. I continued to watch them and so made another discovery. The women in gray, who uttered a different sort of cry, had a very different effect on the fighters. The fallen they cried over were not dead, and when the keen had ended, these men rose and rejoined the battle. Unlike the death mourners, these gray ladies seemed to have no effect on the Fomorian soldiers, nor did they minister to them.

They were healers, I realized. This was good news indeed.

A few of the women had now reached the hilltop, and I called to them to make haste.

"I need healing," I said to the first gray lady to reach me on the tower—a crone perhaps fifty years my senior.

She reached out and touched my shoulder, then tipped back her head and keened. I closed my eyes, listening to the clear, pure voice, and a warm pulsing sensation moved up and down the length of my arm. The heat in my shoulder grew quite intense, and I began to tremble. But before it became intolerable, both the keen and the heat began to fade.

Flexing my fingers, I raised my arm gingerly toward the sky, but the pain was gone, replaced by a pleasant tingling. And my heart, too, had been lifted, filled with a sense of hope.

"Thank you," I said to the old woman. Studying her more closely, I recognized her from the night I was carried across Achill Island.

*The night I was carried.* How had I forgotten?

"Call the others," I said to her.

I saw now that with a little guidance in deploying their efforts, the banshees could perhaps play a very real part in this battle.

## EDWARD

As soon as the Morrigan set us down atop the tower of Drumcliff Castle, I whistled for the water horse, Aughisky, and she came galloping across from Sligo Bay. By the time I took leave of Ada, the mare was waiting for me on the lawn below, and I mounted and galloped into battle.

Isolde had embodied her warrior ancestress, Maeve, in all her glory, and a golden chariot had come through the fairy gate for her at the commencement of the battle. While I was occupied with Ada, the queen and Finvara had used the chariot to relocate to the lower slopes of Ben Bulben. Now I, too, must cross to that higher vantage point—a grassy bulb near the eastern end of the mountain.

I could have crossed the battlefield on the friendly side of the line, as they had, but I found myself riding a wave of Diarmuid's eagerness to join this fight with his ancient enemies. Moreover, the threat to Ada had fired my blood—the white-hot rage that flooded my chest when Balor broke her body had yet to recede.

Once Aughisky charged through the battle lines, I was amid the enemy, and as I swung Great Fury in wide arcs to my right and left, the sword showed me how it had come by its name. For it could smite three goblins or cleave the head from a giant in a single stroke. My ancestor and I had found our stride. I felt his power coursing through me, and I made use of it. My body possessed the strength, but the memory of the movements required for this form of combat came from his centuries-old consciousness. Dark and ancient magic was at work in our collaboration. Yet it felt natural, and it felt fated. Only one other time had I felt so alive.

I hazarded a glance back toward the castle, hoping to reassure myself that she was safe. But from this distance, I could not see her. I had glimpsed her women moving across the field of battle, and I knew they would find her. Diarmuid seemed to believe that they would protect her even more fiercely than would the men I had stationed on the grounds below the castle. It would have to be enough.

*Have we not come to the end of your doubting her, after all?*

Ignoring this just chastisement, I raised Great Fury again and took out my anger at myself on the leather helm of a boar-faced giant that had stumbled on the slick and casualty-littered ground. The blade easily sliced through and down into the pig skull, and the sound he made was indeed like that of a wild beast.

I cut my bloody way across the field, and Aughisky attacked

the steeply climbing slope on the other side. Soon I had rejoined the others.

"Is she whole?" Finvara demanded.

"No thanks to you," I muttered. I wasn't sure whether Diarmuid or I hated him more. "Perhaps your powers are weakening."

"Desist, idiots!" barked the queen. "Or I shall order you both executed for dereliction."

She directed our attention to the battlefield. "I should have anticipated the inefficacy of our firearms," she fumed. "We have not had to contend further with the eye, at least."

"With thanks to Ada Quicksilver," I said, still awed by what she'd had the presence of mind to do despite being terrified and badly injured.

"Indeed," replied the queen. "But they outnumber us, and my men are not seasoned in this kind of combat. My ships ..." She gazed across the few miles to Sligo Bay, biting her lip in frustration. "I assume their cannons are disabled, and without cannons they are useless."

The moment the seal was broken, dozens of enemy ships had landed on the strand, unmolested by the queen's fleet of French-made midcentury ironclads stationed in the waters just beyond. These enemy ships were not Gap galleons, but Norse-style vessels with oarsmen. Fomorian warriors streamed in a continuous line from strand to battlefield, where they joined a host of dark fairies who had slipped through the gate behind the Danaan while Balor was raining down terror and destruction on the main body of Isolde's troops.

"They don't need cannon to sink those smaller ships," replied Finvara, sounding more like Duncan than he had since Brú na Bóinne. "Nor steam, either, unless they've forgotten how to use their sails."

"They do need wind," I observed, glancing at a small hawthorn tree growing on the slope above us. Its foliage was gone with the season, but every twig on every branch was as still as the grave.

A tense silence ensued, but finally Finvara said, "I might be able do something about that."

The queen turned to look at him. "What are you waiting for?"

He shook his head. "I'm not Dana or the Morrigan. I can't hope to do it from here."

Isolde muttered an oath. "Then we must get you *there*." She glanced at me. "What about the Morrigan? Perhaps she would carry him as she carried you."

"We dare not trust her," I told her. "Our interests run counter."

She frowned. "Is not war her purview?"

"Precisely, and she will prolong it if she can."

While she and Finvara continued discussing our options, a light snow began to fall. Turning my attention once again to the castle, I saw something strange approaching in the sky from the southeast.

## ADA

As the banshee host gathered around me, lifting me from the castle's tower, I began to search for Edward. Cliona had advised me to look for the black horse, which he always rode into battle. I found them scrambling up a steep hillside near the eastern end of the long, narrow mountain that enclosed the battle along the northern edge of the plain.

"There!" I cried. Edward made it to the top and drew up his mount next to two other figures atop the hill.

The banshees bore me forward on their shoulders, far above the flying arrows and near the battlefield's eastern boundary, out of range of the catapult.

I could feel the moment Edward saw us approaching. Though

I could not yet make out his expression, I didn't need to see him to know that he would be less than pleased to find me outside the relative safety of the castle.

The three figures on the hill followed our progress as we approached, and to my surprise, the banshees placed me directly into the arms of Edward, who waited below us on his great black horse. This was not precisely what I had asked them to do, but they knew the earl, the Danaan warrior, *and* the horse, and perhaps they could not be blamed for taking this initiative.

*Or perhaps they did what you* wanted *instead of what you* asked.

I let this observation from my ancestress pass.

"*Acushla,*" Edward murmured, settling me before him on Aughisky's back.

The Irish term of endearment translated to "pulse of my heart." I could feel the electric presence of Diarmuid, and the low timbre of the earl's voice raised a shiver in my body.

"My dear," said the queen, "that was quite a useful parlor trick. Perhaps your women might likewise spirit Finvara across to my fleet so that he may endeavor to run down these enemy ships."

This they would not do; I knew it without asking. The request would only confuse them. Their interaction with the living was limited to death warnings and healing. As Cliona's descendant, I was an exception. They considered me one of them.

I explained this to the queen, but I also told her, "I will send for Enbarr. She will carry Finvara if I accompany him."

The earl stiffened behind me, but he had sense enough not to protest. I certainly felt no eagerness at the prospect of joining forces a second time with the faithless fairy king, but ending this battle with as little bloodshed as possible trumped all lesser considerations.

"Make haste, then," replied the queen.

I twisted on my perch in preparation to slip down. I had forgotten the considerable distance to the ground, but Edward caught me around the middle as I pushed off, helping to ease me down.

"Your shoulder?" he asked.

As my eyes met his, the tenderness and regret in his expression squeezed my heart. But I gave a brisk nod. "I am well, my lord. The gray ladies are healers. They have been restoring our wounded in the field. It could give us an advantage."

"More good news," pronounced the queen.

Two of the banshees had remained close while the others dispersed to the edges of the rounded hilltop. I called to them and relayed my orders. One left us immediately, in search of a gull to carry a message to Manannán, the sea god, while the other led the gray ladies down to the battlefield. I had ordered that the death mourners remain behind. They were a distraction, and there would be plenty of time after the battle for keening over the dead.

"Now what shall we do to make *ourselves* useful, cousin?" the queen asked Edward.

"I shall ride down among my men," he replied, and it was my turn to feel a stab of dread. "Great Fury should not remain on the sidelines."

"Nor the most accomplished warrior of the Danaan," said the queen. "Leave your bird so I may send for you if I have need."

Looking up at the sky, Edward whistled, and soon I saw the slight figure of the kestrel moving across the heavy backdrop of cloud. She floated down to us and landed lightly on the queen's shoulder.

Then the earl's eyes came to rest on me.

"Take care, my lord," I said through the tightness in my throat.

He held my gaze a moment longer, and the tender, regretful expression returned. "And you, my love."

Finally, he urged Aughisky forward, and they plunged down the hillside, my unspoken pledge trailing after them.

*My heart goes with you.*

# STILL A MAN

## ADA

The gray ladies returned to their work healing the fallen, and my eyes followed the dark figure of Diarmuid as he joined the battle, swinging Great Fury about him with preternatural speed, leaving a wide swath of destruction in his wake. Spear after spear they hurled at him—as well as lances, pikes, and arrows—but the sword's motion created a protective bubble around him that no weapon could penetrate.

Yet he was still a man. Would he not tire?

*God and Dana protect him,* whispered my ancestress.

*God and Dana protect him,* I agreed.

"Miss Q, I fear I owe you an apology."

I turned to find that Finvara had drawn near. But Finvara was not in the habit of calling me "Miss Q."

"Duncan?" I said, searching his eyes.

He offered a smile orders of magnitude dimmer than his usual brilliance. "Indeed, at last."

"I have missed you!" I cried, reaching for his hand.

He laughed, squeezing my fingers. "And I you. But I have not really been gone. Only in a sort of prison." He frowned. "Not unlike your own. I am sorry for my part in that."

"I fear Lord Meath was more to blame than you."

"Perhaps. But certainly, Finvara had planned it before receiving Edward's note."

I couldn't help feeling a fresh pang at this reminder of the earl's betrayal. "Well," I replied softly, "that does not much surprise me. And it makes little difference now."

"How, then, did you escape from Knock Ma?" he asked.

"Billy Millstone." I looked up at *Death Rattler.* The Fomorians were reloading their catapult. "It was a trap, but the poor fellow redeemed himself in the end. When this is over, I hope that I shall be able tell his story, for he deserves to be remembered."

I looked again at Duncan. "Have you banished him, then? The fairy king?"

Duncan shook his head. "I have found my strength again, and that is all. He is with me. But I made him understand *I* would no longer be banished."

"I am glad," I said. "I would not like to lose you. And we shall need *him* for the task ahead, if it involves spells."

"Aye, we shall."

I shifted my gaze west across the battlefield and all the way to the coastline, noting the continuing march of Fomorian reinforcements. The Irish army was holding its own, but I didn't know how long that could last with this steady influx of fresh enemy warriors.

"She comes," said Duncan, and I followed his pointing finger. A white figure was indeed approaching swiftly across the countryside just north of the Fomorian procession. We lost sight of her as she veered around the north face of Ben Bulben, presumably to avoid the battlefield.

"Let us be ready."

Enbarr soon joined us on the hillock, her sides heaving and lathered. We mounted at once and plunged back down the hillside, curving, as she had, around the north side of the mountain.

Snow stung our faces as we rode back toward Sligo Bay. The scenery around us blurred, and I sank against Duncan for warmth.

"We'll make for Streedagh Point!" he yelled over the wind in our ears.

Streedagh Point was the site of the Spanish shipwreck in the sixteenth century. It was situated at the near end of a narrow peninsula that ran parallel to the coastline. Its strand was sandy, with dark, craggy rock formations. Duncan stationed himself on a shale stack that looked like a ship's prow pointed out to sea. I remained astride Enbarr on the sand just below. We were very exposed here, with the winter ocean all around us and dark clouds looming overhead. The snow was light but steady—icy white grains that made a pecking sound as they struck the sand and water.

But the sea was quiet, and the sounds of the raging battle still reached us. I could see *Death Rattler* hovering above Ben Bulben and knew she was launching her deadly missiles.

The queen's ironclads were becalmed on the black and mirrored surface of the bay, their cannons and steam engines apparently defeated by magic. The Fomorian boats, propelled by oarsmen whose captains drove them by shouting commands, flowed effortlessly between and around the queen's ships. Fomorian soldiers swarmed over the strand like ants over a dead wasp. A few of the Fomorian boats had been caught by grappling hooks thrown from the ironclads and were abandoned. Bodies shot with arrows lay sprawled inside these open vessels and on the shore. But it was plain that the queen's fleet had been mostly ineffective.

I glanced up at the shale stack and saw Duncan—or Finvara—on his knees, head bowed as if in prayer or perhaps deep concentration. I could hear his chanting tones but could make out only an occasional poetic phrase, such as "riders from the four directions" and "upon shale and strand."

After a few moments, I felt a new chill against my skin. Was a breeze picking up? I watched the fleet closely, holding my breath, afraid to hope. Did I imagine that flutter of white? The slight rocking of the closest ship's hull? The creaking of masts?

But soon I heard the distinct ruffling of sails, and sailors' rising voices.

He had done it!

The breeze begat a wind, men shouted orders, and sails filled. The ironclads began to creep like giant beasts waking from hibernation. I watched with fevered anticipation as a vessel called *Manannán* picked up speed, seemingly on an intercept course with one of the Fomorian boats.

I gave a cry of triumph as the larger ship broadsided the smaller, smashing through its wooden hull and driving it into one of its brethren, fatally wounding both ships.

"You've done it!" I cried as Fomorian fighters hurled themselves into the sea.

Two dozen ironclads were moving across the bay. I discovered that the water, too, was moving when a wave slapped the base of the sea stack. Enbarr whinnied and danced into the spray.

"Easy, my lady," I murmured, tightening my grip on her mane. "We'll send you home soon enough."

With the wind filling their sails, the queen's modern ships were more than a match for the feebler Fomorian boats, whose spears and other projectiles bounced harmlessly off the metal-sheeted hulls.

"I'd give a great deal to be captaining one of those vessels!" Duncan shouted, laughing into the wind.

His enthusiasm was contagious, and I was beaming when

I turned back to see the growing gap in Balor's stream of reinforcements. If Finvara could keep up his spell, no more Fomorians would be landing on the beach. And with the banshees healing Isolde's wounded in the field, Ireland and her allies might gain an advantage.

Looking again to Ben Bulben, I glimpsed something strange approaching from the north—almost like a rapidly moving fog.

"What is that?" I wondered aloud.

Cold crept along my spine, and I felt my ancestress's dread before she spoke. *The dead.*

At first, I could not understand it, but in watching the way the mass moved—like a flock of giant birds—I recalled a passage from my own thesis.

> The Sluagh, though a classification of fairy, are in fact a host of the restless dead. The souls of the unforgiven. At night, they are cursed to rise from their rest, gathering like flocks of geese in the sky. They circle the earth, especially at All Hallows, tormenting and frightening the living, until through forgiveness they find their release.

The host picked up speed and swooped down over the battlefield. Individual figures dispersed from the fog and plummeted to the earth one by one, their corpse cries cutting shrill above the din of battle. As each shadow figure swooped up again into the clouds, it released something that fell quickly back to earth.

By the horrible cries that accompanied these maneuvers, I understood that the Sluagh were dropping soldiers to their deaths.

These beings were so numerous, they were an army unto themselves—hundreds, perhaps a thousand or more. Soldiers fell like fruit from a shaken tree.

"We must do something!" I said. "Can they be killed?"

But I knew the answer: they were dead already.

My mind was struggling to make an important connection. I sensed it, but horror had frozen my intellect.

*An army unto themselves,* I thought. *No mortal man can oppose an army of the dead.*

Then suddenly, it came to me.

"Duncan!" I cried. I gripped Enbarr's mane, and she began to skitter and dance in readiness. "Duncan!" I shouted over the noise of the waves. "I must go! Will you be all right?"

"Aye!" he called, and I could hear in his voice the exhilaration of battle. "I will find my own way back!"

With that, I threw my leg over Enbarr, which hiked my skirt up almost to my waist, and dug my heel into the mare's side until she spun about and galloped back toward the battlefield.

Hurtling at top speed across rough ground had been hard enough when I was anchored by Duncan. Now I clung desperately to the mare's lathered neck, closing my thighs against her broad back, praying I would keep my seat. But Enbarr had a practiced, even gait and was never tripped up by stone or loose earth.

When I rejoined Isolde, I, too, was clammy with sweat, and a few moments passed before I could catch my breath enough to do what was needed.

The queen was peppering me with questions, but I shut out her voice, and as soon as I could speak, I called to the death mourners, who still kept a respectful distance from the queen.

"Gather your sisters," I ordered. "Then show those bedeviled souls their way home."

As soon as I gave this command, the banshees left us, swarming out over the battlefield.

The queen stood at Enbarr's shoulder. I could feel her impatience, but to her credit, she watched and waited. Up close, the Sluagh were even more dreadful, with shrieking, broken-toothed maws, gaping eye sockets, grizzled hair, and the talon-like fingers of those long in the grave. It sickened me to think of the terrifying last moments of their victims.

*May I not have been wrong,* I prayed breathlessly, still gripping Enbarr's mane in my two fists.

The banshees formed an active cloud, as small winged insects do, and when the cloud first enveloped some of the ghastly Slaugh, the figures went rigid. Then they shot across the sky like falling stars.

"Huzzah," murmured the queen in a tone of curious surprise, and I let out the breath I'd been holding.

The keening women maintained their cloud-like formation and moved with more purpose than I had yet seen. They caught up a dozen or more of the dead at a time, and the ranks of the Slaugh began to thin. Were the banshees healing or merely banishing? I wondered.

*Both, let us hope.*

Soon, the departing Slaugh were more numerous than those still hunting, their forms leaving blue trails of light against the clouds behind them. It made me think of the storm of the Leonids that had happened in my grandparents' time.

"Nicely managed," said the queen, and I was surprised to find her earnest and thoughtful as she continued to observe this strange release of souls.

But it was not to last. "What news of my ships, Miss Q?"

I had to lower my gaze to look at her from the back of Enbarr, yet I still managed to feel small. "The ships are again sailing, Your Majesty. Duncan has blocked the flow of reinforcements."

"Excellent!" She clapped her hands together as she stared out over the field. "Between Diarmuid's sword and your healing women, I think we shall turn this around."

I followed her gaze and located the earl, still cutting through the enemy. It was clear how the Danaan warrior had earned his reputation. I wondered, would we have to kill every last one of them? Or was there hope of surrender?

A shadow passed over the battlefield then. It drew my attention because there was no visible ray of sun. The shadow belonged to the Morrigan, whose crow form circled just beneath the low clouds.

The hair at the nape of my neck stood up, and a bolt of silver lightning forked down from the sky. I screamed as it struck the ground where I'd last spotted Edward, and for a horrifying frozen moment, I saw him suspended above the field, arm raised, Great Fury glowing with hot blue light—as if he wielded the lightning itself.

Then the flash was gone. Aughisky shrieked and reared, and the earl toppled and slumped to the ground, his enemies closing around him.

Without thought, I kicked Enbarr and pounded down the hill with the queen shouting after me. I screamed orders at the banshees.

The thunderous approach of Enbarr was enough to stun enemy and ally alike, and a path opened before us.

I jumped from Enbarr's back, tumbling to the ground and landing hard on one hip at Edward's side. Ignoring the stab of pain, I grabbed Great Fury and scrambled to my feet, swinging the weapon in a circle around us.

"Get back!" I shouted, my voice raw with fear and fury.

The Fomorians flinched back as the sword flashed. They hissed and spat, taunting in a language I could not understand. But I knew that it was a language of menace, vengeance, and death.

I felt the pulse of power in the weapon I held. It wanted to cleave and rend, and so did I. Even now the enemy warriors were pressing closer. Two Irish soldiers managed to break in among us, but they were viciously cut down by an ax-wielding goblin with corpse flesh and bloody fangs.

I swung Great Fury in a violent arc, and a goblin hand, ornamented with spiked rings, dropped into the mud while what remained of the owner's arm sprayed me with silvery blood.

Before I could lift the sword again, the fist of another goblin smashed down on mine, knocking the weapon from my hands.

I felt the strange stirring of the air as the first banshee reached me. "The death song!" I commanded.

The woman was young, with luxuriant black hair that reached to her bare feet. Her dark gown of mourning was of rich cloth, like a garment made for nobility. Her delicate chin tilted back, and she let out a keen that rolled forth like a herd of wild horses over the battlefield. Every creature in our vicinity stumbled to its knees, heads falling upon breasts, some even dropping their weapons. I could feel their despair—it pulled at me too—but I forced myself to kneel at Edward's side.

I bent low, turning my ear to his lips. His flesh was pale, his breath gone. I laid a palm against his chest, which was quiet and still.

"Diarmuid!" I shouted, channeling despair into a broken and pointless rage. "What kind of god are you?" Raising my fist, I brought it down hard on his leather breastplate. Pain coursed through my hand, but I raised it again, and tears streamed down my cheeks as I beat at his lifeless body.

When my strength was spent, I fell across his chest. My body heaved with sobs, and suddenly, he jerked beneath me.

The gray ladies then pressed in close around me and raised their voices in the healing song.

Edward's eyes opened suddenly, and he looked questioningly into my face. His chest filled and emptied, and laughter escaped my lips. It was a giddy and half-crazed noise, I knew. The swings in emotion, made extreme by the supernatural mourners, had unhinged me. He took my hand in both of his and whispered soothing words that I could not focus on well enough to understand.

The moment the keeners fell silent, the enemy began to revive. Edward grabbed Great Fury and sprang to his feet, pushing me behind him. I stayed close, watching for a chance to grab a fallen weapon. But we could not last—not like this, without Aughisky to keep us above the fray. Enbarr, too, had fled in the chaos, and the earl was handicapped by having to shield me.

In this moment of desperation, I thought to call again on the banshees for a temporary reprieve, but then I saw the great battle crow swooping down on us from above. She alighted on a hill of fallen warriors that we had backed against for protection.

Without words, she called to us, offering a chance to end this. We could not trust her—I felt it keenly. But before I could speak, Edward had lifted me onto her back and climbed up behind me. The Morrigan's wings swept open, and she carried us above the battlefield. Edward raised his sword, deflecting the spears and arrows that reached after us.

As we winged over the battle, I watched Danaan warriors close in around the knot of enemies that had threatened us, and I saw that the queen's line had shifted to the west.

"The tide is turning, Edward," I spoke urgently. "We need not agree to be a part of her schemes."

"I am not sure we shall be given a choice." His voice was low and hard. I could not have said whether it was the earl or his ancestor who spoke.

We were passing now over the hill from which Isolde was directing her army. From above, the queen was vulnerable. One of her generals had joined her, and her personal guard kept watch just below, but none of them could stop a lightning bolt.

"That lightning strike was no coincidence," muttered the earl, whose thoughts seemed to be running in a similar vein.

Even had the Morrigan not intended to threaten the queen, we had accepted the war goddess's offer of assistance on the battlefield, and now we would face the consequences.

"Are you injured?" asked Edward.

"No," I assured him. I thought some small bones in my hand had been crushed in the fight, but since the healing song of the banshees, I felt no more pain. "I lost my head for a while," I admitted, grimacing as I recalled the relish with which I'd bloodied my enemies. "I did not know myself."

He grunted dismissively. "What you did was succumb to battle fever. What you *did* was fight fiercely, and then you saved my life."

Fierceness having fled me now that the immediate danger had passed, I glanced self-consciously over my shoulder. "How could you know that?"

"Have you forgotten I am half immortal, with a shadow in another world?" He studied me intently, the light of the Danaan burning bright in his countenance. "I know that you fought the Fomorians to protect me, and I know that it was you who called me back into my body." He bent closer, speaking into my ear. "I know that had you stayed locked away in Knock Ma, I would still be lying lifeless on the battlefield."

Something that had been holding taut within me released, but I had no time to consider his words or reply. The Morrigan had carried us to the tabletop summit of Ben Bulben. We slid down from her back onto the rocky ground and watched as she assumed her womanly form.

"How may we further amuse you?" the earl asked darkly.

Her black lips split into a cheerless smile, and we heard a roar behind us. Balor had disembarked from *Death Rattler* with his Fomorian guard and now led a charge across the mountaintop.

Edward raised Great Fury, eyeing the Morrigan incredulously.

"So we're to be slaughtered now? You have been in this for *them* all along?"

She raised the tip of her bone staff and knocked it three times against the ground. With each knock, the earth rumbled and shook, stopping the enemy's charge and causing us to stagger backward. I lost my footing on loose, snow-dusted stones and tumbled close enough to the edge for a dizzying view of the plain below. Edward caught me around the waist and hauled me back to firmer ground.

When the mountain stopped shaking, the earth before us suddenly broke open. The soil rose in small hillocks, and sticks of wood broke suddenly through the loosened earth.

*Not sticks,* but skeleton-thin limbs with leathery brown skin.

"Stay back!" warned Edward as the corpse men clawed their way out of the earth.

When the creatures were free, they reached back into their holes and hauled out six bulky burlap sacks, which they tossed in a heap at my feet.

Glancing up, my eyes met those of a bog man wearing a rude crown woven of twisting roots. I stepped forward with a curtsy. "King Máine Mór, I am your servant."

"The king is *thine,* lady," rasped the bog man, and he made a courtly bow. He and his two-dozen followers leaned their frail weight against ancient spear shafts. In the other hand each held a wide, leaf-shaped Celtic blade.

The foes on the opposite end of the table were stirring, recovering their footing, and again Balor let loose a savage battle cry. If I had questioned whether these bog men had the strength to raise their weapons, I now received an answer.

Shouting their own earsplitting challenge, the leathery figures rushed across the barren tabletop toward the Fomorian guard. Blades crossed time-hardened spears, and sparks flew.

Edward raised Great Fury and stepped onto the field.

The Fomorian king, baring his teeth in gruesome mockery of a smile, raised a massive double-bitted ax. His deadly eye was closed and crusted over with dried blood. It would affect his aim, would it not? I was no student of physiology, but so I hoped.

"When I have bled you, Danaan princeling," bellowed Balor, his voice shuddering with rage, "I shall take my time with your woman. Small cuts, one by one. How many before her fair flesh begins to peel apart? How many drops of blood before her heart stops?"

Edward let out a roar of hot fury and charged across the field. Ax and sword clashed, their blows again shaking the ground beneath our feet.

Once this one-on-one struggle commenced, I could no longer keep track of the bog men's battle, though several times the air rang with the screams of goblins plummeting over the side of Ben Bulben, and I thought I glimpsed more of the skeletal hands poking up through the ground, grabbing at goblin legs. I was also vaguely aware that another Gap galleon had appeared in the sky next to *Death Rattler,* and the two vessels were trading catapult shots.

But Edward, along with Diarmuid, was locked in the fight of his life.

*And your Edward has but one.*

My throat tightened. My ancestress was not taunting me. She was understanding something about me. Something about *us.* Diarmuid and Cliona would never lose each other. Edward and Ada had *this* moment in time.

"Edward!" I cried, my voice raw from emotion and the strain of the day. "Remember the story of us!"

Halfway through this rallying cry, the world slowed down. I watched as the bog men, running with a strange, suspended motion, made a final charge across the field, driving half their remaining foes over the edge with unearthly screams of terror.

A huge stone struck the figurehead of *Death Rattler*, knocking it, along with a chunk of the bow, clean off the hull. The ship crackled and groaned, tipping backward and tossing crewmen overboard. The aft end struck the edge of the tabletop, sweeping the last of the Fomorian fighters over the edge before rolling and tumbling down the side of the mountain.

Horns called out from the battlefield—a clear signal the enemy was routed—and from our high vantage point I saw them turn back toward the sea.

And in the only yet undecided battle, Balor raised his ax in the air, preparing to strike a final, deadly blow.

The Morrigan bowed her head, and her body sprouted the feathers of transmutation. She spun in place, levitating from the mountaintop, and shot straight into the air like an arrow, soaring higher until naught but a speck, and then, finally ... nothing and nowhere.

The gears of time spun free, Balor swung his ax, and in the last moment, Edward dropped and rolled closer, throwing off his one-eyed foe's already handicapped aim. Then Edward launched to his feet and swung Great Fury, lopping off the ax-wielding arm. The giant teetered, and Edward hurled his weapon, the blade plunging into the middle of the massive chest.

The Fomorian king crashed to the ground like a toppled monolith.

# THE GREEN HILLS

## ADA

Edward pressed his boot against his fallen enemy and pulled his sword free, then let its tip sink against the earth. He hunched over the weapon, taking great, heaving breaths of frigid air. He scanned the field until he found me; then he closed his eyes and let his chest and shoulders go slack. His hair hung in sweaty waves around his face, which was smeared with enemy blood. The day's violent exertions had wrought deep, dark furrows in his countenance.

Drawn to him, as I always was in his moments of vulnerability, I stepped forward. But Máine Mór stepped into my path. Holding his sword before him, the bog king bowed his head.

"We've brought thee sacksful of ill intentions, lady," said the king.

For a moment, the significance of these words eluded me, and I studied his bog-tanned visage warily. Then I recognized the reference to our first meeting.

"Potatoes," I replied with a smile. Though glancing down at the burlap sacks resting beside me, I saw that other forms of blighted herbage—beets and turnips, stalks of wheat and oats—had spilled or protruded from their openings.

Words came to me then, taught by Finvara to my ancestress. *Wisp's light, burn bright, elfin charm against the night.*

I turned, raising my hand over the pile of tainted food, and softly spoke the incantation—for a spell was to be coaxed, not commanded. Blue flame sprouted from my hand, and I watched it burn a moment before tilting my palm and letting it slip onto the sacks. The burlap caught despite the damp air, and soon a fire was blazing.

The snow had changed—big, soft flakes replaced the icy grit and gave off a faint hiss as they touched the flames.

I looked at the bog king. "Perhaps one day I shall do something for *you,* my lord."

His lipless mouth curved in a smile. "Perhaps, and perhaps not." He lifted his chin, appearing to sniff at the air. "'Tis enough to walk the green earth once again. To feel the snow on my face." His gaze settled again on me. "To feel the lips of a beautiful lady."

I curtsied again, and he made a noise that sounded like a chuckle. "Now we must go, before the battle crow's spell fades away. I care not to rest my bones in unknown ground or in such a high and lonely place. Fare thee well, lady."

"Fare thee well, King."

With that, the bog men crept back into the ground, slowly pushing bony limbs into the broken earth, until at last the soil closed over their heads. All accounted for but a few, who must have fallen from the mountaintop in battle. I hoped we would be able to find them and at least return them to the ground.

I joined Edward by the side of his fallen enemy.

"So he is dead," I said as the earl reached for my hand.

"For now," he agreed.

I did not like the sound of this. "You believe he will return?"

Edward shrugged. "Diarmuid has defeated him before. But this blow was severe. He will fade away for a time."

"Let us hope it is a *long* time."

He offered a weary smile. "Shall we board the *Queen of Connacht* and return to the others?"

We glanced up at the one remaining Gap galleon, holding her position above the mountain.

Flightless mortals stranded on the summit of Ben Bulben, we had to yell to attract Captain O'Malley's attention. She lowered a rowboat and her crew hauled us aboard.

As her ship carried us down to the plain, we congratulated Captain O'Malley on her defeat of *Death Rattler,* and she told us her story of guarding the Gap gates, and the three Fomorian galleons she had destroyed before joining our battle. She appeared to have high hopes that the spiritual scales would now balance in her favor, but it was difficult to imagine such a person retiring quietly to the Land of Promise, which I rather imagined to be a place of peace and rest.

We joined Queen Isolde and Duncan, who had borrowed a farmer's nag and returned to us, all boisterousness and high spirits. There was much to discuss now that we had rejoined the others, and I began to fear that Edward and I would never get a moment alone.

In truth, I feared that our moments alone had been doomed from our very first meeting. But we were alive and whole, and that counted for much.

"Ada," said the earl, as if reading my thoughts. "Could I speak with you?"

Our party had assembled inside the castle, before a roaring fire. Servants of the queen were preparing a feast so we might break our day-long fast, discuss the outcome of the fight, and make plans for honoring and burying the dead. Drumcliff Castle was of recent construction and offered all the modern comforts. We all had washed now and taken a glass of whiskey or wine and were resting and awaiting the call to dinner.

"Come," said Edward, and I followed him up the stairs to a library in the top of the tower, where we could gaze out at the moonlit snow on the slopes of Ben Bulben. On the plain below, the banshees kept silent vigil over the fallen. But the fires from the soldiers' encampments, and the lively music that drifted across the battlefield, were cheering reminders of the day's victory.

The earl and I stood before the window, neither hands nor gazes touching. His dark countenance was somber and thoughtful. He touched his hand to the breast of his jacket, then smiled thinly and lowered it to his side. A crutch he had leaned on so long, he reached for it out of habit.

"I have been very wrong," he said.

I took a deep breath. "You have, my lord."

He flinched at my honesty but replied, "I know it. And I have no excuse for it, though I will tell you that when I saw you and your women on Caer's tapestry, all of you standing in the shadow of Balor, I felt a dread that I could not master."

Ah, the reason for his betrayal. For his sudden decision to *encourage* the very thing he had most feared: Finvara locking me away in Knock Ma.

I studied his profile, waiting for him to continue.

He turned to me. "And yet it was *you* who saved *my* life this day. It was you who saved *many* lives. From the eye of Balor. From the malice of the dead. You managed even to win the respect of a malevolent redcap and an ancient, withered king. No one has underestimated you, in fact, but I."

"And why is that, do you think?" There was no accusation in my tone. I did not intend to punish him. But I needed to understand. I believed that I had begun to, but I needed to hear him say it. "What was it about me that so convinced you I could not manage without your protection?"

"Nothing," he admitted with regret. "Nothing at all. You and my cousin are the most self-sufficient women I know." He laughed dryly. "In truth, you are more capable than most of the men I know."

He sighed as he stared out at the night. The snow had stopped falling, but a pristine white blanket covered the mountain, and in the clear moonlight it glittered like diamonds.

"It was a gentleman's upbringing, in part," he continued. "A soldier's instinct to protect the vulnerable. An Irishman's inclination to look out for a traveler." Turning and fixing his eyes on me, he said, "In the end, it was no more than a man's instinct to protect the woman he loves—a woman who could be carrying his child."

Heat spread across my cheeks and breast, and I dropped my gaze.

"I believe this is the first time I've discovered you in uncertainty today," he said gently.

My throat felt thick as I replied, "About some things, I am not uncertain."

"Tell me what it is that worries you, Ada."


# EDWARD

Color had stolen into her cheeks, and she shivered as I pronounced her name.

*Could bode well or could bode ill.*

Indeed. Was it possible for her to forgive such a betrayal? Could she trust me again?

I bent my head, trying to catch her gaze, and suddenly she looked up at me.

"I understand you very well, Edward," she said, but her voice trembled and her expression was sweetly confused. "As much as you have frustrated and even infuriated me, I can see that your misguided choices have stemmed from a ..." She wrung her hands, and I resisted the urge to take hold of them. "... have stemmed from a warm regard," she concluded.

I held my tongue, waiting for her to collect herself and continue. I would not have interrupted her for the world.

"My concern is, what will become of us now? Half mortal and half *other*? What of these beings that are both part of us and separate? How are we to go forward from this?"

Now I did take her hands in mine. "Do you recall reminding me about 'the story of us' on the peak of Ben Bulben?"

She nodded. "Of course."

"I know that you intended to rally my courage, but did you *mean* what you said, Ada? Do you want such a story to be written?"

Her lower lip trembled, and she steadied it with her teeth. A single tear slipped onto her cheek, and she nodded. "Yes, Edward. I want that more than anything."

I drew in a great breath, breaking the constriction in my chest. My heart swelled and my blood sang. I pulled her into my arms. "Then let us speak with them. Let us find out under what terms they will permit that to happen."

Her body was warm against my chest. How I had longed to hold her just like this after striking down Balor. I had been bloodstained and sweating, stinking like a great beast—and mostly I had not been sure whether she would have me. Now that I was sure, my heart could scarcely contain it.

"No terms," she murmured against me.

I stood back from her so that I could see her face. Her complexion glowed as if from within, and her eyes were bright and intent. "Ada?"

"No terms," she repeated.

*Cliona.* "My lady?"

"Diarmuid?" she replied.

I felt him come forward, moving like a shadowy presence between us. My vision dimmed, and my instincts urged, as always, that I resist him. But I knew that I must accept this meeting between them were we to have any hope of compromise. I could not spend my life fighting him for the woman I loved.

"*Acushla,*" whispered Diarmuid, taking her into his arms.

Their lips met, caressing lightly. The gentlest of reunions. But something enormous was building, like snowmelt raging down the mountain to inundate a meandering stream.

Her mouth opened, inviting him in, and he clasped her against him. His hot hands moved over the curves of her body, pulling at her clothing.

We had become a channel for centuries of hunger, and now came a moment from which I knew we could not return—the physical union the two immortals had longed for must come, as no power on earth could stop it.

Yet in that moment, she went still in his arms.

His breaths came hard and fast, and he trailed kisses down her face and neck. She reached for his hands and pressed her palms against his, lacing their fingers together. She murmured sweet, soft words against his cheek—tender words of sorrow and regret. A plea for forgiveness, and a pledge of ageless love.

Eventually, his confusion got the better of his passion, and he drew back to look at her.

"We are going," she said to him. "We have had our story, and they shall have theirs. I'll not be responsible for taking it from them."

Despair crashed within me like waves on jagged cliffs. Yet in that same moment came relief, like still waters after a storm. If I needed further evidence that it would be a maddening existence sharing my body with him, here it was. Yet I would have done it happily had it been the only terms we could agree on.

Already I could feel him drawing away, and the light in Ada's countenance was fading.

"Where will you go, lady?" I asked her.

She smiled at me. It was a kindly smile, and yet unlike the smiles of Ada's that I knew so well.

"We shall wander the green hills until all the green hills are gone. Then we shall wander only in men's memories."

The sweet wistfulness of these words tugged at my heart. "Will we see you again?"

She closed her eyes, the smile fading from her lips, the last of her light draining from Ada's face. "Time will tell."

I glimpsed a movement on the ground below the window and bent closer to the glass. Two shadow figures strode into the garden, hand in hand, their backs to us. They left no tracks in the snow and passed through the gate without opening it.

## ADA

"They have gone," I said in wonder.

Edward wrapped his arms around me. "They have gone," he agreed.

"It feels strange. There's a spaciousness in my mind that I had forgotten. And yet the memories she shared with me, the stories she told me—all of them remain." I looked into his eyes. "I shall miss her. In a way, she was family, something I have not had for years."

He raised his hand to caress my cheek. "I should like to remedy that."

My heart thrummed, warm and eager in my chest. I smiled. "How so, my lord?"

"May I once again offer you a husband, my dear Miss Q?" He bent forward, kissing my lips. "And perhaps, one day, a child?"

These questions sang within me, firing my blood with a joyous hope. But I took a steadying breath and did what I knew I must.

"That will depend, my lord."

Undaunted, he nuzzled my hair and took my earlobe lightly between his teeth. I gave a quiet gasp, and heat pooled in my belly.

"Upon what, lady?" he whispered.

My breaths had shortened, making it harder to think, but I persisted. "Shall I be permitted to continue my studies?"

He laughed, and his breath was warm in my ear. "You may earn twenty degrees, if you so desire. You may do a hundred other things, with or without my consent. Don't imagine I shall ever stand in your way."

I smiled, satisfied with this answer. "I should like to begin *now*," I said.

He trailed kisses down one side of my neck, his lips brushing past my collarbone before starting down my chest and into the cleft between my breasts.

I gasped again as his voice rumbled against the tender flesh there. "As you like. *How* shall we begin?"

I took his head in my hands, and he rose. "Let us study what it will be like to be man and wife," I said.

His smile was roguish indeed, and I trembled as his hands slid down to my hips. The hem of my gown tickled my flesh as it traveled up my legs.

"The dinner bell is ringing," he murmured teasingly, his hips pressing closer to mine.

"Let it ring, my love."